PASSION

By Louise Bagshawe

Career Girls
The Movie
Tall Poppies
Venus Envy
A Kept Woman
When She Was Bad . . .
The Devil You Know
Monday's Child
Tuesday's Child
Sparkles
Glamour
Glitz
Passion

Louise BAGSHAWE

PASSION

headline
review

First published in 2009 by HEADLINE REVIEW
An imprint of HEADLINE PUBLISHING GROUP

1

Cataloguing in Publication Data is available from the British Library

Hardback 978 0 7553 3608 1
Trade paperback 978 0 7553 3609 8

Typeset in Meridien Roman by Avon DataSet Ltd,
Bidford-on-Avon, Warwickshire

Printed and bound in Great Britain by
Clays Ltd, St Ives plc

Headline's policy is to use papers that are natural, renewable and recyclable
products and made from wood grown in sustainable forests. The logging and
manufacturing processes are expected to conform to the environmental
regulations of the country of origin.

HEADLINE PUBLISHING GROUP
An Hachette UK Company
338 Euston Road
London NW1 3BH

www.headline.co.uk
www.hachette.co.uk

This book is dedicated to Harrie Evans,
a wonderful editor and a wonderful friend.

Acknowledgements

Thanks especially to Harrie Evans for reading *Passion* through and picking me up on every inconsistency. She's worse than my mother! It made this a far better book and I'm very grateful. I would like to thank Michael Sissons my fantastic agent at PFD for seeing another book through to the finish, and for putting up with babies, politics, and other distractions; particular thanks to the whole team at Headline, who somehow manage to make every book better than the last one with minimal help from me. In particular, can I thank Martin Neild, Jane Morpeth, Kerr MacRae, Louise Rothwell, Lucy Le Poidevin, Emily Furniss, Peter Newsom, James Horobin, Katherine Rhodes, Diane Griffith, Paul Erdpresser and Celine Kelly.

ACKNOWLEDGEMENT

Prologue

Dimitri slid the photograph across the desk.

They were on the fourth floor of a nondescript office building. Outside, rush-hour traffic was just starting to build up on the Königstrasse. He had already been at work for four hours.

The hunt had started.

'The first.'

His operative took the picture, studied it for a second. The subject smiled, glossily handsome. He wore an expensive white-tie suit. The woman by his side was a brunette, rail-thin, in red satin. Several other dinner guests were glancing their way. He was the centre of attention, pleased with himself.

He had a lot of money, a lot of power.

He'd be dead soon.

'Not a problem.'

'Another.' He passed a second over. 'You probably don't recognise this one. She's not as important.'

'You have a name and a location?'

'Of course.'

Then that target was dead too. The operative shrugged. No need to state the obvious. Dimitri looked across his desk, taking the measure of her reaction.

Her name was Lola Montoya, and God, she was a cold bitch. It would be only the third time he had ever hired a female. The first two had not ended well, and most bosses in his world didn't make a habit of it. This girl was different. Dimitri had had to search around for nearly a month just to make contact with her. Her price was excessive, because she was one of the best killers in the world. Easily the best female. His gaze trickled across her impressive body. Large breasts, a tight, curvy ass, narrow hips. But her pretty face was marred by her eyes; ice-blue, and as a cold as a snake's.

She was efficient. She was merciless.

He turned his attention back to the targets.

'The third one is a politician. American, so there will be major protection.'

That was slightly more interesting to her. Dimitri tapped the latest photo. 'A US senator, connected in our field. Rumours of a Mossad contingent assigned to her security detail.'

A slight smile. 'Mossad are overrated.'

'You think so?' he asked.

'I've taken out several. And various of their protectees.'

He shook his head. 'You think everyone is overrated.'

'These targets are not a problem.' The girl was getting bored. 'They will fall as easily as the professor did. One week for all of them, ten days at the most. You wire the money to my accounts. I can be on a plane in an hour.'

Dimitri nodded. There was no point in arguing that payment was on completion. The world's best worked on their reputations. And once he had solved this little problem for his group of global clients, he would become too big to cross. The price was nothing, really. He nodded. 'It will be done, right away.'

'Then you'll get a call. We're done here?'

He almost nodded again, then on second thoughts pulled one last photograph from his drawer. He studied it. A young girl, long brown hair, pale skin, very pretty. She was about eighteen, playing hockey in a school uniform. Regulation navy blue skirt, dark socks, studded boots, a pale blue T-shirt that suited her complexion. No make-up. She was so full of life.

To him, suddenly, the picture seemed strangely erotic.

'She knows about all this?' Lola asked.

'Not at all,' Dimitri said confidently. He shrugged. 'But kill her anyway. Just to make sure. She's older now, teaches at Oxford.'

'Sure. Who is she?'

'The daughter,' he said.

Chapter One

The Past

She was his passion. The first time he laid eyes on her, he knew it.

'Will.' Jock Campbell tugged at his elbow. 'Pay attention, for fuck's sake! Get in the lineout!'

He nodded, reluctantly. 'Right.' Wrenched his eyes back from the slight figure on the touchline. Hard to do.

She was standing there, watching the rugby with a light frown of concentration, like many girls did who didn't have a clue about the game. She wore a pair of tight jeans and a fisherman's sweater that looked like it was borrowed from a boyfriend. Whoever he was, Will already hated him.

The girl had candied chestnut hair, long and glossy, whipping around her face. Full lips. Her skin glowed. Her cheeks were pink from the cold. She smiled at someone. It was Mark Crosby, from Hertford, and he had the ball. He lifted it and threw it towards his team.

Will propelled himself up from the ground and caught

the ball, easily. There were murmurs of 'Fucking hell,' all around him. That was one hell of a jump. Now he was supposed to pass it to one of the backs. Instead he tucked it under his arm and headed towards the line.

There were shouts and screams from the touchline. He imagined the girl watching him. Hertford's finest flung themselves at him. He brushed them off, like flies. Crosby came up behind him and grabbed at his legs. He knew it was Crosby from the way his feet fell on the muddy grass, Will registered details like that. He turned his leg, pushing backwards. On a pitch full of muscular students, Will Hyde had the measure of them all. He was the strongest. He was the most determined.

His lungs screamed for air. He ran on. It was a close game. The line loomed into his vision, but now four of the bastards were on him, hanging on to him like human limpets, forcibly trying to drag him back, away from the white-chalked grass. Will squared his shoulders and grunted from the effort. His quadriceps muscles tightened like iron cords under the skin. They couldn't hold him. He reached out, the ball firm in his grip. His hand put it down, two perfect inches on the other side of the line.

Oriel were all around him, cheering. The ref blew the whistle. Reluctantly the Hertford guys let go. Mark Crosby spat on the grass, expressively. Fuck him, Will thought, that rich bastard.

Crosby was the heir to a brewery in Oxfordshire. His parents lived in a Queen Anne rectory. He drove an MG around the town and was considered quite a catch.

Will was not considered a catch. He had no parents. He'd been raised in a Barnardo's orphanage. The staff were great, but they changed frequently. Will had been bullied as a young kid, and had learned fast to fend for himself. He'd got into sport, then proper running, lifting weights. And he had studied; maths was his speciality. It was such a pure discipline, no emotion to it at all. Will tried to dampen his emotions. They did nobody any good.

His life, as a child, had been a mixture of longing and hope. Wanting to be adopted, fantasising that his real mother would come back for him. But the parents that visited the orphanage were usually looking for babies. The older he got, the more hopeless it became.

Will tried to keep steady. He was a survivor, like most of the kids there. They weren't mistreated. Everybody was kind. And he had friends; some of them came and went, in and out of the foster system. Will was a boy, naturally strong; he looked older than his age. Nobody wanted him. He came to prefer the stability of the orphanage and of school. He was good at school, and the teachers piled encouragement on him. He might go to university. The LSE, Oxford or Cambridge, even. He could become a big success. Other Barnardo's kids had done it before him.

Will heard it all, the kind words and sympathy. It wasn't that he didn't value it. He just knew the difference between kindness and love. Maybe he could be a success. He wasn't sure. But what he really wanted was love.

Mathematics was an escape from the loneliness. In English classes, in languages and history, you had to deal with humanity in all its rawness. Will much preferred science. Specifically, he liked the impersonal poetry, the pure logic, of maths.

He was gifted and strong. He worked out, spent time with his friends at the orphanage, and studied. By the time he was sixteen, the friendships were fading, because he was so far ahead of everyone else. But he kept going anyway. He needed to get out into the world. He went up to Oxford for interviews and aced them; and received three grade As and two grade 1 S levels. There was a tremendous sense of escape. His life, Will's own life, could finally begin.

So there was a social gulf between him and Mark Crosby. So what? At uni they were all equals. Crosby had money. But Will Hyde was stronger.

He fell back into position as the fly half settled in for his kick. The ball soared through the posts, and as Oriel's supporters cheered, Will looked at the touchline again.

There she was. She shrugged expressively at Mark, who cursed. Will's eyes lingered. She was amazing. Beautiful, vibrant, the sympathy on that pretty face. So feminine in her chunky sweater.

As the referee blew the final whistle, Crosby jostled him.

'Hands off,' he said, following Will's eyes. 'That one's my girl.'

'Yeah? Then how come I saw you with Lisa Smith in

the Union bar last week?' Mark had had her half under the table, his tongue down her throat.

Crosby grinned. 'What she don't know won't hurt her. She's not even at Oxford. She goes to St Mary's.'

Now Will was surprised. He looked again. A schoolgirl?

'Don't worry, she's seventeen. Perfectly legal.'

'Are you sleeping with her?'

He was surprised how much the idea bothered him.

'What do you think?' Crosby sneered. Will could tell he was lying. He relaxed.

'Back off her, Mark. I'm going to ask her out.'

'I said she's dating me,' Crosby replied, with bravado.

Will turned towards him. Crosby was a prop forward like Will, but Will had twenty pounds of pure muscle on him. And everybody knew Will's background. Nobody wanted to mess with a man like that.

'Not any more,' Will said.

He walked over, without waiting for a reply. The girl was hovering, waiting for Mark, who had started to talk to one of his mates. Coward, Will thought. She had looked his way, seen him defeat her boyfriend. There was that unmistakable spark of interest in her eyes.

'Hey,' he said. 'I'm Will Hyde.'

'Nice try,' she replied. Her eyes were full of laughter at the ambiguity. He liked her. He smiled.

'Melissa Elmet,' she said. 'I'm here with Mark Crosby. I don't know if you're his favourite person right now.'

Will grinned. 'Don't take this the wrong way . . .'

'Uh-oh,' she said, grinning back. He felt a surge of pleasure. There was an instant connection. Emboldened, he pressed on.

'Mark's not a bad bloke, but he isn't for you. He cats around with loads of girls in the university. I saw him kissing one last week in a bar myself. And she was nothing like as gorgeous as you are.'

Melissa digested this. She looked mildly annoyed, nothing more.

'Really?'

'Yes,' he said earnestly. 'Would you let me take you out for lunch or something?'

'I don't know. Have *you* got any girlfriends?'

'None.' He shook his head. It was true. Like most rugby players he'd had a few one-night stands, but that was all.

'Then lunch would be nice,' she said. He saw her gaze trickle over his dirt-stained body, and she blushed. He was charmed. How many girls blushed these days?

'Great. Just let me get changed. Can I pick you up somewhere?'

'I'd rather meet you at the restaurant. Less explaining with the parents.'

'I get that.'

'Where?'

Will's turn for embarrassment, but he had to get it out of the way. She had been going out with Mark, and Mark had money.

'It'll have to be somewhere cheap. I'm on a student

loan. Got a job at night at a pub, but it doesn't pay much.'

She didn't flinch. 'How about the Blue Boar, then? Right next to your college. And mine.'

'Perfect.' He paused. 'Your college?'

'Well, Dad's. My father's Richard Elmet . . .'

'I know him.' For the first time, Will had a slight frisson of foreboding. He had taken a few extra lectures with Professor Elmet. How could this stunning girl be his daughter? She was so happy, full of laughter. Elmet, a brilliant physicist, was a pinched, sour man, harsh on his students, demanding perfection. Will hadn't liked him. The man was obsessed with climate change. He thought the idea of man-made global warming was scaremongering nonsense and stated in his lectures that he was going to disprove it. Halfway between a genius and a nutter. 'Were you adopted?'

She hit him. 'Dad's not that bad.'

He didn't argue. 'Meet you at one thirty?'

'OK.' Another of those dazzling smiles. 'Will.'

In the changing room the lads crowded around him, teasing and shouting.

'The Professor's daughter,' Jock said. 'Better watch out there, Hyde.'

'Shut up,' Will grunted. He laced up his shoes, smiled to himself. She was a fantastic girl, a great wash of sunshine appearing out of a cloud-bank. He'd have to take this slowly.

'I think he's in love,' Peter Little, the hooker, announced.

Will didn't say anything, mostly because he thought so too.

Melissa was waiting for him at one thirty. She ordered cheap fish and chips and half a cider. She was taking her A levels next year, English, History and French. She'd read history at Oxford if it all worked out. After that? Who knows, she told him. She wanted to have adventures.

All Will wanted was to settle down. Get a good job and a good house somewhere. A home. He didn't want to talk about himself. She was far more interesting. But she probed, gently enough, and found out the truth. Her sympathy was genuine, but not cloying. She told him she was sorry and then moved on to his future. He got the feeling she was a girl who lived in the future. Something not quite right in her home. He asked her out to the cinema.

'Yes. Thanks. That'd be nice.' She looked him right in the eye, and Will got the sense she had to force herself to do it. Vivacious, but a little shy. 'Any time. I can get the tickets.'

'I'm asking you out, so I'm buying.' He smiled. 'It just means I can never take you anywhere expensive.'

'I can chip in.'

He shook his head, firmly enough. And she didn't argue. She could see he meant it.

'Can I pick you up at your house?' Will asked.

Melissa shook her head. 'Best not. Like I said, things aren't so great at home with boyfriends.'

He didn't argue. He could meet her parents later, a lot later. What mattered was that she'd said yes. He was going to see her again.

After the cinema, she let him walk her home. At their next date, he kissed her. She was awkward, unpractised. Light as a dandelion seed in his arms. Will burned with desire for her, but forced himself to push away. She wasn't ready yet, nothing like. Most girls couldn't wait to hit the hay with him; skint student or not, he was muscular and handsome, a rugby player, had a reputation as a brain. The orphanage background was a turn-on for a lot of them too, although most weren't crass enough to say so. Will Hyde was street tough. A risk. A little bit dangerous.

Melissa Elmet never put him into a box. She was a schoolgirl, but in the sixth form. Extremely clever, a little starved for love. Her parents were obviously uptight. She was not. She was kind and adventurous. If they went out for a picnic – romantic and cheap, so he did that a lot – she always wanted to climb trees, or strip off her tights and paddle in the stream.

She was sexy, clever. And fun. Lots of fun. The more he saw her, the more he wanted to see her.

Will fell in love. He tried not to – he was only nineteen, she was seventeen. He knew it was young. But he could not help himself. He watched her reservation, watched her struggling not to fall too hard for him. None of that mattered. Melissa couldn't fight it either. When he arrived at their rendezvous, she'd be early, waiting, and her eyes would gleam, her face would brighten, like a child at Christmas. She was interested in anything he liked. Her fingers would trail across his chest, toy with his biceps, and he felt her heart-rate accelerate as she leaned against him, her breath quicken, her pupils dilate. Forcing himself to wait for her was the hardest thing he had ever done. But he managed it, because he was in love.

A week after her eighteenth birthday, his two house-mates flew to Dublin to go to a Five Nations match at Lansdowne Road. Will couldn't afford the tickets or the flight, cheap or otherwise. But that was fine with him. He had their slummy little house all to himself. He invited Melissa round for dinner.

She came. It was a spring night, balmy enough, and twilight over Walton Street, with the students cycling past and swallows swooping low towards the grounds of Worcester College. Will's last paper had received an Alpha and his tutors were convinced he'd get a starred first. Even though he was overtired from working two jobs, they told him his future was truly bright. He had saved up, splashed out on a bottle of champagne, on discount at Victoria Wine, some fillet steak and strawberries. The curtains of the tiny Victorian parlour were drawn against the dark, and Will had cleaned the house and lit a fire in the grate. He was full of happiness, full of optimism. Every day he was with her, he realised, felt like this. Because she loved him. He loved her. The darkness of his childhood fell away when he was with her. Melissa filled that longing. It was no mere infatuation, he was certain. It had been months, already. The girl was his life.

When she knocked on the door, his heart leapt. He opened it, and there she was, exquisite in a cotton dress, white with pink roses, and a silk jersey wheat-coloured sweater. Her long hair tumbled loose around her shoulders. She wore a little make-up, and there was a sexy gloss on her lips that Will immediately wanted to kiss off.

'So where are Matt and James?' She glanced around as he closed the door.

'In Ireland till Sunday.'

'No wonder it's so tidy.' She looked at him, laughed. 'Am I safe with you?'

'You'll always be safe with me.' Will smiled, kissed her. Those lips were so soft and yielding. 'I'm glad to see you,' he said, and he realised he was. That was the perfect word for it. He was deeply, profoundly glad to see her. His entire body suffused with joy. 'Come in, Missy, have some champagne.'

She followed him into the living room and purred with pleasure. The pine logs crackled in the grate. 'What are we celebrating?'

Will handed her a glass, chilled and full to the brim

with the golden, bubbling wine. 'Your birthday. Us. The future.'

Melissa tipped her champagne flute against his and they drank. Her head tilted back slightly, and her long hair gleamed against the firelight as it flickered. Will was caught with a stab of desire so intense it hurt him.

Gently he took her glass from her hand and set it on the table, with his. His hand went under her chin, tilting her face up to him. His left arm went around her waist. He pulled her close in to him, close enough that he could feel the heat of her blood pooling in her belly, see her lips part. His right hand moved to the gentle swell of her breast. He caressed it, very slightly, through her dress, and felt her respond.

'Will . . .' she whispered. 'I've never . . . I don't know . . .'

'I love you, Missy.' His breath was hot in her ear. 'I really love you. It's OK. You can trust me.'

She thrust herself against him, and he felt her legs trembling with need, her skin hot and flushing. She gasped with longing, letting herself go, letting herself arch against his touch . . .

Chapter Two

Melissa cycled home, slowly. It was late now, gone eleven. She didn't want to be out here. She wanted to be back in Walton Street, in bed with Will.

But her parents would be waiting.

It was cold, but she didn't feel it. Her whole body glowed. The aftermath of the sensations he'd put her through still throbbed through her body. She blushed as she pedalled. Surely it must be obvious. Surely the whole town could see it?

She wasn't a virgin any more. You built it up to be such a big thing, and then afterwards the world was exactly the same. That was weird. Did she feel different? Not truly; only that she was so much more in love with Will Hyde.

Somehow, she wasn't afraid that he'd dump her now, the way her friends said men did. Maybe other men, other students. Not Will, though. He'd asked her to trust him. She did. Utterly. They'd get married, right? Surely he'd ask her. Surely they'd have a wonderful wedding, somewhere romantic, with just the family and his best friends. And then a great life together.

Just one tiny thing to get through.

The road was widening now, stretching out past the Martyrs' Memorial, and Melissa's heady glow began to fade. She couldn't wait to get out of school. Her first year at Oxford would be Will's last. They'd be together all the time, once she was out of her parents' house.

Of course, she loved them. And they loved her. But . . . Major but.

Here it was. Lights still on in the front room. She dismounted and opened the door, leaning her bike against the wall in the corridor.

'Melissa.' Daddy's voice, low but insistent.

She sighed inwardly. It was so embarrassing when he tried to do the father thing. Daddy had always been around, but his nose was forever in his papers. Or he was at the lab, doing concrete experiments. Dad had risen fast in the tiny world of Oxford academia; his papers on solar flares and global temperature had made his name. And his work on nuclear fission responses had cemented his reputation. He was a tight man, bad with money and concerned for his reputation. That more than anything. Daddy wanted his peers to respect him, to acknowledge his brilliance. Forget his marriage or her birth, Melissa knew that the day they'd given him a chair at Oxford had been the happiest of his life. And the day the Queen knighted him for services to the Royal Society had been the happiest day of Mummy's. No cash to speak of, but her mother was now Lady Elmet, and she relished that title every waking moment.

Melissa wished it had never happened. Her parents were now socially ambitious. That spelled trouble for her and Will. It was why she'd kept him from them. She loved him, and he was the best thing in her life. She wanted to protect him. More than ever, after tonight.

'Hi, Daddy,' she said, coming in and giving her father a peck on the cheek. 'Is Mum in bed?'

'Of course. Look at the time.'

'It's only quarter past eleven.'

'You should have been back hours ago.'

Melissa stiffened with annoyance. 'I am eighteen, Dad. I've finished my exams, remember?'

'Were you with that boyfriend of yours?'

Her father was facing their fire, a scrawny little thing compared to Will's effort. Was he calculating something about the flames when he looked at it? she wondered. Daddy never gave her his complete attention, even when he was telling her off.

Melissa squared her shoulders. All that her darling Will had gone through in his life, she could deal with parental disapproval. 'Yes, I was, Dad. Like I said, I'm eighteen years old. A legal adult.'

'Living in my house.' Sir Richard stirred the fire. 'Your mother is concerned about this romance, Melissa. The young man has no family, no prospects, he's a barman . . .'

'A student job, Dad, he's paying off a loan. And what does it matter?'

'Melissa.' With an effort her father turned to look at

her. 'Date him if you must, but please remember you're still in school . . .'

'Till the end of this term.'

'At any rate, you are far too young to get serious. Both of you,' he added, with a transparent attempt to sound fair. 'We haven't even met this boy.'

Melissa sighed again. 'Like you said, Daddy, who knows if it's serious? Why don't I just see how things work out?' She could pretend, too, she could pretend detachment. 'I could bring him home if it ever gets that way.'

Her father's shoulders visibly relaxed. 'You know how your mother worries. You are her only child.'

'I know.' Melissa felt a twinge of guilt. She loved her mother. Mummy was snobbish, but at least she'd always been around.

'So come home on time. As you point out, it's only for a few more months. Then you'll be an undergraduate.'

'If I get in.'

Sir Richard puffed up his thin chest. 'You are *my* daughter. Of course you'll get in.'

Melissa went over and patted her father on the shoulder; he gave her an awkward embrace. They wouldn't like it when she told them she wanted to marry Will Hyde, she thought as she went upstairs to her bedroom. But they'd have to get over it. Will Hyde was her future. They would never be apart.

Chapter Three

The Present

Melissa Elmet never scheduled her tutorials before ten. She was a morning person, and did her best thinking right after breakfast, when the city was still asleep. She loved to take her coffee – good coffee, sent over from the States by friends, not supermarket swill – and sit on her window seat, watching the sun come up over the classical beauty of Peckwater Quad. It was one of the most attractive views in Oxford.

Her students were still sleeping off hangovers at nine. She preferred them to be fully awake, ready to go. It was important they did well in their exams. Good results were a major part of her job, and she needed this job. Her fellowship provided everything; not just her meagre salary, her living quarters too.

She published papers, the bare minimum for an academic, but there was never enough time for true research. Melissa's career depended on the examination grades the undergraduates got. History was a traditional college strength, and if she didn't keep those starred firsts coming, she'd be out. Melissa could not afford to lose her job. Outside of Oxford, she had nothing. Her days were always tinged with worry. About money, her job performance, her lack of a house. And her relationship. Especially that.

Melissa tapped the keys on her laptop. They were sticky, which annoyed her, but she couldn't afford to replace it. This computer was four years old, a dinosaur. Her calendar opened up, next to the notes for today's tutorial. Her freshman undergraduates would read their essays on Alfred the Great. Melissa hoped young Kevin Ross showed a bit more imagination in this week's analysis. He was heading for a lower second or worse, and he'd be wrecking a perfect group of students. Melissa hated confrontation. But one was coming with Kevin. He was a rower and thought he was untouchable. Senior dons protected him because he was being considered for the university crew and the Boat Race. Melissa didn't care; he was *not* going to spoil her crop of firsts. She would rusticate the guy first, send him away from Oxford for a year to get his act together. There were so many bright young kids who had longed for Kevin's place in this college. She would discipline him if she had to, and let the boaties squeal and moan all they liked.

Her computer pinged. Appointment reminder. *Dinner with Fraser*, it said. *Eagle and Child*.

An overwhelming sense of weariness gripped Melissa. How did this wind up being my life? she thought.

She stood up, and walked to the mirror over her magnificent fireplace. Her rooms were sumptuous, a tutor's digs in the middle of this elegant college. Bought privately, a flat like this in central Oxford would have cost a fortune. Only a millionaire could afford it. Someone like Will Hyde.

She was instantly annoyed with herself for thinking about *him*. She had to grow up. Her mind was drifting deliberately in that direction far too often these days. William Hyde was her past. And he was long gone, distant from her in all sorts of ways. Melissa had stopped taking the Sunday papers. She hated it when photographs of him appeared on the front of the business sections. Or worse, in the magazines. The style sections adored him. But Melissa had long since stopped reading those.

She stared into the mirror.

Her reflection gazed back at her. Brown hair, once a rich chestnut, that had lost its lustre. A neat enough face; she could still see the traces of her former beauty. But her eyes had no sparkle; they were bloodshot, she was not sleeping well. Anxiety and stress had dulled her skin. Melissa never bothered with much make-up, and her neat skirts and trouser suits were merely practical. She still had the odd good dress, and a string of pearls from her father. Once a month or so, when Fraser took her to dinner, she had to trot them out and put on high heels, and start the tedious business of dolling up.

But Melissa always felt a little stupid dressing up for

Fraser, like she was a tourist in some other woman's life for the night. Flirtation was not her thing. She was a proper academic now, in the old-fashioned sense. Truly her father's daughter. A great flat, good food at high table, silver cutlery and petits fours with coffee; and then back to wondering how she would ever scrape up enough for a deposit on a place of her own. Even a studio would do. Because Melissa, herself, had nothing. When she shopped, she was used to checking the prices on everything. Her clothes were from the high street, and bought in the sales. There were no holidays abroad. Her savings crept up, sure, but infinitesimally slowly.

It's the price I pay, she thought. Hundreds of research fellows would kill for this position.

True. But was it enough?

The academic life had its compensations. Long holidays, her luxurious surroundings, intellectual challenge, and the beauties of Oxford.

Melissa sighed, and turned away from the mirror. Her low-grade disappointment with her life was bothering her today, a lot more than usual. She wasn't looking forward to dinner with Fraser.

Fraser Macintosh. Her fiancé of six months. Melissa idly lifted her left hand, looking at the small solitaire diamond that glittered on her third finger. It summed him up: respectable, unflashy. Fraser was eight years older than her and a professor, full chair, of theoretical physics. A scientist, like her father. What would Dr Freud make of that? Fraser wasn't handsome, nor particularly ugly; he was tall, with blond hair that fell about in a mop, and his words tumbled quickly out of his mouth, as though they could not process his brilliant thoughts fast enough. He did have a first-class mind, and that impressed her. He exhibited a streak of solid common sense, too. He had actually bought his house from his college, Worcester, right before the boom, and it had a lovely little garden that backed on to the Isis. He also, he told her proudly, had a wonderful pension scheme and some yearly dividend money from a share portfolio. His total assets were a hundred thousand, excluding the house. And with her own modest salary added to his more substantial one, they could live together really quite comfortably.

Melissa thought she could make that deal. OK, so Fraser didn't excite her; but she did like him. He respected her, didn't push her to move in before she was ready. She could keep her own name after marriage, he said. Yes, he wanted children.

He had surprised her with the ring one night, as they took a twilight walk in the summer evening down in the Botanical Gardens. It was a romantic setting, and Fraser seized his moment by an old elm tree, dropping rather awkwardly to one knee and producing the jewel. It was his grandmother's.

Melissa had made an instant decision. Yes, she wanted children, she wanted to be settled. Fraser and she were comfortable together. Passion – the passion she'd had with Will – true, that wasn't there. But passion faded, like beauty. Marriage to Fraser would remove some of those money worries; it would guarantee her a comfortable home and a family. And the love part could come later.

She had worn his ring ever since.

Last week, though, something had changed. Last week Fraser had casually suggested a wedding date. November 22, at St Mary's. Close friends and family. A small party, around twenty-five.

How could Melissa say no? Not yet? We should wait? She had no family left of her own. Sir Richard had been killed last year in that accident in Venice, leaving her mostly debts. Her mother had been dead for the last decade. There was one aunt, in Ottowa, and a cousin in London who kept to himself. So the wedding and reception would all be for Fraser's benefit. Melissa didn't feel ready, but when were you ready for something like that? She was past thirty already, and her life of genteel poverty and growing boredom was making her desperate.

She agreed.

Fraser took over. He had commissioned the stationery, hired the caterers, booked the Master's garden for the reception. The university photographers would record the event. Melissa's new mother-in-law was flying in from the south of France. Fraser was busy, juggling all the details with his academic schedule. Melissa was only in charge of her wedding gown and the bridesmaids.

Only they were now one month away, and Melissa

hadn't asked any of her friends to attend her. She did have a dress on order – a simple sheath gown with three-quarter sleeves and a boat neckline; elegant, not tremendously exciting. Thinking about flowers made her head pound, and she had ordered a bunch of plain cream roses with dark leaves. Fraser would hardly dissect her choice of bouquet.

And still Will Hyde kept coming into her head. Sometime this week she would have to see the vicar, privately. Their brief marriage had been legally annulled, but Melissa had never got round to the church paperwork. Fraser didn't know she'd been married before, and she never wanted him to find out.

She tried to ignore her reluctance to take care of the final paperwork. It was her last thread of connection with Will, from so long ago. Don't be stupid, she thought, annoyed with herself. You haven't spoken to him since he walked out. You will never see that man again.

OK, fine. But did she want to see Fraser again? Did she truly want to see him at the altar, and every morning after for the rest of their lives?

The phone, balanced precariously on a stack of textbooks, buzzed, and Melissa jumped. Few people called her. Oxford was a small town, and her guests mostly just dropped in. A great disadvantage of digs in college was that everybody knew where you were.

'Hello?'

'Morning, darling.'

'Fraser. How are things?'

'Fine. Dad emailed from Grenada; he wants to know if he can bring his second wife.'

'That's between you and your mother.'

'If I say no, he won't come.'

Then why are you asking me? she thought disloyally.

'Up to you,' she repeated.

'Ready for our date?'

'Of course.' That jokey tone set her teeth on edge. She glanced down at the ring on her finger, curled around the receiver, and came to an instant decision. 'Fraser, could we meet earlier?'

'Fine. Half six?'

'I'll be there.'

Melissa hung up, and carefully slid his grandmother's ring off her finger. She laid it gently on top of her copy of Asser's *Life of Alfred*. A great wave of relief washed over her. She had been chewing on her unhappiness all morning, and hearing Fraser's voice had crystallised things for her. Melissa was very fond of Fraser, very grateful to him. But she just didn't *love* him.

No wonder she was thinking about Will. One failed marriage was enough for any girl. Better to still be poor, and be on her own.

Melissa wasn't going to marry Fraser Macintosh.

Now she just had to tell him.

Chapter Four

The Metropolitan Museum of Art is home to some of Manhattan's greatest parties. The charity benefits are a way for the world's richest people to enjoy champagne, caviar, great cooking, and the fabulous sight of themselves in evening dress and diamonds, minus any inconvenient white liberal guilt.

William Hyde sipped a chilled flute of Cristal, enjoying himself. His other arm rested around the slim waist of Olivia Wharton. She wasn't a model, but she could have been. She was divinely elegant tonight, wearing a clinging gown of silver mesh that made her look like a mermaid. An eighty-thousand-dollar necklace of aquamarine and pearls glittered at her throat. His gift. He was proud to have her on his arm.

Olivia had glossy dark hair, a red slash of lipstick, nice surgically enhanced breasts, and a medical degree from Harvard. She had specialised in oncology, but didn't have the personality to cope with death all day long. He could hardly blame her. Dr Wharton was charming and gorgeous; a butterfly, not a death's-head moth. She was retraining in dermatology, with vague aspirations to work in skin cancer. But she'd been dropping hints lately that she would give up the whole thing if only Will would propose. Stay home with their future children, graduate from being a perfect girlfriend to being a perfect wife.

Will was relaxed about it. If it was some girl he was sleeping with, she only needed to be gorgeous and skilled in bed. But girlfriends were different. He'd been intrigued to find a woman as pretty as Olivia who was also a doctor. That marked her out from every other rail-thin society broad hunting a big-game husband like himself. She had her own life, and her own achievements. Plus, she was a good sport and willing to try new things. Partly as a test, for their first date he'd taken her to a burger joint on Coney Island and then out for a spin on the rickety wooden rollercoaster. She had sat with him in the carriage, her manicured fingers gripping the sides, screaming with laughter. He liked her immediately. She'd ordered a cheeseburger, for one thing. He preferred a girl who liked sports and the gym to the ex-models who obsessed about calories.

They'd been dating a long time. Eighteen months. That was longer than any other woman since he'd moved the bank from Virginia to Manhattan. Tonight she was the hottest woman in the room. Yet again.

The Mayor of New York was flirting with her. William looked on, amused. He splayed his fingers imperceptibly against her rib cage, to feel that telltale squirm. Very responsive girl, Olivia. From a good family, had her own money, intelligent. He was toying with the idea of asking her to marry him. Olivia laughed at the Mayor's joke, and Will liked the sound. But there was no answering glimmer of interest in her eyes as the grey-haired man chatted her up, of course. What did he think would happen?

No mere politician could impress any girl of Will's. He was confident about that. Multi-million stock options had made him confident in all sorts of ways.

Next month it would be more. The Lassos deal. His bank was moving to manage a sovereign wealth fund for the government of Greece. Those big national contracts were where the real cash was made. Once the deal was finalised, the bank would split its stock again and he would be past billionaire status, if he wasn't there already. Will was a little hazy as to exactly how much he was worth. Perhaps it *was* time, he thought idly. Marriage. Kids. Every empire needed an heir.

'William.'

A touch on his sleeve. He turned.

'Senator.'

Ellen Jospin was the senior senator from New York, and she wore the title like it made her the Queen of England. She was very left-wing, and very rich, always clad in couture. It was rumoured that she wore her diamonds to bed. Her eccentricities were one reason they had never asked her to run for president.

Her silver-white hair was held neatly in an updo, and her crêpey neck was concealed behind a Tiffany choker of black pearls and platinum. She wore a Balenciaga skirt and jacket, and a signet ring stamped with the American eagle.

'Looking forward to seeing you next week.' Her dark eyes narrowed. Senator Jospin didn't take any shit. 'In front of the committee.'

William smiled. He had encountered far tougher foes than the senator.

'Looking forward to it,' he replied.

Ellen Jospin stiffened. He had not added the usual deferential 'Senator'. Her committee didn't like his bank. They specialised in 'commercial intelligence'. Companies up and down the Dow Jones used Virginian Prospect Bank for lending facilities, then had their M&A department find out the weaknesses of their competitors. This Brit had made his fortune that way. But if knowledge was power, William Hyde was becoming far too powerful.

He had invented a whole new industry. Taking the techniques of personal search firms like Kroll, the masterful private investigator, William Hyde had applied them to money. Of course there were plenty of 'opposition research' consultants already; Ellen used them every time there was an election, and left her opponents' reputations broken in the gutter. But William Hyde was different.

He hired spies.

Actual spies. And bankers, and forensic accountants. The private foibles of the board of directors, the slushy accounts, the libel cases, the malpractice victims, any- thing and everything that was wrong with your takeover target, Hyde Tracking, a division of the bank, brought it to light. Two New York companies he had exposed as overvalued, with the executives' hands in the till, had closed their doors just last month. As a Democratic senator, Ellen publicly applauded them being brought to justice. But her patch was losing jobs. *She* was losing votes. And she blamed the handsome young Brit.

'Now you're moving into advising governments?'

'Those with sovereign wealth funds. Yes.' He gave Ellen a brilliant smile, and she seethed inside. She knew the type.

When she was younger, she'd lusted after men like him. Muscular, dark-haired, arrogant. But she'd married a grey banker with the personality of a Dover sole. A safer choice. Obligingly, he had died young and left her all his money.

Still, Ellen loathed people who stoked up her regrets. Men like Will Hyde. She had no time for regrets. She was busy ruling.

'That might not be in the national interest. Virginian Prospect is an American company.'

'We can discuss it in front of the committee.' Another smile, and he was turning away, towards the exquisite young woman on his arm. What a glittering couple they were, with all that wealth and beauty. Her own Central Park West apartment and beach house in Nantucket could not compare. 'Oh yes, Ellen.' He turned back, and the Senator got the distinct impression that this foreigner was throwing her a bone, as though she, not he, were the supplicant. 'Remember, our expertise is also available to our friends in New York. For a price.'

Senator Jospin stared at his disappearing back. That was how William Hyde spoke to the chairman of the Senate Intelligence Committee?

Her party had a majority of the House and Senate, and the President was an impotent old fool who couldn't even veto his wife's choice of tie. It was wrong for a Brit to be over here, lapping up the limelight and the dollars as he destroyed corporate reputations. Many of her donors hated Will Hyde. Suddenly she wanted to teach him a lesson. To *stop* him. Even if it meant tying up the legislative session . . .

William steered Olivia through to the dining room. He loved jousting with politicians. Especially those with the big egos, which, let's face it, he thought, was most of them. Ellen Jospin's dislike was written bright on her face. And he didn't give a goddamn, anyway. If he had a vote, it would be Republican.

Will smiled as he ran his fingers across Olivia's spine, feeling her shiver pleasantly. She had learned to let go in his arms, learned that he would overlook any lack of technique but never a lack of responsiveness. He couldn't help assuming she was playing her cards, trying to hook him into marriage. But he didn't want that to poison the time he spent with her. He consciously attempted to be fair to women. What had happened, long ago . . . they were both teenagers. He was not about to blame every female for the misdeeds of someone else.

And Olivia looked like she was going to get lucky. She was the one holding the parcel when the music stopped. For he was half sick of gorgeous charity balls like this one, skiing parties in the Alps and weeks on this billionaire's private island or that mogul's giant yacht. The thrills had to come bigger and bigger these days just to stave off boredom. Will Hyde recognised the signs. He knew he was getting stale. It was time to admit he was no longer the young buck. Time for a new adventure, a real one: settling down and having children. A real family, for the first time in his life.

Olivia had a good sense of humour, and he'd watched her at her sister Alice's exclusive nursery school on the Upper East Side, once when she didn't realise he was there; her warmth with the kids was real. She'd make an accomplished wife and a great mother. It wasn't a crime that she liked him being rich. He liked her being gorgeous.

'Let's get out of here,' he murmured in her ear.

'Sure,' she whispered back. Ready to go at once. Will smiled in anticipation. Women rarely argued with him, and Olivia Wharton was no exception.

Yeah, she was a sweet girl. And he was going to take her home and make love to her until her long red nails were scratching at his back and her hair was falling tousled and sweaty on to the pillow.

And then, for the second time in his life, Will Hyde thought he might ask a woman to marry him.

Chapter Five

At first, Will dreaded the charity galas. A commercial banker shouldn't hog the limelight. But his PR firm persuaded him otherwise. He wasn't an operative any more; he was a CEO. The more Will's face got out there, the better the bank's share price. Call it the Donald Trump effect. Will Hyde, they told him, *was* the brand.

Will succumbed to the *GQ* photoshoot, the mentions on Page Six, the paparazzi and the business press. He was a human-interest story, and it sold the company; the ex-spy, although he never admitted it, comes to America, buys out struggling, tiny bank, is instantly successful. A rush of small deals making way for bigger ones. Hyde living in a tiny walk-up apartment in Richmond, Virginia, ploughing every red cent of profit back into the company. No cars, no house; he was buying his shoes at Payless. The money went on people: better executives, retired or unhappy, tempted by six figures and stock options and, when he moved the headquarters to the big city, the Manhattan nightlife. And the top men brought more skills, furthered his reputation, and took more jobs.

For a year, even in New York, William Hyde used subway tokens and bought his dinner at the local deli, a Styrofoam container full of noodles and fried vegetables, while his employees drove Mercedes and took their wives out to Broadway shows. But he didn't care. He had no attachments, God knew. The girls he met were young and anonymous, out for a good time. William gave them that, but connected with nobody. He didn't want baggage, and it was easy to disappear. He lifted weights, went running, got laid. It was an easy year, a good year. Plenty of stuff to do in the city for free. He was foreign, and New York still excited him.

After one year exactly, Will Hyde put on the cheap suit he'd bought at Warehouse for Men, took the subway down to Eleventh Street and went to see his accountant.

'It's been a successful year.' Carl Goldberg pushed his glasses up his nose and regarded his young client. Cool as the Hudson in November. Hyde's low-rent existence was eccentric, given the money the firm was making. But something about his eyes had told Goldberg not to argue.

'I can hire more people.'

'You have men in your offices now with free time. You are at capacity, unless you want to expand your branch network.' Goldberg hesitated. 'My advice is that you now start paying yourself. With the revenue stream of the bank at this point, questions will be asked by analysts if you do not regularise your position.'

Will nodded. 'And what would be regularising the position? I believe in investment. You're a financial officer of the company.' He shrugged. 'Give me a cheque for the minimum possible salary.'

Goldberg said, 'The minimum.'

Will nodded.

The older man hesitated, then scribbled out a cheque. He ripped it out and passed it across to Will.

It was for one million dollars.

At the time, Will had thought that was a lot of money.

It had passed by in a blur, much of it. The fast cars, the townhouse in Brooklyn, the penthouse on Fifth, the estate in the Hamptons. The designer suits, shipped from Savile Row back home. He wore antique watches and bespoke shoes. He dated girls, carefully. Will was becoming so rich now that they were fighting to get into his bed. And he was exceptionally cautious. No paternity suits. Certainly no marriage.

He wasn't into that. Made that mistake once, long ago. No more. Will was enjoying himself thoroughly. Building the business was his passion now. Finding and funding his new departments, applying forensic dissection techniques to company records, sleazy executives, lying balance sheets. Every deal he made, every client he landed – it was a buzz. The women were a pleasant diversion. And he was generous.

'It isn't you,' he'd say to the girl of the month, or six weeks, as soon as he got bored. 'You're gorgeous. You'll make some man very happy.' A shrug. 'I'm just not ready. You need to meet your husband, and I'm in the way.'

Mostly they accepted it. Some of them cried. But Will became an expert at softening the blow. A warm statement of enduring friendship, when the gossip columns asked; public invitations to his next house party; presents of magnificent jewels from Tiffany or House Massot. One girl, Mary Allen, who'd been as skilful in bed as she was demure in public, got an Aston Martin. His reputation preceded him. Will sometimes got the impression that some of his women were almost looking forward to the break-up.

Whether that was true or not, he always moved on. He'd been brutally hurt when younger. Never again.

Melissa Elmet. The daughter of Professor Richard Elmet and his waspish wife Miranda. When her husband was knighted for services to science, Miranda Elmet's joy in life was complete. She trotted out her title at every opportunity. And became ever more socially ambitious for Melissa, her only child. The Elmets had a small Victorian house in Oxford, with a cramped garden, all the way out on Northcliffe Road. But Lady Elmet determined that her little girl would marry splendidly, and live in the luxury to which she herself was sadly unaccustomed.

Melissa was clever, fearless, fresh-faced and pretty; not stunning, with the exquisitely even features and perfect grooming of the models Will dated today. Far more attractive than that. How un-plastic she'd been. He had a pang thinking about it, even now. She laughed, all the time; even at seventeen, when he first met her, she loved climbing trees. She was agile and ready for adventure.

He'd been a new undergraduate at Oriel, reading mathematics, on a scholarship. But he had come up to Oxford as a success story: a Barnado's orphan, with nothing to recommend him but his brains. He remembered being poor. Student loan, a pub job. Struggling to take Missy to the cinema.

She didn't care. They were nineteen and seventeen. They fell deeply in love. At least, he'd thought it was love.

Those first months, when he courted her! She was young, still a schoolgirl. He was just two years older, but seventeen, sixth form, was miles away from the knowing chicks that hung around Oriel's junior common room. Melissa had that innocence, that perfection, and Will didn't want to rush her. He just wanted to be with her, like a plant turning towards the sun, drinking it in. The petty horrors of his childhood, the loneliness, the poverty, everything fell away when he was with Melissa. He'd never resented her middle-class comfort. He admired her stiff, unemotional father for scraping to put her through a minor public school. And Will thought he'd like the same life, to become a research fellow, a professor in due course, and keep Melissa in comfort. All that would come, once he passed his exams.

Desire for her grew too strong. Will started to think about Melissa daily, nightly. He asked her to sleep with him; she refused. That only made him want her more. He started to touch her when they were together, to caress her. Melissa, damn, how she had responded.

Clumsily, but with such passion. Fighting herself, and her desire. Fighting him. It was maddening, delicious teenage love. When she finally surrendered to him, in the front room in Walton Street, it was the greatest night of his life. She was tense, but Will loved her. He was patient; by the end of the night she scratched and bit at him, sobbed with passion, and at last, drained, in love, fell fast asleep in his arms.

Will remembered barely closing his eyes. He lay there, listening to her breathing.

When Melissa woke, she panicked.

'Oh no! It's almost eleven.' The moon was already high outside his grimy window. 'Mummy – Dad – they'll know I've been out all evening.'

'It's OK.' He stroked her hair. 'I'll meet them. We're going to be together.'

'Meet them . . .'

'Don't you want me to?'

'Of course I do, of course I do!' She chewed her lip, and he wanted to kiss it. 'But they're very protective, Will . . .'

'Yes. But you're eighteen now, an adult. And you're the one.' He shrugged. 'I know it.'

Her whole body shook as he said that, and the stiffness went out of her.

'Me too.' She kissed him, and he took her again. No guilt. Will had never believed in God. But something stirred, and he felt profoundly, incredibly grateful. He was not sure to who, or to what. It was there, nonetheless.

The next day, they were walking down by the Meadows, past Christ Church, where Melissa had just applied. He lay in the grass with her, on a blistering summer day, his tinny little radio tuned to Classic FM, playing Handel. Will loved classical music, and Melissa was trying to learn about it. She was completely artless; she just wanted to please him. He had his arms around her as she settled back against his chest. She was his family, at last. God, she's everything to me, he thought.

'Did you ever want to go to America?' Melissa asked idly.

He teased her collarbone with a blade of grass, enjoying how her breathing got shallow almost immediately.

'It's a dream of mine. Always was.'

'Me too. Maybe Boston. They have great colleges there. You'd love it, it has the Handel and Haydn Society, that's the oldest in the United States. I should take you to the Symphony Hall there.'

He rolled her over, kissed her. She gasped softly with desire.

'Melissa.' They were under the spreading shade of an ancient elm tree, its leaves sending dappled shadows across her face. 'I love you. I'll never stop loving you. Will you marry me?'

'I think not,' her father said.

Will was distracted by the leaden tick-tick of their ugly nineteen thirties clock on the mantelpiece; very loud. For a second Professor Elmet's words hardly registered.

His expression did, though. Tight, and angry. Not happy, not grateful. It was the look of refusal. As a boy, Will Hyde had come to learn it well.

'What did you say?'

'I said no.' The Professor stood up and began to pace around his small study. He was a thin man, lanky and graceless as a daddy-long-legs. 'Her mother and I want somebody special for Melissa. She is a very attractive girl.' He examined his watch. 'And comes from a good family.'

Will bristled; he had no family.

'I don't have money now, Sir Richard, but I'm confident that after I graduate . . .'

'The time to assess your prospects will be then.' The Professor turned back to him. 'I want you to understand, my decision is final. In my opinion, teenage marriages rarely work. The statistics say the same thing. My intent here is to save my daughter heartbreak and the cost of divorce. Her mother and I certainly don't want to see her a single mother.'

'Divorce?' Will tried to smile. 'I haven't even married her yet. With respect, Sir Richard.'

'If you *do* have respect, you will give Melissa up. She's too young to marry and we intend her for . . .' He hesitated. 'She's just too young. I'm sorry to be so blunt, but it's better you should surrender this idea at once.'

They were young. Sure. But Will heard something else in the older man's voice: contempt. Will wasn't just too young, he was not good enough. Sir Richard was making that very clear indeed.

Will Hyde had no idea where the voice came from, but he heard himself reply, utterly calm: 'Sir Richard, I've asked your permission out of a sense of tradition, and to make Melissa happy. I would prefer your blessing, but I love your daughter and I *will* marry her anyway, whether you like it or not.'

'We'll see about that,' the older man snapped. 'I'll ask you to leave my house.'

'Very well.' Will was shocked, but he didn't want a scene. 'I hope you'll change your mind, sir. I'm a hard worker.'

'I won't. It's for the best.' Sir Richard's thin arms reached out to grab him, and shoved him rudely towards the door. Will was a rugby player and could have had the Professor in a half-nelson within thirty seconds, but he thought of Melissa and swallowed his rage.

That night they met at the pub. He was thrilled to find her just as calm. Her face was stained with tears, she was pale and shaken, but she was determined to go through with it. They agreed to work on her parents. He'd write letters, she'd talk to them. But they would marry anyway.

As he slept alone in his rooms, though, young Will Hyde, a penniless orphan living on benefits, asked himself if Sir Richard had been right. If Melissa was too young, and he'd never be good enough for her. But his heart insisted the Professor had it wrong. You made your own destiny – he was in Oxford, wasn't he, best university in the world? Will believed in himself. He determined he would be a greater man than the old curmudgeon could ever dream of.

Melissa was religious, and Will didn't care. He agreed to instruction in the Anglican Church. They would marry in a nearby church as soon as the banns had been read. Melissa was of age; she couldn't legally be stopped.

The day of the wedding, she sneaked into town in a taxi, wearing a simple white shift dress.

'You're beautiful,' Will said.

She blushed. Her hair was loose. She had tied a string of seed pearls around her long neck. He recognised them: they were a gift from her godmother. His ring, a minute diamond, was on her left hand. In the early-morning light she looked utterly radiant.

He had arranged for the vicar to marry them in the morning, half past eight, while most undergraduates were still asleep. Since Sir Richard and Lady Elmet didn't know about the wedding, there would be no other guests. The verger would be the witness.

The ceremony was fast, but he remembered every word. Love, honour, cherish. How she stood there, slim, shaking a little, breathing fast. He thought he might explode from love of her. She was defying her whole world to marry him. You're mine, he thought as he slipped the wedding ring over her finger. Now it was a fait accompli; surely the parents would accept it. They had no choice, not now.

He'd saved up and booked a room at the Randolph Hotel in central Oxford; expensive, but private. They had a wedding breakfast, with champagne, and then he took his bride and made love to her for hours. Melissa was on the pill, but Will couldn't help hoping it would fail. His passion for her was incredible, and he wanted lots of small happy children. They might have no money, but it would work out. On that morning the world seemed bright with hope. Everything will come right, Will thought.

She kissed him at last, at lunchtime, and said she was going back to the house.

'I'll come with you,' Will said.

Melissa shook her head. 'I have to do this alone. They're going to be devastated. Let me at least tell them by myself.'

'OK.' Will kissed her. 'OK, darling.'

Later, looking back, he couldn't say when he knew it had gone wrong. Not the exact moment. She didn't return at tea. She didn't return at supper. He called the house; her mother simply hung up on him. He called again.

'She doesn't want to speak to you,' Sir Richard barked down the line.

'Bullshit.' The time for niceties was over. The bastard was ruining his wedding day. 'Let me speak to *my wife* or I'll come over there and get her.'

There was a pause. 'Hold on.' He barked for Melissa. Will waited, his heart thudding in his chest. He could hear her coming down the stairs; he knew everything about her, even her footfall.

'Here.' Sir Richard's voice.

'Will?'

His heart dropped. She was crying.

'What's the matter, darling? Come home.'

'I can't – we can't get married.'

'Bit late for that,' he said, although he didn't feel like joking. 'Melissa, what have they done to you, what have they said?'

'I'm coming over.'

'No!' Sir Richard again, in the background.

He heard them argue. Then she said, 'I'm coming,' and hung up on him.

Will waited, sick with anxiety. She arrived fast, not more than twenty minutes of sheer bloody agony. Her eyes were red and puffy; she looked defeated and sick, and she was wearing jeans, a T-shirt, and neither of his rings.

'I have to annul the marriage,' she said, when he'd shut the door.

'For God's sake, you can't mean it.'

'I do. It's Mummy.'

'Fuck Mummy,' he said brutally.

Melissa shrank away from him. 'Will, she's dying! Dying of cancer. She told me, Dad told me. They've been keeping it quiet. She cried . . . she said she can't go to her grave seeing me ruin my life . . .'

He reeled backwards, sat down heavily on his old IKEA couch.

'I'm sorry. Very sorry.' He struggled to know what to

do. 'We . . . we could say we annulled but just not do it. I can be your boyfriend, court you for longer. Win them round.'

Melissa shook her head. 'No, no, Mummy was hysterical, Will, if you'd seen her . . .'

He had a very bad feeling about how this conversation was going. Hatred of her parents surged in his heart.

'How do you know it's not all an act?' he demanded.

'It's not,' she said, defensive. 'She wouldn't do that. She only asked me . . . to take some time . . .'

Her eyes slid away from him, and he realised what she was trying to say.

'You don't want to see me any more? That's it . . . your mother's sick, so goodbye, Will, don't frighten the horses?'

'Don't be bitter.' Melissa straightened herself. 'It's just for a little while. Our love can survive that. A short separation . . .'

'A little while? No.' Will shook his head, reached out and took her hands. 'My love . . . your mother hates me because she thinks you can do better. Giving in to her won't help. If you stand up to them now, in a month or so she'll see for herself how happy we are. That I *can* look after you. All of you! That's the only way to bring them round. We have to go through this *together*.'

Melissa wrung her hands, and for a second he was angry, despising her weakness.

'We're married,' he insisted. 'I'm your husband now. I'm family too.' And you're the only family I've ever had, he wanted to say.

She sobbed, a great wrenching sob that shook her small chest, and stood up.

'I'm sorry,' she said again. 'Look, let it blow over, don't call for a day or two.'

'I won't annul this marriage!' he exploded.

'It's up to me,' she said. 'Sorry, Will. I love you.'

The light in her eyes had gone out. As he looked at her, his heart breaking, he could see the hateful truth: that she had made her decision, chosen her mother over him

'But that's not enough,' he said. 'Is it?'

Melissa walked out and Will shut his eyes, partly because he didn't want her to see the tears. He heard the door shut.

And he never saw her again.

Chapter Six

Will found the notice of annulment the next morning in his pigeonhole in the Porters' Lodge. He went back to his room immediately and packed his bags. He wrote letters to his tutor and the Senior Censor and delivered them through the college mail system. They were short, affectionate letters. Will Hyde was resigning his place at Oxford in his second year as an undergraduate.

He didn't wait for a response. The tutors were good men; he knew exactly what they would think, how they'd be concerned he was chucking his life away over a teenage infatuation that would blow over. But Will knew better. His life had emerged from the darkness of a childhood all on his own into love, real love, and now Melissa had betrayed him, put him second; she'd taken everything from him. Will couldn't stay in the same city as her. He didn't really want to stay in the same country as her.

He headed straight for Aldershot and joined the army. The recruiting sergeant didn't ask too many questions. Hyde was a prime physical specimen of the type he rarely saw these days: thickly muscled in the chest, large biceps, strong thighs. He wasn't surprised to learn the kid was a prop forward. He'd dropped out of Oxford, fine, but he had three A levels at grade A and leaned towards maths and the sciences.

'I'm putting you in for officer training.'

Will wanted to die, to disappear. He didn't want responsibility.

'I'd rather be a private, Sarge.'

The older man looked up. 'I don't give a bugger what you would rather. You're going in for officer training. Sign here.'

Life at Sandhurst was brutal enough. It suited Will Hyde perfectly. He got regular pay, and enough physical torment to get him through the day. His broken heart didn't bother him as long as his arms and legs were screaming. Will excelled at every discipline. He was the most intelligent cadet in his year; other young men with his degree of intellectual ability didn't join the army direct, they went on to college. Will had arrived physically strong, but he left stronger. He rose before the other cadets and went down to the weight room. He tailored his diet, loading up on protein. He became leaner and larger. His uniform had to be refitted, twice.

The single-minded dedication got him noticed, fast. He was a dead cert for the Sword of Honour. But he would never make it that far.

It was his second year of training. Will was twenty-two years old. He was leaning over against a tree stump at the end of a run, red-faced, gasping for breath, when they came for him. Two men in dark suits, not military uniform.

'William Hyde?'

'Yes, sir.' Will treated all civilians with excessive politeness, but he was annoyed. He was wearing his jogging gear; it was dark with sweat. He needed a few moments to recover from his blistering ten-mile run.

'We need to speak to you.'

He glanced at his watch.

'I'm afraid I have to be in the lecture room in twenty minutes and I need to shower and change.'

'You've been excused from the lecture, Cadet Hyde.'

William straightened himself slowly. He knew instinctively that these men were not kidding. Who would turn up at Sandhurst in a restricted area, out of uniform, and demand to see him? He wasn't a criminal, and he was devoid of rich uncles who might suddenly die and leave him a large legacy.

'M15?' he asked.

They glanced at each other. He saw a flicker of a smile on the thinner one's face.

'M16.'

'We want to recruit you,' his companion said, unnecessarily.

Will smiled the first really genuine smile to cross his face for six months.

'What kept you?' he said.

They trained him amazingly quickly. He was a natural spy. His ability to decode, to blend in, to assess was first rate. Commanders wanted him in the field as soon as possible. He was sent to Jordan, to track down an operative of Abu Yusef, a major Saudi terrorist who was committing banking fraud, a difficult target. The man was sunk inside the establishment and polite society. Agents had spent a year trying to track him down and made only modest progress.

Will joined the hunt, and had the guy identified in eight weeks. He was immediately promoted. Over the next decade, they kept him busy. It suited him very well. He was young, with no dependents. He lived on the road, on the job, in hotels and safe houses, sometimes in more basic quarters. He ate what he was given. He slept with local women, consular officials, other spies sometimes. Those girls made good lovers. In the midst of so much death, you were sometimes eager to prove you were still alive.

His pay was reasonable; better than the army cadets, anyway. There were performance bonuses, hazard bonuses, bribe money his station chief shrugged and said he could keep. And Will Hyde had no expenses. He owned no property, had no roots. When he finished one assignment he asked for another.

The money, in his secure Liechtenstein bank account, began to pile up.

Will had an excellent grasp of business, and his line of work honed it at the sharp end. The men he hunted were experts with more than guns. They stole, defrauded, hid, transferred; they swam in illicit money and traded on information. As Will tracked them, he began to see patterns.

One night, from his small motel room in downtown Cairo, Will Hyde called Farrell & Gironde, the most secure private client brokerage firm in Europe. They told him their minimum deposit was fifty thousand pounds sterling. Will gave them seventy and instructed them to make three trades. Cordex, Brut GMB and Microsoft, a small technology company from Seattle.

Microsoft rose at once, by a small amount. Cordex jumped ten per cent in the next week. Brut GMB lost money.

'We can put on a stop loss, get out of the position,' his broker said.

'Hold,' Will replied.

The stock suffered further losses over the next month. Will refused to abandon his position. It hardly mattered, since his other two picks were now off to the races. He was already sitting on paper profits of forty per cent.

'Mr Hyde, I really think . . .'

'I'd rather you just traded. Or didn't trade, in this case.'

'Very well,' the broker replied angrily, thinking this young pup was arrogant enough for somebody who'd lucked out with two trades. 'We'll hold.'

Two months later, Brut GMB was taken over by a Moroccan shipping company. William Hyde's stock quadrupled.

The next time he called to trade, his broker didn't ask

him any questions. Over the next two years, William Hyde made various calls. A few failed; most, eighty per cent, rose, their performance ranging from the merely good to the truly stupendous.

After six months, his broker started to wonder if Hyde made the bad trades deliberately, to mask his insider knowledge.

After a year, he quietly started to copy Hyde's trades with his own broker at another house. It was the best move he ever made.

William Hyde stayed alive, on top of the brutal game he had chosen. And all his money went into investments. He checked the stock market wherever he was in the world, using day-old copies of the *Wall Street Journal* if he had to. Once he passed four hundred thousand, one of the brass bands of humiliation, squeezed tight around his heart for so many years, finally snapped.

Four hundred thousand was a magic number to Will. That was the figure Melissa had told him Sir Richard was worth.

When he passed one million for the first time, Will Hyde relaxed. He had taken the Elmets' verdict that he was worthless, and smashed it into rubble. That night, he thought about looking Melissa up, but then dismissed the idea. He had a mission to finish in Tel Aviv; no women necessary. And certainly not that woman. Melissa had betrayed him. He saw no reason to risk his heart a second time. There was no pain any more; his wound had scarred over. He was not going to break it open again.

He killed his fourteenth target, an Al-Asqa martyrs' brigade assassin, a month later in a cramped alley in Tunis, swiftly photographed the man's body, then stole his car. He drove to the heart of the tourist district, purchased a new Western suit, then booked passage to Morocco on a small ferry boat. Only from Fez did he catch a plane to London. Once he had landed at Heathrow, Will Hyde made a single telephone call.

'This is Evans.'

'Good afternoon, Roger,' said the unflappable switchboard operator.

'Tell Jason I'm coming in.'

This was against procedure; he was supposed to be in a hotel in Paris, waiting for details of the next job.

'Any hassle with the traffic down there?' she asked pleasantly. Requesting a code word from an agent possibly under duress.

'Yes, it was brutal,' he said. The code for free speech.

'Fine, I'll pass that on.' Click.

The bantering tone of the exchange was quite marvellous, he thought, knowing full well what consternation it was causing at HQ. They'd be running around squawking, contacting the hotel and his station chief. But Will was gone. It was over.

An hour and forty minutes later, he walked into the bland grey building on the banks of the Thames that housed one of the world's most sophisticated security agencies and signed himself in at reception. His pass was still active. He took the internal elevator to the nineteenth floor and walked into the lobby of the Egyptian/Moroccan section.

'It's William Hyde for Sir Rafe.'

Sir Raphael Court was about to celebrate his sixtieth birthday and had no intention of retiring. He had reached the upper echelons of a world nobody talked about, and one of his greatest joys was talent-spotting. William Hyde had stood out, as early as Sandhurst. Rafe had briefly studied the boy's background, and been certain he would turn into an outstanding recruit. And his confidence had proved brilliantly justified. It was well known at headquarters that Rafe regarded Hyde as his star pupil.

'Of course. Take a seat, please.' The receptionist was an older woman and immune to the charms of the younger agents. Will much preferred it that way. He sat down on a nondescript brown leather sofa and picked up a copy of the *Times*.

'Mr Hyde?'

He was flipping to the sports pages. Arsenal vs Portsmouth, so far away from all that death and destruction in fly-ridden ghettos in the Middle East. London hardly seemed real to him any more.

'Yes?'

'The Chief will see you immediately.'

'Very good. Thanks.' No point in prolonging it. He folded the paper neatly and walked into the office.

Sir Raphael was sitting at his desk, studying the daily reports. He didn't use a computer; felt they were too easily hacked. He was an old man with a young mind, and had instituted radical policies during his time in the job. But his office was traditional, a gentleman's den of dark wood, green baize and burgundy leather.

William shut the door behind him. The office was completely soundproof, with the glass windows treated against long-distance spying equipment, and it was swept for bugs twice daily.

'You have some sort of crisis?'

William shrugged, holding his boss's shrewd gaze. 'Not personally, sir. But I *am* here to resign.'

'You can take a leave of absence. It gets wearing.'

Say that again, Will thought. Wearing. How very British. He thought of the screams of the assassin, who'd died like the coward and bully he was.

'No, sir. I've had enough altogether.'

'We have excellent shrinks,' Sir Rafe said. 'No disgrace. Better men than you have used them after a rough time in the field. The mind needs healing when it's injured, same as the body does.'

Will shook his head. 'I'm not traumatised. I just want to quit.'

'And do what? Do you want a desk job?' He tilted his head, considering it. 'Bloody waste of a fine field agent, but you do have a first-class mind. I can stick you in analysis. You might even be more use to us there.'

William smiled thinly. 'I plan to be of use to myself, Sir Rafe. I'm going to leave the service altogether. My military commission expired six months ago. The debt is paid.'

The Chief blinked at the finality in the young man's tone.

'So you plan to . . .'

'I'm going to start a bank,' William said. 'Make my fortune.'

He was not joking. Sir Rafe pushed his chair back, genuinely shocked.

'Start a bank? Make money?'

'It's not illegal.'

'I don't think you understand. You are one of the best field agents we have recruited in the last decade, Will. You've been marked for promotion. We expect you to play a major part in defending this country against terrorism.'

'Others can do that.'

'So Queen and country means nothing to you?'

Will Hyde shrugged again, and Sir Rafe realised, as he looked into his protégé's eyes, that he was empty of all the feelings he had projected on to him. His excessive brilliance, his physical tirelessness; they came from something, but devotion to duty wasn't it.

'You can keep your patriotism, sir. It doesn't mean anything to me. I did the job I was paid for. Some bad guys are dead. It's my turn now.'

Outside, on the street, Will Hyde stretched in the sun. His security pass had been taken from him, paperwork signed. He was a free man. He owned nothing physical but the clothes on his back. Even his mobile phone and credit cards had been removed.

But there was money, quite a lot of money. Will had

moved it around in a sophisticated net of transactions, and he knew exactly what to do with it. He checked himself into Claridges, and slept for the better part of the day. Then he ate a steak, medium rare, with deliciously crisped thin-cut fries and a good salad, and downed half a bottle of Château Margaux. It all tasted incredibly good. Will did not begrudge himself the fine food and the sensation of his impeccably ironed crisp linen sheets. He was marking out the ending of one stage in his life. If he thought about Melissa at all, that night, it was only in passing. He was ready to move on. Literally.

There was no difficulty in getting to sleep that night, either. Will had run on petrol fumes for almost a year, and his body was trained to recuperate when and how it could.

He set his alarm for half five, woke, and went down to the gym. Very few men were awake at that hour: a couple of City boys, and their envious glances at his rock-hard body amused him. Will had no intention of losing his field agent's fitness. When other men left the service, they often sank into softness, alcoholism and depression. Not him. The job had been a prelude, working something rotten out of his soul. Melissa Elmet, and what she'd meant to him.

That frenzy had passed, and he was ready for the next chapter. He had tested himself in the crucible, and his self-confidence was total. Will showered, and changed into another new suit. Then he checked out, barely glancing at the bill, and took the Tube to Heathrow, because it was quicker. A tour of the desks procured a business-class ticket to Newark with Delta. Will Hyde never booked in advance. It gave his enemies too many opportunities.

Nine hours later, he passed through immigration into the United States. Having slept on the plane, he was fresh and ready to go. He jumped in a yellow cab and negotiated a rate to Richmond, Virginia, where he paid an unannounced call on Mr Louie Ferranto, one of a number of targets of the man he had just killed in Tunis. Mr Ferranto was the sole owner of an undercapitalised S&L bank, a real Mom and Pop outfit, with two Virginian branches and one in Delaware. Unfortunately for him, he'd dabbled in the big time by taking on some Arab clients who wanted total secrecy. But the bank was in difficulty, and their money was no longer safe. People, plenty of people, wanted Louie Ferranto dead.

Will Hyde knew this. He introduced himself, close to the truth, as a private investor with excellent sources. The bank was in trouble, he said, and he thought he could rescue it where conventional finance would fail. He offered Louie Ferranto fourteen cents on the dollar for the business, and Louie took it gratefully. He wanted to get out with his skin intact.

By June of that year, William Hyde, with a newly legitimate investor visa, was living in the United States full time and running his own bank. And Melissa Elmet, so he heard, was back at home, scrabbling for a research fellowship and trying to survive.

Chapter Seven

The sun was sinking down over the old grey spires of Oxford. The view never failed to calm and impress Melissa. She loved the town; whatever disappointments there had been in her life, whatever tragedies, she had at least always been surrounded by beauty. And the villages and meadows that fringed the city were no less attractive. But tonight, she had the strangest sense that her life here was coming to its end.

Breaking up with Fraser Macintosh was obviously not going to be much fun. Melissa poured herself a small sherry as she dressed, to counteract her nerves and depression. She had no real fear of breaking Fraser's heart; he was, like herself, settling. That wasn't a flattering thought, but she knew it to be the truth. Fraser wanted a nice, halfway pretty, suitably intelligent girlfriend to provide him with good genetic stock, so he could father another generation of children who could move on in their turns to a starred first and Worcester. He might be mildly embarrassed, a little regretful. The days when she could take a man's heart and smash it to pieces had long gone. Melissa was too intelligent not to see that, quite clearly.

As she picked up her little crystal decanter and poured her drink, the loneliness of the gesture suddenly hit her. Oh God, her heart cried. Is that what I've become? The academic spinster with the small sherry and the dowdy wardrobe, piles of papers to be marked on the shelf?

She reached out to steady herself against a small walnut table, suddenly feeling dizzy. When the moment passed, she stood up. Her eyes were moist. Angrily she dabbed at them with a tissue, resenting her own weakness.

Who said? Who said she had to be this? Daddy had gone now. He was dead.

The fury that had simmered in her heart against her father threatened to boil up again. Melissa reached for the sherry and tossed it down the back of her throat. *You're only here because of him*, said the little voice inside her head.

Her parents. The arch-manipulators. Her mother, breaking up her love affair with Will because she swore she had terminal cancer. And Melissa finding out, two months later, that they knew all along Mummy was in no danger. Thankfully, it had been Hodgkin's, and a mild form at that. Her parents weren't above using it against Will.

She tried to find William in London, but he had gone, disappeared without trace. For months Melissa jumped at the ringing phone and raced to the post every morning.

Until it became clear he was not coming back.

The weariness had settled over her then. Everybody remarked on it. Her mother, who started to complain that her bloom had gone. 'Plain Melissa,' she would say, with a little laugh that had an edge to it. That hurt, because despite it all Melissa did love her mother, she always would. Without Will, it was hard to live with her parents. She became an undergraduate herself, but she didn't date or socialise. She turned down all the rich kids Lady Elmet tried to push at her. The distance between Melissa and her parents increased. She retreated, into her studies.

Mummy died five years later, but not of cancer. She was admitted to hospital for a routine operation on a knee joint and collapsed in the theatre. The autopsy confirmed a previously unsuspected hole in Miranda's heart. Melissa, and her stiff, unbending father, were both devastated.

The day after the funeral Sir Richard called Melissa into his study.

'Your mother has left us both a small legacy.'

Melissa shrugged. Her heart was smashed: the loss of Will, and now this. She didn't want money, she wanted her mother back.

'Yours is put in a trust until you reach thirty. After the unpleasantness –' that was always how he referred to her early marriage – 'your mother did not trust you to inherit anything at the usual age.'

'Fine.'

'Don't answer me in monosyllabic grunts.' Sir Richard's voice was thick with emotion. 'And I never want to hear you mention the name of William Hyde again, not in my presence. Your constant bleating about him put your mother under intolerable stress. All the pain you caused her, moping around the house, refusing to talk to any of the young men she introduced you to . . .'

Melissa winced. That was brutal. Just because she hadn't agreed to date any of the chinless wonders her mother had shoved at her, now Daddy was blaming her for Mummy's heart?

'But I loved him!' she cried.

Sir Richard went grey, and Melissa rushed over to him, overwhelmed with remorse. He clutched at himself, and in her grief Melissa panicked that he was going to die too.

'OK. OK, Dad,' she said soothingly. 'No more talk of him. He's gone and forgotten about.'

'You promise?'

'I promise. Time to move on.' She forced a smile. The words tumbled out of her because they were true. It was years since Will left. And he'd clearly put Melissa Elmet clean out of his mind.

She'd been as good as her word, plunging herself into her studies, desperate to make it at Oxford on her own merits. As a gifted graduate, she was singled out for her precise mind and detailed grasp of argument; her love of history, another world to escape to, was evident. Where her parents had carped, her tutors lavished praise on her.

Melissa absented herself from socialising with the other doctoral students; she was still mourning, and had no desire to be courted. The boys thought her cold and pallid. She didn't go on many dates.

And there was always Daddy to look after. Her brilliant father; he loved ideas, not people. When he did come home, he locked himself in his room, consumed by his papers. White pages covered with arcane equations littered the house. Small sheets of metal were everywhere. Part of his climatology studies.

Melissa hoped they'd be closer. She was becoming an academic too. At least they could talk about university politics.

'Yours is a different field,' Sir Richard said blandly, when she tried to bring it up. 'Things are different in the sciences.'

Melissa bristled. 'How so?'

'Any physicist can make a discovery that changes the world. Look at Stephen Hawking. He's famous. Rich.'

Daddy was respected, but he desperately wanted to be famous.

'Historians can't do that.'

'Studying people matters as much as studying the sun and clouds, Daddy.'

Sir Richard smiled thinly.

'You've never come close to a discovery like Hawking's, though, have you?' Melissa asked, stung. She wanted to hurt him. 'And you're well into your fifties. You won't be changing the world.'

'You have no idea what I can do,' Sir Richard said coldly. 'One day my research will be published across the globe. How much do you think the sun and clouds matter? Hawking will be a footnote.'

Melissa arched a brow, and had the satisfaction of seeing him angry.

He refused to engage a housekeeper. Melissa cooked his supper and tidied the house, even as she tried to master her own studies. She was soon exhausted, and even less interested in looking for romance. She just assumed she'd be following in her father's footsteps, and caring for him as he sulked and grimaced into old age. His sorrow for her mother prevented her from complaining. She was still full of guilt.

After she took her DPhil and obtained a coveted research fellowship, Melissa gradually went home less and less often. Her father had withdrawn from the teaching life and he was too brooding, too gloomy to bear, working on his experiments with energy, determined to punch a hole in the global consensus on climate change. She couldn't abandon him, but she attempted, once college granted her rooms of her own, to stake out some independence.

One Saturday in August, she served him a Pimm's at the house – that was his favourite, with rough chunks of cucumber and apple – while a dish of mutton chops with braised cabbage and leeks was simmering on the stove. Sir Richard took a long sip, then looked at his daughter and cleared his throat.

He sounded nervous. Unusual for him.

'Darling,' he said. Also unusual. If he addressed her at all, it was as Melissa. Her heart clutched. He was still her father, after all.

'Yes, Daddy? Are you all right?'

He lifted his head, startled, she thought, at the concern in her voice; an expression flickered across his face, something like regret.

'Oh, perfectly fine. Don't concern yourself. Look, Melissa, I have something I have to do. I've been invited by a big firm to do some specialist research in Rome. There's a grant – it's being funded by David Fell.'

Melissa knew that name. 'The oil billionaire?'

'Yes. He has plenty of money to spread around, so it's a very good salary, and quarters.' Sir Richard puffed himself up. 'I'll be off soon. Maybe tomorrow, if he can get me a flight. It's all a bit last minute, but I've been thinking about work outside the university.' He hesitated. 'There may be some business opportunities out there as well, commercial applications for the research. There are some exciting things in climatology these days.'

Exciting things in climatology! Sure there were.

'I might stay for a while,' Sir Richard went on. 'Do you think you'll be all right here?'

She tried not to look relieved. 'Oh, fine. I've got loads of work to do. Preparing eight weeks of tutorials.'

'Then I'll be in touch.' Her father exhaled. 'Will you move out of college back here?'

'I'd prefer not to,' Melissa said reluctantly. 'It's convenient to everything . . .'

She didn't want to be stuck in the fusty old Victorian house by herself.

'You can rent the place out if you like. I'll set up a power of attorney for you with Simpson and Partners before I go.'

'Are you going to be gone that long, then?'

'It might be six months,' he admitted.

Melissa was ashamed of how her heart leaped with relief. She'd spent so long with her parents. A little freedom sounded very good.

'Then I'll take care of it all,' she said. 'Shall I get supper on the table? Are you hungry now?'

Her father gave her another odd look, then reached over and kissed her on the forehead, awkwardly. 'You're a good girl,' he said. 'Take care, won't you?'

He left the next morning, after bacon and eggs, and Melissa didn't see him again for months.

There were phone calls and letters, very infrequently. He always sounded distracted and busy. Melissa leased the house to another academic and his wife, and got on with her own modest life.

With his distance came clarity. They visited each other, now and then. Melissa flew out to Rome or Venice, and her father embraced her, dragging himself out of his laboratory; they went for meals together, and visited churches. But it was always awkward. Melissa seldom stayed longer than a weekend. Her mother was the glue that had held them together. Now she was gone, and her father's lack of interest was plain. He did the right thing, called on her birthday and flew home at Christmas. But the two of them were comfortable being apart. As the months passed into years, their long-distance relationship seemed more suitable.

When news came of her father's death, killed in a motorboat accident outside Venice, Melissa mourned, but only briefly. She flew to collect the coffin and arranged burial back home, next to her mother. There was a good complement of his former colleagues at the funeral; he would have been pleased, she thought. She didn't feel much more alone than she had when he'd been alive.

Melissa was his sole heir, but there wasn't much to the estate. Sir Richard had large undisclosed debts, and when the house was sold she was left with barely fifty thousand. After tax, a lot less. It supplemented her salary for a while, and now it was mostly gone.

Was that why she had grabbed on to Fraser? As a lifeline?

She was grateful when Fraser finally mustered the courage to ask her out. Someone was still interested. A respectable, kind guy. Fraser would save her from spinsterhood. That was something – right?

Fraser was a good man. But not for her.

The sherry burned in her throat. Melissa looked around at her gorgeous rooms, and felt the walls closing in on her. The college owned them. Melissa needed to change her life. She'd been in Oxford far too long. Her heart had shattered long ago, but she was still breathing, like it or not. Time to end it with Fraser, gently, and start living.

A clean break. Then a fresh start – somewhere else.

She checked herself out in the mirror. It was an outfit Fraser liked: a warm dress of navy flannel with mother-of-pearl buttons and a little white cardigan, a matching navy bag and flat shoes, so she could walk away quickly when it was all over. Her clothes suddenly seemed horribly dated and prissy to her. Her body was slim but soft, not like it used to be. She wanted to change that, change everything. Buy some cheap shoes and start running.

Melissa took her bag from the hook on the door, locked up and set off. Relief mixed with the nerves. At least now she was making a decision.

Chapter Eight

Fraser spooned some more brown sugar into his espresso. Must be the consistency of treacle now, she thought. He had an incredibly sweet tooth and never put on an ounce. She couldn't say the same.

The candle was burning down in the glass bottle in front of them. Melissa had listened to Fraser banging on about his trip to a flea market in Witney for most of the meal, only nodding her head. She wanted to bring the subject up, but there was never a quiet moment. The tables in the pub were too close, and the waiters very attentive.

'Let's get the bill,' she suggested.

'I'd like another coffee. Irish coffee this time.' Fraser was a bit flushed; he'd had three glasses of wine, and couldn't hold his drink very well. Melissa saw her opportunity.

'Let's walk to your house, then. We can stop off on the way and buy some really good whisky. Much cheaper. More private.'

'Mmm,' he said, his eyes focusing suddenly. They

hadn't had sex in almost a month. 'All right then, darling.'

Night had fallen over Magdalen Bridge. It was crowded with students, townies and tourists cycling up the high street or walking to Magdalen or St Hilda's. Fraser's house was just a little to the south, about a fifteen-minute walk from Christ Church. Melissa screwed up her courage. She didn't want to do this inside his living room. She wanted it over with.

'Fraser.' He reached to take her hand, but Melissa deftly moved away. 'We have to talk.'

'Sounds ominous.' He gave the high-pitched giggle that set her teeth on edge. 'Wedding stuff?'

'More serious than that, I'm afraid.'

That got his attention. He slowed, and looked at her with something like real dismay. Melissa's heart sank. Perhaps this wasn't going to be the clean break she was hoping for.

'Melissa, what's this about?'

She faltered. 'Look, I've been thinking a lot lately, and . . .'

'Are you breaking up with me?' he said, a touch too loudly.

'No,' Melissa said. She stopped. 'Actually . . . Fraser – we've had a wonderful time together, you and I, and you're very dear to me . . .'

'I don't believe it. You are.' He staggered back. 'You're breaking up with me. Calling it off,' he said clearly.

'I just don't think marriage is what I want right now,' Melissa said imploringly. 'We rushed things.'

He chewed his lip bitterly, like a man who'd been publicly humiliated.

'You could have told me this any time. I've spent thousands on the wedding. I've notified all my friends, all my relations. What am I supposed to tell them?'

'Say I couldn't go through with it. Or that we mutually called it off . . .' Melissa felt helpless – he looked so angry and so hurt. 'I'll write to them all if you want to give me the list. Nobody will blame you.'

'Give me my grandmother's ring.' Fraser held out a shaking hand. 'You were bloody lucky that I asked you, Melissa. I should have known better, going for someone like you . . .'

She fished the ring box out of her purse and handed it to him. He hadn't even noticed she wasn't wearing it at dinner.

'Someone like me?'

'Well, you've done it before, haven't you? Let a man down?'

Melissa flinched backwards, as though she'd been struck. Nobody had referred to Will in her presence since her father left the house.

He laughed unpleasantly. 'Surprised? People talk, you know. I offered you a second chance and you flung it in my face. I don't think many men will want to try for third time lucky.'

She tugged her cardigan round herself. 'Sorry you feel

that way.' He was starting to weave in and out of the crowds. Perhaps he'd had more to drink than she thought. 'Fraser, I can walk you home and put on a pot of coffee. We can talk it through tomorrow.'

Fraser shook his head. 'Nothing to discuss. I can get home just fine, thank you, *darling* . . .'

He swerved to avoid a jogger plugged into his iPod, oblivious to the bodies walking around him, and lost his footing. Melissa leaped forward, frightened his ankle was going to twist. She reached out and steadied Fraser's shoulders.

Then a bullet blasted his skull wide open.

People dived to the pavement, scattering and screaming in every direction. Melissa froze still, gaping in horror. There was a hole, a large gash, in the top of Fraser's forehead. She saw grey brain matter. The wound was bleeding, a lot of bright red blood. There was blood dripping on to her hands. Her fiancé's eyes were still open, but they were dull and dead. His body tottered and slumped to the ground.

The movement broke the spell. Distantly she registered the sound of a second gunshot, but her knees had crumpled and she was slumped over Fraser's body, retching. Hysterical screams were all around her. The sound of a car crashing on the road. Melissa fell forward, her fingers scrabbling to find the ground, just to hold herself up. The world was spinning. Fraser was dead. She felt strong arms, men's arms, grab her by the waist, turning her over. Somebody said, 'She's alive,' and then Melissa fainted.

*

The Radcliffe Infirmary was short of beds. It was clear the ward sister wanted her out of there. Fine with Melissa. She had to go. But the police were coming, and the doctors insisted she wait. Her clothes and shoes had been taken in evidence, and a college scout had been sent over with some replacements from her rooms: jeans, a sweatshirt, running shoes, even clean underwear. The humiliations piled up.

The policemen stood at the side of her bed and asked her questions over and again, until the nausea rose in her throat and she had to reach for the grey plastic bucket on her side table. What had she been doing with Fraser Macintosh? How long had they been engaged? Why did she break up with him? Did he have any enemies? Did she? Was she his heir? Did he have life insurance? Was she the beneficiary?

Melissa finally convinced them that she was innocent, just a bystander. She supplied them with full contact details for Fraser's parents. They would take care of everything. When the policemen left, she was utterly exhausted, too tired for anything, too tired to grieve. Nobody else had been shot, they told her. It looked more like a murder than a random attack by a crazed gunman. Melissa was helpless; she couldn't imagine a single person who would wish Fraser harm.

The police had offered her counselling, which Melissa turned down. She was shocked and grieving, but a shrink wouldn't help. The nurses came in once the detectives left and fussed about her a little, as their momentary celebrity. The incident was now featuring on the news bulletins, and the manner of the orderlies had softened. She was almost famous.

Melissa refused visits and calls from concerned colleagues at Christ Church. The day after, she woke up completely clear-headed. She asked for a pen and paper and wrote a long, tactful letter to Fraser's mother. She decided not to tell her about the broken engagement. Instead, she wrote some of the truth. What a brilliant man Fraser was, how good he'd been to her.

She couldn't face seeing Mrs Macintosh right now. The funeral would be soon enough. She wrote that she needed to get over the shock. She was going away for a few days; she knew Fraser would have wanted his birth family to arrange the funeral.

As soon as Melissa dropped the stiff paper envelope into the hospital postbox, she felt an overwhelming sense of panic. Once that was taken care of, her farewell to Fraser and his family, the full horror of her situation rushed upon her. She had been walking with him when he was murdered. She had watched his head crack open right in front of her. An inch the other way, Melissa understood, and it could have been her. What if it had been?

The foul sense of death, Fraser's death, her witnessing of it, hung over the hospital, over Oxford. Melissa felt choked by it. The longing to get the hell away, to clear her head, to be out of this city where the shooter was still at large – because no news bulletin said they'd caught him – was too intense. What if this man had a grudge against Fraser that would extend to her? She had been his fiancée, after all. Melissa's heart thudded; she simply did not feel safe.

Her instincts told her to run. To run immediately and as quietly as she could. She could return here at any time, but for now, it seemed to her that she absolutely had to get away.

She slipped her bare feet out of bed. Her clothes were packed up in a plastic bag next to her bedside table. She gingerly unpeeled the bandage and slipped the IV of fluids from her arm. Then she tugged on her jeans, T-shirt, sweatshirt and shoes, and retrieved her bag. Her purse was in there, with some cash, and her passport. She thought about taking the lift to the front entrance, but one of the nurses had mentioned that the local TV stations were there with a crew, and she definitely didn't want to be filmed.

The door was open at the end of the ward. Melissa walked through it, pacing the corridors randomly until she saw a sign for a goods entrance. There was a freight elevator, and she glanced around, then punched the button and took it down to the basement. A few cars and ambulances were parked around; Melissa walked through them, up a bank of grass and into the street. A glance over her shoulder assured her that yes, there was indeed a small knot of journalists camped out at the front entrance of the hospital.

Melissa headed south. She wouldn't go to Oxford's railway station – too many of her friends commuted to London all the time, and she couldn't face questions. There was a boat service that ran twice a day from the Folly Bridge down to Caversham Bridge in Reading. She would get out there and get on a direct to London, not the Oxford route. After that, she wasn't sure. She started walking, as quickly as she could without breaking into a jog. Fraser had been murdered, right in front of her, and every cell in her body was telling her to run. She needed a break, a little holiday, time to regroup, figure out what to do with her life. Maybe work hard, for the first time, on laying the ghost of William Hyde.

Up in the A&E ward, a young man, olive-skinned and attractive, wearing jogging gear, pushed through the swing doors carrying a huge bunch of flowers. He walked confidently up to the nurses' station and asked to see Melissa Elmet.

'She's not taking visitors,' Nurse Linda Smith responded. 'Sorry.'

'Maybe you'd ask if she'd see me?' He fished around in his pocket for a driving licence. 'I'm Carlos Elmet and I'm her nephew.'

'Carlos . . .'

'My mama, her sister, went to live in Andalucia.' He smiled confidently. None of these women would ever see him again, and the man on CCTV didn't exist and therefore couldn't be caught. His nasal prosthesis, wig and contact lenses were manufactured by some of the best in the business. Certainly he was completely untroubled by the thought of scrutiny from Thames Valley Police.

'Of course. Come this way.' The nurse got up from behind the station; she was fat, and made a production of it. He could wait. There was no rush.

The toxin he had to kill Melissa Elmet was a slow-working thing. She would be unconscious instantly, but would not die until several days later, by which time he'd be in Brazil, enjoying the favours of some barely pubescent girls and two million American dollars.

He followed as the nurse waddled down the corridor and whisked back a curtain. The bed was empty.

'Oh! Look at that, she's gone. Never told us she was leaving. She must have discharged herself. Do you have her mobile number?'

He stared disbelievingly at the bed. He had been complacent and slow. He should have been here an hour ago. Lola Montoya would not be pleased.

'Don't worry.' He collected himself enough for a brilliant smile. 'I'll catch her.'

Chapter Nine

Moira Dunwoody was the chief librarian at the New York Public Library. It was a major position, and she was proud of it. She had reached the zenith of a quiet life spent dedicated to public service. She was married to a fellow librarian, Jack, whom she'd met late in life. There were no children, and that didn't bother her. Moira had plenty of nieces and nephews, and the one thing she really valued was peace and quiet. She adored books, and her eyesight was weak.

Moira had a very pleasant life. Her husband had inherited a townhouse on Brooklyn Heights, something he could never afford if they'd had to purchase it today. They had converted the first floor into a separate apartment and enjoyed an income from Mr and Mrs Kravits, a retired policeman and his wife, good tenants living off an excellent police pension. Moira bought good-quality clothes and organic fruit and vegetables. She and Jack had both been vegetarians since the sixties. They were lean and fit, walking several miles a day, and hoped to live long into a comfortable retirement.

Moira pecked her husband on the cheek on Tuesday morning as she left for work. There was a function on this evening, a fundraiser for the NYPD, and Moira was overseeing everything; a private exhibition of some of their more notable manuscripts was to be the star attraction. She would also make a welcome speech. The Governor, Senators Allen and Jospin, the Yankees' shortstop and a whole bunch of Manhattan's richest would be in attendance. She had prepared thoroughly, and now she was looking forward to a great evening. There would be a fee for the party, and Moira Dunwoody got paid by results.

'I won't see you later,' Jack said, stirring Sweet'N Low into his cinnamon coffee.

'It won't be done till midnight. You can come if you want, honey.'

Jack liked to sleep early. He was five years older than her and needed the rest these days.

'That's OK. I'm going to stay in and watch *SportsCenter*.'

They both smiled at the lie. Jack had the same interest in sports that he had in computer games. Zero.

'Then I'll see you tomorrow.'

He patted her lightly on the back. Good companions, they rarely slept together. Life was full of drowsy contentment, without jagged edges or ecstatic peaks.

Moira selected a light Burberry raincoat and stepped out on to the street.

*

Lola watched her for three blocks; there was no rush. Moira Dunwoody would be an easy kill. She loved her routine, and she loved the open air. On the fourth block Moira stopped at a newsagent and left holding coffee in a cardboard holder and a magazine. She was following a pattern, on her way to the subway.

Lola walked forward as Moira turned towards the subway. She hung back, two or three people behind her, lowering her head once when the target looked round. They boarded the same subway car, and Lola stood in the middle, strap-hanging, with Moira Dunwoody just inches from her, sitting staring into space, knees pressed tightly together. Lola wore slim jeans, a faded T-shirt and a baseball cap with glasses; most men didn't look at her twice. Moira was in a red dress, which would hide the blood and be hard to run in.

They exited at Penn Station, which was perfect. She followed Moira up the steps, the crowd spilling around her. Lola was completely anonymous, and her head was partly lowered, to dodge the cameras. They had filmed her on five continents and never caught her. She varied everything periodically, even her gait.

Moira, humming to herself, exited into the bright sunlight and started to walk towards the library. She had no sense of danger, but then they were in the middle of Manhattan. Lola weighed her options. A more elaborate kill, with the benefit of later discovery, was doable, but she preferred to get it over with and get out. There was unlikely to be much investigation. As Moira turned on to

Eighth Avenue, Lola moved closer to her, her left hand withdrawing a syringe from the outside pocket of her purse. She stumbled against the librarian, cursing.

'Shit! Oh, excuse me.'

'It's all right,' said Moira. 'Don't . . .'

She gasped, in surprise, then horror. Lola had pricked her, and the cyanide had entered her bloodstream.

'I can't . . .' she gurgled.

Breathe. No. Not while you're metabolising cyanide.

She choked a little, and Lola caught her as she teetered. They were standing in the entrance to an underground garage; there were cameras mounted on the wall. Lola carried the jerking body of Moira Dunwoody into the garage, just inside, by the wall. She drew out a knife and stabbed her several times; in the back, the stomach, the heart, moving aside so the blood did not splash her; then she grabbed her purse. Moira would not feel the knife; she had already been dead for ten seconds. But the blood was pumping, and the coroner wouldn't know any differently. Moira Dunwoody, just another mugging victim on the streets of Manhattan.

Lola walked away with practised calm. One block south, she headed west, out towards Hell's Kitchen, away from where an assassin would go. There was a diner on Tenth Avenue and she stopped there for an omelette. They'd be scouring the streets, and she'd be nowhere to be found. After the cops gave up on the subways, she'd get a cab to Brooklyn, then take the train to the airport, hang there for a few hours. The big prize, the Senator, was due to be killed that night. Then she'd have earned her money.

There were nerves in her stomach. It was a big job. Females were rare in Lola's business. The courage and disposition were too often lacking. She enjoyed her reputation, though, and this would enhance it.

Lola had studied up, and knew herself to lack empathy. Not surprising, considering what had happened to her in childhood. What her mother had done. Her psychology didn't bother her. It made her good. She ate well and rehearsed tonight in her mind. The client paid tremendously and assumed the job was done. If not, then she herself was as good as dead. A clean, untraceable kill meant more than money to an operative like her. The mystery was sustained, and the clients loved and feared you. That was essential. Because as soon as they stopped fearing her, they would start hunting her.

Lola had a goal and a plan. Twenty million, US. She knew just where to hide it, and when she disappeared, it would be for life.

Moira Dunwoody was worth a hundred grand to the client. But Ellen Jospin was worth two million.

Yes. Big day today.

Chapter Ten

The roof garden was Will's favourite part of his penthouse. He had a palatial apartment, six bedrooms on three floors, and then this eyrie in the sky. One of the hottest hotel designers in the world had built it for him; clever use of internal walls as windbreaks, mountain plants, and fountains. He liked the sense of the open sky, loved breathing air where it was high enough to be fresh. The traffic below him crawled, windscreens glittering in the sun like tiny diamonds. Everything was peaceful up here.

In the centre of the garden he had placed, at colossal expense, a large swimming pool, surrounded by clear glass. William swam fifty laps in there daily, morning and evening; he'd fucked countless women in there; he lay on a floating mattress sometimes, staring at the stars. There was nobody there to bother him; no ringing phones, no gossip columnists, no fawning sycophants.

Olivia was waiting for him inside. She liked to swim in front of him, nude; her body was good, lean, with perky fake breasts, although he didn't object to that. He'd seen lusher girls, but Olivia was good. She did know how to press his buttons. There was that delicious contrast between the socialite and the sexy girl; she was unattainable to most guys, but not him, of course. Other girls had tried the same trick, but Olivia Wharton was special; she was funny, she was sweet, and she was an accomplished doctor.

The stars were bright; it was a cloudless night. He shivered. Olivia was stunning in that dress. She was sitting on the side of his pool, her bare feet dangling in the warm water, and all the lights of the city's concrete towers behind her. He could see her high-heeled shoes perched on the tiles. The careless gesture was endearing.

Will opened the glass doors and went in. Olivia smiled; she was an incredibly beautiful girl, better than many models he'd had. He walked around the edge of the pool towards her. The water was lit up at night, and shadows danced all around the enclosure. He enjoyed the way they dappled the walls. It was deeply relaxing, familiar and safe, like this girl, whom he'd known for quite some time and who had never annoyed him.

'Hey.'

'Hey,' she said. 'Great party, wasn't it?'

She laughed, a good rich laugh.

'You're not into that?'

'I like a nice party. But they all merge into each other, don't they? Those affairs.' She grinned. 'Senator Jospin has a bug up her ass about you, babe.'

Irreverent. He liked that about her. Yes. It was time, right now.

'Olivia.' He felt a bit stupid; this hadn't been planned before tonight. 'I don't have a ring. I'll get you one, get you a great one.'

'Will . . . ?' she turned her head to him, and those big blue eyes glittered with joy and hope. She clasped her hands together childishly.

'Will you marry me, sweetie?'

She shrieked with joy. 'I will! Of course I will.'

He kissed her, then took her into his arms and started to peel the dress from her shoulders, rubbing his thumbs down across her smooth skin, and she pressed her body into his, eager and hot for him.

When Will woke up, at six, Olivia was still sleeping. That was fine; he didn't need much rest. He left her there in the bed and stepped into his power shower. It was carved from a single slab of jet-black basalt and studded on the inside with the stars and moon picked out in gold. Showers were one of the things Americans did best.

His valet had laid out the day's clothes for him the night before. Will shaved and dressed in under five minutes. He hated wasting time, particularly when there were deals to be done. This morning he walked into the kitchen, where the housekeeper had laid out his breakfast: a pot of Jamaican Blue Mountain coffee, a bagel and lox. He ate fast, enjoying the scent of the coffee filling the room. Not a lot of time, today or any day. The

New York Times and *Wall Street Journal* were laid out for him, along with the *Times* and *Telegraph* from London, arrived on the first flight of the morning. His twenty minutes over breakfast were sufficient to scan them all and process whatever he might need to know. Dull headlines; a crunch in the price of oil, flooding in the Cotswolds, the President's son arrested for DUI.

Will put the papers down and turned to the *Journal*. Still worth reading, even in the days of the internet. He pulled out his phone and checked his appointments for the day. The Japanese bankers from Nomura at noon; some guys from KKR at ten; he was seeing management from a takeover target at eight thirty . . .

Every minute of his day was accounted for. He put in a note: cut the afternoon session with his brokers. He needed half an hour to go to Tiffany's and buy Olivia a ring. The Americans liked solitaire diamonds; the British used coloured stones. He would get her something perfect: a coloured diamond. He thought a perfect canary diamond, a glittering round cut, four or five carats, deep saturation. They might not have it in the store, but they would source it for him. A golden stone for his golden girl.

His eye flicked back to a headline in the English *Telegraph*, lying where he had casually thrown it, on an inside page.

Oxford Academic Shot.

Oxford academic? That was very unusual. The English didn't even allow guns. He drew the paper close to him, scanned the report, and stopped dead.

Fraser Macintosh's fiancée, academic Melissa Elmet, who was present when he was shot, disappeared from a local hospital on Thursday without checking out. Police sources say that Ms Elmet remains an important witness, and they are appealing to her to come forward.

His chauffeur, waiting in the building's garage, and his seven a.m. with the guys from Bear Sterns suddenly seemed far less important.

Melissa Elmet had been caught up in a shooting. She had run from hospital.

She had been about to remarry.

He laid the paper down on his granite countertop. The cold black words in print meant nothing to Will.

He picked up the *New York Times* with intent, wanting to read the American paper to see if it had anything more in it. His forefinger quickly raced through the pages – nothing about an obscure murder in England.

But on the third page there was something that caught his eye. The Chief Librarian of the New York Public Library had been killed. Mugged, they said. Dragged into a garage by some punk, stabbed in multiple places, her bag stolen . . .

Moira Dunwoody. He knew the name. And she had known . . .

A sick feeling started to build in Will Hyde's stomach.

A mugging, he thought. Get over it. Who was Fraser Macintosh, though? Shot by a sniper? A sniper. In

Oxford, that sleepy little town. Connections, Will thought. Coincidences. He did not believe in them.

Stop that. You're paranoid, he thought. Old habits. You haven't been in this game for years. Random violence is a fact of life.

He turned on the television to Bloomberg to pick up the overnight news from Japan. The bank had a lot of investment in the Pacific Rim.

A rolling news scroll was crossing the screen underneath the soothing stream of stock prices. A tornado outside of Dallas, a shooting in a Wyoming church.

'We anticipate an easing of light sweet crude this morning, as—'

'I'm sorry to interrupt, Dave, but I have some breaking news,' the anchorwoman said, being handed a piece of paper. 'We're getting word that Senator Ellen Jospin, the senator from New York, has been found dead at her home on Pennsylvania Avenue in Washington DC and that murder is suspected. Senator Jospin's body was found alongside that of her chauffeur and a Secret Service agent in the underground garage of her apartment building. The cause of death has not been released at this time. The—'

Will Hyde flinched with shock, as if he had been hit. He switched to a news channel. He recognised Jospin's sumptuous building, not far from the White House. He had met her there a couple of times when she served in the Department of Energy. A while ago, now, and it had stuck in his mind because . . .

He put his mug down on the granite countertop and called his chauffeur.

'Jack, are you ready?'

'Yes, sir, Mr Hyde.'

'I'm coming down. Let's get into the office.'

There were other places that he could have done this, but his office was the safest. Will had it routinely swept for bugs, and the telecommunications were absolutely secure.

'You got it.'

Inside his limo, Will settled back against the silver-grey leather and picked up the phone. It was early yet, but he thought Rob would be up. If his old habits were anything to go by. Will had carefully cultivated a few of his contacts from former years. Not many, but one or two key players. Rob Wilson was a communications man. He had access to the databases of most telecoms companies, and knew others who could get where he couldn't.

'Yeah?'

'Rob, it's Will Hyde. I want a number.'

'Cost you. How fast?'

Will glanced at the traffic.

'Ten minutes. Can you send it to my phone?'

'I can do just about anything, but for that kind of speed we're talking fifty.'

'Do it faster and I'll get you a hundred.'

He laughed. 'I love dealing with rich bastards. Sure, why not? It's your money. Who are we looking for?'

'Melissa Elmet, UK, resident of Oxford, recently disappeared.'

He had never told anybody about Melissa. The name meant nothing to Wilson.

'Call you back,' his contact said, hanging up. Will wondered how long it would take. When his mobile buzzed less than two minutes later, he was not surprised. Melissa's number wouldn't have been secure; ex-directory was meaningless. And Rob would jump to it for a man who was offering him a hundred thousand dollars for a few seconds' work. Will smiled, and transferred the money via his phone. He never spoke to a person when making these kind of payments. The less of a trail, the better.

Lincoln Town Cars and yellow cabs jostled and honked outside his tinted windows, Manhattan's bankers and traders on their way to work. The financial district was choked. He often traded in his car at this hour. Will Hyde was fully mobile. But this morning, he was distracted. The Japanese deal, the takeover, it had all faded for him. The world was shrunk to the little number glowing on his cellphone screen.

He might be mistaken. Thinking like a spy, like the soldier he'd been long ago. Melissa Elmet was nobody to anybody, surely. What if there was no connection? What if she was perfectly safe? He had not spoken to her since the day she walked out on him, and he had no desire to do so now. Last night he'd got engaged to a stunningly beautiful woman. He was a wealthy man, moving in another world. Melissa was still teaching at Oxford. She'd been with another guy, and Will Hyde wasn't even bothered. They had both moved on. Calling her would stir things up that should lie dead.

He thought it through for eight minutes, until the limousine parked in his personal bay at the bank's offices. A private elevator lifted him from the car directly to his office. His principal and secondary assistants were already sitting outside.

'No calls, Janet,' he called.

'No, sir.' His secretary was a beautiful brunette, married with two kids in junior school. She had a crush on him, but he tolerated her because she never made a move. Janet wanted Will Hyde, but she wanted her ninety grand salary and generous pension scheme a lot more.

Will closed the door. His office was large but functional: panelled walls and relatively small windows. The view could be distracting, and he didn't care to be in the sights of anybody with a decent telescope. He checked his watch. In England it was noon. Then he moved to his phone, with a slight sigh. He had not done anything like this for a decade.

'Radcliffe Infirmary.'

'Put me through to A and E, please. Nursing station.'

'Who's calling?'

'This is Sergeant Brooks of Thames Valley Police. I need to discuss the circumstances of Melissa Elmet's discharge.'

'Hold on, Sergeant.' There was a pause. His training came back instantly, as though he had never stopped being a field agent. Will spoke with authority, his voice softened to an Oxfordshire burr. In his experience, hospital security in England was lax.

'This is Sally Mount.'

'Sergeant James Brooks, Thames Valley. Sorry to be bothering you again, but they want me to check something in the statement.'

A sigh. 'All right, but we're very busy . . .'

'Miss Elmet checked herself out.'

'We told you, not even that. She just left.'

'And she still hasn't been in contact?'

'We don't expect to see her again. She was only being held for observation. Didn't want the therapy, so I suppose if she has problems she'll go to her GP.'

Will asked his main question. 'OK, almost done. How many visitors came looking for her?'

'Just her nephew, the Spanish one.' Will heard giggles, the phone being muffled. Sally was hissing at her colleagues to behave. 'Carlos.'

'Bit of a charmer, isn't he?'

'Oh yeah.' She relaxed, seeing it was all right to joke. 'The girls are all hoping he comes back.'

'And Carlos came after she left.'

'Brought her some flowers.'

'Thanks, Nurse, you've been very helpful.' He hung up, punched another button on his phone. 'Janet, cancel all my meetings.'

'But sir, your first is due in ten minutes. They're in the lobby.'

Shit. Will hated being rude. 'OK. Get Jack Sansone down here to take it. Tell him I said to make conversation, don't offer anything, and cancel all my other meetings. Personal commitment. We'll reschedule. I'm out of the office for today.'

Jack was Will's deputy chairman, more than capable of gladhanding a few small businessmen from the Midwest. He was older than Will, headhunted from Wachovia and exceptionally ambitious. Will had put him on the board because he was capable. The lust for power of lesser men didn't bother him.

'Right away, Mr Hyde.' Janet Navarro never argued with him. Few did.

Will picked up his phone and headed for a second elevator, right into the lobby. He was going to speak to Melissa, and he wanted to do it in the open air. The idea that they would be talking was very strange, even disturbing, but he had no doubts.

He decided to walk uptown towards Tiffany's. Concentrate on buying Olivia the most spectacular ring, one his wife could wear proudly. That thought assuaged some of his sense of guilt. It wasn't logical to feel guilty, and Will hated it when his emotions were out of control.

Chapter Eleven

Melissa stood in the middle of Paddington station, feeling a little bit stupid. She had found a train and almost automatically headed to London. She had no clothes other than the ones she was wearing, a bag with her passport and purse in it, and that was all. Not even a toothbrush. The escape planning hadn't got that far. So she wanted what, a holiday? Where? What did she want to do with her life?

The crowds in the station were making her a little claustrophobic. It had been crowded that night on Magdalen Bridge too. She breathed in and walked out of the station, to the front, where there was a long queue for taxis. Melissa joined it, more to give herself time to think than anything. Perhaps she would go somewhere very quiet and calming. The British Museum. No, too many tourists. The National Portrait Gallery would be better. She could walk up and down, look at some of her favourite paintings, make some decisions about where her life was going.

Her phone buzzed in her bag, startling her. Calm

down, Melissa told herself, you're way too jumpy. You're at Paddington station, in broad daylight. She fished the mobile out and glanced at the screen. Not that many people had her number, and they were all programmed in, but the screen said *Unknown*.

A telemarketer perhaps. She was embarrassed at her attack of nerves. She had to get over this, what had happened to Fraser, the senseless violence of it, or she'd be living the rest of her life like some coward, shivering at shadows. There was nobody to look after her but herself.

'Melissa Elmet,' she said.

'Melissa, this is Will Hyde. We haven't spoken for a long time.'

Her fingers tightened around the phone.

'Will?' she gasped.

Dear God. It was truly him. She would know the voice anywhere. A decade's absence, more, was wiped away in a few beats of her pounding heart. Will's voice. The same as it was the day she walked out.

A sweat broke out right across her body, and she felt her face flush scarlet. She was dizzy, lightheaded. She steadied herself against the shock.

'How did you get this number?'

'I've got a lot of contacts. It's not important. Look, Melissa, I saw what happened to you, and I'm very sorry for your loss.' His tone was brisk. That was good; she didn't want his pity, wanted that less than anything. She regained control.

'Thank you,' she said coolly. 'I hope you're well.'

'I didn't call to socialise with you, Melissa. I don't want to alarm you, but you have to listen to me very carefully.'

She blinked with surprise. 'What?'

'I want you to be safe. Whatever might have happened in the past between us.'

'Why wouldn't I be safe?' she asked, frightened. None of her fantasies about hearing from Will again had involved a conversation like this. The dizziness returned.

'Look, there's no easy way to say this. In my opinion, the bullet that hit your fiancé was meant for you.'

She stumbled out of the queue, leaned back against a wall.

'Are you waiting?' a fat woman in a blue coat asked her. Melissa shook her head numbly, gestured to her to go forward.

'And why do you think that?'

'People have been killed here, too. Senator Ellen Jospin of New York. A woman called Moira Dunwoody. She was the Chief Librarian of the New York Public Library. A businessman called David Fell, in Venice.'

'I'm sorry, but . . .'

Her denial trailed off. That last name rang warning alarms. David Fell. He had funded Daddy.

'Every one of them is connected with your father. He died too, I believe, in some kind of accident.'

'Yes,' she said numbly. 'But Will, I've never heard of the librarian lady . . . or the senator. And I lost contact with Dad a while before he died.'

'Your father took two meetings with Senator Jospin right before he went back to Italy and died out on the lagoon. I remember noticing it in the press. They weren't big meetings. She was serving on the energy committee then and he came to speak to them on conservation. The two met privately. I track what the politicians in my area do, it helps with business.'

Melissa shook her head. So her father had met some American committee, so what? He was a scientist and loved to grandstand. It didn't surprise her. He might have come back to Britain to visit her, though. But then his career had always come first.

'And the librarian?'

'On the same visit. He sat next to her at a benefit dinner that night; he was a guest of Columbia University. I know, because I attended as a patron. He saw me.' Will paused. 'It was an awkward moment, as you might imagine. It stuck in my mind.'

Melissa winced. What agony, what humiliation for her father. To see Will Hyde in all his billionaire glory at some bloody dinner in New York. The boy he had rejected, dragged Melissa from, able to buy and sell him a million times over.

'Did you talk?' She would pretend this detail meant nothing to her.

'We were both busy,' Will said diplomatically. Melissa closed her eyes and wriggled a little in pure shame.

'Two women meet my father and then they're dead? Come on, he must have met thousands of people.'

'I don't believe in coincidence. Not with my background. And David Fell, the third man, was funding your father's research in Rome.'

'But who killed them? Why?'

'Don't know that yet. I'll find out.'

'How will you do that? You're a banker, Will, not a detective.'

A pause on the end of the line. She could almost see him struggling with himself. It was quite clear he wanted to convince her he was serious about this threat he was imagining.

'Before I took over this bank I worked in MI6 for many years,' he said.

She was completely silent. A strange mixture of emotions raged through her. Regret. Desire. Fear. She was almost grateful for the fear, because the ice on her heart was cracking open, against her will, like a glacier moving and melting at the advent of spring.

Will Hyde, her Will, a spy. That brave. A British spy, and then a self-made man.

'That's how you got my number, then,' she joked weakly.

'Yes.'

'I don't understand what any of it has to do with me, Will.'

'Do you have any brothers or sisters?'

Had he forgotten her so completely? 'You know I don't.'

'Step-siblings, anything like that?'

'No.'

'Melissa, a man claiming to be your nephew Carlos, from Spain, came to the Radcliffe Infirmary right after you walked out, carrying flowers. The nurses took him to your bed.'

The fear was stronger now, crowding out the sudden rush of longing for him.

'A journalist, a tabloid writer,' she suggested. 'Why didn't they check his ID?'

'They did. He had a proper driver's licence in the name of Carlos Elmet. Journalists don't usually go to that much trouble. And they couldn't have obtained a false one in the time from the shooting to when you walked out. That is the mark of a professional.'

Her throat was dry. 'A professional killer.'

'I might be wrong. I don't want you to take any chances.'

She thanked God for the wall at her back. The world was threatening to start spinning again, and she did not want to faint. She didn't want Will Hyde to think she was weak.

'I've – I've got my passport. I can take the under-ground to Paddington and get on the Heathrow Express. Barcelona or Geneva or somewhere . . .'

'Definitely not,' he said sharply. 'They'll be watching the ports and airports for you right now. Later, maybe. But don't use your credit card, don't check into a hotel. Don't get money at a cashpoint.'

Now she was panicking. 'But I only have sixty

pounds in my purse, Will. What the hell am I supposed to do?'

There was another pause.

'Will?'

'I'm thinking. Don't panic, Melissa, they didn't find you at the Radcliffe and they don't know where you are right now. What I want you to do is to go to a hotel, the Victrix in Covent Garden. There will be a reservation waiting for you in the name of Olivia Wharton.'

'Olivia Wharton? Who's she?'

'My fiancée. She won't mind.' His words hit her like a fist in the solar plexus. Of course it had to happen, Melissa told herself, and the only surprise was that he'd been single this long. But her eyes were wet, and she was deeply grateful he couldn't see her dash her hand across them. 'You will not need to present any ID. There will be a suite set up for you, and food inside it. Now this is very important.'

'OK.'

'I do not want you to open that door to anybody but me. Not room service, not housekeeping, nothing. The hotel will be instructed not to bother you. Don't order anything, do not leave the room. Are you clear on that?'

'Perfectly clear.'

'Maybe I'm paranoid, but if not, your life could depend on it. It's as important as that.'

'I understand, Will.' She forced the words out of her mouth, half choking on them. 'And thank you.'

Another momentary pause. 'Go there now. Get in a

taxi. I'm coming to get you, and then we can figure out what to do.'

'You're in London?'

'New York. But I'll be on the next plane.'

She said in a daze, 'All right. I'm on my way.'

'See you later.' He hung up, and Melissa realised she didn't have any way to call him back. Tears were flowing freely now, and she was shaking. Other travellers moved away from her, embarrassed. Melissa didn't care. She grabbed a tissue from her bag, and mopped at her face. It was important to get herself together so she didn't make a scene at the hotel. She wished desperately that she had brought some make-up with her. Of course, there was a branch of Boots just yards behind her in the station. But Will had told her to run, and she was quite certain, from his tone, that he was not joking.

The cabs lined up quickly and the passengers piled into them. Melissa was at the head of the queue within five minutes. She asked for the Victrix and the driver sped off without needing further instructions.

The hotel was jaw-dropping, but Melissa did not have time to take it in. A vast marble lobby, complete with an enormous fountain and massive modern art canvases; sleek, minimalist Italian designer sofas; massive, cinema-sized television screens, playing the news. A slice of Manhattan in the middle of London.

She was intimidated, but walked up to reception anyway.

'Yes. Can I help you?'

Melissa thought she saw a flash of disdain in the young woman's eyes as they scanned her jeans and sweatshirt.

'Yes. I believe you have a room for me, name of Olivia Wharton.'

The girl tapped a couple of keys. Clearly there was a note appearing on her screen. She scanned it, and went slightly pale.

'Oh yes, of course, Dr Wharton. I am so sorry. Your suite is all ready for you. Can I take any luggage . . .'

'No thank you.'

'Let me get the porter to conduct you to your suite.'

'That's OK,' Melissa said, taken aback. The girl was so deferential, she was falling over herself to suck up to her. 'I'd rather just take the key card. I prefer to be by myself for a while, if you don't mind.' She managed a smile. 'I'm exhausted, want a good sleep.'

'Of course, ma'am. Just a second.' There was some frenzied tapping of keys, then the receptionist handed over a smart little wallet. 'You have the Windsor Suite, it's the best in the hotel, Dr Wharton. If you take any elevator, the suite has a dedicated button.'

'Thank you.'

'We do hope you and Mr Hyde are satisfied with the accommodations – if there's anything else you need, or anything you want changed, please let us know.'

'Thank you,' Melissa said again, feeling a bit foolish. She took the card and walked to the lift with the uneasy sense that they were watching her; because they thought she was the new queen of the Hyde empire, and they wondered, no doubt, why she dressed like that. She hit the button and the lift was mercifully waiting. When it swallowed her up, Melissa exhaled with relief. She pressed the light for the Windsor Suite, and the elevator whisked her upwards with a satisfyingly quiet whirr.

The doors hissed open, and she found herself in a corridor lined with thick carpet and walnut panelling. Her card slotted into a door, the only door in the hallway, and it swung open.

Melissa gasped in amazement. It was a fantasy – a colossal room spread out across almost the entire floor of the hotel. There was a vast Louis XIV bed, two couches, desks with computers and faxes on them. To her left she saw a cavernous bathroom lined in travertine marble, with a Jacuzzi, a power shower and a bath you could swim in. To her right was a separate sitting room with its own cinema-sized wall-mounted TV. Behind the bedroom was a walk-in wardrobe and a small gym; there was a weights machine, a treadmill and a bike for spinning. Arrangements of fresh flowers were everywhere.

In the centre of the living room a table had been laid with food. There were pitchers of water and juice, a silver bucket with a magnum of Krug – Melissa smiled at the gesture; she was hardly likely to be drinking champagne – and trays of sandwiches. She noticed smoked salmon, cucumber, and roast beef. There was also an entire roast chicken, an enormous basket of fruit, a tray of cakes, bread rolls and croissants. Somebody had set up a small fridge freezer, and Melissa opened it to find bags of salad, a dressed crab, ice creams, milk and cream. On the table was an enormous box of Charbonnel and Walker chocolates, and a card in a little envelope.

She couldn't help smiling at the colossal waste. Perhaps Will thought she was morbidly obese or something; she would never get through this amount of food in a month of Sundays. The little card, in its envelope, was sitting there. Melissa couldn't help herself; she ripped it open. In a hotel employee's neat print it read:

Please eat something and try not to worry. I will be there as soon as I can. Yours, Will.

The friendliness, the pity in the note tugged at the cords around her heart. She meant nothing to him, she saw that; he wasn't bothered that she had had a fiancé, and he was getting married himself. No, he was coming for her not on a white charger to rescue his true love but from some sense of loyalty, protectiveness to an old flame who might be in danger of death.

Melissa tried to imagine the beauty and youth of whatever girl he was with now. She was appalled that she cared so much, with Fraser, poor Fraser, dead not forty-eight hours. She wanted to crawl into a hole and just curl up and die. Will was coming, and he would see her just as she was: no make-up, her hair in need of a cut, her roots untouched, years of worry etched on her face, plus lack of sleep and a few days of fear.

But none of it could be helped. Perhaps he'd got it all wrong, but she didn't want to take the risk. Despite everything, she loved life. She wanted a fresh chance, and she had no desire to die.

So let him come.

Melissa walked slowly into the bathroom and peeled off her clothes. There were two voluminous white towelling bathrobes laid out warming on the towel rack. Carefully she ran a quarter of a bath, and using the free Floris bubble bath they provided, she started to hand-wash everything she was wearing. Then she hung as much as she could out on the hot metal rails, and placed the rest on windowsills, to dry in the sun. It was a bit rough and ready, but she wasn't going to meet Will Hyde wearing dirty clothes. If they were damp, they were damp.

It was the early evening. Outside her vast windows the sun was setting over London, the sky streaked with coral and gold. Suddenly Melissa was absolutely exhausted. She drained the water and ran a fresh bath, sliding into it gratefully. She scrubbed her hair with the free shampoo; there was, mercifully, a small travel kit with a razor, a toothbrush and a tiny tube of toothpaste.

She pulled on one of the robes and slid her feet into the matching pair of snow-white cashmere slippers, embroidered with the hotel's crest. This might be the most luxurious room Melissa had ever been in in her life. She was simply grateful to be decent. The fluffy white robe she drew around her like a comfort blanket.

Nobody was there, and at last she allowed herself to cry. For Fraser, poor inoffensive Fraser, shot in the head. For her father, and whatever he'd got mixed up in, because perhaps he'd been murdered, perhaps he'd been terrified. For herself, and her danger. And because she was about to see Will Hyde again, but it would be nothing like the fantasies, nothing like the joyful scenes she'd imagined for long, hopeful years after they split up.

She did not want to see him. And yet she did want to see him, desperately. It was like being a child, picking at a scab even though it hurt. She couldn't stop.

Hungry after her crying bout, Melissa forced herself to eat a couple of sandwiches. She took a long drink of water, brushed her teeth. It was early yet; perhaps she should watch TV. But she was afraid, scared of seeing herself, scared of seeing the pictures of Fraser's body being loaded on to an ambulance. Instead, she peeled off her robe and crawled into the massive bed. The sheets were deliciously cool and crisp. She wasn't used to being nude in bed, but she was physically drained. She closed her eyes, her damp hair tumbling about her on the pillow, and she was soon fast asleep.

When she woke it was five in the morning. She was disorientated; she had no idea where she was. She sat up, frightened, blinking, looking around the hotel, until it all came back to her.

Gingerly she headed for the shower, then blow-dried her hair. She could not look beautiful for Will, but at least she would look respectable. She reached out and touched her clothes; thank God, they had pretty much dried overnight.

She got dressed. She was ravenous; the sandwiches had dried out slightly, and their corners were turning up, but they were still edible. She ate two, then a banana, and made herself a pot of English Breakfast from a tray with a kettle and various sachets of coffee and herbal tea. She was hungry enough that it all tasted delicious.

On the large desk by the window, the hotel had provided writing paper and a Mont Blanc pen. Melissa started to make notes, as the sun rose over the city. Will Hyde would whisk her out of here, but he would not stay with her. Melissa was still foggy about some of the stuff he'd said yesterday, but she trusted that Will would get her away safely from whoever, whatever it was. Beyond that, she still had no plans.

She sipped tea and thought about it. Maybe she would go somewhere quiet and write a novel. That was risky, though, no guarantees. She decided she would head south, to Rome, where she had contacts in the government's archaeological department, where her father had worked. She would take a job teaching students or putting on guided tours for rich tourists. She was bilingual, and knew a few city officials. It shouldn't be impossible. At the very least she'd wind up in a city full of good food, good wine and sunshine. There were worse fates than that.

Maybe there would be a man there for her too. A

divorcee, or a widower. Somebody she could feel passionate about.

Melissa's mind jumped to Will, and she fought the impulse to run to the mirror, straighten her hair some more. Pull yourself together, she thought fiercely. He's gone. Long gone. And you can't really believe he's the only man in the world for you. You're a bit too old for fairy stories, Melissa Elmet.

OK, so Fraser Macintosh hadn't been the one. But had there been a chance for her to find anybody? She'd locked her heart away so carefully, not even she could find it.

That would have to change, if she didn't want to die an old maid. Melissa knew she had treated Will badly, made the wrong decision. But she had punished herself over it far more harshly than he ever could . . .

On the paper, she started to write a list of names, from memory. Professore Gina d'Almattia. Don Angelo Ruffini, Carlotta Leone, Signor Buttuoco . . .

There was a knock on the door. Melissa jumped out of her skin, automatically leaping from her place. Her chair toppled backwards on to the floor, and she pressed a hand to her heart.

'No thank you,' she called loudly. 'I don't want room service.'

'Melissa. It's me,' Will said.

She didn't have to ask him to say it twice. She would recognise the voice anywhere, any time. Numbly she picked up the chair from the floor and straightened it. She walked to the door, and unlatched it.

He was standing there, in a dark suit. His shirt was crumpled; clearly he had just got off the plane. He was bigger than she remembered, the muscles of the chest broader. His biceps were huge; Melissa could see them even under his well-cut clothes. He looked tired, and he had five o'clock stubble, but he was tanned, strong and incredibly attractive.

She couldn't help herself. She flushed scarlet.

Will came into the room, carefully shutting the door behind him.

'Hey.' He looked her over, and she had the horrible sensation of his being shocked, and not in a good way. 'Melissa. How are you?'

'Fine,' she said. 'Given I think all this is nonsense.'

'Quite possibly. I'm being cautious.'

'I don't have a lot of cash on me, Will. I need to access my money. Otherwise, what can I do?'

He wasn't paying attention; he had been looking all around the room, scanning it. Melissa was instantly aware that he had noticed her, taken her in and found her undesirable; he was not shaken, not affected by seeing her. She was just the fact of his old girlfriend, an object to be protected. Olivia Wharton had nothing to worry about.

'We'll sort all that out, don't worry. Will you come with me?'

She swallowed hard; swallowed her pride, and her heart. 'Of course. And I know you've been up all night coming to get me. Thank you, Will.'

He looked at her then and smiled lightly, and it broke her heart. There was sympathy there, kindness, but no desire, no passion. She felt horribly unattractive.

'You think I would leave you in danger?'

She had to say it. 'Will – what happened – I'm sorry.'

He looked at her then, his dark eyes holding her blue ones. 'Don't be, Melissa. We were both young. We've got different lives now. Come on, let's get out of here.'

'Where are you going to take me?'

Will shrugged. 'How about New York? I work there, and I've got plenty of places where I can put you up. You'll be safe enough. Just until I figure out what's going on.'

She looked away, not wanting to meet his eyes. 'I can't stay in one of your apartments for ever, though. I have to get back to Oxford, get back to work.'

Will didn't know she'd quit, and she didn't want him to.

'There are lots of good schools in Manhattan.' *Schools*, not *universities*. He'd been in America so long, he'd acquired a slight mid-Atlantic twang. 'Columbia's Ivy League, perfect for you. I'm sure they'd love an Oxford academic.'

'And you've got influence?'

'I've got influence.'

Melissa flushed, hating that she still wanted him. It was so humiliating. Anger made her terse.

'I'll come, but I've got to get some money. I need to buy things. Fresh clothes, toothpaste, make-up. Basics.'

Will sighed. 'It may be nothing, but I'd much rather get you back to the States. If you are being followed, then shops are an open opportunity. My jet is waiting for you. I'll call ahead and have a selection of clothes that fit you and good make-up waiting in the apartment. Toothpaste, shampoo, the kitchen stocked, the whole bit.'

She stiffened. 'I'm not a pauper, Will. I have savings from my salary. I can buy my own groceries and dresses.'

'I know that. I'm not suggesting . . .' He ran his hand over his hair, exasperated, a gesture she knew well, that brought their dates flooding back to her. 'It's not for you, it's for me. If you let me call ahead it will save me hours of time. We have a departure slot booked. In New York, the bank is in the middle of a takeover deal. If I miss stuff at the office it could potentially cost me hundreds of thousands of dollars. Do me a favour, Melissa, let me get your stuff for you. Just once. I'm trying to be efficient.'

There was no answer; she knew it. She tugged her bag around her shoulder.

'Fine, it's your money. And, you know, thank you again.'

He said shortly, 'I wouldn't let anyone hurt you. Shall we go?'

She nodded and looked around for her room key.

'Don't worry about that. Come on.'

Melissa followed Will along the hall to the lifts.

'We'll take the stairs,' he said. 'Indulge me. Force of habit.'

'No problem,' she answered. But he was already ahead of her. Melissa saw he moved quite differently now from the man she remembered; and nothing like a banker. His shoulders were tense, his body sprung, his head lifted, like a cat's. He was listening, his neck taut, his eyes scanning the stairwell. She hurried behind him, not wanting to be far from him. He was a warrior, suit or no suit. She wasn't sure if the thrill that coursed through her was desire or terror.

They reached the ground floor. Will strode through the lobby. Melissa put her hand on his arm, timidly.

'What? Let's go. Car's waiting.'

'I haven't checked out,' she said. 'I had a bottle of mineral water.'

He stared at her, then laughed. 'Emma.'

'Yes, sir?' asked a uniformed receptionist, walking past them to the desk.

'Charge this lady's room to my account, won't you? Check us out.'

'Of course, Mr Hyde.'

The staffer walked on without blinking an eye. Melissa shrugged, looking away so he didn't see the expression crossing her face. She had lived a decade in Oxford without meeting a single man like Will. Fraser included, Melissa thought, then despised herself for her disloyalty.

There was a limousine waiting out front: a Lincoln Town Car. A uniformed chauffeur stood in front of it. He tipped his cap to Will.

'Hiya, Jake,' Will said. 'Out to Heathrow, please.'

'Sure thing, Mr Hyde.' He smiled at Melissa and leant forward to open the door for her.

She almost wasn't sure what happened next. There was a soft, negligible sound, a *phut*, and then Jake the chauffeur was standing up, bewildered . . . and there was a hole, a large one, in the sleeve of his jacket.

'What the hell was . . .'

Will stepped forward and shoved. Melissa gasped, sprawling forwards over the back seat as Will slammed the door. She rolled over to see a blur of bodies. Will Hyde had jumped into the driver's seat, the chauffeur was stumbling backward, up the steps of the hotel, Will was spinning the wheel. They had already started to move. The car screeched into traffic, Will expertly weaving his way at high speed. There was a loud bang, and her head whipped round to see a spider crack in the rear windscreen.

Melissa moaned in terror. 'Somebody's shooting at us.'

'Yeah.' Will's voice was grim. 'This car has bulletproof glass. But I'm not armed. I should have been, Melissa, I'm sorry.' His eyes were on the street, on the traffic building up around Tottenham Court Road. 'I'm going to do some very illegal stuff now, and I want you to do exactly as I say. Don't hesitate. Got it?'

'Yes,' she said, her voice shaking.

'Stay close to the door. You'll be getting out.' He wrenched the wheel and took the car into the bus lane. Melissa twisted her body around to look behind her, but the window was white with hairline cracks. There was another thud, and another; bullets splintering into the metal of the car, into the rear window.

'Oh my God,' Melissa gasped. 'We're going to die.' She wanted to pray, but now she was sitting in the back of this car, the words wouldn't come. There was nothing in her head but the road, the traffic, how good that bulletproofing really was . . .

'Yeah. But not today.' He suddenly spun the wheel and the car mounted a traffic island and ploughed across the road, into oncoming traffic. Melissa screamed, but Will floored the accelerator and the vehicle plunged through a tiny gap of road into a side street, with horns blaring behind them, people shouting abuse.

Pedestrians scattered. The Lincoln Town Car mounted the kerb.

'Get out. Run after me,' Will said, and she wrenched the door open, shoved past a woman with a pushchair, who was yelling at her. Will was running forwards; she followed him. He was going slowly for her sake, she knew. She pushed her legs, sprinting, and caught up with him. There was an office building right ahead, a printer's.

'Shall we go in there?'

'No. Closed end.' She had no idea what he meant, but followed him anyway. Will ran through an alley and on to Grafton Way. 'Come on!'

Her heart was bursting, but he gestured across the street and she saw it: the squat brick gatehouses leading into the colonnaded façade of University College, rising up like a sanctuary. Will turned and grabbed her hand.

'Melissa, take a deep breath, you have to be relaxed right now. Look normal. Got it?'

She nodded. But as she did so, she heard the unmistakable sound of footsteps round the corner, running, getting closer. Will grabbed her hand and led her across Gower Street. Melissa sucked her breath in, trying to regulate it. Will Hyde had already recovered. She guessed that was what happened when you were super-fit. Will walked up to the gatehouse.

'This is Professor Melissa Elmet from Oxford University. She's got an appointment with the bursar.'

'Can I have your ID, please?' the guard said.

Melissa fished around in her bag and produced a Bodleian Library card. That seemed to do the trick. He pressed a button and the electronic gates swung open. There were crowds of students everywhere; laughing, carrying files and piles of books. Will said nothing, but his hand was pressing firmly into the small of her back. Melissa let him push her forwards, up the steps and through the stone pillars. She turned her head to see a hooded figure speaking to the guard; head lifted, it caught her staring, leaped over the gate, started to run . . .

'You never look back,' Will hissed. He shoved her forwards, and the shadows of the tall white stone pillars blessedly swallowed them up. Now they were in some kind of central hall. There were crowds of kids.

Will took her hand. 'Just walk with me. Like we're together.'

She smiled nervously. His fingers rubbed across hers.

The students crowded around them. He was walking quickly, but not running. They went down another corridor, into a room, out into a courtyard.

'We'll head straight back to the main road. Turn left,' Will ordered. She saw it ahead of her, Euston Square Tube station. Will glanced back with the slightest movement of his head.

'He lost us in there. Get inside.'

She did. Will pulled out an Oyster card, swiped it twice, and she was heading into the tunnels.

'Metropolitan line,' he said.

Melissa obeyed him. Her heart was thudding in her chest. Any second now she expected to hear that sound again, the feet of an assassin thudding towards her, running through the tunnels, hood over his face. But there was nobody. The train was pulling in as they reached the platform. Will pushed her to the back, by the doors, and stood in front of her, his body directly blocking hers. His eyes scanned the platform.

Nothing. The train pulled out, into a tunnel.

Melissa knew better than to speak to Will now, or ask where they were going. At Baker Street he got out. Melissa hurried behind him, and he led her through the tunnels to the Circle line.

'Going back the way we came?'

He didn't reply. 'You got your passport, right?'

She patted her handbag. 'Yes.'

'We're going to Belgium. On the Eurostar.' He grinned. 'Have you ever been to Bruges?'

'No,' Melissa said. 'I'd like to go, though, I hear it's beautiful.' Then she blushed, because she was making small talk while somebody was trying to kill her. 'But your jet . . .'

'They'll wait all day. Or at least till I can contact them.' He smiled bleakly. 'I'd expect these people to have a number of operatives at the airport. We'll go to New York, from the Continent.'

'OK.' Melissa wanted to say more, to thank him again, to clutch at him, to beg him not to leave her. She was past embarrassment now, almost past desire. She couldn't stress out at her make-up-free face and mid-thirties teacher's body. Will Hyde was keeping her alive. That was all she could think about.

A creaky old train trundled through the tunnel like an angel of mercy. Will satisfied himself there were no killers in the carriage, and she rode back to St Pancras next to him, head down, not wanting to make eye contact with anyone.

They emerged into the sleek new station. Will led her up to the ticket desks.

'We're on a date,' he whispered. 'Look happy, look like we're in love.'

Melissa forced a smile; Will was more natural. He slid a strong arm around her waist, and she could feel his muscles through the thin cotton of his shirt. She felt her skin thrill at his touch, the tiny hairs standing on end; of course, she told herself, because you're practically hysterical and this man is all that stands between you and a bullet.

'Hello, sir, can I help you?'

'Dunno. Can you?' Melissa noticed the mid-Atlantic twang had disappeared; his old Oxfordshire burr had replaced it, and he was slurring his words very slightly, like he'd had half a glass of wine too many. 'I want to take my girlfriend abroad. Just for lunch. 'Cos we can.' He beamed at the ticket agent. 'We got our passports. You have two seats?'

'For which destination?' The ticket agent was a forty-something man, and completely immune to Will's charm.

'Don't care, mate. Whatever you got. Last-minute, see?' He shrugged. 'How about Belgium? I did Paris last year.'

There was some interminable tapping. Melissa tensed. Every second she expected the hooded man to come barrelling round the corner, the long nozzle of his silenced gun pointed directly at her forehead . . .

'I do have two tickets to Bruges for the twelve fifty-seven departure, but only first class remain.'

'Not a problem, mate.' Will squeezed Melissa and placed his lips to her forehead. 'Cash do you?'

He pulled out a wallet thick with fifty-pound notes and laid the money on the counter. The agent scooped up the notes and printed out two tickets. He managed a tiny smile. 'Enjoy your trip.'

'We're going to,' Will agreed. He took the tickets and put them in his jacket pocket, ushering Melissa towards the barriers.

'No.' She was firm. 'I need five minutes.'

'For what? They could be anywhere.'

'If they could shoot us, they wouldn't wait,' Melissa said. 'Right, Will?'

He shrugged. 'Probably.'

'I just have to brush my teeth. I have to. There's a Boots round the corner, right in the station.'

He hesitated, then wavered. 'All right, but be as fast as you can.' A smile. 'And bring me a mineral water.'

She half ran around the corner to the shop. They had a rack of travel toiletries; she grabbed toothpaste, a brush. She looked longingly at the make-up. She wanted to get some, fix herself up a little for Will. Vanity, on the run? She mocked herself; there was no time, was there? And no point. Will Hyde was long gone, like her youth.

Melissa picked up the bottled water, paid, and ran to the lavatories. It felt so good to do her teeth. Just being clean was better than nothing. She smoothed down her hair in the mirror and ran back out to him.

'Thanks for the water,' Will said. 'You look refreshed.'

Melissa smiled weakly. He was being polite; he cared enough to save her, but it was painfully obvious he was no longer attracted to her. She was filled with the urge to get to safety and then get away from him. While she was afraid, her heart was not aching; but the aftershock of this meeting was going to be brutal.

She just wanted to get through this. Afterwards, she would go somewhere far, far away from Will, and do . . .

Her mind stopped there. She had no idea what she

might do. Her whole world had shattered.

'We won't stop for champagne. Not now, anyway. Let's just get on the train.'

'OK,' Melissa said. The tension leached into every pore of her skin. 'I'm tired,' she added.

Will nodded. 'Sleep on the train. I'll be there, you'll be safe. The Eurostar is harder to attack than a plane. And I don't think they'll be looking for us there.'

He turned and led her into the boarding area; there was a large crowd of travellers, and Melissa pressed herself close to Will. He presented the tickets and passports for a final check, and they were standing on the platform, with the sleek red and yellow train hissing into the terminal. Passengers dismounted, the crowd flowed around Melissa; she tried not to panic. Will's hand closed over hers, and his thumb brushed against her skin. Reassuring her.

Melissa leaned her head in, close to him.

'Will.' She was timid, but she asked him all the same. 'Who are these people? Why are they trying to kill me? I'm just a lecturer. I've got no money . . .'

He shook his head. 'Too many people.'

She bit her lip, feeling stupid. And totally out of control.

'We'll talk properly later today. I'll tell you everything I know. Trust me, OK?'

'Sure.' Like she had any other option.

Will put his hand on her shoulder and guided her into the train; they found their seats, in first class, by the window.

'It would be a good idea for you to go to sleep now,' he said.

She was puzzled. Passengers were striding past them, finding their places, stowing hand luggage. 'What? Now?'

Will gestured with his hand, and moved his body. Light dawned. She swallowed.

'Like this?' Melissa murmured. She turned her face to the window, and her back to the carriage; her face nestled against the fabric of the seat. It could not now be seen by anyone walking through the train.

'Just like that,' he said, voice soft in her ear. 'And Melissa – if you can really sleep, do. A professional can tell when somebody's pretending.'

'I'll try.' She closed her eyes, she didn't want to look at him anyway. He was physically with her, but his heart was miles away; the distance of an ocean, and long bitter years. Her mind was too full. The brutal events of the last few days played themselves out like a movie in her mind. She had questions . . . so many of them. And somebody was desperate to make sure they never got answered. She saw the chauffeur flinching away, the hole in the sleeve of his jacket. She saw Fraser crumple, the obscene gash in the middle of his forehead, the light visibly fading from his eyes. She saw Will at her door, his look of friendly concern; the complete detachment in his eyes . . .

I can't bear it, Melissa thought. But she had to bear it. She had to endure. The main thing was to get safe, and the second thing was to get away from him.

For that matter, why was she trusting him? He'd got her unlisted number. He had appeared from nowhere, like a ghost. He knew all the connections between her father and three people who'd been brutally murdered.

But her soul had the answer to that one. Will Hyde would never physically hurt her. She knew him; that was simply not in his character. Not possible. However much being with him might wound her, break her heart, she trusted him completely, and she would trust him until the day she died. Which might be sooner rather than later.

The train shuddered gently, then started to move. Nothing was happening, nobody was pointing any guns. Emotionally exhausted, Melissa allowed herself to sink into sleep.

Chapter Twelve

She was woken by a gentle hand on her shoulder; Will shaking her. Passengers were getting off the crammed train.

'Brussels Midi. We'll change here.'

'We're still alive, then.'

'You don't sound very excited about it.' He touched her forearm gently. 'It'll get better, Melissa. We'll figure this out. Come on.'

She walked out of the carriage with him, glad to stretch her legs. 'Where do we change for Bruges?'

'We're not going to Bruges. Come on.'

She had no wish to argue. He took her into the heart of the station and bought tickets on the underground. Within twenty minutes they had left the glossy Eurostar terminal and were at an older, dingy station in down-town Brussels. Will walked her through it to a bus terminal. He exchanged words with the ticket seller in flawless French; Melissa spoke pretty good French herself, but she was too nervous even to try it right now. He flashed their passports, joking around with the man, who didn't bother checking them. Will paid for the tickets in cash, pulling a couple of twenty-euro notes from his pocket and grumbling about the fare. As though he were another poor backpacker. The queue was rumbling, and they climbed into the coach, which filled up quickly. Will checked his watch; at noon exactly, the big creaking vehicle pulled into grimy traffic, and they were off.

'Rotterdam,' he told her quietly.

'Bruges is nicer,' Melissa said.

'But our tickets go to Bruges.'

She shivered. 'Is this spycraft?'

'It's basic, low-level evasion stuff.'

Melissa was suddenly angry. She was running for her life, with the last man she wanted to see on the face of the earth, and he hadn't told her a goddamn thing.

'I want answers,' she said. 'I'm not a child, Will.'

'We're on public transport,' he said mildly.

'Look around you.' The bus was full of impoverished students, a mumbling drunk, and a few tired-looking parents with young kids. 'None of these people are Carlos the Jackal.'

Will stared at her, and saw the determination in her reddened eyes. Brave, he'd always thought she was brave, at least until she gave up on him. 'OK.' He leaned his head close to hers, lowered his voice. His warm breath on her neck was disturbing. She turned her face away and stared out at the grey buildings of Brussels as she listened. 'Tell me exactly what you want to know.'

'Who's trying to kill me, and why?'

'I don't know. We have to find that out. There are clues I can investigate. The other victims all have some connection to your father. He must have been more than an academic. People around him are dying.' Will kept his tone low, steady, like a man murmuring endearments into her ear. 'The connections are tenuous, though, and I think it's something to do with knowledge. He told these people some sort of secret, and now they're dead.'

'He didn't tell me any secrets.' She struggled not to sound bitter. 'We sort of drifted apart. By the end, we were hardly speaking.'

'There's more.'

'I'm not going anywhere. Tell me whatever you've got, Will.'

'OK. I don't want to scare you.'

'That ship has sailed.' A smile. 'Look, I don't have time to be scared. Tell me.'

'These guys are serious professional killers. They took out the other victims carefully; I saw the pattern because I'm trained to look for one. The failure to hit you was a shocker. You were very lucky, Melissa, lucky to get out of that hospital when you did.'

'Lucky you found me?'

'I didn't say that.'

'How do you know all this, Will. What happened to you?'

He stiffened beside her; Melissa sensed it, attuned to his body, before he said anything.

'I could ask you the same thing. You were my wife.'

'My mother . . .'

'I was your husband.' He kept his voice quiet. 'Your family tried to make me feel like dirt. It wouldn't have worked, until you consented.'

She lowered her head. 'What do you care? You have your money, you have your own girl.'

'You never called me.' He sat upright, falling silent; when he leaned closer to her again, his tone had changed, like he'd got a grip on himself. He was dispassionate now. 'But you're right, that's the past. I went into the army, then the security services. When I left those, I emigrated to America and bought a small bank. Which I turned into a large bank.'

'Security services. So was it James Bond?'

'It's not glamorous. People die, quite often.'

'No women?'

'There were always women. I wasn't about to become a monk.'

She wanted to joke, lighten the moment; she was distressed at his anger, and at how badly she wished she had been one of those women. But he was unyielding, and she dared not face his eyes.

'What are you going to do?'

'Protect you,' he said.

A crackle of lust ran lightly over her skin. She ignored it.

'How are you going to do that?'

'I'll get you back to New York. Joking aside, I will

place you in a safe house. Then I'll make calls. I have a network, a good network of contacts. We'll discover who's paying these killers to track you, and why. Then I can put a stop to it. You don't know anything; we demonstrate that publicly and clearly and it brings too much heat to kill you, plus it's not necessary.' He put a hand on her shoulder. 'I won't lie to you, Melissa, that may not be enough. Sometimes players will kill a witness because to fail to do it shows weakness, so they keep coming.'

She trembled. 'I don't want to die, Will.'

'If I sense that there's some kind of vendetta thing going on, I can still help. It will be traumatic, but you'll be safe.'

Melissa turned from the window. The bus was pulling out of Brussels now, rolling through the ugly houses of the suburbs towards the motorway.

'It's pretty traumatic at the moment,' she said. 'Shouldn't we tell the police?'

Will grinned.

'What's so funny?' Melissa asked, surprised into annoyance.

'I'm sorry. The police . . . OK. Look, these people are professional killers. Amateurs don't get to take out a United States senator and her Secret Service bodyguards. The police could not possibly stop them, and anything you tell a police force you may as well advertise on the front page of the *New York Times*.'

'Are you saying they're corrupt?'

'They don't have to be. Police info is held in multiple places, on hackable computers, in paper reports. Police HQs the world over are easy to infiltrate if you're a spy with connections. You don't even need good connections, just a gullible friend in law enforcement. If it's a criminal, you go to the police. If it's an assassin, you go to another professional.'

'The US Secret Service, then?'

'A senator's been killed. They're already on the trail. And so far they aren't coming up with much.'

'How do you know that?'

Will just looked at her. Melissa felt foolish. She tried to stamp on an immediate pang of desire. He was just so good at this. Clearly he'd been something else, back when he was in MI6.

She needed to concentrate on how that made her safer, not how masculine it was. Smarten up, girl, she told herself.

'OK, then. No police force. So what could you do, Will? How could you help if it is a vendetta?'

He considered it for a second.

'I'll have professionals fake your death,' he replied, 'and then I'll get you into the Federal Witness Protection programme. New identity, new life. Maybe surgery. They're very good, and they've kept people safe from the Mafia for years.'

Her eyes widened. 'Witness protection? New life as a small-town bank clerk, that kind of thing?'

'As a last resort.' His eyes trawled over her face. 'And

it would mean total assumption of a new identity. No friends, no contact, even with family.'

'I have no family.' She wouldn't miss her university friends that much either. The one person . . . well, Fraser was dead. And Will was here, with her.

'You and I would never see each other again.'

'I never expected to see you again in the first place.'

He smiled coldly.

'No big deal then. I can make sure they give you a really good job somewhere, and that you get a decent salary. About a hundred thousand a year, US. Anything more and the small towns start to talk.'

'Thank you,' she muttered.

'It may not come to that. Let's get you back to New York first.'

The bus had moved on to the main road, and she saw signs to Rotterdam in three languages; the motorway was straight and monotonous, and the country flat and sludge green. Melissa wished to hell she were back in Peckwater, in her beautiful rooms. With her glass of sherry.

'What will your fiancée say when you show up with me?'

He smiled. 'How do you do, I guess. She's a bright woman, you know. She won't mind.'

Sure she won't, Melissa thought. 'It'll be good to meet her,' she lied. 'Thanks again for helping me.'

'No problem. We'll be in Rotterdam by two, then we'll get something to eat, and you can buy clothes.'

Will fell silent, and Melissa leaned her head into the seat, closing her eyes again. But sleep would not come so easy this time.

Chapter Thirteen

'I don't understand,' Dimitri said again, although he clearly did understand. 'You're supposed to be one of the best in the world. You've been paid five million dollars for the job.'

They were sitting together on the deck of his ninety-foot yacht, one of the smaller, more discreet vessels in the private fleet. Around them the crystal waters of the Al Seef marina lapped gently around the pale beige wood of her hull. Across the creek, a heatwave was rippling the view of Dubai's old city; low-built apartment blocks, the odd desert house, and skyscrapers looming in the background.

It was a country dizzy on new money, lots of it from the West. English was almost as common in the bars and restaurants as Arabic. There were lots of very rich men indeed floating around the Al Seef. Nobody paid her client much attention here.

'I understand,' Lola said.

'They told me I was a fool to hire you as an assassin.' Dimitri's lip curled. 'You are, in the end, only a woman.'

His operative looked back at him steadily. 'Others have thought the same thing. They're all dead now.'

'Not this old maid from Oxford.'

She pushed her hair back from her eyes impatiently, and for a moment Dimitri assessed her, as a female. Certainly a pretty girl, but damaged; ice-cold. Which was why she was so superb at killing. A functioning psychopath, brutally intelligent, she had channelled her energy into the hunt. Legend had it that her first kill was an abusive teacher. After that, she took money, and nobody in the business knew where she kept it.

Her record had been one hundred per cent. Up until now.

She was right: the incongruity of the female assassin had served her well. They called her Lola, although he was sure it was not her real name. She was slightly built, and as a result, very few targets saw her as a threat. She was martial-arts-trained, and had once killed two men with almost eighty pounds on her by smashing the bridges of their noses with the flat of her hand and ramming them into their skulls. She was small, but total muscle. Even so, in a plain fight he could have her on the ground, writhing under him, in thirty seconds, he thought.

That was why she avoided fights. She used cords, surprise, and bullets. There was no better female shot out there. She could get close, and use a syringe. She was expert at administering toxins.

But she had failed to kill the daughter, even using a

male accomplice to keep her away from the hospital's CCTV. Admittedly, the daughter had only been his afterthought; she probably knew nothing. But he had not risen in the world by making assumptions. Melissa Elmet was a loose end.

And now the key players were gone. Richard Elmet's secret was almost safe. Except that the loose end was still around, and he feared, desperately, that she would unravel everything.

He looked at the attractive woman in front of him with disfavour. He was a man of great ruthlessness. If she failed to deliver the kill within a month, he would have her eliminated. If possible, though, he decided, looking at the ripe swell of her breasts and her delicious, narrow athlete's waist, he would bring her back here and rape her first. He had a vast sexual appetite, and he had never met any female like this one. It would be good to fuck her. And she should not go to her grave thinking herself the equal of men.

'The woman has help.'

He knew this. From her sombre tone, he gathered the details would not make pleasant listening.

'Go on. Tell me.'

'It is an American banker called William Hyde.'

He sat up straight on the sun lounger. At the bottom of the stairs going down into the cabin, one of the models – they were all whores, really – he had invited on to the yacht emerged from the bedroom to smile at him. She was a French girl with glossy chestnut hair, white teeth and a deep golden tan. She wore a tiny string bikini bottom with nothing but a silken thong at the back, and a short, see-through white silk robe. She let it fall open to show him she had removed the top of the bikini, and winked at him.

He waved her away. She pouted and went back inside to chop out another line. There would be time for a woman later, if he was in the mood.

'William Hyde. Of Virginian Prospect Bank?'

Her deadpan expression flickered briefly. 'Yes.'

'You do understand he is one of Wall Street's most celebrated executives?'

'I kill. I'm not a spy. He's not my target.'

He slammed his hand down on the antique Moroccan table next to them. 'Stupid bitch. He has money – lots of money. And resources. And he is well known. You will be inviting the press into the whole thing. How is it that a businessman is able to evade you?'

She actually flushed. 'Hyde is more than a suit. He used to be a spy, for the British. A good one.'

'You're kidding.'

'I made some calls when I discovered she had checked into a hotel. His phone was untraceable, but I discovered he'd rung from New York by pulling records on hers.'

'Why is a billionaire banker calling a nonentity from an English university?'

She sighed. 'They were briefly married when they were very young. She had it annulled. He went into the army, then MI6. As far as I know, he contacted her only after the shooting in Oxford.'

Anger subsided fast; he had to think.

'Does he love her?'

'Rumour has it that he got engaged just before coming to England. The woman was also engaged. It appears to be merely a desire to protect her.'

'Why was the marriage dissolved?'

'Her colleagues believe her parents objected. Hyde was an orphan and had no prospects.'

'Her parents.' He breathed in sharply. 'Then Hyde knew Sir Richard.'

'Over a decade ago, yes.'

'So he comes to protect his former woman. Which means that he understood her to be in danger.'

'I thought of that,' she admitted. She was sitting before him, fidgeting, practically writhing under his displeasure. 'He must have detected the prior three killings.' The police had not done so; she was proud of being one of the cleanest workers on the circuit. 'But as I told you, he was a spy for a very long time and he was excellent. He is a player.'

He rose and moved to the rail of the yacht. The blazing Gulf sunlight sparkled on the waters of the creek. In an hour, he had to prepare to dine with the Emir. There was a state banquet, and deals to be done over a regional oil-piping network. Several billion dollars were at stake. Sovereign wealth funds were involved. And this woman's sloppy work was giving him a giant headache.

'So now I have a former spy with massive financial resources, who may also know Sir Richard's little secret, protecting this woman. Do you have any idea where they are?'

'They went to Belgium. I had people at the airports . . .'

'But they took the train. Can you track them through the woman's mobile phone or credit card?'

'They've not used their cellphones and appear to be using cash. They're off the grid. For now.'

He thought about this for five minutes.

'He has a bank to run, and a fiancée waiting. He will need to make contact. He is now your target. I want him dead. He will certainly seek to discover who is hunting the daughter, and why. You are insufficiently talented to take both of them out alone.'

She coloured. 'I have hunted far more important, far richer people.'

'But none who are professionals. This was not a complicated job. This was simple.'

He considered having the girl killed, right this minute. Two of his best bodyguards, burly men, ex-KGB, were standing right behind him. At a signal from him they would have her pinned to the floor, ready to be disposed of however he saw fit. But then, reluctantly, he dismissed the idea. She was trained and already in place; she had studied Elmet and got close with Will Hyde. There was no point in punishment now. Her situational knowledge was useful.

'I will assign you a team. Three operatives and two men from our own intelligence service.' Operatives was the current polite word for assassins. 'You will brief them on everything you know. The spies will be contactable, to provide you with information you may need on the road.' He was plotting while he was talking. 'Your operatives will work separately.' Assassins were never good together. 'You will co-ordinate and report back to me.'

Lola chewed her lip. He could see she hated the idea, but then she had messed it up. And he was clearly right: Will Hyde was not your average target. He would be a hard kill, a rich man who could act as his own protection. 'I will be the one to take Hyde out.'

'Of course.' He inclined his head. She had to make that boast, her reputation depended on it. 'You will head back to Belgium?'

She shook her head, and the strawberry-blonde curls bounced attractively around her face. He began to recover his appetite. Yes, sooner or later he would definitely fuck her. Whether she survived after that would depend on if she redeemed herself now.

'I won't waste time searching for a pro who's gone off-grid. I'll go to New York. He has to come back there.'

Yes, he does, her client thought, and suddenly, gloriously, a possible solution opened up for him.

Will Hyde would take his old flame back to America. And he, Dimitri Alexeivitch, would ensure there was more than one kind of trouble waiting for him there.

Lola the assassin was answering to him. But Dimitri had his own masters. The stakes for them could not be higher. And they would not be interested in excuses.

He waved a hand and barked something in Farsi. One of the crew turned away and began to tack the yacht back to the marina. A small electric motor hummed, and she moved through the still waters.

'I will contact you with names tomorrow,' he said, then stood. The hard little bitch made him want to assert himself. While this job was being done, she was untouchable. The girl in the string bikini, however, was lying on the bed in his stateroom. She was nicely curved, skilled and pliant.

Will Hyde thought he was a master of the universe, but he was no match at all for the kind of money Dimitri had access to. And his bank, well. That was easily taken care of.

He walked away from Lola, down the stairs. The girl waiting for him had better please him. He was not in the mood for more disappointment. The assassin did not need tender farewells. She had fucked up, and she would be heading towards the airport as soon as the yacht touched the harbour.

He had managed others like her before. They were at their best after a setback. So much to prove, such rage and hunger. He did not envy Will Hyde now. Of course, the girl remained a target, but she was almost an aside. Once Hyde was gone, she would be an easy kill.

The door to his cabin was open. The French girl was

sitting on a chair, reading a magazine. As he entered, she saw the light in his eyes and shivered a little, afraid. He smiled. Eager to placate him, she stood without a word and let the translucent scrap of silk slither to the floor. He walked towards her, the day's problems momentarily forgotten.

Chapter Fourteen

'No, as I said,' Olivia Wharton tried to hide her annoyance, 'Will's not here, Jack. Sorry. He left for work on Thursday morning and I haven't seen him since.'

Hadn't seen him. Hadn't even heard from him. Not a text, not an email. Was he having some sort of commitment crisis? He'd promised her a massive ring and then suddenly disappeared.

In a way, Jack Sansone's persistence was strangely reassuring. Will was up to *something*, or he'd have been in contact with the bank. This wasn't about her. She hadn't finally landed him, after a dedicated campaign, only to see him run off in a total panic. Anyway, that wasn't her Will. He was one of the good guys. Protective, very masculine. Never cheated on her. The two of them had fun together. He wasn't the type to lead a girl a dance like that.

Will was reliable. Olivia kept telling herself that. But this was the clincher: he'd never neglect the bank. And she had some vague memory of a big financing deal going down.

So where was he?

And that pushy Mr Sansone had been on the phone twice a day.

'If anything changes, I'll surely let you know,' she said. Olivia kept her voice sweet and light. Everything was a constant audition for the role of Mrs William Hyde, and that certainly included being a gracious hostess, and not blowing up at Will's lieutenants.

'OK.' Sansone sounded distracted. 'It's just that things are happening at the bank, and we need Will to make some major decisions. Quite soon.'

'I'm certain Will knows his business. I just keep on working at my dermatology clinic.' Dr Wharton was due in her Fifth Avenue offices in a couple of hours; she found she was looking forward to the day she could give that up. Will's wife should concentrate on charity. Anything else would be absurd.

'You don't think anything's *happened* to him?'

She smiled; Will was the hardest, toughest man she'd ever met. Any mugger that came up to him would get his face ripped off. Nor was he likely to fall under a bus.

'No. And I think we need to wait and see. It's only been a couple of days. If we don't hear anything in the next forty-eight hours we can file a Missing Persons report,' she said reluctantly. Will would not thank her for making a fuss; Olivia instinctively knew he'd want his fiancée to be cool in a crisis.

'Maybe that's the best thing to do.' Sansone sucked his breath in. 'I won't lie to you, Olivia, the board is getting very anxious. We have a large amount of VED collateralisation. The credit crunch is very nasty. If we don't reduce our exposure there could be trouble. Much faster than you might think.'

She shivered. Every socialite in New York knew a player who was getting ruined, stock by stock. Look at what happened to the Lehman Brothers bank. One of the oldest and biggest names on Wall Street. One day its executives were eating hand-prepared blowfish at Nobu with a chaser of Cristal, and the next it was crashing and being sold off cheap for cents on the dollar. Fortunes were built on sand. *Even Will's fortune.*

'You're in the house,' Sansone went on. 'Do you think there's maybe anything there we might use to contact him . . . a computer with a secure email, perhaps a special cell phone?'

She hesitated. Would Will want her letting anyone into his house? But he'd proposed . . . that made it her house too. And Jack Sansone was someone she knew socially, through Will. He was a senior executive at Prospect. Will trusted him.

Olivia made a snap decision. She would let Jack Sansone in. She desperately wanted to hear from her fiancé. And besides, if she helped Jack out, she'd always have an in at the bank.

Dr Olivia Wharton was old school about things. She collected charities, artworks, and people. She also collected debts.

'Why don't you come on over, Jack,' she purred. 'And

you can see if there's anything in his study that might help.'

'Great.' Sansone was thrilled. 'We need that line of financing.'

'I'll see you in a bit. I'll have the maid brew some coffee.' Olivia replaced the receiver and chewed a little on her pretty lip. Where the hell *was* he? She wanted that ring on her finger. She wanted to go out to Le Cirque or Trump Tower and flash it around in a series of carefully artless gestures. Read it and weep, ladies.

Will was off on an adventure somewhere. Finding a new diamond mine in South America. Something like that. He was in a hidden gas field in Siberia, ready to do another big deal. But her own adventure couldn't start until he came on back here.

Olivia would try anything, if it would bring Will back home.

Jack Sansone stepped out on to Lower Wall Street, where his limo was waiting. The chauffeur opened the door and he got in, without thanking the man. Nor did his driver offer any conversation. Sansone was a hard man, and didn't fraternise with the help. They all knew that. There was no tipping, no birthday wishes and no Merry Christmas. He paid a handsome salary, and expected the little people to melt into the background. There were lots of them quite happy to take that deal.

'Where are we going to today, sir?'

Jack hadn't phoned his instructions ahead as he usually did. This little trip had better be private.

'Mr Hyde's house. I have an appointment to see Ms Wharton,' he added, then kicked himself. Never complain, never explain.

'OK, sir.' Roberto didn't seem to have noticed. He just put the car in motion, and it swam into traffic, beautifully hushed behind the soundproofed, tinted windows. Sansone really enjoyed all the trappings of wealth. Made him feel like a rock star. Made him feel like Will Hyde.

In the privacy of the car he grimaced. Man, he was so fed up with smiling at his young boss all the time, laughing at all his jokes. Will Hyde's success annoyed him intensely. Yes, the rise of Virginian Prospect had made him a very rich man. Will had turned the bank around. But Jack was a perennial number two.

In the early days, Will had wooed him very carefully. Recruited him from Wachovia that was doing some daring mortgage financing at the height of the boom, and had soon expanded to four times its size. Jack Sansone had resisted. Why the hell would one of the best banking executives of his generation leave sunny LA, full of sililcone-breasted models and white sandy beaches, for dreary Virginia with its faded clapboard houses and cold, dark winters? He was Chief Operating Officer of his own bank. He had a local reputation. When Ernest Stein, the CEO, retired in a year or so, he was the designated heir. No way, he was going nowhere.

But Will Hyde was persistent. He offered Jack stock – a full ten per cent of the bank. A permanent seat on the board. A twenty-four-hour chauffeur, a zero-rate mortgage. And there was still more.

'I'm going to make Virginian Prospect the hottest bank in Wall Street's history,' he said. 'Five years, we'll be as big as Wachovia. Ten, we'll bury Bank of America. This is your shot at the big time, Jack.' Pause. 'And if you don't take it, I'm going after Rick Connell.'

Jack Sansone knew that name well. Connell was a sharp young lieutenant at Berkshire Hathaway with a growing reputation as a serious stock picker.

He swallowed drily. Suddenly, he had a vision of a golden future, dandled out before him by a far younger man, slipping from his grasp and running down the drain. For the sake of some sunshine and a few cheaply bought pretty smiles.

'I understand, Mr Hyde. I'd like to take up your offer.'

A chuckle. 'Excellent. Can you be on a plane to DC tomorrow morning? We've got a lot of work to do. And Jack, call me Will or you're fired.'

'Will.' He'd forced a smile. And he'd got on the plane. But it rankled, even back then. Will Hyde was ten years younger than Sansone. It was Hyde who should be excited at being recruited, Hyde who should be eager to please. Jack had taken the executive route – and he was very good at it, amply rewarded. But Will Hyde had gambled his own money, and owned the entire bank. Jack was to be offered ten per cent, for getting in on the ground floor. But Hyde would have ninety.

Jack Sansone had a clear set of priorities. He took the deal, moved to Virginia and spent every waking moment turning Virginian Prospect into a success. Will Hyde made big, clever investments, and Jack parcelled out debt derivatives. His young boss had an eye for talent as well as for women; there were several other underlings recruited who made almost as much difference as he did. Every department expanded, from underwriting to M&A. Will Hyde married investment banking with retail banking. Within two years, they had moved from Virginia to Manhattan. It was still cold in the winter, but the white picket houses were a thing of the past – unless he took his helicopter to Dutchess County to go shooting.

Jack was now a very rich man indeed. And his work at Prospect had been part of that. But there was no denying that Will Hyde had done the lion's share of the deals, made the right tactical moves, and got all the glory.

Jack was worth almost fifty million dollars. A bunch of cash. Way more than any S&L salary.

But his young boss was a damned billionaire. And Jack absolutely hated that, hated that difference.

Now Will had swanned off somewhere, God knew where. Leaving no way to get in contact. No note, no nothing. And he was *needed*. They had to reduce their exposure to paper as fast as possible. What if the other banks called for their money? Supply was tight. Prospect did not currently have the cash on hand. Moves had to be made, and none but William Hyde could make them.

That flat-out sucked. Jack was deputy chairman. He should have that power.

Was William hurt? Dead?

I couldn't be that lucky, Jack thought. For a second he felt guilty, but then stamped on it. No, he thought. I've been treated with disrespect.

If he *was* dead, though, somewhere . . .

Delicious visions of a naked Will Hyde, trapped in a penthouse with a hooker, maybe, having taken a hot dose of some intoxicant, danced in his head. He'd sure love to see the guy humiliated like that. Of course he'd defend him to the press, express bewilderment, look grave. 'Not the William Hyde I knew . . . that's all I have to say.'

He leaned back against the moon-grey leather seats and smiled.

If Will didn't come back, what then? Who got the bank . . . his stock? Will never talked about his background and came down like a ton of bricks on any employee caught speculating. Journalists were too scared to displease him – he was friends with every newspaper man in town. But from his very discreet enquiries, Jack had discovered there were no heirs. No family members. Will had come from England, where he had attended an orphanage, of all things. There were several charities he supported, but he was not the type to give away stock to an institution. Friends? Godchildren? He had acquaintances and plenty of them, but no friends.

Ambitious employees had asked him to godfather their kids; the answer was a polite no.

Which left what?

Surely only the girlfriend.

The thought hit him between the eyes, and he turned and stared out of the window as Lower Manhattan flowed past it, seeing absolutely nothing. Olivia Wharton was undoubtedly one step up from the several beautiful pieces of eye candy Will had draped over his arm through the years. She had stuck around longer; she was less obviously a gold-digger. Jack himself had heard Will laughing with her, several times. Maybe that was why Will had moved her in. She was the first girl to share his house. She must be the heiress, if it came to that.

Jack himself was newly divorced. The ex-wife and their eight year old were quite happily ensconced in a mansion in Connecticut. He could flirt with Olivia, and there'd be no consequences. And if Will *was* dead, he could woo her, marry her. And then take complete control.

The thought of fucking Will Hyde's woman was a powerfully erotic one. But Jack wasn't stupid. Hyde was probably alive. He didn't value his future at the bank – or anywhere – if Hyde caught him so much as making eyes at Olivia. The man was territorial, in a particularly old-fashioned way. Jack affected to mock his virile machismo, but secretly he hated it. Because it disturbed him.

Still ... some sweet words for Dr Wharton were definitely in order.

The car pulled into Fifth Avenue. He was going to rifle through Will Hyde's personal papers, walk round his house with his woman. As far as Jack Sansone was concerned, Will could stay away as long as he wanted to.

Chapter Fifteen

They clambered out of the bus. Melissa felt sticky and tired; she was starving, and thirsty. Her stomach had rumbled embarrassingly in front of Will. The adrenaline that had sustained her since the morning was fading; nobody had tried to kill them on the coach. She wanted to shower, to get fresh clothes.

Will drew her away from the dismounting passengers. Melissa waited until they were a good distance before she dared to speak. They appeared to be in the city centre; Rotterdam was a sleek, architecturally modernist city, lots of glass and carefully designed buildings, skyscrapers and traffic.

It looked like an excellent place to get lost in. Not much tourism, signs mostly in Dutch.

'So what now?' she muttered. 'I suppose you'll be taking us to some flea-ridden bed and breakfast where you can pay in cash?'

He chuckled, and she bristled at the thought of him patronising her.

'No. I think you've had enough. We'll go to a good

hotel, very discreet, where I know several of the managers. It's right next to a massive shopping centre. You can stop there first, buy some clothes, whatever you might need. Then we'll check in together.'

A hotel! She was almost faint with relief. A shower. A bath, even. Room service. Her belly crunched with hunger. 'My own room?'

He shook his head. 'The reason I know the managers is that I've taken people there on several occasions. They're used to me paying in cash and using a false name. You will share a room with me.'

'What kinds of people?' She couldn't stop herself. 'Women?' He nodded. 'Hookers? High-priced call girls? Models?'

'Those things aren't synonymous, you know.' He shrugged. 'Both, at different times. You object?'

'How can I object?' Melissa replied stiffly. 'Your life is your own business.'

'I thought so,' he said, amused.

Damn it! He was infuriating. She smoothed down the rumpled cotton of her sweatshirt. 'The hotel staff will talk. I could hardly pass for a hooker. Or a model.'

Will, striding a little in front of her, stopped. He turned and regarded her slowly, his eyes trickling over her face, her breasts and body.

Melissa caught her breath, her heart thumping.

'You underestimate yourself,' he said.

Then, as though shaking something off, he caught

himself and turned to the front. 'Here. The Plaza Shopping Centre.'

She looked up; it was huge, a vast grey building.

'They've got everything in here that you're going to need. A luggage store. Clothes. A pharmacy. Can you shop fast?'

'Very. I loathe shopping,' she said truthfully.

He crooked a brow. 'Me too. My girlfriend loves it. She can spend hours just trying on shoes.'

'I can be fast.' She had to, she was starving. 'I want to get to the hotel.'

'Come on, then.'

'I can do it.' It would be a relief to be away from him for a while. 'I can meet you out at the front.'

He grinned. 'Like I'd let you out of my sight today.'

'But we haven't been followed.'

'Neither of us can be sure of that.' He gestured, and she walked after him through the main double doors.

They were in some kind of superstore. Melissa walked forward, and Will followed her; she grabbed a couple of shirt dresses, two sweaters, a pair of plain heels and some brogues. Next she found jeans, T-shirts, and two pairs of cotton pyjamas. They had little ducks printed on them. Will snickered, but Melissa ignored him; she was too tired for modesty. She passed the clothes back, and he draped them across his arm. The store signs were in Dutch, but she could work it out. Lingerie was in the back; unembarrassed, too weary, she selected some knickers and two bras, with some basic tights and black socks. Lastly, on impulse, she grabbed some workout gear: a modest one-piece swimsuit, a sports bra, a jogging suit and a pair of Nikes. She might really need running shoes, she thought grimly. She was, apparently, on the run.

Will took her purchases to the counter; they came to five hundred euros.

'I'll pay you back,' she said, blushing.

'Don't be dumb.' He handed the notes across. 'You must know this kind of money doesn't bother me.'

She did know. She felt stupid. Will saw her blush, and relented. 'But it was nice of you to offer, Missy.'

Don't call me Missy. That was the name he had used when they were courting, when the world was OK. 'It's Melissa now,' she said sharply.

'Fine.' He took the carrier bag with her purchases. 'This way.'

Will obviously knew the mall. She wondered what he'd bought here for his other girls. He strode out into an internal corridor, turned left, and they were at a luggage store; he selected and paid for a plain blue suitcase, then unzipped it right in the shop and dumped her purchases inside, including the little bag she'd clutched since St Pancras, with its pathetic cosmetics and toothbrush. 'Pharmacy,' he said, holding the case and walking her into a large store called Escura, full of French make-up. 'Get whatever you need.'

Melissa watched as he picked up soap, a toothbrush and paste. She hurriedly grabbed some brands she recognized: Maybelline and Oil of Olay, with a Clinique facewash. No point in looking at the prices. Like he said, he could afford it. On a whim, she grabbed a square package of perfume; Amarige, by Givenchy. One of her favourites. Will took them all up to the counter, paid for them with more banknotes. She wondered just how much he was carrying. He glanced at the scent, and she wished she hadn't indulged herself. What would she need perfume for? Or rather, who? She fought the temptation to remark that she just needed cheering up. She wouldn't draw further attention to it. Will was too sharp. And she didn't want to be teased any longer.

He tossed their purchases into an outside zipped compartment of the soft suitcase. 'Are we done?'

'I am, anyway.'

Will glanced at his Rolex. 'Eleven minutes. Not bad at all.'

'So where's this hotel?' She stumbled after him; he walked so fast, like an athlete. She was desperately out of shape. Not fat, of course; her body was slender, but it had the softness of the academic, the girl who lived in the world of the ninth century. Today was the most exercise she'd had in years.

'Right over the road. Look.' They had come out of the shopping centre, and he'd turned left, down a side street, into the very heart of the city. There was a museum of some kind to one side, and a sign for a zoo in English. Clearly Will knew his way around, Melissa thought. Rotterdam – and most places. She felt herself so small and provincial. But she wouldn't give him the satisfaction. So what if she wasn't travelled? She was an Oxford don; learned, respected. And she hadn't done anything to deserve this. I didn't ask him to come, she thought. She ignored the feeling that she was glad he had.

Will was pointing to a sleek, modern, curved hotel, the Westin, a fantasy of glass and steel. It looked expensive. It looked luxurious.

'Really?' she said hopefully.

'Sure. You need a break.' He picked up the case and strode across the street; Melissa hurried after him.

The lobby was sleek, glass and marble with a domed ceiling. Businessmen in well-cut suits were everywhere. Uniformed waiters served coffees to guests perched on minimalist cushions. Reception was quiet; Melissa hung back while Will went to the desk, chatting up a staffer in a neat navy shirt who smiled flirtatiously at him. The woman glanced at Melissa, gave her a smile which didn't reach the eyes, and then handed Will a room key. She giggled, and Melissa heard Will laugh.

He walked back over to her and slipped his arm around her waist. She felt his thick biceps through her sweatshirt. His head lowered to her, and he kissed the side of her temple, his lips brushing on her skin. Melissa trembled, involuntarily. It was torture. She wanted him, so much. Too much.

Immediately she pulled stiffly away from him. No way would she let Will know what she was thinking. He frowned; she was his date, the cover story. Melissa pasted on a bubbly smile; she put one slender hand on his thick chest.

'Let's go upstairs,' she purred, as best she could.

He grinned. 'Sure, baby. Lifts are that way.'

Melissa headed off towards them, and Will playfully swatted her on the rump. She grimaced, ready to slap his hand off. But he was at the lifts, with their case. The door hissed open; she was almost too weak, and when they got out at the fifth floor she could barely wait for the door to open. Every step along the corridor was agony.

Will halted outside a door at the very end of the corridor. Melissa glanced up at it; it said *King Willelm Suite*.

'A suite?' she asked, as he produced the key.

'Anything less and they would have talked. Normally I take the penthouse.'

'Of course.'

He looked at her, then pushed the door open. It was a colossal suite, with modern minimalist furniture, floor-to-ceiling windows overlooking the city, a sitting room with a computer, a bowl of fruit on a walnut box of a table, and a vast bathroom clad in rich brown stone with a separate power shower, a Jacuzzi tub, and a deep square stone bath. Hanging from the door invitingly were two fluffy white robes.

Melissa stood paralysed. She half wanted to cry. She walked unsteadily to the bowl of fruit and selected a peach. It was heady, scented and ripe. Famished, she bit into it. A drop of juice fell down her cheek; embarrassed, she licked it off, then looked up to catch Will staring at her.

He immediately looked away. 'You're hungry.'

She didn't bother to answer.

'I'll order some food, shall I? You can sleep, or bathe if you like.'

'There's only one bed.'

'It's big enough for both of us.' It was – a gigantic superking. 'Don't worry. I won't molest you.'

'Why would I worry about that?' she snapped. Pause. 'Excuse me, Will, I'm tired.'

'Here.' He pushed the suitcase towards her. 'Take some clothes in there, lock the door, have a bath – I know you hate showers . . .'

He remembered that, she thought, and blushed. What a strange little detail to stick in his mind.

'That way when you're done you can come out fully clothed. You have nothing to fear from me, Melissa. I'm not here to hurt you.'

'I know.' She relented.

'Besides, I can call Olivia.' That was his fiancée. Melissa almost flinched at the name, but Will didn't notice it. 'She'll be going nuts. I should let them know we're safe. And I have some other calls to make. We'll be heading back to New York first thing tomorrow.'

'OK.' She wanted to know how, but didn't dare ask. And anyway, drained of calories and emotion, she didn't care. She crouched and removed her clothes from the suitcase, quickly packing them away. She selected one of the new bras, and some pyjamas, and stumbled into the bathroom, locking the door.

For the first time since London, she was completely alone. Thank God, she thought.

Quickly she hurried to the fancy bath and turned on the taps. The hotel offered free L'Occitane toiletries – she emptied the bubble bath under the flow of water, letting the room fill up with the blissful scent of lavender, and stripped, climbing into it. The warm water flowed around her tired limbs like a caress, and she let herself relax, briefly, revelling in being clean, the grime and sweat of the running, the train and the bus slipping from her. They had shampoo; she grabbed the mixer tap, washed and conditioned her hair, and started to feel slightly more human. When she was done, she stepped out and dried herself off, then pulled on the bra and pyjamas and wrapped the fluffy white robe over them. She cleaned her teeth again, and looked in the mirror; better, a little better. She wanted to make herself up, but dared not. He would read into it that she wanted to attract him; she was already dressed to sleep.

The bathroom had its own dressing room. There was a comb and a hairdryer provided. Quickly, carefully, she combed out the knots and tangles of the day and blew her hair out, letting it fall around her shoulders. It felt wonderful just to be clean.

Melissa realised she had been too long in the

bathroom. Will would want a shower. She jumped up and unbolted the door, guiltily.

A fantastic aroma hit her: lemon and rosemary. She looked at the centre of the room; there was a room-service tray, groaning with food, and Will had drawn up two chairs at the table.

'I didn't know what you'd like, so I ordered a few things.' He gestured. *'Pollo al limone*, they do good Italian in the hotel. *Stamppot*, that's a traditional Dutch stew, very tasty. A fillet steak. Pasta primavera.'

She almost moaned with hunger. 'Thank you, Will. Don't worry, I'll eat it all.'

He chuckled, surprised. 'You're joking – that's a good sign.'

He was sitting at the table. Melissa slipped into the chair opposite him and helped herself to a bowl of stew. It was very good, herby, with beef and vegetables. She felt the warmth sink into her bones.

'Aren't you going to eat?'

He was just sitting there, watching her. It was disturbing.

'Sure.' He looked away, broke the moment. He reached for a plate of pasta. 'I'm starving too. You really should eat whatever you can manage in these situations. You don't know when you'll be able to eat again. Strength matters.'

'And you've been in these situations.' Not a question.

'Many times,' he confirmed.

'So how do you go from doing that to being a banker?'

'It's rough work, very rough.' He fell silent, and she wondered what he had seen. Had he seen men die? Had he killed them? She realised the answer to that one was almost certainly yes.

'You were a spy for a long time?'

'Spy is a bit of a misnomer. I gathered intelligence, carried out missions. They're not all collecting KGB microfiches from Russian embassies.'

'What kind of missions?' How vital, how alive his job had been. She thought of herself, marking papers for surly students, hungover or lazy; living on the charity of the college, dating a man she hardly found attractive. A safe life, sure. But one that seemed light years away now. Melissa ate another spoonful of stew. It was so delicious. When had she last been this hungry? Even though she was frightened, bewildered, she suddenly realised she was feeling more alive than she had done in years.

Will grinned. 'I can't tell you.'

'Right.' She changed the subject. 'Why did you spend so long doing it, then? You're obviously very good at . . . at money. Why didn't you do that first?'

He took a sip of water. There were two bottles of mineral water and a pitcher of freshly squeezed orange juice, but no wine, no spirits. She understood without needing to ask that alcohol was not permissible. If a sharpshooter blew the window out, or something, Will wanted their reflexes to be at their best.

'Good question.' His eyes slid away from her. 'I had to get something out of my system.'

'What was that?' she half whispered.

'You know exactly what it was.' His knuckles tightened a little round the stem of his water glass, and Melissa shrank back. 'Don't play games with me.'

'It's OK for you.' She was bitter. 'You didn't have parents to please. Maybe you have no idea what it means to love two people at the same time. My mother was dying. You were cruel.'

His eyes flashed. '*I* was cruel?'

She shoved the bowl away from her, and made to stand up. 'I've lost my appetite.'

Will's hand closed like a vice around her wrist. With a very slight movement he pulled her back to her chair.

'Eat,' he ordered.

Melissa's eyes filled with tears of fury. 'I am not a child.'

'And I haven't put myself and my business in danger by coming to get you just to watch you throw a tantrum. We're not safe yet. Not till I have you in a safe house in New York. The risk is slight, but it's there. If they come back you must be at your physical best, do you understand me?'

She bit her lip, angry. It was worse because she knew he was right.

'Very well.'

'It's not a date. Eat some pasta, eat some meat and drink the juice. That gives you carbohydrates, protein, vitamins. I'm happy to go to the other end of the room if it bothers you.'

'No. It's fine. I understand.' She grabbed a plate and heaped it with fettucine, looking down at the food, eating methodically. Will's eyes were on her, but she would not look up. After a moment, he started eating his own meal. Melissa cut herself steak, and poured out some of the golden orange juice. Mechanical, just mechanical, she told herself. Listen to him when he's right. Feed your body. Charge your system.

She finished the meal, enough to sate her hunger but not enough to make her feel ill. Will was still eating; his body was much bigger than hers, of course. He had moved from the steak to the chicken. Melissa pushed back her chair and went over to the chest of drawers. She pulled out some clothes and headed back into the bathroom.

'What are you doing?' Will demanded.

'Getting changed.' She looked at him defiantly. 'If it matters that much, then I guess I can't wear pyjamas. We might be running at any time.'

Will nodded; she had the small pleasure of seeing him look startled. She shut the door behind her and quickly changed into the tracksuit, the socks and the trainers. Practical, comfortable. When she was done, she came outside. He had finished with his meal, and was standing staring out of the window.

Melissa wished she could erase all the awkwardness. Will mustn't think she was still hung up on him. Nor could she allow herself to slip into that. This was a high-octane moment, and she was determined not to be humiliated, not any further. He had a model girlfriend and a dream of a life without her, and he was going back to it. Once he had got her to safety she might never see him again.

She steeled herself. Her job now was to get to New York. Start a new life. Something with passion, at the very least. No more teaching. No more academia. Perhaps she'd be a journalist, something like that. She had to focus on her new life, and not shame herself with Will.

'I hope your fiancée was glad to hear from you,' she said, boldly. 'She must be out of her mind with worry.'

His back tensed slightly. 'I didn't talk to her. In the end it seemed an unnecessary risk. We'll be on a plane tomorrow at dawn.'

'OK, so you'll see her soon. That's great.' Wow, it was easy enough to be light and breezy, when you put your mind to it. 'And your company the same, I suppose?'

'Yes. Although they're going through a sticky patch. Nothing I can't fix when I get back.'

'When I'm safe I must call Fraser's mother. They don't know why I ran.' She sighed. 'I hope the police don't think I was involved in it.'

'If a lover disappears after a murder, people do tend to make assumptions. We'll have to clear that up.'

Melissa picked up the hotel services brochure and flicked through it. A lover. Yes, she had been Fraser's lover, once in a while. Very infrequently, and always with distaste. Melissa remembered guiltily the unease, the shame she'd felt while he fumbled inexpertly over her body, how she'd lain there in the dark – always the dark, because she hadn't wanted to see the skinny chest on top of her. The best you could say about Fraser was that he was finished quickly. Melissa always had to get slightly drunk, just to endure it. She'd convinced herself that bad sex was the price she'd have to pay for the companionship and security of marriage.

But she had not forgotten what it had been like, so long ago, with Will Hyde. Her heart fluttered from sheer disappointment with herself. I'll never do that again, she vowed. Better to be alone – a million times better – than to sleep with a man she had to endure instead of enjoy.

'Fraser was a good man,' she said, to assuage her guilt. 'His parents are very nice, too. They will always wonder why he was shot. I'll need to tell them.'

'I understand.' Will didn't look round.

'Will.' She couldn't cope with the tension, the desire, the frustration, the fear. There were too many emotions washing through her, and Melissa wanted to get rid of them all. 'There's a gym in this hotel, a good one. I'm not like you, I'm not fit. Not much call for it marking essays in Christ Church. I want to go and . . . and work out.'

He turned round, surprised. 'You want to work out?'

'Like you said, we might be on the run for longer than we think.' She didn't like her body's softness and vulnerability. 'Can I? Do you think it's safe?'

'You're taking this very seriously.'

'That can happen when somebody tries to kill you.' It

was important to her. 'What happens if you put me in witness protection? You'll never be able to see me. You won't be around to help. I'll need to stay fit, and . . . and learn how to fire a gun.'

'Yes, you will.' Will nodded. 'I'm sorry to say it. A girl like you . . . shouldn't be involved in stuff like this. But it's a distinct possibility that we may never be able to relax completely. Right now I need to work out who's after you and why.'

Melissa swallowed. 'Then I have to change. Starting with getting fit. Can I go down to the gym, Will?'

'No, not alone. Too exposed.' He sighed. 'I'll come with you.'

She climbed on to a treadmill. Behind her, Will Hyde was lifting free weights. He wore the outfit of a personal trainer of the hotel – a word with the concierge had magicked it up instantly. Melissa had averted her eyes. She had no desire to see Will in a white T-shirt, the fabric stretched against his strong chest, as he curled an enormous chrome weight. He would not use a machine, so he could be free to grab her if anyone tried to attack.

He had always looked good, but the Will of today was a different person. Success had made him confident. And physically, his body was iron. She couldn't look at it without feeling a shock of desire. How foolish, she taunted herself, the mousy little professor getting so worked up by such a clichéd vision of masculinity.

But the feelings were undeniably there. No way could she look at his muscled body straining against the weights without staring. And she'd rather die than let him see her lusting after him. Her feet walked briskly, and she jabbed at the controls, sending the belt faster, until she was out of breath and had to slow down. Perhaps, behind her, he was watching, amusing himself with her amateurishness. No matter, Melissa thought. She was learning this all over again. She had to pace herself. Even Will would have started somewhere. She found her pace at a steady six miles an hour, and as her body heated up, she relished the exercise. With every deep breath, every pounding stride, she felt the maelstrom of feelings fall back in her, blessedly, until there was nothing but herself and the treadmill, her heart pumping, the blood and the oxygen singing in her veins. She ran, punishing herself, for thirty minutes. When she was done, she slowed to a walk, got off, and stretched. Her muscles were sore, but in a good way.

As she straightened herself, mopping at her face with a towel, Will came over to her.

'I'm impressed, Missy. You've got willpower.'

She panted, not bothering to correct the name. 'I've got motivation.'

They both grinned. She suddenly understood that she liked Will a lot. They could even have been friends, if she wasn't so attracted to him.

'Are you done?'

'I'd like to lift some weights.'

'I'd prefer if you went back to the bedroom. Every time we leave it, there is a small exposure risk.'

'OK,' she sighed.

'But don't worry. You don't need weights to strength-train. I've done it daily, whatever hell-hole I was stuck in.'

She followed him back to the lifts. 'How did you do that?'

'Push-ups, crunches, tricep dips, lateral leg raises. I can show you.'

'All right.'

'The weight of your body is all you need. Remember that. Useful skill.'

'So you're teaching me craft?' She smiled. The whole thing was so ridiculous.

As the elevator doors hissed shut, he put one hand on her shoulder and looked down into her eyes.

'You're teaching yourself. And that's good. I want you to stay alive.'

Melissa said nothing. Because he loved her? He cared for her, that was all. And it wasn't even close to being enough.

'When do we leave?'

'We leave at first light,' he said.

'Then I'll shower and go to bed.' Her question hung in the air.

'I will sleep the other side of the bed from you.' He was definite. 'Quality sleep matters. I'm trained to sleep very lightly. I won't touch or disturb you.'

'That's absolutely fine,' Melissa said. She could hardly demand he lie on the floor. She was alive only because of Will's good graces. He was looking after her; nothing more.

She hated how much that disappointed her.

Melissa waited while Will showered. Then she washed herself, pulled on a T-shirt and jeans, and climbed into bed. She felt the coverlet move, felt him settle beside her, facing the door. Her back was to him. She did not turn round. She hardly dared to move at all. Besides, she knew he would protect her. For now, she was quite safe.

It had been a long day, and the exercise had tired her. She closed her eyes, gratefully, and fell into a soft, dreamless sleep.

'Wake up.' His hand was on her back, on the small of her back. 'Time to go.'

'Will,' she said, sleepy. Then consciousness rushed up on her. She tossed back the bedding and sprang on to the floor, frightened, looking at the door.

'Hey. Hey,' he said, soothing her. 'It's OK. Just wash up fast as you can. We've got to go.'

Outside, the city was pitch black. The vast windows oversaw an inky night punctuated with neon and the dull orange glow of street lamps. She could see the illuminated portholes of ships, moving in the harbour.

'Sure.' She didn't bother to ask the time. If Will said go, she went. Melissa grabbed a few clothes and jumped in the shower. She washed herself and cleaned her teeth in two minutes flat, put on basic make-up and changed in another three, emerging from the bathroom tying her long hair back into a pigtail.

'Fast,' he commended her. Melissa smiled.

'I can be. Not much of a girlie girl when it comes to that sort of stuff. Are you going to wash?'

'Already did it.'

'I'll pack.'

'It's done. And I've checked out.' He held up a little white envelope; she saw that the blue case was by the door. 'Follow me and stay close.'

He took her down the stairwell this time. Melissa was beginning to get it; at day, with plenty of people, Will would use the elevators; the threat was greater when the hotel was empty, so they were walking eight flights. On the first floor, he took her into the corridor and they summoned the elevator, so they'd emerge into the lobby in the least conspicuous way.

There was a night clerk on reception and a janitor mopping at the marble floor. Nobody noticed them as Will dropped the envelope into the early-checkout box. There were cabs already waiting out front. Melissa murmured surprise.

'Lots of businessmen use this hotel. Lot of early flights. Like ours.'

He led her out of the glass doors into the first cab waiting, and said something in Dutch. The guy grunted and flung their suitcase in the back.

'How many languages do you speak?'

'Eight,' he said, matter-of-fact. 'You learn fast when you have to.'

She leaned back against the ripped leather of the seat. The car smelled of must and smoke. Melissa cracked a window as the driver clambered in and drove off. Her hands clenched nervously on her thighs.

'What is it? We're going home.'

Not her home, but she didn't pick him up on it. 'It's just that you've been very clever, Will, giving them the slip and taking buses and paying in cash. But we're going to the airport now. Our name will appear on the flight list at some point, won't it? It's no use – you can't get on a plane without showing a passport. What if these people . . . what if . . . I don't know, if they can hack computers? As soon as they know we're coming, what if they have people waiting for us?'

He smiled. 'You're learning fast, too.'

'They did track you, even you, at first. You didn't expect them to be outside the hotel.'

'I did not.'

'So that says to me they're quite good at this stuff. Whoever they are.'

'Yes.'

'They could be waiting for us,' she said, and she pulled closer to him.

Chapter Sixteen

The Sultanate of Nadrah, off the Straits of Hormuz, was small but wealthy. Dense oil fields packed the plains to the south, and a mountain range sheltered the desert from the temperate north, well served by rivers and pleasantly green. As the petrodollars flowed in, in the sixties, so did the investment; the Emir became a sultan, the population exploded, gleaming white skyscrapers thrust upwards almost right away. Nadrah did not have much habitable land. The flat plains were dry and needed for drilling; the rivers and flood plains were the nation's breadbasket. In the small cities that were left, they could not cope with the influx of people. Houses were demolished, apartment complexes took their place. Then even they were discarded in favour of soaring towers. An absolute monarchy and a liberal brand of Islam flourished amongst the high wages and the dreams of traders and property developers. Soon the immigration policy tightened. The Sultan exempted the wealthy from tax, if they could employ his people. The policy mimicked that of the trashy Grimaldi family of Monaco;

nobody with a net worth less than a million US dollars, cash in the bank account, was permitted permanent residence. Nadrah, tiny in geopolitical terms, became a paradise for anyone lucky enough to live there. It was known as the Manhattan of the Middle East, a scrap of land that was nonetheless a player, and the place where everybody wanted to be.

The palace of the Sultan was set high on the hills overlooking the sparkling waters of the strait. It was whitewashed and domed, in the traditional manner, with high walls set around it. Within the grounds were Italianate gardens, villas and minor palaces, several private mosques, barracks for the guards, fountains, rivers, streams. The highest level of modern security, from gun towers to laser-beamed alarms, operated at all times. The soldiers who patrolled every entrance, with their ghutra headdresses and traditional loose white robes, were highly trained mercenaries, many of them Ukrainian or Serb. The ruler of the country, Haroun bin Faisal, had no interest in being assassinated or shot.

It was Nadrahi policy to stay out of the limelight. The country was rich; the people were rich. The Sultan stayed at home, travelling rarely, and only ever within the region. He sent emissaries to OPEC conferences. But he stayed in control, perfectly, the spider at the centre of the web. If the world did not notice Nadrah, that was fine with Haroun. Discretion and neutrality were the watchwords of the state, and all its ministers.

His Majesty the Sultan, as a Westerner would style

him, sat outside, on one of his private terraces, feeling relaxed. He affected belief in God, for political reasons, but unlike his devout father and two sisters had always been a private atheist. He had just one wife, and treated her kindly, with all appropriate honours heaped on her position; she had whatever she could wish for, and he came to her bed at least once a month. The Sultana, young and beautiful, a native Nadrahi girl and popular in the country, had delighted his people by producing two sons and an adorable princess. They lived in their own apartments in the palace, and treated their father as a friendly stranger. It was a perfect arrangement. As the boys grew older, Haroun planned to be closer to them. His heirs, later on, would matter. The kingdom was wholly in his gift; he would need to determine which should follow him on to the ivory throne. The relative distance of his family left him free to pursue his own pleasures. Which he did with great vigour. He kept a villa, on whose balcony he now sat, on the edge of the compound, filled with beautiful, willing girls. Some were true whores, the highest-class girls from Paris or Beverly Hills. Some were slutty little model types who trolled around the French Riviera looking for a rich husband, where his talent-spotters found them. Sometimes, although rarely, he brought in a local woman. That was dangerous, for the people would hate the scandal. But he found the dark eyes, modest confusion and olive skin of his own people especially attractive. Forbidden fruit always was.

There was no need to rape or compel any of them. Each of them understood the position. She would stay in the royal villa until summoned, keeping herself from all other men. Before the Sultan, she would do exactly as she was told. Sometimes, when faced with the reality of his chamber, the girls were frightened. He enjoyed that; it was more erotic. He had never hurt a woman yet, but his power was absolute, and he loved feeling them squirm and wriggle, striving to please him. It was especially satisfying to give such a girl pleasure. More than once, they had tried to profess love at the end. Though he would never be interested in whores.

The women were rotated out of the compound when he tired of them, usually after a month. His longest concubine had stayed for five. When he was done, they were summoned by an administrator, paid money in an envelope – Haroun did not bother with jewels; he wished the nature of their prostitution to be quite clear to them – and driven back to the airport at Fadiz. There they found waiting a one-way ticket, first class, to wherever they had come from. A local girl could pick her own destination. The warning not to return to Nadrah was implicit, but very real.

Few of them complained. There was a lot of money in the envelope, more than most would earn in a lifetime, on their backs or otherwise. Haroun did not want any whiff of scandal. He did, however, want his pleasures. And he had the money to ensure that they were delivered.

The girl who had just left was a blonde, twenty-two, from Ontario, and quite exceptional. She soothed him. Her pale skin had ripened to a deep golden tan under the Middle Eastern sun. She was responsive and eager and she seemed to enjoy having sex with a king. He'd kept her longer than most, three months already, and was in no hurry to send her to the airport.

As he looked out over the magnificent view, the skyscrapers of his capital city of Jibaz jabbing into the air above the harbour, Haroun's relaxation started to wane. The girl was a splendid distraction, but all his problems were still there. There was the possibility of his entire world coming to an end. The money would dissipate, the jobs and prosperity would go. Nobody cared about his dictatorship when times were good and riches were everywhere. If that changed? He could be dead before sundown. All the mercenaries in his palace could not withstand the sustained force of an angry mob. It had happened before, many times. The Shah of Iran had been lucky to escape with his life.

Others would be affected, also. His brothers. This region would be utterly devastated. And the shock reached further yet, beyond the Middle East and out into Russia. The entire global economy would shudder. He had no intention of shivering out his last days in some cold townhouse in London. No, if their money was taken from them, Haroun bin Faisal predicted war. Lots of war. From the Gulf to the Steppes. He shivered in righteous indignation. It was the correct thing to do, really, taking out the Englishman and his connections. Elmet had brought it on himself. He had dared to look into the sky and read the mind of God. He had wanted wealth, and position. Instead of which he got a cheap, anonymous death on the water, and those to whom he blabbed went with him.

It had been merciful. A couple of expendable lives balanced against castastrophe, for Haroun, for Nadrah, perhaps for the world.

They were safe again. Until the American banker came for the ordinary-looking young teacher. And now his world was once again on edge.

He snapped his fingers and a manservant dressed in the gold and purple livery of the royal house hurried forward. Haroun barked a command. In seconds, a tall, iced glass of mint julep was placed in front of him. It was his favourite cocktail, by far the best thing ever to come out of America. He took a long draught of it. Before he'd attempted to calm himself by fucking the little blonde Canadian, he had taken a call which disturbed him, very much. From Qatar. And then a second, from Jeddah. Everything came through on secure lines. Presidents and regents, they were talking directly, without the baggage of ministers. They could not afford ministers. The fewer people who knew, the better. Earlier in the day he had spoken to a Nigerian and the President of Mexico. Already it was leaking. That was a disaster. To the Nigerian he had been curt, denying knowledge, laughing it off.

This must not spread. They *must* get the banker and his female, whatever it might take.

'*Malik.*' One of his viziers was by his table. He bowed low, and touched a hand to his chest. 'Your visitor is waiting in the office.'

'Bring him out,' Haroun said. 'And then clear everybody from the office. Nobody is to approach. Do you understand?'

'Of course, *Sidi.*' He bowed again, and withdrew. Haroun looked expectantly at the glass doors that led out to the terrace. Yes – there he was, the Russian. Haroun's dark eyes held the man's.

'Majesty,' the Russian said, without deference.

'Sit.' Haroun frowned. 'You understand this is not good.'

'I do. The operative has been rebuked, but she has good understanding of the targets. I have expanded the hunting field.'

'How many *hashashin*?' he asked, pronouncing it in the original way.

'I have engaged three of the world's best in addition to Lola. You know her kill record. The man she failed to remove had been an operative himself.' He reached behind him and handed a slim file across the table. 'He works clean, but this is what we have been able to gather. He is a billionaire now. He owns a mid-sized American bank. Retail money and M&A.'

Haroun swore.

'Where is he?'

Dimitri hated having to answer. He cursed Lola silently. 'We are not sure. We anticipate he must come back to New York.'

'You will need more than three. You will need bodies on the ground, many bodies.' Haroun thought hard. 'I can mobilise CISEN.' The Mexican secret police, the Centro de Investigación y Seguridad Nacional. 'And the Mukhabarat. They are reliable. They will not understand why they are looking, but they will look.'

Dimitri exhaled. The Sultan was not about to have him killed, then; he was turning his mind to solving the problem.

'If you can give me that much manpower, get somebody in every airport, at the very least.'

'It is done.'

'If they have an easy shot, they should take it. Otherwise, reports should be made to the centre so the operatives can gain control. It is unhelpful for the entire world to believe that Miss Elmet is being hunted. Still less her billionaire friend.'

'His wealth is an issue?'

'Very much so, Majesty. He is somewhat famous. And he has resources. Neither of which assists our present mission.'

Haroun looked at the Russian as though he were stupid. 'Then remove his resources.'

'I am investigating it.'

'We have an excellent team of banking specialists in the intelligence ministry.'

Dimitri inclined his head. 'That will be most useful. It is my plan to bankrupt his institution, or possibly just the man himself.'

'Are there men who will take his bank?'

'More than one.'

'Then ruin just the man. To take the bank itself risks publicity.'

Dimitri agreed.

'Of course, if you kill him first, it will all be moot.'

'We will get him. He's been retired for years. Little more than a lucky amateur.'

'Be sure that you do.' The Sultan turned to his drink. The interview was clearly over.

Dimitri got to his feet. 'How quickly can you order the watch at the airports?'

'My senior officer will contact you,' Haroun said. 'Men will be on their way before you have left the palace.'

'My thanks.' Dimitri would not bow, but he inclined his head. This one was sharp, not like some he had dealt with recently, corpulent and complacent or drunk and corrupt. He had the impression that the Sultan understood the threat very clearly. He turned on his heel, and left the Nadrahi to his drink.

Carlos Morales was the name he'd been using for the last six months. He moved quietly through Rotterdam airport. Of course it was a waste of time, surveillance at a pathetic regional hub. The international flights all went through Schiphol. He consulted his secure mobile again, looking intently at the pictures of the targets. A mousy girl and a rich American banker with matinee-idol looks. Who had apparently spent years in the life and was damned good at it. His station chief added that he had retired and been on Wall Street for years. Lots of cash. Lots of resources.

He mooched around duty-free, his eyes scanning the check-in desks, the shops. So dumb to have him out there. They should assign more pairs of eyes to Schiphol. This two-bit joint was for the drunk English tourists and the fat Dutch and Belgians cramming themselves into low-cost flights to Italy. Billionaires would not fly from here. Spies would know it was too small, not enough crowds to slip through.

He kept looking anyway.

'Hotels.'

Sultan Haroun was thinking. This office, hidden away in his capital city, was one of the best equipped in the Middle East. He faced a bank of screens, computers and satellite terminals. He had personally ordered the sheikh in charge of his security service to move away from weapons, and expensive field operatives, and to invest in technology. Nadrah now had one of the best interception units in the world, after the Americans and the Chinese. And very few people knew about it. Haroun believed you could always farm out to an operative. What mattered was knowing where to send them.

His Chief of Station looked up at the Sultan with

respect. Although the prince was not a spy, he had an instinctive sense for what mattered in this crisis. This man, this Anglo-American banker, a decadent son of the West, one who ran with whores and lived like a caliph, he was very important to the Sultan. More so than their current top targets in the region. The Chief could tell. The order for the hunt had been given to so few people, and with a studied casualness that suggested keeping it quiet was top of the agenda. Normally, they hunted like a pack of jackals.

And other agencies were involved. That was rare indeed. What did the man have, what had he done? The Chief had never heard of him, and he knew every important player for the last five years. William Hyde had been totally off the radar. What should the Nadrahi Mukhabarat care about some random American businessman? Go to Mauritius and you could hit ten of them.

But the Sultan was here personally. He cared very much. The Chief sensed that no more important target had come his way since he had been promoted. Other station chiefs, other intelligence directors, would be hunting this man. He was determined that he and he alone should have the glory of the capture.

Sultan Haroun dealt ruthlessly with failures. But those who won his approval lived lives of unimaginable opulence. The Chief wanted Will Hyde dead. He was desperate to impress his ruler.

They were watching the airports and stations. Even

the ferry ports. It was a massive manhunt. The girl and her rich bodyguard should not stand a chance, in theory. He, Abdul al-Ishmael, did not play by theories, which was why he was already station chief and only thirty-five.

'Hotels, *Malik*?'

'Have people make discreet enquiries in all the hotels in . . .' The Sultan thought about it. They had gone to Belgium. He studied the map. 'Every establishment within a three-hour drive of Brussels. Do not stop at major chains. Gather what you can from the smaller places, bed and breakfast, apartment rentals, even the hostels.'

Chief Abdul nodded. 'Yes, *Malik*. Of course, it will take hours, and many men.'

'Get it done.' He did not want excuses.

The Chief turned to one of his men. 'Rashid, have a ten-man team go into the computers of the travel agents. All reservations in the major chains, all rooms booked for a man and a woman together in the same radius.'

'Yes, sir.' The older man turned to obey him. He leaned his head close to their team of geeks, young, ardent fanatics with sharp brains and advanced computer-programming skills. There was even one convert from America, who affected a long straggly beard, but whose hacking ability was second to none in the directorate.

The Chief slipped into an empty chair in front of a terminal himself and began to tap at the keys frantically.

It was important to inspire in battle, even if that battle took place purely in the mind. He was a programmer himself. He hacked into the hotels.com database, and started to peruse reservations in Brussels.

'Call me when you have something.' The Sultan walked out.

Less than an hour later, Jamal bin Khaled, one of the Chief's youngest staffers, ran across the air-conditioned office and tapped him on the shoulder. 'Boss, we have them.'

The Chief blinked. 'You have them?'

'Yes, *insh' Allah*. One of our men on the ground in Holland. He asked around his contacts. They were at a hotel in Rotterdam.'

He shook his head. 'I already checked the database on every place in that city.'

The kid would not be put off. 'No, they did not show on the computer. The contact is a maid at the hotel. They checked in with a false identity and he requested the reservation not be logged at all . . . She says the hotel obliges him because he is rich and a good customer and tips well.'

The Chief jumped to his feet. 'Fantastic, fantastic work, Jamal. Rotterdam.' It was a hub, a port. 'Get men to the harbour right now. To every train station, the subway, the car-hire places.'

'Yes, *Sidi*.'

'We already have men at the airports?'

'Yes.'

'Send more. They must all be armed. If they see them, they are to shoot, also the woman.'

'The airports have armed police.'

'A necessary risk. Whoever dies eliminating this man dies a martyr.' He wasn't sure if that was true, but it was a useful line in the situation. Jamal's eyes gleamed with fanaticism.

'Yes, *Sidi*.'

'I want you to communicate to the men in place. They are there. In the region. They must be prepared.'

Jamal ran to obey.

Carlos's pager buzzed at his hip, startling him. He immediately moved to a magazine rack and withdrew it. It was the code for his Dutch superior. He walked smartly to a phone rack, not running, and punched in a series of numbers, then another as a code.

'They left Rotterdam forty minutes ago.' CISEN did not bother with code phrases; those were best left to the movies. When you needed to get information out fast you did not risk confusion. 'I want you to redouble your efforts. Other operatives are on their way. Shoot to kill, understand?'

His heart leaped. He hated Holland; it was cold and miserable. If he took out these two fuckers, perhaps they would assign him back to Caracas, or Madrid at the very least.

'Yeah. Got it.'

'Don't make the mistake of thinking they'll avoid a regional airport. The man is good. And use visuals. He has selected multiple identities.'

'Understood.' He hung up and spun around, walking fast throughout the airport lobbies in a planned sweeping motion. They were not there. If the man was that damned good, Carlos decided, he wouldn't check in anyway. Let the other guys keep an eye on the baggage handlers and the queues for passport control. He was going out to the planes.

There was a door behind him, ajar, by the cleaning station. Carlos slipped inside. He knew this airport, and Schiphol, well. In a dingy grey room they had piled up uniforms. He selected a baggage handler's outfit and had changed within twenty seconds. There was a fake ID badge in his pocket. He pinned it on, and walked out to the luggage carousels. From there it was going to be easy . . .

Chapter Seventeen

Will felt Melissa pull close to him. He laid one hand reassuringly on her shoulder. Poor girl, she was right to be scared. Whatever she had done, she did not deserve this, none of it.

Her heart thumped. She was frightened. He had an urge to pull her closer, but resisted it. Olivia wouldn't like that. She must be going frantic. He was not looking forward to the conversation they would have when he got home. Olivia wasn't the type to challenge or defy him – not like Melissa, he thought, amused. She was exquisitely beautiful, ten times more attractive than Missy, and far more concerned to please him. He understood very well that she wanted to get married, and she wouldn't do anything to jeopardise that. But it wouldn't stop her silently resenting every moment he'd spent with his old flame. Will didn't want to see her gorgeous face hurt and sullen.

A ring would take care of that. Unfinished business that he had in New York. Guess now it'd have to be even more spectacular than before.

Olivia needed to understand, however, that he had no intention of letting Melissa Elmet get hurt. Taking care of her was a duty. He understood duty. And something else too, he decided. It meant that he could finally lay the ghost to rest. Melissa had hung in the background, over his life, ever since she had walked out of his door. In the army, in MI6, even in Virginia. He had thought about her once or twice a month, at least. She had been there with most of his girlfriends, no matter how stunningly beautiful they were, no matter if they could wipe the floor with her in bed. Because she had not been real. She was the ghost of his first love, and everybody knows you can't kill a ghost.

But when she was here, with him, running for her life, she was not a ghost any more. He could see her, the real woman. Nothing magic about her. She was flesh, blood. She was true. And mostly, he just felt pity.

He could be completely objective about it. Her face was the same, she had not put on weight, but everything he'd fallen in love with, so deeply and passionately, had vanished. Her eyes were dull, her skin had no smoothness, no fire. She dressed to be invisible. All the fight had gone out of her. She was a disappointed woman, and it showed. Stick her in a room with Olivia Wharton and no man would give her a second glance.

He had gambled with his life, and won big. Melissa had been her father's daughter, stayed in Oxford, followed the comfortable path. She had inherited his house, that must be worth something. She had a teaching job and, until these bastards came along, a fiancé. He wondered if Sir Richard would have approved of him. Probably. Another don, with a little money of his own and a family. Melissa had gotten for herself exactly what her parents wanted. The safe life. The ordinary life. Will had thought she was so much better than that. But perhaps he had projected on to her his desires, his dreams, when she was really just Melissa Elmet, and no better or worse than millions of other girls.

It had been shocking to see her, that first moment. He felt he should hardly have recognised her. It was not the same as it had been.

She had no passion.

Will had immediately decided to get her to safety, and then get on with his own life. With Olivia. Her shadow, after this, wouldn't be quite as long. It was sad to see her that way. His anger and resentment had turned to compassion; compared to Melissa, his life had been the good one.

And yet . . .

Something had changed. When his chauffeur moved to let her into the car, when the assassin started shooting. He'd been careful, sure, but he'd never really expected them to be there. They were. And they were quite serious. Melissa had surprised him; she ran well, she didn't argue, she had an instinctive grasp of the danger. No complaints. She remained brave. And from time to time, there had been moments, flashes – he hated to admit it – of the old attraction. She was unexpected.

Somebody was out to destroy her, had forced her from her world. Will was well aware that he was showing up with gunfire and promises to change everything, cut her off from all she knew, but Melissa was strong. When she'd asked to work out, he had been impressed. She was unfit and soft, but she was taking immediate steps to change that.

Melissa was no longer sweet-faced, and carefree. But . . . he could discern, even today, a trace of her old attractiveness. When she was gutsy, when she fought him. Once or twice he'd actually felt desire return to him. When he caught her looking at him.

But he was probably reading her wrong. She hadn't pined for him, all those years. She'd dumped him and eventually got engaged. Did she want him now? Will knew he was a good-looking guy; he had the testimony of countless girls, all hitting on him, to tell him that. It happened often enough with total strangers that he knew it wasn't merely a function of his money. Melissa knew more of him than those girls. Of all the females he had pleasured, none had responded so hotly, so overwhelmingly, in his arms than she. Even today. Even Olivia.

So maybe there was something, an echo in her of what he felt himself. Will determined he would ignore it. She needed safety, and space. He knew from long experience that life-and-death situations inflamed desire in hunters and hunted. Whatever fleeting moments of lust he might feel would not survive landing in New York and an encounter with his fiancée. And if Melissa wanted him ... well. She had not come to find him when he resurfaced in Virginia, even New York. Even when he was well known, in most of the papers, and she could hardly have avoided reading about the bank. She had never got in touch. So how real could it be?

Even moments of fondness might lead to his being weak. He had to be careful. It was a matter of discipline, just controlling himself till he got home.

Will sat up straighter, the movement pushing him away from her. At once, Melissa responded; she drew herself back, proudly, no longer seeking him out for comfort. He suppressed the feeling of callousness. There could be nothing between them.

'You wanted to know if they would be waiting for us at check-in. There's a strong possibility of that. Some of the better operations can hack into flight reservations quite easily.'

Melissa paled. 'But how can we avoid it? To get to the US you need a passport, you need to book. Right?'

'You need your passport, yeah. We're not flying commercial. We won't appear on any reservation lists or in the departure areas.'

She was silent for a second. 'Are you going to tell me what's going on, Will?'

'I still have connections.' They were approaching the road to the airport. Will pulled some notes from his pocket and handed them to the driver, speaking a few words of Dutch. '*Einde hier, tevreden.*'

The driver grunted. *'Hier? Bent u zeker? De luchthaven is die manier.'*

Will nodded and smiled. The man pulled over, and Will indicated to Melissa to jump out. The guy popped the trunk and he lifted out her pathetic little suitcase. This was about all she had in the world right now.

She looked at him, but waited until the driver had sped off. They were standing on a grass verge by the side of the road, with a wire fence to their left. Will could see a large oval of green grass, and several planes already on the tarmac. His target was the other side of the field.

'Follow me. Walk as fast as you can without running. We don't want to attract attention.'

Melissa nodded, but her eyes were sparkling with annoyance. Will grinned; he couldn't help it. She was a feisty little thing for a penniless fugitive.

'And where are we walking to?'

'Just follow me.'

'Hey. If they're here and they shoot you and I get away, I want to know where I'm supposed to be running.'

He laughed out loud. 'You're quite right. OK. We're heading to that squat plane over in the far corner.'

She squinted; uniformed men were loading stuff on to a ramp, large boxes and crates.

'Cargo plane?'

'Yes. A military cargo plane. US Air Force.'

She breathed in, deeply. He could see she was

impressed. She was struggling with herself, and looked away.

'How did you get passage on a military plane, Will?'

'The CO was a buddy of mine, back when I was in the service. I called him last night, when you were in the bath. He's taking us home, no questions asked.'

'That's great. Let's go.' Melissa turned her back and started walking. The moment passed.

Will moved behind her, the little blue suitcase in his hand. Whatever the girl felt, she would not surrender to him. He liked her for it.

Carlos moved away from the KLM flight to Heathrow, subtle in his movements. One of the other baggage handlers shouted something out. He looked back, swore in Dutch about his supervisor, and shrugged. The man turned back to his task.

Beyond the small jet there were several charter-flight prop planes. Carlos scanned them. Nothing. There probably would be nothing. Unlikely that an operative would fly on a prop plane; they didn't go high enough, too easy to shoot down. Whatever. He was all out of ideas. He kept looking.

Melissa walked across the tarmac, her eyes focused on the cargo plane. Soldiers, thank God. Young men with guns and combat training and all the expensive equipment of the US Army. It was a stroke of genius by Will to get them on this flight. He must have incredible pull, to put two civilians on a military flight. You didn't get goodwill like that for nothing. She wondered exactly what he had done for MI6, what missions he had fought alongside the Americans. She tried to give herself a pep talk as she walked. *So, OK, it's impressive. I can't let it affect me. I can't let him affect me*. There were men out there who wanted to kill her, and that was absolutely all that could matter.

Will had said to walk straight ahead.

She was nervous. She kept moving, but her eyes switched to the left, back towards the airport gates where the jets were parked, and the passenger buses were bringing tourists and businessmen out to the propeller planes, further back. The passengers moved like ants; flight staff milled around them.

And then she saw him.

'Will.'

'Just keep walking.'

'Will, please. There's a guy. He's coming for us. Please!'

She knew he was. The man wore an airport uniform, but he had halted, and he was looking at them across the expanse of tarmac, and she didn't like it. Will was right behind her; she could almost feel his hot breath on her shoulder.

'OK.' His tone was serious. 'Melissa, run for the plane, honey. Run and don't look back.'

She tried, but the compulsion was there. She glanced for half a second to her right. The man had run towards them at frightening speed, and he had a gun out in one hand, and was speaking into a phone with the other.

A bullet blasted out of the gun. It whistled past her, missing her by inches.

'Run!' Will shouted. 'Run!'

She screamed, but she ran, faltering, stumbling steps towards the cargo plane. There were sounds, the *phut-phut* of more bullets. He was shooting. He was shooting. She turned her head, her body. Will. Dear God.

'Will!'

He was back there, doubled over, on one knee. Melissa was terrified. She screamed. 'Will!'

She turned on her heel and ran back to him, back towards him. He groaned and shouted at her to run for the plane. She ignored it. There was nothing now, nothing but her fear, and him, and the bullets.

'Will! No!' Melissa was in a blind panic. He was down, dear God, he was down! She reached him – he was bleeding from the upper arm. She tugged him to his feet, stupidly.

'For God's sake, woman! Get to the fucking plane!'

'Will, come, please – come . . .'

But he was running, he was already running, faster wounded than she was whole, and his arm was on her, his hand like a vice, and he was half pulling her along. The man was after her, he was yelling and shooting. And now, she dimly perceived, there were other men behind him, appearing from nowhere. There was a siren in the background; she could hear the screech of police vehicles . . .

The whine of sirens was growing louder. Bullets flew past her; they were getting closer, more accurate, as the man ran towards them. Melissa's knees crumpled, but Will's hand was carrying her, not permitting her to fall, dragging her forwards. Somewhere she registered that it hurt. His grip was iron, even though blood was leaking through his shirt and had doused his forearm. She was tremendously frightened he might lose too much blood and faint . . .

And then there were shouts, and bodies came pounding towards them from the other direction – soldiers, running from the plane, unholstering side-arms. A burly man dropped to one knee beside her, ignoring her and steadying his weapon. Then another.

'Drop your weapon!' some man shouted. 'Drop your goddamn weapon!'

Another guy, just in front of her, fired. It was incredibly loud. She understood the assassin must have used a silencer. Her ears hurt. She would have fallen but Will held her up, impervious to pain, impervious to anything. And suddenly other arms were there, uniformed arms, separating them, and Will disappeared, surrounded by uniforms, and she cried out, but multiple hands were on her, lifting her bodily and rushing her towards the plane in a cocoon of men. It was moving, slowly, a behemoth, taxiing forward on the tarmac.

'US Rangers, ma'am.' A thickset man with a moustache was talking to her. 'You're OK. You're safe. Let us get you in the plane.' Behind him two more men fired. Melissa was suddenly, savagely glad. They were firing. This man had tried to kill Will and now soldiers were firing back at him. They were not helpless targets. She decided at once that if she lived, she would learn to fire a gun. In America it was legal to have guns. Legal or not, she needed one. This stuff was real. She, Melissa, needed weapons training. God, she thought. How the hell did I get here! What's happening to me?

'Thank you,' she said weakly. They weren't listening anyway. She was bundled into the back of the plane, up a ramp, like she was a sack of potatoes. Men were sitting on one side of the plane and more hands grabbed her and manhandled her into a seat, strapping her in tightly. Melissa turned her head to look at Will. He was in a corner, tied down to a gurney. A soldier was leaning over him, wrapping a tourniquet around his arm, brutally tight.

The men were shouting. Soldiers, the guys who had been shooting she guessed, tumbled into the plane behind them. The ramp was rising. The men rolled on to the floor, shouting about AK-47s. The plane moved forward, forward, gathering speed. Melissa was seated by a small oval window. She looked out, her heart crashing in her chest. There were two bodies prone on the airfield and sirens going everywhere, but more men – she saw at least five – were still running towards the aircraft, firing. One of them had a machine gun. The plane was still moving, speeding up properly. She leaned back against the wall, dizzy, and closed her eyes, feeling sick. Oh God.

Oh God. What if one of those men had a rocket launcher? They would all die; she would have got Will killed and all these brave men too. The plane would disintegrate, or they would burn to death. They were now moving too fast for the men on the ground; she looked behind her to see them hanging back . . .

The plane lifted into the air. It felt like Melissa's whole body, her breathing, was in suspension. She looked at the soldiers sitting around her. They studied their knees or stared straight ahead. They were totally impassive. One kid was chewing gum. How could they do that, how could they be so calm?

The plane lifted, lifted. Melissa waited for an impact. It didn't come. The plane went higher, it seemed at a sharper angle than commercial flights. The pilot wasn't wasting time. Her stomach flipped and dropped against the angle of the plane.

She looked across at Will. He turned his head on the gurney, staring at her. Melissa couldn't read his expression.

'You shouldn't have come back,' he said. 'I told you to run, damn it.'

He was OK. He was going to be OK.

She groaned. They were high in the sky now, above the clouds and away from the airport. Safe. A wave of nausea rushed up on her. She swallowed desperately, not wanting to puke. The blood thumped in her head. She felt dizzy. Spots swam in front of her eyes; her head lolled, and she fainted.

*

Melissa had only a vague impression of landing. She was groggy, half asleep. She heard Will's voice, talking, and lapsed into unconsciousness again. Hands picked her up, carried her limp body somewhere. She tried to stir her limbs, but they would not obey her. She slept again. In a little while, she was placed in the back of a car. A soft cashmere blanket was wrapped around her. Will was thanking somebody. He was there, with her. She leaned her head against him, and his firm body supported her. She slept some more.

When her eyes opened, the car was heading over a huge suspension bridge. Melissa stirred uneasily, tried to focus. There was water below them, a very wide river. On the far bank she could see skyscrapers.

She looked around her. She was in a limousine, a long car with pearl-grey leather trim, leaning against one of the windows. There was a navy blanket draped over her knees. Will Hyde was sitting on the other side of the car, talking into his cell phone.

'Hold on. I'll call you back.' He clicked the phone shut. 'Welcome back. How are you feeling?'

'Where are we?'

'Coming into Manhattan.'

She blinked. 'I was out for that long?'

'You passed out, and then they sedated you.'

'What?'

'It's perfectly harmless. And besides, that was a secure

plane and they were an elite combat unit. You could not be permitted to know the flight plan or see various things on that plane. I thought a mild sedative would be better for you than a blindfold. We also landed on a military base.'

She wanted to argue, but the drugs were still in her system. Maybe there was no point. 'What about your arm?'

'The boys shot me up and tied it up. I got stitches when we landed. It's fine.'

'There was so much blood.'

'Minor wound. The important thing is I can still flex all my fingers, see?' Will made a fist. Then he frowned. 'Melissa – you came back to get me.'

'You were on the ground. He could have killed you.'

'My risk to take. I'm a soldier.'

She scoffed. 'You're a banker, Will.'

He ignored that. 'In this mess we're in, whatever it is, you have got to be prepared to listen to me. I want you alive.'

'I wasn't going to stand there and watch you die.'

His face softened slightly. 'And what could you have done to stop it? Did you have a gun? A helmet or a Kevlar vest stuffed in your handbag?'

She flushed. 'Stuff you, Will Hyde.'

'It was a sweet gesture.'

She said nothing. Her emotions in that moment were better not faced. She changed the subject.

'And what about that scene at the airport? What will happen?'

'We'll worry about that when we need to. OK?'

'OK. Where are you taking me now?'

'To the secure apartment I discussed with you. Melissa, I want you to do exactly as I say for a day or so, OK? No phone calls, in or out. I will leave you a secure mobile phone with a code for me. Don't use it for anything else.'

'All right.' He looked relieved to be discussing practicalities, she saw, and she hated that.

'I'm going to send things over to your apartment. Clothes, things like that. It's already stocked with food. I will bring fresh stuff over myself. Don't order in and for God's sake don't leave the apartment for any reason.'

She nodded.

'Look, I know it seems like a prison, but it won't be for long. Just a few days while I figure this out. Who's doing this, why, and how we protect you.' He saw her dismay and leaned forward, pulling out a drawer in the base of the seat in front of them; it was a miniature bar, lit with tiny spotlights, with a crystal whisky decanter, gin and mixers, and bottles of mineral water. 'You want a drink?'

'I'm just thirsty.'

He fixed her a sparkling water with ice from a crystal bucket and a slice of fresh lime. Melissa sipped it. It was so luxurious. A soundproof screen separated them from the chauffeur. 'Thanks,' she murmured.

'The apartment is a penthouse. You'll get lots of light. It has books, a massive TV screen. No computer – forgive me, but they can track people through computers.'

'That's fine.' She thought for a moment. 'Does it have gym equipment?'

Will lifted a brow. 'You were serious.'

'Deadly serious. I don't know how long I'll be running.'

'There's a fully equipped gymnasium and pool complex in the basement, but I don't want you going out of the front door of your flat.' He picked up his phone, dialled. 'Leon, this is Will. Yeah. Good, thanks. Look, can you have them take a complete set of free weights and a treadmill up to Apartment B? Get some aerobics DVDs in too. Pilates. Olivia wanted it. Yeah, right now. Thanks. And clear everybody out of the lobbies. I'm coming in twenty and I want privacy. Security too. I'll tell you when they can come back.'

He hung up. 'That should work for you. I recommend Pilates for flexibility.'

'Never heard of it,' Melissa said.

'Works with the strength of your own body. So you can train when there's no equipment around.'

Melissa swallowed hard. 'I'll try anything.'

He was silent for a moment. 'I hope you won't have to run for ever.'

She shrugged. 'From now on, whatever happens, I'll always be ready to run.'

His eyes met hers for a long moment, and Melissa had to force herself to look away. This was agony, this was such agony. She wanted him. Surely it must just be lust, a natural survival response to a life-threatening situation. You need to get into that apartment, away from him. Let him go back to his fiancée and his high finance. She was looking at a life of witness protection, she knew it. She would never see Will again. He would marry this girl and be very happy. Melissa needed to get over him, fast.

'I know,' he said.

'You can't get a firing range up there, can you?' She forced a joke.

'Not without inviting too much comment.' He grinned. 'But when you get out of there, I'll teach you.'

She flashed on Will standing behind her, his strong chest pressing into her back, his thick arms around her slender ones, his hand steadying hers on the trigger.

It was a powerfully sexy image.

'No thanks,' she said firmly. 'I'd rather do it myself with an instructor.'

'I'm a very good shot.'

'Not short of self-confidence, are you?' she snapped. 'You won't always be there, OK? I have to learn to handle myself. You can't make me dependent on you.'

'Fiery,' he said, and to her fury she saw him trying to suppress a smile. Melissa bit her lip with anger, and turned away from Will Hyde, to stare out the window.

He walked her in to an anonymous-looking skyscraper on the Upper West Side. It had sleek granite sides, and was surrounded by similar buildings. Nobody paid them any attention. A Korean guy in a suit strode past them on the street. Melissa kept her head down, her mousy-brown hair tumbling in front of her face. Will was pushing her into an elevator. He put his head close to hers.

'Keep your head down. CCTV camera.'

She stared at a polished brass floor for ninety seconds, while the express elevator rushed them to the top of the building. It must be high, Melissa thought; her ears popped. The doors opened, and she was glad to get out. They were on a small landing; she realised she was looking around, checking for the stairwell. It was next to the lifts. There were two doors on that level.

'This one goes to the roof, for maintenance. You might hear men coming and going. Ignore them. This building is as secure as they come. I have bodyguards on every floor, the best. Some are ex-Mossad. Three are former SAS.'

'That must be expensive.'

'It is.' He took a small key and opened the other door. 'Your temporary home.'

Melissa glanced around the place as Will shut the door behind her. Unable to be cool, she gasped in amazement.

Apartment didn't really begin to say it. It stretched out over the top floor of the building. She was in an entrance hall that led into a drawing room, bigger than the entire downstairs of her father's house, furnished with gorgeous low-slung leather minimalist furniture, glass coffee tables, sharply designed bookshelves. Across one wall was a gigantic television. Melissa walked forward, hesitantly. She could see through an open door to the master bedroom suite; there was a king-size bed, antique Chinese cabinets and wardrobes, and beyond it a master bath with a gigantic tub and separate shower.

'There's another bedroom suite the other side, past the kitchen,' Will said. 'Let me show you that.'

'Sure.' Melissa blushed, she didn't know where to look. She understood that Will was very wealthy, but being confronted like this with the fact of it was extremely disturbing. And to think that this wasn't even his house. It was just one of many apartments that he had, one of a stable.

The kitchen was vast and intimidating, set with appliances in burnished steel, gleaming black marble floors and cabinetry in smooth modern walnut. It was one of those designer magazine things, she thought, where they hide all the handles and you have no idea where you keep the mugs.

She asked where everything was. He chuckled, and showed her. There was a steel panel that turned out to be a fridge; a walnut wall slid open to reveal a wine cooler and a fruit rack; there was a proper old-fashioned larder cupboard hidden away, too, and everything she could possibly want.

'Nutmeg grater?' she teased.

Will, taken aback, had the good grace to laugh. 'Nutmeg grater, yes. Here. And here,' he pulled at a shelf to reveal a two-foot spice rack, 'are some fresh nutmegs.'

Melissa laughed with him. She shook her head. She

was so relieved to be alive and able to make fun at him over the nutmeg.

'Will.' She suddenly had an impulse to say it. Just say it, so there was no more skirting around the elephant in the room. 'You've done very well for yourself, making all this money. Congratulations. I'm truly happy for you. You deserve to be happy.' She swallowed hard. 'I'm sure your Olivia must be a lovely girl, and I hope she makes you happy too. And – whatever may come now—'

'Melissa . . .'

'No, please. Let me get it out. Thank you so much for coming to get me and saving my life. I'm sorry you were injured.'

'That was nothing.' He moved towards her, and she couldn't make out the dark look that crossed his face. 'Melissa – I would never let you get hurt. That wasn't even a question. I . . .'

His phone buzzed. He glanced at it.

'It's Olivia.'

The moment had shattered, the spell was broken.

'I have to go.' Will pulled out a phone from his pocket and laid it on a marble counter top, a little awkwardly. 'I'm on speed-dial one. It's set so only I can call in, so it's safe to answer. There are clothes in the closets for you, shoes; workout gear is over there.' He pointed. 'There are big windows here but you're safe to stand by them, because the glass is tinted like a limousine. Do not answer any of the other phones. I'm going, I need to make quite a few phone calls. Try and find out what the fuck is going on. Will you be OK?'

'Absolutely,' Melissa said, forcing a smile. Her little blue suitcase from Holland was behind him, in the corridor, pathetic on its own. 'Take your time. I won't expect to hear from you for a while.'

He came closer to her, put one hand on her shoulder. 'I'll be in touch.' His eyes raked her face, as though he were about to say something, do something. But he hesitated, and turned away.

Then he turned on his heel and walked out of the flat. The door closed heavily, and she was quite alone.

For a moment or two Melissa just stood there. If there were tears, they wouldn't come. She was all by herself, the way she'd wanted to be. In a moment, she went back to the front door to retrieve the suitcase. She carried it back into the master bedroom and started to unpack. When that was done, she would bathe and lie down. It was important to sleep off those drugs.

And when that was done, Melissa decided, she would get the hell on to her treadmill. Because the luxury of her surroundings did not fool her. She was in secure accommodation, and she hadn't stopped running.

Chapter Eighteen

Olivia Wharton's phone rang in the bedroom. It startled her so much she dropped the cut-glass tumbler of green vegetable juice all over the gleaming kitchen floor.

She snapped her fingers at a passing maid. 'Quick, clean that up.'

'*Si, Señora.*'

The bedroom phone. That was Will, that was how he rang her. Only he had the number. Oh God! He was home, he was home!

Her heart thumped like a schoolgirl's. Jack Sansone had found absolutely nothing, no clues, no way to contact him. She had begun to fear he might be dead. And now he was calling her.

Olivia started to run, never mind about her teeteringly high Christian Louboutin shoes. She could move when she wanted to. She flung her wiry little body across the satin coverlet of their oyster-white bed and grabbed the phone.

'Hello?' she almost shouted.

'Livvy,' he said. 'It's me. Will.'

'Where have you been? Are you OK?'

'Europe. I'm fine.'

'I've been panicking, Will. Jack's been panicking too. They're going frantic over at Prospect . . .'

'Jack and Prospect can damned well wait.'

Olivia recalibrated slightly. It wouldn't do to be seen to be concerned about his bank stock. 'Where are you now? I miss you, Will. I've been out of my head wondering . . .'

'I'm in Manhattan now. I'm at a payphone. On my way, I should be there in ten minutes. I'll tell you everything I can.' He sighed on the end of the line. 'It's a long story, Livvy.'

'I have all the time in the world,' she said softly. 'Hurry home, sweetheart.'

She hung up, placed the phone in its cradle and stood in the bedroom, frantic with indecision. This wouldn't do, this staid little Chanel suit she'd worn to lunch with Emily Drasner. This said social lioness, not sex kitten. Help! She only had ten minutes. Olivia slammed the bedroom door shut and ran into her walk-in closet, frantically flipping through the racks. Relax, she told herself. You're a brilliant dresser. Instinctively she pounced. A cute little Empire-waisted sundress by Armani, yellow cotton with a butterfly embroidery; it was deceptively sexy, because it had a modest length, but it clung to her breasts. A little slither of a shrug in pale cream jersey, to emphasise her tan. She tugged at her hair, pulling out all the diamond clips so artfully set there by her personal hairdresser Gianfranco, and letting the raven locks tumble loose about her shoulders, how Will liked it. Scent; he loved her in Hermès. Stockings . . . yes. She slipped a pair of Wolfords out of their box and up her slender, well-turned calves, and matched them with a pale yellow garter belt and a tiny scrap of white cotton panties, almost virginal till you got to the thong at the back. In a stroke of genius, she decided she would not wear high heels. Instead she slipped on a cute pair of white drugstore flats.

She pirouetted in front of her floor-to-ceiling mirror. Perfect. It was the sexy-girl-next-door look, hot in a way you couldn't quite put your finger on. Will Hyde was never into the obvious sexpot thing. She'd seen many girls flounder horribly with him by coming on far too strong. When she was sexy for Will, it was always half secret.

Quickly she bent down and scooped up her Chanel suit and T-shirt, dumping them in the dry-cleaning bin. There was a tube of KY Jelly hidden in her shoe closet; Olivia applied just a little bit. Will was big, and he hurt her sometimes. When she'd first been dating him, she hadn't needed it. He was too strong, too hot. She'd been responsive, enjoyed herself. But gradually, as she became aware exactly who he was – *what* he was – she knew she had to marry him, and paradoxically, then it was harder. Because everything she did was geared to making Will propose. Sleeping with him became a performance test. She had to work to please him, incredibly hard, and it made her nervous.

He had been away for days. He was a supremely lusty

man. She half dreaded it. At least now it wouldn't hurt her, and more important, Will wouldn't know she was tense.

OK, Olivia thought. I'm ready.

You don't need to be this nervous. He proposed. You got him.

She would say nothing, absolutely nothing about Jack Sansone coming over. Damn that guy. Mind you . . .

Her mind flickered back to Jack in the house. Full of compliments for her outfit and her taste. His eyes smiling at her appreciatively. She'd been so grateful. He was flattering. He smiled widely and flirted outrageously with her. When he left, empty-handed after touching Will's computer and looking through his desk, Olivia had regretted it. She'd stood there and watched him go . . .

Her daydream snuck up on her, and she started, guiltily. Of course she didn't want to have an affair with Jack Sansone. He might be more sensible than Will; she didn't think he'd leave her for days without a word of notice, but so what. He worked for Will. He had ten per cent, Will had ninety. She was not the kind of girl to go for the beta dog . . .

'Hey.'

Olivia gave a little squeal, jumping out of her skin. She spun on her heels, facing the door. Will was standing there, in a shirt and pants. He had some kind of bandage on his upper right arm. He looked tired, really tired.

'Oh my God!' she squeaked. 'You scared me!'

'Sorry, baby.'

Baby. The term of endearment was so welcome to her.

He still wanted her. He still loved her. This little jaunt to Europe wasn't some fear-of-commitment thing.

Olivia ran forward and flung her arms around him, lifting her carefully lipglossed mouth to kiss him, parting her lips, pushing her tongue towards his . . .

'Ah.' He winced and hung back. 'Honey . . . not right now.'

'Not now?' She stumbled and fell back.

'My arm hurts. I got shot. It's fine, it's fine' – he put his left hand at her waist – 'but I want to leave it a day or two.'

'Aw.' She pouted, to hide her relief. Then his words hit her. Her eyes widened. 'Wait. You got *shot*?'

'Don't worry about it.'

'I do worry. Can I see it?'

He drew his arm back.

'Trust me, I'm a doctor,' she joked, and was relieved to see the answering grin.

'It's been looked at by a medic. Long story, Livvy. It's late. Let me tell you over dinner.'

'OK. A date, that'd be lovely.' He wasn't hurt, so she was the bright, bubbly girl again that he enjoyed so much. 'Where shall we go?' she cooed. 'Twenty-One? Jean Georges? Masa? Maybe Le Bernadin? I haven't been there in a while. I hear they have a divine peach soufflé at the moment.'

Will's face clouded. 'You want to go out?'

'Not if you don't,' she said, correcting herself instantly. 'I've had a long few days. Maybe we'll just have a quiet evening in. I just want to be with you right now, Livvy.'

She melted, kissing him on the cheek. 'Oh, sure, sweetie. Of course. I'll tell the chef to make us something simple. How about . . .' She had blanked out on his favourite dishes. 'How about just a nice steak, some thin fries and a salad? And a bottle of Margaux. What do you say?'

'Fine.' He sat down on the bed. 'Even better because it's quick. Tell him I want mine rare.'

'Sure thing. They can get it to you in twenty minutes.'

'Great.' Will rubbed his eyes. 'You look terrific, Liv. Let me shower and change. I've been on a plane most of the day. I'll tell you everything over supper, OK?'

She was bursting with curiosity, but she tossed her head and smiled engagingly. *Don't argue, don't nag.* It was her number-one rule. 'That's just perfect, sweetheart.'

The candles were flickering in their private dining room. Will had had one built, out on the terrace overlooking the townhouse's beautiful walled garden. It had one wall of solid glass, and the rest was oak panelled; it was the right size to sit four, and was approached through the bedroom. The formal dining room, downstairs, was a massive affair and mostly used for her charity parties. This was where Will came when he wanted to date, but not to go out.

Beeswax candles, solid silver candlesticks, Irish linen napkins and fine bone china – everything was set just so. Olivia had had the chef bring up the food in a catering trolley with tiny warming plates, and then dismissed the staff. She poured the water and wine herself, and helped Will to his food delicately, bending over as she did it to give him a good look at her breasts.

'You look better,' she ventured, slicing off a tiny portion of his fillet steak. It was meltingly good. Will's chef used Kobe beef, massaged in beer, and never cooked it a second too long. Will was attacking his with gusto, and the crispy fries as well, perfectly hot and dry. Of course, she would never touch carbs like those. Looking good took work.

Will looked at the wine swirling into his glass. Olivia poured it very delicately. He had always admired her feminine grace. She looked beautiful, too; the antithesis of tired, natural Melissa. Livvy's hair was blow-dried, soft and gorgeous, raven black with lowlights of chocolate and caramel. Her outfit was absolutely perfect; girlish but elegant, and he could see how it set off her breasts to perfection, without being obvious. Olivia Wharton was never obvious. Her nails were neatly shaped and finished with a French polish, her eyebrows were plucked into a sassy arch; she had the perfect pair of low-cost shoes, the right touch of rose-pink blush, mascara on her eyelashes, and neutral shades on her lids and lips.

She was the epitome of the high-maintenance American rose: fresh, gorgeous, and groomed to within an inch of her life. If one of his business contacts had walked into the room right now, Will would have felt proud that Olivia was his girl. Still he looked her over, beautiful and polished as she was. Did she love him for him? Or for his money?

A little of both, he concluded, without rancour. Olivia Wharton was a beauty from a good family; she had at least a couple of million of her own. It was expected of her to date a rich guy. She was one of the most attractive girls on the circuit, and being chased by several eligible guys when he'd decided to beckon her over. But she had chosen him. And anyway, Will liked to think he was not naïve. A woman couldn't separate a man from his money, unless the man had inherited it. He had made that money. It proved his worth in today's hormonal jungle; he was the hunter who could fell the biggest mammoth. He was not bitter at women for finding his success attractive. Olivia was like him, in some ways. She was going after the biggest prize she could see.

She had a sense of humour, she was kind, and she was feminine.

So why did he feel so awkward?

You have to get a grip, Will told himself. Stop wallowing in nostalgia. You enjoyed protecting Melissa, admit it. You enjoyed going back to those days and nights on the run, where the concern was the next meal, not the next deal. Of course something has transferred on to the girl.

Here's Olivia. She's younger, thinner, and better groomed than Melissa Elmet. And she obeys you unquestioningly; she doesn't scowl or argue the toss. She understands your new world as Melissa never could.

She's willing in bed, if not as hot as she used to be, and she'll make a perfect hostess . . .

Time to stop mucking around. Time to get that ring.

'Tell me why my man has a gunshot wound in his arm,' Olivia teased.

He motioned that she should sit, and she did so, taking a tiny sip of the good wine. Olivia drank to keep him company, but she watched her figure quite obsessively. He had never seen her drunk, not even tipsy.

'Here's what happened.' He breathed in. 'Do me a favour and listen to the full story before you give me your questions, OK? I think you'll understand better if you hear the whole thing.'

She nodded and smiled. 'That's fine, honey.'

Will told her, as calmly as he could, everything that was safe for her to know. The bare bones, but the truth. He included the early marriage and how Melissa had it annulled; that he'd gone into the army and then worked in intelligence. That he had seen Sir Richard before his death, and it had prompted him to see a pattern in the other killings.

'I thought she was in danger. I couldn't let her die, because of what we had once been to each other.' He saw Olivia's face contort gently; she was clearly desperate to speak out. 'Go ahead.'

'So you still loved her . . . a little bit?'

'No.' He was glad he could be firm. 'Not even a little bit. I cared for her, that's different. It's way different. She was engaged to this guy who got shot.'

227

Olivia's lip curled. It was clear she didn't think some dead penniless professor could be much competition for a handsome live billionaire.

'Is she pretty, Will?'

Again he could tell the truth. 'Not compared to you, baby. She isn't even in the same league.' Now he felt a pang of disloyalty to Melissa, but what the hell. She had hurt him, and she was not here to listen to his assessment.

'What did you think . . . I mean, when you saw her again after all that time?'

Olivia should have been a lawyer. Most men would crumble under the cross-examination. She went straight for the emotional jugular.

'I thought . . . how beaten down she looked.' He held his fiancée's gaze. 'If you want the truth, I just felt sorry for her.'

'Yeah. Well.' Olivia's tone was sharp, surprising him. 'She should have stayed married to you. She missed the boat.'

'We got shot at, outside the hotel.'

Olivia's delicate hand lifted to cover her mouth.

'They chased us through London, I got her away safely. Took her to Belgium on the train, then a bus to Rotterdam. The next day they found us at the airport. That's when I got shot. But it's only a flesh wound; it's nothing to concern you. We took a charter flight home,' he lied. 'She's safe now. I have to figure out who wants to hurt her, see if I can call them off. If not, get her somewhere safely permanently. It should only take a month or so, but I'm not about to put her in danger.'

He said the last sentence very firmly. Olivia had to understand there was no point arguing about this.

'And darling, that's about all I can tell you. I don't want anybody but me knowing where she is or what her status is. These people on her trail are pretty serious. It's best for you that you have no idea about her, so this is the last conversation we'll have on the subject.'

Olivia bit her lip, hard.

'I'll tell you when I have Melissa stowed someplace safe,' he conceded. 'So you'll know it's over.'

'So.' Olivia waved her French-manicured nails as if to dismiss all that. 'You stayed a night in Rotterdam? Separate bedrooms?'

'We slept in the same bed, for security. Don't worry. I didn't touch her once. I didn't want to.' Was that last bit true? He ignored the question. 'It was a big bed.'

Olivia glanced down at the table, and he hated seeing that her eyes were wet.

'Baby, come on. She's a friend whose life was in danger.' He reached out across the table, and Olivia meekly put her hand in his. 'I'm not going out to Tiffany's tomorrow to buy *her* an engagement ring.'

Olivia lifted her head; her eyes were sparkling now, the moisture in them lit up with joy. 'Really?'

'Of course really. I promised, didn't I?' He wanted her to be happy. 'It's not all that romantic, but you can come with me if you like. You can choose.'

She clapped her hands childishly, with pure joy. 'Honey! *Thank* you.'

Women were strange, he thought affectionately. The smallest things made them happy. A piece of jewellery, a new dress. He bought tailored clothes and good watches, but none of them gave him particular pleasure. They were utilitarian. But if the fact of the ring gave Olivia happiness, that was fine with him.

She had him. Melissa made her nervous and upset. She was tense over this girl, Will thought, the girl who had married him and dumped him and broken his heart, shattered him completely for more than a decade. Melissa, who was less pretty, less groomed, less everything than Olivia. Except intelligent, perhaps, and courageous . . .

Whatever. He glanced out at his garden, carefully illuminated with small spotlights. Melissa deserved his protection, nothing more. She had hurt him brutally. Olivia Wharton was concerned only to please him, and her ultimate ambition was to be his wife.

'When we've finished dinner, go and call the *New York Times*.' To this day he never referred to it as the *Times*. 'Put the announcement in.'

Olivia squealed with joy. She pushed back her chair, jumped up and ran across the room to him, covering his face with kisses, careful not to touch the wound on his arm.

'Oh Will, thank you. You're wonderful. I *love* you.' Another kiss. 'Hurry up and get better,' she purred. 'I want to get you into bed. Oh baby, I'm gonna make you *so happy*. I swear it.'

Chapter Nineteen

Melissa lowered the eight-pound dumbbell, her face red with strain. She was sweating, her hair matted to her head. Done; done. Slowly she began a series of side-steps and gentle kicks, cooling down, bringing her body temperature back to a resting state. You didn't stop this exercise stuff suddenly. The DVDs in the apartment's fitness library were teaching her that.

Two days, and already her body was completely different. Melissa had little else to do; she was putting herself through a rigorous training programme. Every day she did an hour on the treadmill, morning and evening; mid-morning, she worked out with weights; mid-afternoon, she did Pilates strength training. Provided there were sufficient recovery periods, there was almost no limit to how hard she could work. And the time spent jogging was blissful; her treadmill faced the window, and she could see the steel and glass caverns of Manhattan, with the little cars crawling past them on the ground below. As her tired legs and body fell into the rhythm, her heartbeat pumped out oxygenated blood; all her anxieties and heartache faded, and for a little while there was nothing but the sky, the city and herself.

Her heart rate slowed, returned to normal. Melissa bent over, as she had been shown, and went into a long series of stretches. It wouldn't do to rush any of this. Her goal was to get firm and fit as quickly as possible. She must avoid injury.

The muscles in her calves and thighs felt good, stretching. She was calm now, breathing normally. The pleasure she felt after exercise began to flood her body; not a high, just a strong sense of well-being and achievement. She clung to it. It had kept her sane, kept away the sadness that had been there ever since Will walked out of the apartment. Getting herself fit was a mission now, something she could do even though she was trapped in this apartment. It handed back a sense of control. And in these confusing, frightening days, control was something she needed.

She went back into the living room and laid herself down on the couch, flicking on the giant TV with her remote. Soaps, local news, comedy sketches. Melissa flicked through them. A baseball game. Trapped here, she had actually started to figure out baseball. It was relaxing noise in the background, at first. Then she had started to study it. But she wasn't in the mood for baseball right now. Something light. Something fluffy. Unreality was good, when you were trapped in a penthouse apartment, guarded by former Mossad soldiers with guns, in fear for your life. Melissa flicked to E! Entertainment. And gasped.

There was Will, on the screen in front of her. He was at some gala event, standing on a red carpet. He wore black tie. Her eyes slipped to his arm; the bandage was beneath the shirt, very discreet. There had been nothing about Will and her on the news, no mention of an incident at Rotterdam airport. Somehow he had managed to keep it all quiet.

He looked urbane and handsome. She thought of the strong muscles hidden under the crisp white shirt and the tuxedo. She preferred him in a T-shirt, covered in dust, his chest and biceps easy to see. Just to look at him made her heart crunch with longing. She breathed in, sharply, from the sheer pain of it.

But it got worse. There was a woman standing beside him, an incredibly beautiful woman. Melissa stared at her, fascinated. Compared to her, this woman was like a doll: petite and slender, no more than five foot five. She had glossy jet-black hair, swept back from her face with a sparkling diamond barrette. A chic dress of solid gold sequins clung lovingly to her tanned skin; her toes were barely visible under the floor-skimming hem. She clutched a polished gold metal bag with a small chain loop, and she was smiling brightly with carefully painted scarlet lips. She was easily the equal of most supermodels on the circuit. Melissa pushed her damp hair back from her glowing face. Impossible to imagine this girl with a set of free weights in her hand. If she worked out, it might be ballet, or a few laps in a pool. She would not be sweating and groaning like Melissa, and she doubted she'd have fixed herself a bowl of pasta for lunch either.

'And here we have two *fabulous* benefactors to the city's Red Ribbon Gala for Aids,' the presenter gushed. She was a blonde with that ditzy cheerleader thing down. 'Billionaire Will Hyde, long known as one of New York's most *eligible* bachelors, and hostess with the mostess, socialite Olivia Wharton, and guys, I hear you have announced some wonderful news today, is that right?'

She shoved the microphone forwards. Melissa thought she saw a wince on Will's face, a flicker of distaste, but perhaps she was projecting. Olivia, at least, had no such qualms; she stepped close to the microphone with a brilliant smile, and her gaze flicked between the reporter and the camera. It was as though she were looking through the screen, right at Melissa.

'Yes,' she said. She had a breathy, high-pitched voice, soft-spoken and girlish. 'Thank you, Elise, we do have some good news. Will proposed and we've announced the engagement.' She paused, as though for emphasis. 'We're getting married, and we just could *not* be more thrilled.'

'Wow! That's awesome!' the presenter squealed. 'And the ring, can we see the ring?'

Olivia laughed and blushed but, Melissa saw, she extended her hand readily enough. On the third finger there gleamed a simply enormous solitaire diamond, a massive emerald-cut stone; even under the artificial klieg lights behind the reporter, Melissa could tell it had a coloured tint.

'Oh my God!' screamed the reporter. 'What is that? Is that real?'

'It's a canary diamond,' Olivia said modestly. 'From Tiffany's, of course! Will had the ring engraved with my name yesterday – they did it especially quickly. Just for me.'

'How many carats is that thing?'

'I'm not sure . . . I guess . . . it's approximately twelve carats.'

Melissa snorted. She bet that girl knew the weight of the stone to three decimal places, and everything else about it too.

'That is incredible!'

'It is very pretty,' Olivia agreed, 'and it's internally flawless, which is nice.' She squeezed Will's arm. 'He is soooo good to me!'

Will smiled. 'Shall we go in, darling?'

'Of course.' Olivia waggled her fingertips at the TV reporter. 'Excuse me! Love you, guys!'

'We love you, Olivia! Congratulations! Congratulations to you both! And here are another adorable power couple, Donald and Melania Trump . . .'

Will and Olivia were walking up the red carpet now, out of range of the microphone. Olivia's gown had a plunging back, tied up at the neck, and Will's hand was resting on the small of her back. They were talking to each other, and his fingers were splayed out over her skin, stroking it gently.

Melissa felt sick. She switched off the TV.

There were no tears, because there was no point. She stood up, and headed into the bathroom. Will had made sure there was an enormous range of cosmetics in the mirrored bathroom closets, including boxes of hair dye of every shade. They had briefly discussed that she might need to change her appearance. Melissa dully picked up a box of auburn dye. She would colour her hair, something she'd never done before. Whatever would help to throw them off the scent. Her mousy locks were gone. She was going to be a redhead. And while she was about it, she would cut her hair. Grabbing scissors before she could change her mind she chopped off a good few inches.

It was important to be as ready as she could, because Melissa had determined one thing. She was getting out of here and away from Will Hyde. He could set her up in witness protection or whatever he wanted, but dealing with him, talking to him day to day, she realised now, was too much pain. She could face the facts calmly now. Indeed, she had to. As Melissa shook the plastic bottle and started to squeeze the strong-smelling dye all over her head, she admitted it openly to herself, so she could grieve his loss and try to move on.

Will had come back, and she had, once again, fallen helplessly and hopelessly in love with him. But there was to be no mercy, no respite from her teenage mistake. He might forgive her one day, but the love had gone. Time and distance, experience, money; everything separated them. If he knew she loved him, he would assume it was for the money. The Will Hyde of today was lost to her.

That thought was a comfort. Melissa scrubbed the dye into her scalp, covered her hair with the plastic shower-cap, and threw on a towelling robe, settling down to wait. The idea that he should think her a gold-digger was intolerable. Much better to be openly hostile. Pride made her dash her hand across her eyes and dry her tears. She would change her hair colour, work out hard, and wait a little while. And think what she might do after she left New York, where she might hide. Away from the men who wanted to kill her, and away from Will.

Will was in his study at home. He looked down at his pager, impatiently.

Jack Sansone was buzzing him again. That guy could be very annoying. Will was needed in the boardroom, apparently. Because Sansone and the other directors he paid millions of dollars per annum couldn't run a bath, let alone a bank.

He looked at the screen again, and then back to his notes. They were illegible scribbles to anybody but him, an old shorthand code with a random key. There was no way to decipher it except to get the code through old-fashioned torture, and Will didn't plan on submitting himself to that.

Melissa. Her father. David Fell. Senator Ellen Jospin. Poor, quiet Moira Dunwoody, librarian. What was the connection? Why were they killed?

Who was doing it?

He had taken the second question first. That was

easier to answer. Will had a photographic memory, something useful for both banking and spycraft. He recalled everything. He had replayed, in his mind, the events of the last few days over and over again. The shots in London. The chase. The hooded figure in the crowd. The man at Rotterdam, that became men. Everything that had happened told him something.

Start with the basics. The problem lay with Melissa's father. She had done nothing extraordinary with her life to merit this, he was sure. She had no connection to Jospin or Dunwoody. No, Richard Elmet was the common link. A few phone calls had established what he left her – very little: a house, with a lot of debts, just a scrap of money when all was said and done. His lawyer contact had got back to him estimating forty-five to fifty thousand British pounds. Maybe that was a lot, in relative terms. Will dealt with numbers that were so big these days that he had lost sight of what the guy in the street might consider wealthy. However, there was no question that an inheritance had anything to do with this. Fifty grand wasn't worth bothering with. And if it had been something physical, such as a microfiche or some stolen plans for a nuclear reactor – the normal objects spies followed each other across the world trying to grab – assassination would not have been necessary; repeated burglaries, sweeps of an office late at night, that sort of thing, would have happened instead. Perhaps a kidnapping to force the relative to cough up the location. He shivered at the thought. He had been trained to withstand torture, and eventually to give up false information convincingly. On a couple of occasions he'd had to put it to the test. Missy had no such protection. The thought of someone hurting her was unbearable.

No object; no money. There was no gift of land that might have ruined a major development or contained oil or diamonds. That left information, damaging information. You killed when you did not want information spread. It fitted.

Will thought hard. His mind processed information like a computer, running the analysis.

First: information. Something she knew, or they thought she knew. Some knowledge that Moira Dunwoody and Ellen Jospin had also had access to. He set that part of the puzzle aside for later. It required facts to complete.

Second: who. They were rich. That went without saying. To hire some jerk with a gun was easy; pissed-off husbands and wives did it on a regular basis. To get a professional, one who could track Melissa under a false name to the Victrix Hotel, a crack shot, that needed money. And he was not merely focused on his own hunt. The instigators of this had the resources to send operatives to America and to Europe. Ellen Jospin was the key. She was a US senator. It was very, very hard to take out a senator. Most professional killers would not touch that job. The full might of the CIA and the US Secret Service would be on their trail immediately. Who wanted that kind of hassle? The Jospin killing told him some hard facts. The organisation, whoever they were,

were exceptionally rich and utterly ruthless. Ellen Jospin's killer would not have been some common-or-garden shooter. It would have been a major assassin, one with a worldwide reputation, one who could go after, and deliver, a government target, even a US target.

That did not bode well for Melissa Elmet, Oxford academic.

It also narrowed down the possibilities.

To this day, there was no progress in the Jospin investigation. The killer had been exquisitely clean. World-class, then. There were not too many of those.

He had more information. The fact that somebody was waiting at Rotterdam. He had told almost nobody except his good friend Chuck Robertson of the Rangers, and he'd served time in the Jordanian desert with Chuck. There was no way at all the leak came from that end. There was nobody else. The hotel, though, was always a possibility. He was known by sight.

Think, Will, think. Work backwards, he commanded himself.

Leak from the hotel, then. Meaning they had the resources to ask all the hotels in the area. They might have found him on the Eurostar, the last time he had used his passport. Again, data searches like that were the province of . . .

. . . of state security agencies.

A wash of adrenaline rocketed through Will. His heart rate sped up, and sweat dewed his skin. Melissa was being hunted by a state agency. That was very bad news indeed. They could rarely be bargained with. There was almost no point taking out their operatives. There were always more, and always more money.

Like the Terminator, they just kept coming and coming. Kill one bad guy, they sent more. They had lots. And the target had just the one life.

He made himself be calm. He would not let her die. More information, he needed more information. He replayed the chase again in his head, every moment of it . . .

Starting with that first bullet.

The figure running through the streets. Hooded. Lithe. Will shut his eyes and concentrated, till he could hear the sound of the footfalls thudding around the London streets.

His subconscious served up the information.

It was a woman.

Will almost jumped out of his skin. God. Yes. A female. Her slight build and the light, too light, sound of her feet on the stone. A man running sounded different. He was aggravated he had not noticed before. Distracted by Melissa, by his emotions. A dumb rookie mistake.

Not just Will's. Theirs, too.

There were probably fewer than five top-class female assassins in the world today. It would be easy to identify her. There was footage, CCTV footage, of the murderer of Moira Dunwoody, a simple stabbing. The killer had been hooded and muffled, but Will would be able to tell who it was just from her body. He would call down at One Police Plaza later today. He had fantastic contacts in every branch of law enforcement, and every agency, in both Britain and the States, right down to the DMV. He would see that video and determine who the girl was. A few more enquiries would find out her recent client list, or something close to it.

For the first time that day, Will Hyde felt a glimmer of hope. If you knew your enemy, there was a way to defeat them.

He didn't have endless time. They would regroup after Rotterdam. Obviously they knew he was based in New York. They would come after Melissa. The first priority was clear enough: get her out of his flat into a proper safe house. But after that? He had no idea.

Will didn't want to leave her alone.

His life was here. His bank, his company. His girl. It had been a little boring, listening to Olivia coo and trill madly over the ring and the engagement. But it was a big moment in the life of a woman. He put up with it, just like he had to put up with listening to the doorbell ringing all morning; her jealous girlfriends falling over themselves to send flowers. It was Livvy's victory parade. He was just meant to be good-natured about it.

And she tried to please him. She had insisted on making love to him when they got back from the charity gala; his second night at home, and Olivia was bursting to get out on the town. He'd been uneasy all night, spooning up caviar and a little taster menu including smoked salmon, mango coulis and a ginger cheesecake; good food. Yet all he could think of was Melissa, stuck in that apartment, afraid and alone. She was safe. But it was little consolation.

Olivia had forced him to take a glass of claret, to relax just a little. And it was an important thing that those watching him – as they surely were – saw him settling into his normal life, not knowing if he'd abandoned Melissa, what he'd done with her. They did not want discovery, he knew that. Questions might be asked. He was safe in his own world, one of the most prominent members of Manhattan society. They would likely fear he had some early conclusions in a sealed envelope with a journalist, ready for publication on the event of his death. The fact that they'd come after Melissa last suggested she was an afterthought. On paper, she had been the easiest kill of all. They were probably unsure if she knew anything. All the more reason not to take him out in public, in Manhattan. Messy. Too many questions.

So he danced with Olivia, enjoyed her grace, her sensational body, her peerless social skills. She dazzled on his arm, and not just because of the diamonds. Besides, it had been days since he'd had her. She was all too eager. He couldn't resist, didn't want to. The tension of near-death . . . of Melissa, OK, maybe that too . . . it needed relief. When Olivia got him home, she tugged him by his bow tie, unravelling it, half pushed him up the stairs. He muttered something about his arm, but she pushed him on to his back and had mounted him expertly before she was even undressed. Olivia was good, and he needed it. He had let himself go, taking her harder than he had done in months. Screwing away the guilt, claiming her. She was his woman now; they were getting married. So there was nothing wrong with fucking her, nothing at all. And she was grateful, a little drunk, relaxed and hot. It was good.

He looked at his phone. It was secure. There was no excuse not to call her.

He punched the number, standing up. Time to get into the office after that. The bank had problems. Who didn't? All that was required was to keep it on an even keel, but apparently even something this simple was beyond the wit of his highly paid lieutenants.

'Yes?'

He started a little; it was still weird, hearing her voice. Natural, he told himself. They had not spoken for years, before all this started.

'It's Will.'

'I would hope so. You said nobody else had the number.'

He grinned. 'I have to go into the office. Work trouble. But I've figured some things out. It gets me closer to making you safe.'

A beat. 'I saw you on TV with Olivia, Will. Many congratulations.'

His smile faded. The goddamn crew at that stupid party. The preening and boasting and showing off of the ring he'd had almost no part in choosing, just paying for.

He hadn't wanted Melissa to see that. He didn't know exactly why. Because it was embarrassing, perhaps.

Yes, sure. Embarrassing. That was it.

'Thank you,' he replied. It seemed wholly inadequate, but there it was.

'What you're doing? How long will it take?'

'A day or two,' he lied. He had no idea how long, nor how he was going to secure her. Only that it had to be done.

'Will, I'm sincerely grateful for all you've done for me. I am.' This was obviously a rehearsed speech. 'But I can't stay here. It's no kind of life. And I feel I should keep moving.'

'Melissa, I am a professional at this stuff.'

'I can't stay with you,' she said firmly. And he heard tears behind the voice, tears she was fighting to keep in check.

My God, he thought. Is it Olivia? Does she care? *Does she love me?*

But this was the ice queen, arrogant Melissa Elmet, who had turned from him, allowed her own father to kick him out. Maybe she regrets that diamond ring, he thought harshly. Not me. She never even tried to reach me.

'I believe you are being targeted for assassination by a government or governments. That means lots of operatives and lots of resources. For a start, it will mean people are currently watching every railway terminal and airport, and every subway station and bus stop in Manhattan.'

She breathed in, frightened. He was stern. Better that she should understand the threat and stop bitching. He had enough problems trying to save her skin without hearing it from her all the time.

'You are a rank amateur, and if you leave my protection and try to get out of this city you will be dead within the hour. Do you understand me, Melissa?'

'Yes, sir,' she said.

'Goddamn it!'

'Look.' There was a tiny snuffle and he imagined her dashing her hand across her eyes. 'You have a life, Will, a great life. And I'd like to get one. You must get back to your wedding plans and your bank, and I, I have to get out of Dodge. Isn't that what the Americans say? OK, they might kill me. But I will just have to accept that risk. I cannot stay as your guest, Will. I don't want to be near . . .'

Her voice trailed off. 'I mean, I need to get out on my own.' She spoke up bravely. 'You showed me a lot of stuff. I bet I'm OK.'

His phone vibrated again. 'Melissa, I have to go. I'll come and see you tonight. OK? We can discuss it then.'

'OK, but . . .'

He heard Olivia coming round the corner, heading to his private office.

'Got to go. Bye,' he said, hanging up. He reached for his jacket.

'Oh, are you off to the office, honey?' Olivia stood in the doorway, in an outrageously short purple fringed minidress and killer heels. 'Because Jack Sansone called and asked me if I knew where you . . .'

He stopped dead. 'Jack Sansone called you?'

She blushed and looked shifty. 'Oh, he rang my phone. I guess he'd already tried you.'

'Really?' Will said coldly. 'I didn't realise you'd been hired to work at Prospect, honey.'

She squirmed. 'Oh, I hope you don't mind. I just . . .'

'I don't want Jack or any of them bothering you at home.' He was furious. 'I'll see you later, I won't get back in time for dinner.'

'Sure, sweetheart,' Olivia said nervously.

He strode out of the house without looking back.

The boardroom for Virginian Prospect Bank was on the sixty-third floor of the Deloitte Tower in downtown Manhattan. It had long, narrow windows like arrow slits in a medieval castle; plenty of light, but not enough of a view to be distracting. Will Hyde had preferred that his senior staff concentrate on business. The floor was covered with a soft burgundy carpet, over which lay an enormous, pricess Bokhara rug; there was a long mahogany board table, and the walls were panelled in dark Jacobean oak, imported from France. Against one wall was a TV screen with a live feed from Bloomberg running constantly; next to it was a table with computer terminals and laptops. There were videoconferencing screens set discreetly into the board table, ready to pop up and be activated at the flick of a button.

When Will strode into the boardroom, his top lieutenants were already sitting around the table. Jack

Sansone was at his right hand, with an eager smile pasted on to his face.

Will moved to the head of the table and sat down. They all looked at him expectantly.

'I've been occupied, this last week, on private business. What's up?'

'The bank has been experiencing a severe crisis of liquidity.'

Will suppressed the urge to roll his eyes. In today's climate, that was like announcing that the secretaries had started to gossip or the traffic was a little heavy in midtown. 'So what happened when you went to the Fed for emergency financing?'

They glanced across the table at each other.

'We didn't do that.'

'Why not?'

'We didn't want it to get out.' Sansone taking the lead again. 'Bad for the prestige of the bank.'

Will frowned. 'That's ludicrous. We're living through a global liquidity crisis. Our mortgage book is excellent, we have little subprime business. Applying for temporary funds from the government is a normal part of doing business at this time.'

He could see the suits exchanging anxious looks across the table.

'If Virginian Prospect went public,' Jack said, 'we could offer a rights issue.'

Ah. There it was. The elephant in the room. *They wanted to take his company public.*

'You know what I think about that.' Will refrained from thumping the table. 'I hold ninety per cent of the stock. None of you can compel me to do a damn thing with my company.'

'We're stockholders too,' Michael Watson said. He was a chubby little senior vice-president from M&A and he was a greedy bastard.

'Jack has ten per cent. I have ninety per cent. Everyone here can do the math.'

He was seriously displeased. Damn everything, he thought, damn these guys coming after Melissa *now*. This time last month, and he would be having security escort these losers out and a firm of headhunters on speed-dial. But he might have to take the girl someplace else. He needed his executives, right now, to run his bank. Because he didn't have time to do it.

Management. He was tired of it, suddenly. Tired to death. What was the point of sitting here, in his luxurious boardroom, nannying a bunch of bean-counters who were all ten years older than him? They resented his success. Give them the slightest problem and they fell apart.

'Jack.' He turned to Sansone. 'You think now is the time for an IPO?'

'Some businesses succeed even in a downturn,' Sansone assured him. 'Prospect is almost unique. You have a great mortgage book, like you say. Solid loans. Good M&A division. It's a rock when other banks are shifting. We could float.'

'Will.' Yogi Brillstein, from the retail section, spoke up. Will respected Yogi. He didn't talk often, and when he did, Will listened. 'It's not about the money, really. That much cash would keep us perfectly liquid. It would reassure all the retail customers. They're scared. Banks are failing. Families with mortgages are panicking, too. We floated, we'd be one of the best-capitalised banks on the street. We could attract so much new business. You'd set a lot of minds at rest out there.'

Will paused. Yogi had come up with the only argument that could sway him. From the very beginning, he had insisted on control, right up until the management buyout when he took the bank private.

The sallow faces around the table, all grey from too many hours in the office, stared at him greedily.

Will glanced out of one of the slit windows. The profile of a skyscraper presented itself to him.

What the hell. He was thirty-nine years old.

He realised, suddenly, that he had felt more alive over the last few days, running with Melissa Elmet, looking out for their lives, than in the whole of the last five years. He did not want to turn into these men. He did not want to spend the rest of his life at stuffy, thousand-dollar-a-plate charity dinners.

'I will keep forty per cent of the stock,' he said. 'What the fuck. Sell it.'

Then he stood up, and walked out of the office.

Chapter Twenty

Melissa was naked. She studied her body in the mirror, carefully. Amazing, she thought. Amazing how different she looked. Even a few days could transform a body, if you worked at it constantly. She had a way to go, of course. Her arms were firmer, but the bicep and tricep muscles were tiny. Nevertheless, she hardly recognised herself. Her slim, soft body was now slim and hard. Relentless crunches and sit-ups had shaped her; she had definition. Her buttocks were tight, raised. Her calves and thighs were rock solid. She could run for an hour straight and tire only slightly. And she hadn't even really begun to train seriously.

There was something compelling about this sort of concentrated effort. She accepted she would always be looking over her shoulder. There could be no more soft, mushy life for her, no quiet days spent in armchairs reading or bent over a lamp in a library. Whatever occupation she took up, she would need to be ready to run. To be physically active, to have her passport and some money always stashed away. She would work at self-defence. A woman could never defeat a man; that had been brought home to her, quite forcefully, running with Will; even an older, thin or weak male could best the fittest woman in a fight, quite easily. Television and movies that sold the vision of the kick-boxing Amazon were tricking some girls into thinking it was real, that they could punch a man and not be laughed at. Taking her hunters on would lead to rape and death. But she would learn some techniques in the hope that surprise would afford her a split second to run. And then, lean and prepared, she'd be able to get away.

And more important skills. Evasion. Foreign languages. She would learn Spanish and Portuguese. Maybe go to Brazil, hide on the beaches amongst the tourists. Hide where the crowds were, that was important. And of course, she, Melissa, who hated all firearms and violence, was going to become a crack shot. She would train with a pistol and a sniper rifle. She would carry a small woman's revolver in her handbag. Maybe Will could get her something she'd seen on a movie once, a gun made of plastic that disassembled, with the bullets hidden in a keyring. If that could be done, it was a great idea. She could carry her weapon with her on the way to South America. Get a job teaching English to the children of some *narcotraficante*. Or something . . .

She hadn't figured that part out yet. Whatever. She would wait tables for less than minimum wage until something occurred to her.

There would be a path to redemption. Already, as she looked herself over, Melissa felt stirrings of something new under her fear and heartache. Defiance, perhaps. And self-respect.

Her thin, soft academic's body was coming alive. And the safe, dull life that had sapped all the hope and joy out of her had been crushed into nothing. She would be an adventurer from now on, like it or not. There was a crumb of comfort in that. Seeing Will Hyde, understanding what she had lost, the kind of man he was, made Melissa long desperately for passion.

Her new life would be day to day. Survival and reinvention had one great asset. It would not leave her any time to mourn. Heartache, the agony of watching Will with Olivia; all that would have to wait.

She straightened her body. With no children, her breasts were still taut and firm. Her slimness meant there was no cellulite to contend with. The new muscles were still female and lean; the definition in her calves and thighs was attractive, it made her look younger.

And there were more changes. With time on her hands, Melissa had set about altering her appearance. The less she was recognised, the better. The hair dye had been a revelation. She looked so incredibly different when her own mousy, nondescript shade was transformed into a rich Titian red. It complemented the colour of her eyes; she'd blushed when she finished with the hairdryer and looked in the mirror.

Wow. What a difference. Melissa was red-headed. Her

skin glowed. Her hair looked stunning. She swallowed hard; had she honestly wasted all those years? But she knew the answer to that one; when Will left, she was so heartbroken that she hadn't cared enough to bother.

She ran her fingertips through her bobbed hair. They were shaped, and painted a pearlescent pink. Thanks to a bottle of fake tan her face and body were not pallid and white any more, but were now covered in a golden tan, not too deep, just healthy and bright like a California girl. She had experimented with make-up, too; stuff she never bothered with: a brown eyeshadow to make her eyes pop, mascara, bronzer on the cheekbones, a golden lip gloss. The result took her aback.

She was unrecognisable, unless you looked closely. Not that she looked like a teenager or anything; the new Melissa was a stronger, bolder, better version of the old one. She had had the academic's contempt for shallowness, concern with looks and the like. Yet now she understood what profound things the face and body were. Just by concentrating, applying cosmetics, dyeing and colouring her hair, she had transformed herself from a woman that nobody looked twice at in the street to a vibrant, pretty girl, tanned and confident.

She was not the same person on the outside. And that had changed her on the inside, too. It was a great disguise. And it made her feel just a tiny bit better.

Of course she could not compete with Olivia Wharton. But Melissa did not want Will feeling sorry for her. It mattered hugely to her that if he was going to see her for the last time, she would damn well be stunning when he kissed her goodbye.

Chapter Twenty-One

Lola was impressed. William Hyde had shown himself to be more than astute. She was glad he had escaped Carlos in Holland. Even though Dimitri apparently had no fewer than six men waiting at the tiny regional airport, Hyde and the target had got away on a military flight; one with no flight plan and the ability to scramble radar. They had simply disappeared, as effectively as if he had teleported her out of Rotterdam. And three of the hirelings had been shot dead by the Americans.

Carlos had escaped to face the wrath of his superiors. At least now they would understand that it was not quite so easy as all that to kill this man. And it was almost impossible to kill him quietly. He was a true professional. He had come back to New York – she could not be sure exactly when, since she did not know when he had landed in the United States – and he had, apparently, moved seamlessly back into his own normal life, in the capitalist spotlight of Manhattan, presenting himself fearlessly in front of television cameras and in open spaces without protective armour, giving the impression that nothing had happened. There was no sign of the girl, Melissa. He had another female; Lola had confirmed that this one had been his woman over the last year. They were getting married. It was already news.

All of which made killing him messy.

Lola was getting soft in her old age, she told herself. Her late twenties. She was almost warming to William Hyde. A target. A very impressive target, though. She indulged herself in a brief fantasy about life with a true man, one like that. Not a user like Dimitri, like all those other men. Maybe, when she had finished this job, she would quit, and disappear. Go out on a high. Nobody would ever find her. Could she, even she, have another sort of life? One that included a man like Hyde?

Besides, he had wandered into this. The girl was the original target. Lola had a pro's respect for William Hyde. He would be taken out, but not immediately. He would be expecting an assault. More reason to wait. The girl was not in his house, therefore he had stashed her safely. Lola understood Will, very clearly. He had attachment – a fault – but cunning with it. Melissa was somewhere that she could not threaten his family or business, somewhere he could protect her.

The amateur took a target into the wilderness, hid them in a log cabin in the Adirondacks, or with a grandmother in some remote village. They were conspicuous out there and easy to track. How many of her kills had stared in amazement, even before they were frightened, as she blew their heads off? That someone had found them in Smalltown, South Dakota, was impossible.

So routine. Will Hyde would not have sent his protectee anywhere like that. She was in a city. Probably New York, because he was here. And Lola just didn't think he'd leave her.

She looked at the monitor in front of her, feeding from the surveillance cameras. He had left his board meeting early and he was getting into a limousine. Probably going home to fuck the model. Dimitri had emphasised he was not to be killed, not yet.

He could relax. Lola shrugged. Perhaps he even wanted her to chase him. He was acting irrationally. The female must have significance to him, to receive such a level of protection. It didn't matter; she would not be diverted. The question was, where had he stashed the girl. Where was she right now?

Lola turned away from her screen as the image of the limousine flickered front and centre, heading over towards Tenth Avenue, taking him uptown. She moved out on to the street. There was an internet café three blocks away which she would use to glean some further information. New York was a great city to hunt in. It always had everything you needed.

Dimitri halted, annoyed. He was walking down an alley in Sabana Grande in Caracas, and he was five minutes late. The city was sweltering today, unusually hot; it was choked with pollution and flooded with street hawkers and bums. Adventurous tourists were advised to keep a little money on them to give to robbers.

Two men had approached behind him. Thieves. They were barking something at him in Spanish, calling him *Americano. Give us your money.*

The larger of the two spat on the ground. His hand went to his belt. He had a knife. His companion laughed.

'Get out of my way or I will kill you,' Dimitri said. It would not require English to understand what he was saying. Men like this had heard that tone before.

The bigger man snarled and snatched the knife out of his belt. The other made a grab at Dimitri's jacket.

Dimitri jabbed at his attacker, a perfect hit to the solar plexus. The man crumpled like a concertina, folding on to the ground, gasping for breath. His companion slashed out wildly with the knife. Dimitri's arm shot out, catching the man's wrist. He twisted, using his attacker's weight against him. There was a yelp of agony as the man hit the dirt, his arm breaking. Dimitri took the knife and stabbed upwards, in the rib cage, directly into the heart. A clean knifing. The man's eyes widened, more in shock than fear. He was not aware what had happened. He glanced down, stupidly, but the light was already fading in his eyes. The knife was back in Dimitri's hand, its blade gleaming red. The second robber, desperately, had scrambled to his feet.

'No, señor. No, no, señor,' he croaked, and ran stumbling down the alley.

It would have taken Dimitri seconds to overtake and

kill him. He let him go. He was late. Carefully he folded the knife into the still-warm grip of the corpse at his feet, then walked smartly, not hurrying, out of the alley and across an unremarkable plaza, to the hotel.

His companion was strolling under the palm trees at the Los Proceres monument. A large square of tile filled with shallow crystal-blue water, it was surrounded by white stone. On the steps leading up from the water feature was a statue, the mounted figure of Simon Bolívar.

The water looked inviting and blue. Nobody came here. It was quiet, an oasis in the middle of this revolting city. A good place to meet. Dimitri glanced around, registering the feeling of riches. There were places in Venezuela where wealth seeped from the stones, just enough of it to lift the country from Third World misery. He didn't give a shit about politics; that was how the regular drones managed the misery of their pitiful existence.

But money was another matter. This whole affair could ruin this country, a place that even now teetered on the brink. His contact, like the Nadrahis and the Russians, was a very frightened man.

Dimitri was starting to feel a slight anxiety himself. When he was not working, he enjoyed skilled hookers, luxurious hotels, yachts, retreats miles from anywhere. Eventually age would catch even the best assassin. You could not run for ever. At seventy or eighty, even those two morons in the alleyway might prove a problem to him. Like all operatives, he would need a place to nest, a good plastic surgeon, and an exquisitely kept fortress. Dimitri was going to Switzerland. He had a place in mind, as secure and luxurious as it was anonymous. But global economic meltdown would not be good for him, either. He enjoyed life as it was.

'My name is Manuel Feliz,' lied his contact.

Dimitri shrugged. He was not there for chat, and couldn't give a shit about this clown's fake name. 'They were apprehended at Rotterdam and escaped on a military flight with the Americans,' he said.

'I know all this,' the man replied.

'He has returned to his previous life. There is a fiancée, an American socialite.' Unimpressively skinny, with fake breasts. Not his type.

'Public knowledge,' Feliz retorted. 'You are running this. Tell me what I do not know.'

Dimitri did not argue. He was pleased the man did not waste time. 'Nothing indicates that either he or the girl are aware of the information.' That was how they always referred to it. 'Furthermore, he has been persuaded to float the stock of his bank.'

Feliz nodded. 'Good. Excellent. How much stock will he have?'

'Forty per cent.'

'Can we bankrupt it? Destroy the bank?'

'The others are moving along those lines, yes. It will not be sufficient to ruin the stock of the bank in order to deprive him of funds. He owns property across Manhattan, including entire buildings.'

'Are they mortgaged?'

'No. He has diverse bank accounts, and likely more that we do not know of. He was a spy.'

Both men mused briefly on their own lack of serious riches. Millions of dollars in the single digits felt inadequate compared to Will Hyde.

It would be an especial pleasure to take this man's fortune from him.

'Then he must be barred from his own money.'

Dimitri nodded. 'I am working on a way to ruin the bank and blame him for fraud. Everything he has will be seized. We are just making certain, you understand. He likely knows nothing.'

'But how certain can we be, when the female is still on the run?'

'Lola.' He had received her report this morning and it mollified him. The girl was good; he no longer looked so stupid for hiring her. 'She has found her. Hyde put her in a penthouse apartment in a secure building, ultimately owned by him, but with an impressive paper trail to disguise it.'

Feliz snorted. They both knew that nothing could withstand the combined resources of national intelligence agencies.

'Is she dead?'

'Not yet. The building is heavily guarded. Top-ranked security, recruited from Mossad and Agency retirees.'

Feliz cursed. He leaned against a palm tree and pushed his sunglasses up his nose. 'Damn it to hell. *Esta fregada!*'

'She is breaking in. They are sending back-up. It'll be like a raid. Our people, with guns, in NYPD uniforms.'

He liked that. A smile. *'Bueno.'*

'She already investigated cleaning companies: no dice. He has the soldiers clean the place themselves. They also work maintenance. Some were in the engineering corps. Hyde specifically designed it as a safe house; there are no outside contractors of any description.'

'He is a careful man,' Feliz agreed. Both of them made a mental note to copy this practice when they retired themselves.

'So we're going in the old-fashioned way. When she is dead, you will be the first to know.'

Feliz nodded. 'And now we should start a sweep of all Richard Elmet's colleagues, all the technicians.'

Dimitri shook his head. 'He worked on this in private. He didn't want anybody else to break his discovery. The notes were hand-written and we have burned them all. His house has been dismantled, top to bottom. Even the floorboards were taken up. There are no more copies.'

'I don't give a fuck. Take out his cleaners, everyone. Everyone he ever breathed on.'

Dimitri suppressed a smile. 'Señor Feliz, if we start blowing up buildings and slaughtering illiterate maids, there will be press attention. People will notice. The operation depends on the press not connecting any dots here. We are taking out whoever might have had access to the information. For the present, this will have to do.'

His client grunted. 'For the present. Yes.' He looked at

Dimitri. 'After an interval you are to see to their elimination, one by one. Space it out. Don't rush it. But they must all go. However remote the possibility it is still there.'

Dimitri nodded. 'Very well. It shall be done. But first we eliminate the woman. Hyde made a mistake. He should know there is no such thing, truly, as a safe house.'

They parked the van directly opposite the building in a no-parking zone. Who cared? It was marked NYPD. Nobody would bother it.

It was also wired with explosives. As they came out of the building with the corpse of Melissa Elmet, the van would be blown sky-high with a fireball you could see for blocks. And the team would be scattered. Lola would drive an unmarked Ford Taurus down to the docks and present the body to two men from Dimitri's team. It was cleaner and simpler to stash it in the van and let it be incinerated in the blast, but her reputation was at stake. *Habeas corpus.* They wanted to see the goddamn body, and see it they would.

She felt elation at the thought of killing Melissa. Her last job, finished. It would be amazing to be free. To stop all this for ever.

'Let's go.' Her men nodded. She had twelve, mostly Colombians, one large black guy she thought was a Canadian. They were good and took orders well. There was no jockeying for position or arguing because she was a female. The men behind this operation wanted it done correctly, and had issued orders accordingly.

Lola adjusted her NYPD uniform and jumped out of the van, fake ID in hand. The guys followed behind her, guns drawn. There were a couple of passers-by on the street. A nanny with a kid in a stroller gave a little yelp of alarm.

'NYPD! NYPD!' the black guy was shouting. That was good, he had the best accent of the lot of them. Straight-up Brooklyn. 'This is a raid with armed police! Clear the area, ma'am, sir! Clear the area!'

They didn't need telling twice. They scattered and screamed and ran in several different directions. One of the Colombians moved up a block with his whistle and began to divert traffic.

Lola ran into the lobby of the building. There was a receptionist sitting behind a large, solid oak desk. She looked alarmed.

'Can I help you, Officer?'

The men were gathering close behind Lola now, forming a combat position. Lola flashed her ID. It was fake, but a very good one. You'd need a magnifying glass and some expertise to disprove it, and security here wouldn't have the time.

'Sergeant Lola Martinez, NYPD. We're here to arrest a terrorist suspect being held in the penthouse apartment of this building. I require immediate access.'

Even as she was talking, security men started appearing from nowhere. They came like ghosts drifting through the woodwork, a door here, a passage there. They had bulletproof vests under their shirts, she could tell. Several of them carried pistols openly. One had a sub-machine gun.

'I – I need authorisation from the landlord . . .'

'No you don't. This is the po-lice,' Lola replied, letting her inflection hang a little. 'We gotta warrant.' She produced a legitimate-looking warrant, faked by the Mukhabarat's best guys. 'Produce access!'

'Step away! Step back!' one of the security guys shouted. 'Vacate the building or we will shoot!'

Her men immediately cocked their weapons. There was no answering sound from the guards. Lola under-stood their guns were ready to fire. Shit. Fucking Mossad.

'NYPD!' she bellowed.

'Like hell, baby,' the guard sneered. He pointed his gun at her head. 'You have ten seconds to withdraw. Ten . . . nine . . . eight . . .'

There was a hiss. As Lola stared a protective Plexiglas shield came up from nowhere, rising from the curved desk. In less than a second it had encased the receptionist in a fully protective wall, even with a roof.

'Fuck!' she said. She levelled her gun and shot the guard who had spoken in the head. It exploded, taking part of his cheek and jaw away. He fell to the ground, dead, and his gun fired from the impact, the bullet ricocheting uselessly into the wall.

Lola had already thrown her body aside, with an

athlete's grace, twisting and spinning in the air as she landed against a door to the stairwell, when the bullets started flying. The guards were not watching her; every man in the lobby was diving for cover and firing at the enemy, dropping and rolling. The bullets burst out, sounding like thunder, a hail of gunfire. Odds were with her group, although one of the Colombians was already on the ground, clutching futilely at a gaping bullet hole in his neck, blood spurting over his fingertips as he gasped. He'd be dead in a minute. Nobody was so dumb as to stop to help him.

She had studied the schematics of the building. There was a stairwell, the lower part of which would be guarded. But there was also a central garbage chute. Lola looked around; nobody was watching, the bullets were flying, the dying man was screaming breathily. She lifted the hatch gently and levered herself into the stinking hole.

It was pitch black. She flicked a button on her watch that gave her a tiny light. There was ambient heat from the tied-up, rotting bags of garbage. The chute was sheer, not designed for humans to penetrate. Lola reached into her backpack and withdrew four plastic suction cups. She clamped one on to the smooth steel wall of the chute. It made a sucking noise, but nobody would register that in all this gunfire. The cups held strong. Lola breathed in; the stench of decay didn't bother her. She had known much worse. She affixed the cups securely to her hands and knees. Like the American hero now, she thought, amused; she was Spider-Man. She lifted her left hand, pressed it down, and moved her right knee. Everything worked fine.

To her left, on the ground floor, men were groaning and screaming. Lola ignored the sound. It was merely useful cover. She started to climb, at a good speed.

Chapter Twenty-Two

Melissa had showered and eaten, an omelette and a salad. Deliberately she had resisted dressing herself up for Will. It would have been easy – there were dresses in the closet – but she had nothing much left but her pride, and she clung to that. Let him take her as he found her. She had her routine. It was half seven, and he still had not come. He also hadn't called.

Perhaps something big was going on. Probably wedding plans . . .

She laughed at her own weakness. Worrying at her heartache like she was a kid, and it was a loose tooth she couldn't stop pushing with her tongue. None of that would restore Will to her. Melissa's only job now was to get on with her training routine.

She changed into her workout gear: a sports bra, a good black T-shirt and a tight pair of Nike jogging bottoms. Carefully she laced up her shoes. It was time for another solid run, and she would finish the day off with strength work and long stretches, so she could start again at first light . . .

Bam bam bam bam . . .

Melissa paused. Listened.

Bam bam bam . . .

She had heard that sound before. Much louder and closer. That was guns, the sound of guns being shot.

They're coming for me.

The sound was very faint. It must be at the bottom of the building and down there, it must be incredibly loud. An internal echo, the elevator shaft, perhaps, was carrying the sound up to her.

The elevator took you straight down into the lobby.

Melissa froze for a second, her heart starting to race. She couldn't think. There was only one way out. And it led right to them.

She glanced back at her secure cell phone, on the couch. Grabbed it, and pushed the number for Will.

There was a long beep. It was the answering machine. Damn it.

'Will, this is Melissa.' Who the hell else would it be? 'They're in the lobby. They're shooting. I can hear guns. I'm getting out.' She paused. 'I'm dumping this phone in case they track you. I – I'll try to get in touch, when I can.'

She pressed the button and walked out into the kitchen, with its giant windows on to Manhattan. You couldn't open them completely – just a touch, a couple of degrees. She pressed the button, and the vast sheet of glass eased itself fractionally away from the wall. Melissa took the phone and wriggled her forearm into the gap. Then she dropped it.

It would smash into smithereens multiple storeys below her. She hoped it didn't hit anybody. Nothing she could do. She would rather die than let them track Will's location, and surely the phone had some sort of GPS link.

Behind the kitchen, against the bedroom wall, her backpack was full and ready to go. Melissa moved to it, half sobbing, half laughing. She had packed it up as an exercise: what she would need to take with her if they came for her. There was a toothbrush, toothpaste, some cash, her passport, underwear, T-shirts, socks, jeans, two sweatshirts, a nylon insulated jacket, vitamin pills, a small bag of cosmetics, some disposable razors, anti-perspirant, soap, bottled water, meal substitute bars and a comb. There was even a small bottle of handwash liquid, so she could do laundry on the run.

She grabbed her workout jacket and zipped it up, then slipped on the backpack. Then she went to the door of the apartment and laid her ear against it. Total silence. An assassin could be waiting outside, but Melissa didn't think so. She didn't hear anything.

Lola felt the urgency, the screaming in her muscles. She ignored it. It might have been better to take a painkiller before heading to the building, but what the fuck. Pain was a regular part of her life. She could and did forgo relief.

The hatch for the first floor had popped up two minutes ago. But Lola, with a supreme effort of will, had ignored it. They would be waiting at the bottom of the stairwell, not at the first floor. Nevertheless, it was possible that if she exited at the first floor she would be heard. She continued to climb, the sweat of exertion bathing her strong back and her arms. There was a perverse joy in pushing through that pain barrier, and she clung to it. She, only she, would be the one to take Melissa Elmet out, the little chick under the full protection of one of the best operatives she had crossed swords with in ten years. Never mind the urgency of the client, Lola's principal concern was with restoring her own glory. Politicians and diplomats were easy targets compared to William Hyde and his canny tradecraft. It would be satisfying to kill his protectee.

She grunted with pain and lifted her left hand, ramming the suction cup into the wall again. Time to go. Time to push. Right hand. Left knee. Right knee. Push, girl, push!

Yesss! There it was, the second hatch, illuminated in the ghostly blue pallor of her tiny watch light. A claustrophobe would not have lasted ten minutes in here. There was nothing but indistinct blackness and a sheer wall of metal. Even the stink of the garbage had faded, a long way below her now. She was moving up, up, always up, her muscles pulling her, in the formless coffin-like tunnel of metal, with no light and no fresh air.

But she had just enough light to see, beaming from her wrist. And the endless sheer steel was presenting her again with an outline, a little rectangle cut into the wall of the garbage shaft. They were still fighting downstairs;

the echoes of the gunshots bounced up towards her, the occasional moan or scream. All of it seemed irrelevant. She was where she always was: alone with the target.

Another two motions and she reached the hatch. Despite her shrieking muscles, Lola lay still on the wall, her head balanced gently against the doorway, keeping her breathing under control, listening, just listening, as hard as she could.

Silence. No footfalls, no voices, not even the slightest vibration. Lola sighed with relief and heaved herself up, over the top of the hatch. In a supreme feat of strength she swung her knees away from the wall, detaching the suction cups, and jack-knifed against the hatch with her long legs. It swung open, and Lola's body followed the momentum, her hands elongated as in prayer, a lean line for the narrow space. And then, there she was, in an empty corridor lined with industrial grey carpet, opposite the elevator.

Lola wanted to laugh. So easy. Hyde thought he was good, but he wasn't, not really. She was about to update him on spycraft in the twenty-first century.

She reached out and punched the up button, summoning the elevator. Those hardcore security guys would be fighting it out downstairs. She was on her way to take care of business.

The elevator hummed and shuddered; she could hear it in the shaft. She calmly plucked the suction cups from her hands and knees, rolled them up into a small ball and stuffed them in her back pocket. The light blinked off, the elevator arrived. Lola stepped in and punched the button for the penthouse. Already her muscles were calming down, the lactic acid seeping out of them. A few floors up, with nothing to protect her but a thick door, her prey was waiting, beautifully cornered.

Lola drew her gun and her small laser knife. She didn't bother lock-picking any more. Science made that unnecessary. Melissa Elmet's door would be open in a few moments, and she would be dead in minutes.

It was the penthouse. There was no place to run.

Lola cocked her weapon.

Melissa's ear was pressed tight against the door. Silence. She wished to fuck she had a gun. The largest, sharpest kitchen knife was pressed into her hand, but it was as pathetic as it looked. She hung on to it anyway; she had nothing else.

She said a small prayer. She was surprised to find she still did believe in God after all, after a fashion anyway; enough to murmur incoherently when she thought she was going to die.

If she stayed here, she was dead. There was no choice. She took a deep breath and opened the door.

There was nobody standing outside. Melissa still had one foot in the doorway to the apartment, because Will had not given her a key. She tried to think. Nobody's here, but is someone coming? There was no sound of feet on the stairwell. It was quite quiet, and it would be a natural echo chamber.

She moved next to the doors of the lift. Her finger hovered over the call button.

And it was then that she heard it, a faint but insistent hum.

They were in the elevator. They were coming. They would be here in seconds.

Chapter Twenty-Three

Will Hyde stopped running. He had made a six-mile circuit of Lower Manhattan at a fast speed, stopping now and again for traffic, although the grid system meant you could always run one way or the other. With the epic news of the sale of his bank, and Olivia waiting at home, expecting an early marriage, running was suddenly an escape; not for him the sterile bounce of a treadmill in some luxury gym, a spinning class or a punchbag. Will liked the streets. There was something perfect in the way you could run and actually go somewhere. He would often finish at some anonymous bench, somewhere on the banks of the river, and do a few push-ups and tricep dips. At home, he had an exhaustively equipped weight room, but running with Melissa had turned him back to the techniques he used to practise, when fitness was necessary but gyms were nonexistent.

He slowed to a walk. Within seconds, his resting heart rate had returned to normal. His recovery times were those of an athlete. Will drank the air into his lungs. He was standing by a scrubby patch of vegetation, somewhere below Canal Street. Over his head the Manhattan Bridge reared, taking the traffic across to Brooklyn. God, he loved this city. He had made his fortune here, changed his life, become famous, enjoyed some of the world's prettiest women. What would life be like if he gave up the bank? What would he do with Olivia? Explore the city a lot, he decided, for a start. And cut way back on the socialising. No need to raise his profile with Wall Street analysts any more. He didn't like it, never had. He would fade into the background; one more rich man in a city that was stuffed to the gills with them.

Will leaned over at the waist and touched his toes, falling deeper into the stretch, then straightened and grabbed one ankle, then the other, feeling his quadriceps elongate. Better. He would get a cab back home, shower, then go see Melissa. She deserved to know what he had figured out. He had identified the type of pursuit. The question was what to do about it. For that, he didn't have an answer. He hated the idea of her running alone. She would be in terrible danger. But she might also be in danger staying here. He felt helpless, a sensation he loathed above all others. When he went to fetch Melissa from England, it was out of duty, keeping faith with his past. Now he cared about her, cared immensely. He couldn't settle with Olivia, enjoy marriage, his freedom from the bank, none of it properly, unless he knew she was safe.

He walked back to the road and hailed a taxi. 'Fifth and Sixty-First, please.'

The car pulled into traffic, and Will retrieved his two mobiles, flicking them on, just in case.

The secure one flashed a little light. Poor Melissa, she'd called, wondering where he was. He was late, but he'd had to clear his head. Twilight loomed in the summer sky. Perhaps he'd go over there now, forget the shower and changing.

'Hey, buddy – changed my mind. Can you go to the Upper West Side?' He gave the address, received a shrug from the driver, and put the phone to his ear, playing Melissa's voicemail.

His heart did a slow, sick flip in his chest. Oh God. How could he have been so dumb? And he was in his jogging gear. He had no gun, no goddamn gun!

Will pulled two fifty-dollar bills from his jogging pouch. He tapped on the Plexiglas screen separating him from the driver.

'I need to get there real fast. If you step on it, I got a hundred dollars for you.'

'When you got to be there, man?' the driver asked, flooring the accelerator.

'Yesterday,' Will said, as the guy switched wildly between lanes.

Melissa stood on the landing. The elevator was humming. It was easy, really; she had no option. She removed her foot and put a hand on the front door to the flat, ensuring it closed softly. Then she opened the small door that led out to the roof. There was a metallic staircase leading up to a hatch. Melissa moved in fast, closed the door behind her and bolted it shut. Then she climbed up the stairs as fast as possible, and shoved at the hatch. It was stuck; the paint or something had settled into position. She put her shoulder against it, her whole weight. She was desperate. The hatch gave a little lurch and shifted. Finally it opened, with a loud pop. Melissa suppressed a sob of relief. She climbed out on to the grey concrete of the roof and lowered the hatch gently behind her.

It was cold up here, with no protection from the winds at this height, the oxygen a little thinner, and night starting to fall over the city. Melissa looked around, frantically. The elevator would have arrived below. She must be quiet. They would be looking for ways to unlock her door, or just blast it open. She thanked God she had running shoes on, the quietest footwear possible.

Over in the corner of the roof, on the west side, was a large domed hatch. An engineering thing, perhaps, access to a ventilation system or a boiler. Whatever. Melissa knew nothing about apartment buildings. But it was the only structure on this flat, featureless roof. There were no convenient fire escapes up here, no outside ladders. The skyscraper was too tall for that. She ran over to the hatch, her feet padding across the concrete ground, her backpack tight against her shoulder blades.

Melissa reached forward, the palms of her hands damp with the sweat of her terror. She tried the door to the hatch.

It wasn't stuck. It was locked. From the inside. She could hear the metal bolt rattling against the lock.

She was out of options.

Lola moved out of the elevator, gun in hand, but stashed it in its holster. There was a tiny fish eye set into the door, like most New York apartments. She pummelled on the door with her fist, and pressed the buzzer.

'Melissa Elmet!' she yelled. 'This is the New York Police Department! We're here at the request of William Hyde! Open up, please!'

Silence. Not that she'd expected anything else, but it had to be tried.

'Open up! NYPD!'

Nothing. She paused for a split second and fired a bullet at the lock. The metal crumpled and some of the surface wood splintered, but it made almost no impact. Lola assumed there was a steel safety door under a veneer. Damn that Hyde, he really was something else.

But then again, so was she. She reached into her pocket and withdrew her laser cutter. There was time. Melissa had no place to run. All exits to this building were totally secure.

She turned it on, and applied the raw red beam to the keyhole, watching the metal heat before her gaze. In a moment, it had started to melt. Any second now, and it would begin to bubble.

Her best guess at the thickness of the steel was that she'd be inside that apartment within five or six minutes.

*

Melissa was too scared to cry. She tried to calm her thumping heart, tried to think. First she tried the door again. No. There was the bolt. Even if she had some way of picking the lock, it would not solve the problem of the bolt. OK. She walked around the edge of the building, choking down her terror of heights. The sheer drop to the ground made her dizzy, her head swim, but she had to look. Just in case she was wrong. Just in case there was a ladder, a drainpipe, some scaffolding, whatever.

On the floor below, she heard shouting. It sounded like a woman's voice. Angry shouting.

Bang.

Somebody was shooting at her front door. They were breaking in. They would find the place empty; maybe they'd spend sixty seconds searching it in case she was hiding in a closet. But then they would figure out about the roof.

Swallowing hard, she looked again for a fire escape. Was there *anything* that could be a way down the side of this building?

There was not. Because that would have been far too easy.

She walked back to the centre of the roof. Cold wind swirled around her, lifting her newly red hair away from her face, chilling her. What would Will do? He would think, Melissa told herself. She tried to think.

There was only one way up to this roof and only one

way down. The hatch through which she had come. Although she'd bolted the door, Melissa was under no illusions. A single gunshot would take that out. Equally, she could not secure the hatch itself. Even if she sat on top of it, two strong men could push her aside with no problems.

She looked around wildly. What then? Go back down through the hatch? Confront whoever was there with her kitchen knife? Try to kill them? They had guns.

Hide behind the boiler hatch? Sure – they would never think of searching there, would they . . .

She grinned, gallows humour. So it was wait and die, or fight and die, then. She stared into the distance, looking past the next building, its flat roof just below hers. Bloody lucky bastards, they had a fire escape, a lovely old rickety wrought-iron set of stairs . . .

An idea, a stupid idea, presented itself to her. But no. No, it would be suicide. She couldn't do that, couldn't possibly . . .

Lola turned her laser knife, delighted with its performance. It was making quick work of this door. She was already almost there.

'Come out, Melissa,' she shouted, no longer bothering with pretence. 'I'm not a sadist. Make it easy for me, and I'll make it fast.'

Would she cry, would she beg for mercy, talk about children or pets or whatever? It was interesting to see how people reacted at the last moments. Even the bravest often begged. Life was precious to most humans. Lola thought Melissa might be stronger, though. She was apparently a stubborn bitch.

She felt no empathy for any target. She knew Melissa Elmet's life had sucked; it was one long episode of drone-like boredom. Lola was practically doing her a favour. In the last days of her drab existence, at least she'd had a little excitement.

The door shuddered and moved. Lola stepped back and kicked it. The bolt had melted away. It gave, and she was standing in a cavernous apartment, sumptuously furnished and equipped. There was enough here to feed, water and entertain her entire squad of Colombians for a fortnight.

'Melissa!' she yelled into the silence. 'There's no point in hiding! I'm a pro. Come out!'

No response. She ran into the bedroom and started to fling open the doors to the wardrobes. There was no place the target could conceal herself. But they always tried.

Melissa scuttled to the edge of the building. The gap was narrow, between this tower and the next. Maybe eight feet. But it was eight feet that stretched over a cavernous, dizzying drop. There was nothing between there and the ground, not so much as a restaurant canopy or a row of trees. And nothing to grab on to on the neighbouring building, even if she had the strength to haul herself up; no gargoyles, no balconies or masonry. Nothing but a plain flat roof. The fire escape was to the left-hand side of the other building.

How far below her? Maybe twelve feet. Technically possible. A good chance she might break a leg.

The wind blew strongly. In movies and TV shows they did this all the time, but this was life, this was her life. Wind gusts would slow her, and she hated heights, and she felt dizzy and sick.

Melissa looked wildly around the roof. There was no other way out. It was a ludicrous thing to contemplate. But staying here to be killed was worse. They might not just kill her; they might take her somewhere and torture her, for whatever they thought she'd done or whatever they thought she knew.

Hurriedly she stripped the backpack off. It was heavy. Melissa told herself to get on with it. This was not going to get any easier, the longer she thought it through. *No choice, baby, no choice.* She moved back and swung her arms, a deep, long swing back, letting the weight of the pack be its momentum, and threw it. She gasped as it sailed away; up into the air, what was the angle . . . but it landed, in a second, with a thud on the roof, and lay there beckoning to her.

She wished she had some alcohol. But there was nothing. She wanted to pray, but all that came to her mind was *Oh God, oh God.* She moved backwards twenty feet, facing the edge of the roof, and she started to run.

Her life seemed to slow down, as though she were watching someone else. Her feet pounded, she sprinted, and in half a second the ground ran out from under her and she sprang and her heart stopped but there was nothing she could do now and there was no air and then the flat grey roof tile, a springy weatherproof material, blessedly came up under her, and if she let her legs break they would catch her and kill her anyway, and she instinctively tucked into a roll like they showed on TV when soldiers came out of parachute jumps, and she thumped down, and it hurt, badly, and there was blood on her face and she rolled some more and then she was OK.

Melissa sat up. She breathed in. Her legs, arms were working. Her rib cage hurt badly. Maybe she had broken a rib. It hurt to breathe, but she was not paralysed. She stumbled to her feet and retrieved the backpack, wiping the blood away from the cut on her face with her sleeve. Her workout clothes were black, the blood would not show. She half ran, half stumbled to the fire escape, and moved down it, her feet pounding now, ignoring the noise of her footfalls. At street level, she saw police cars, sirens blazing, moving into position. Maybe these were the real police, maybe they were more spies looking to kill her. She didn't know.

The fire escape ended fifteen feet from the ground. There was a ladder there, but it had rusted to the stairs. Melissa looked at the gap almost contemptuously. She crouched down, hooked her fingers underneath the iron and suspended herself by her arms. Now it was just a nine-foot drop. She crooked her legs and let go.

A bum was walking past with his dog, rubbernecking all the excitement and sirens in the road in front of them. He looked at her and spat expressively into the gutter.

'Crazy bitch,' he muttered.

Melissa smiled radiantly at him. She was alive. Dear God. She was actually alive. She walked quickly down a back alleyway and into another road, reaching into her backpack for some money. A cab was heading towards her, light on. She pasted on a smile – they didn't stop for crazy bitches, did they?

He pulled over. She clambered in. He was Arab, maybe Algerian.

'Where you goin'?'

She was too flustered to think straight. 'Ah . . .'

He frowned. She didn't want to be some mad woman he would kick out of his car. She couldn't name a hotel or a train station or the airport; they would be watching all those places. Somewhere anonymous, with lots of people, and off this tiny island.

'Yankee Stadium, please,' she said, inspiration striking her.

'Sure.' Not a crazy bitch today, then.

Melissa leaned back against the seat leather. She had no idea where she was going, or how to contact Will, or how she could get these people to stop coming. But she was alive. She had money and her basic necessities. And they had not seen the new her, with her short red hair and her tanned skin. She would pick up cheap sunglasses and a baseball hat at the stadium. Those were effective disguises, she thought, especially in a crowd of thousands all wearing the same thing.

Despite the pain in her side and the cut on her temple, Melissa experienced a vibrant surge of exhilaration. They had sent professional killers to hunt her down, trapped in that apartment, and by thinking fast and being brave, she had outwitted them all.

Yeah. She had been brave. And smart. And tough. She had done well. Her side hurt and her heart was still broken, but as she sat there, quietly recovering her breath, Melissa Elmet liked herself a little better.

Chapter Twenty-Four

Lola worked fast, becoming increasingly frustrated. Melissa was not in any of the obvious places. Lola had paused and listened; she had the ears of a bat, and could detect even tiny sounds of breathing in a short space of time. But she could hear nothing.

She made a second sweep of the rooms, banging on the walls, her feet hitting the floorboards, looking for concealed cellars or boxes. Nothing. It was all solid.

Melissa Elmet was not here.

Had she already gone? Had she left the building before they arrived? No; Lola had reviewed CCTV images taken directly from the bodega across the street; the girl had arrived with Will, her head meekly lowered, and not emerged since. There was no exit other than the front door. No way out.

But there did have to be a way out. Lola was not a big believer in God or magic. The girl was not here. It was her job to figure out the reason for that, and to do it fast.

One. The CCTV footage had been doctored and edited and did not show the moment Will Hyde took her out of there. But Lola was an expert in doctored monitor film. It seemed highly unlikely to her that this was the case.

Two. Melissa had found another way out.

The sides of the building were sheer. It was too low down to use an executive parachute. And this floor had no access to a stairwell. It could be reached only by an elevator shaft. Melissa had not used the elevator. Lola went back out to the landing. There was one other door. She chided herself for her stupidity. The idiot girl was hiding on the roof.

They were within sight of the building. Traffic had crawled to a halt; Will could see lights from police sirens, shadows dappling the front of a Rite Aid at the end of the street. He flung the money at the driver.

'Thanks, man,' he said, but Will was already out of the car, and running. He slowed as he approached the end of the street where his building was. A small crowd had gathered. NYPD were swarming around. There was the wreckage of a vehicle of some kind, burning fiercely, which meant it had been wired to blow. An ambulance at the end of the street was taking corpses, paramedics handing them up in body bags.

He looked around, heart thumping. He didn't want to make himself known to the cops. They would take him away, seek to interview him. Waste time.

One man, in cuffs, was being questioned in Spanish by an officer. He was dark, Bolivian perhaps or Venezuelan.

'*No puedes arrestar me. Tengo inmunidad diplomatica,*' he said.

You can't arrest me. I have diplomatic immunity. Will felt sick. He had been right, absolutely right, and it gave him no satisfaction. This idiot was boasting of his diplomatic passport. A goon on direct secondment from the embassy. His station chief might have him shot for such overt blabbing in the street.

Where were his guys? All dead? He looked at the body bags. Melissa, dear God almighty, had he left her there, trapped like a rat?

A hand tapped him on the shoulder. It was Moishe. His arm was bandaged. Moishe was one of his very best men on that building, an old colleague. Will paid him lavishly to run security and never asked questions. He jerked his head, and the two of them walked away calmly, down the street.

'A woman came in with about twenty of these clowns. NYPD uniforms, search warrant, vehicle, all looked legit. They weren't.'

Will nodded. He accepted that sometimes you just knew.

'We were armed. They were armed better. Sub-machine guns. Most of our guys are dead and I think we got eight or nine of them.'

'You have access to my discretionary account. Pay the families one million dollars each. I may be on the run.'

Moishe did not bat an eye. It was expected that Will

Hyde took care of everybody. They did not need to explain themselves to each other. 'OK.'

'Is Melissa dead?'

'I escaped upstairs while they were questioning our other men. They put the blame on the bad guys because of their fake IDs. The woman disappeared. I couldn't figure it, because we guarded the elevator shaft and the stairwell.'

Will thought for a second. 'The garbage chute is vertical and lined with steel.'

'Suction cups or magnets.'

'Fuck.' Will cursed himself. He had been out of the game too long. 'Incredibly muscular girl, then. World-class pro. I think it's Lola Montoya.'

'You're joking.'

'I think so.'

Moishe brooded. 'Jeez, man. Who the hell did you piss off?'

'Tell me, Moishe.'

'Sorry. OK, so she got out at the second floor, then she gets the elevator while we're shooting. I went up there. She had opened the apartment door with a laser weapon, the steel was melted.'

Lola was worth her fee.

'But Melissa had gone.'

'Impossible.'

'There was no sign of blood in the apartment and no way she could have taken her down. Will, she must have jumped from the roof on to the little condo building next door.'

Will stared at the man. 'You're not serious?'

'No other way out. I go round the apartment with my gun. Nobody there. I go to the roof hatch. My gun's out and I'm mad. I find that bitch up there, looking around, like she can't believe it. I start firing. Man, she was so surprised. I almost had her. She was fumbling for a second. Then she kneels and shoots at me, I drop; while I'm down there she winds up and jumps across the gap right in front of me. Lands on the roof, keeps running. I shot at her. Did not get her, boss, I'm sorry.'

'Don't be. She's slippery.'

'If she didn't have your girl with her, and there was no corpse, I'm saying she figured out that's what the chick did. And she must be long gone by now.'

Relief flooded every inch of Will's being. He was almost weak with it. The pure joy, the pleasure of knowing she was OK. He thought of how frightened she must have been. Did she still hate heights? She used to refuse to walk close to him, when they went on outings to the seaside, if he got too close to the cliffs. But she'd understood they were coming, and she had disobeyed him and left that apartment and jumped across the chasm to safety.

Magnificent. He was proud.

'Moishe. She's being hunted by a state or states. Something to do with her father. They think she knows information she doesn't know.'

'What information?'

295

Will grinned. 'I don't know it either.'

'Serious shit, if they hired Lola Montoya.'

'Twenty assholes in good knock-offs of NYPD. That's a major risk. They want her dead pretty badly. I don't want anybody coming after any more of my men. Tell everybody to take a long break. Hundred grand to every one of our forces guys. Call an agency and get regular security guards on the doors.'

Moishe rolled his eyes. 'Fat ex-cops from traffic division.'

'Maybe, but they won't get hurt.'

'OK.'

As he talked, everything was becoming clearer to him. 'Call Bob Katz.' His principal attorney and a man he'd trust with his life. 'You tell him I want to sell my shares in Prospect. All of them. It's going to turn into a public company.'

'All right.'

'Tell him to remove my document from the safe giving him power of attorney. I am going to disappear and find Melissa. And stop all this stuff.'

'How you gonna do that?'

'I have a plan. You shouldn't know it.'

'You have money and clothes?'

Will considered. 'Can you pack a sports bag for me? Bring me some cash.'

There was a diner on the corner. 'You go eat,' Moishe said. 'I'll bring you some stuff.'

*

296

Will walked over to the payphone on the wall and lifted it up. Remarkable, a real relic. You saw so few of these in a big city these days. Manhattan had a handful left, though. People had long memories of September 11, when the assault on the World Trade Center knocked out the cell phone masts. Queues twenty deep had formed at the payphones left on the streets. The diner had retained its own. He was lucky.

He fished out some quarters and rang Olivia.

'Will! Where *are* you?'

'Olivia, they came back. They tried to kill Melissa. She escaped. I have to go and find her. I'll be back as soon as I can, baby.'

There was a little sob of anger and frustration. 'Will! Let her look after herself. She's quite capable.'

'She's in great danger.'

'And you're not? Anyway, you have to come back. It's all over the news.'

Will glanced at a small TV mounted in the corner of the diner, one of the news channels. It was muted, with the news ticker running across the bottom. Nobody was paying any attention; they were nursing their coffees and lunchtime burgers and giant plates of pasta. This was a working neighbourhood, and the diner was cheap. Garage workers and janitors ate here for lunch and they wouldn't be interested in CNN. The TV was only watched during a game.

'I see,' he acknowledged. The van, in flames; his building, surrounded by police. A chopper shot. The body bags being loaded into the ambulance. A muted vox pop with a passer-by, who talked fast and shook his fist at the screen.

'The *police* want to speak to you. They found out you secretly own the building.'

'Not secret; it's all legal.' He stared in horror at the screen. His own face was up there now, in a dark suit, shirt and tie. He was wearing jogging gear and would look unrecognisable – he hoped. He must avoid the police at all costs. If they pinned him down, he was not safe.

'I'll be happy to go see them. But after I find Melissa. They sent twenty very bad guys to kill her and I can't wait around.'

'The *police* can find Melissa. Clearly you can't protect her; just tell them what happened and get her into protective custody,' Olivia insisted. He disliked the weepy, petulant tone to her voice. OK, this wasn't good for her, but he was trying to save a life.

'It's beyond any of that. Olivia, you need to trust me.'

'Of course I do, honey,' she said, with evident insincerity. 'I just want you back.' By that she meant, 'I want our old life back . . .'

'This afternoon the bank will be announcing we are floating the shares. That's all of them. I'm not keeping even a minority stake. I'm retiring, Livvy. We'll take the money and we'll go and travel the world. We just need to decide where to bring up the kids.'

That shut her up. He knew her so well, he could almost see her emotions struggling with each other.

There was prestige in owning a successful bank, and he'd lose that. But his ninety per cent sold on the open market would make her the wife of one of the richest men in America. Olivia was a socialite; Will knew she understood that he was finding her parties and dinners less and less tolerable. But travelling the world would offer her a chance to shine again. A couture gown at the tables of the Grand Casino in Monte Carlo . . . dripping in diamonds at a masked ball in the Carnival of Venice . . . a film premiere or two in Cannes . . . Ladies' Day at Royal Ascot . . .

'I *would* like to travel,' she agreed. 'We could take a year-long honeymoon all round the world . . .'

'Let me take care of this.'

'But you won't be back to sell the shares . . .'

'My lawyer will take care of it all. Relax.' She took a powerful interest in the minutiae of his wealth. Maybe it was natural. He still didn't like it. The sooner he got Olivia out of the socialite world, the sooner it was just the two of them travelling, the better.

Will was painfully aware of the distance between them since he'd gone to find Melissa. Olivia had been his companion, she'd looked after him. She'd made him laugh. Was he starting to pick at minor faults in her now he'd proposed, running from commitment, maybe? How likely was it, he chided himself, that she had changed? It was he who had changed. No good blaming her.

'When I get back, we'll take off. Anywhere you want to go.'

She laughed. 'To the church, to get married.'

Will chuckled, although it made him uneasy. Why was she pushing? He had proposed. Was she that desperate to get a legal claim to his fortune . . .

No, he told himself. What was this? He had asked her to marry him. Was he about to break her heart, to behave to her the way Melissa Elmet had treated him? Never. The situation was putting strain on them all. He *would* come back to Olivia. He *would* marry her.

'If that's what you want, that's what we'll do.' Outside the window of the diner, a motorbike was parking across the street. He saw Moishe get off it, removing his helmet. 'I got to go. You may not hear from me for a day or two, but I'm OK.'

'Yes, darling – do whatever you have to.' Olivia was reassured; she was warm and breathy again. 'Hurry home to me, sugar.'

'Bye,' he said. She blew him a kiss, and they hung up. He tried not to feel relieved. There was enough to do right now without dealing with emotional turmoil. He was getting too old for this shit, all of it. When he was young and angry he'd been a perfect recruit for the service. An orphan with no wife or family – that was textbook stuff. Attachments made you vulnerable and weak. They were a target for your enemies and they slowed you down. Wives complained about your absence. At least he didn't have kids yet.

Moishe, outside the diner, saw him and made a small gesture. Will went up to the counter, paid the bill, forced himself to keep the tip modest. You did nothing to draw attention. Outside on the street, his friend passed over the helmet and a folded black leather jacket. Will put them both on.

'Best way out of town,' Moishe said.

Will nodded. Sharp thinking. A motorbike helmet hid your face completely, and nobody would want to look twice at him. 'Whose is the bike?'

'My kid brother's. Levi. He's about your age. Works for GE in marketing. His driver's licence is in the rear trunk.' A shrug. 'We can get him another.'

Moishe was well known in Mossad; he could produce any fake documents he needed.

'Yeah, I've met Levi.' They were roughly the same height and build, with dark hair. That would be enough. 'Thanks.'

'The trunk is packed with essentials and ten thousand in tens and twenties.'

'Great.'

'If you contact me on the road, I can send you to people who can help, wherever you are.'

They had sleepers everywhere in the US, of course, treaty or no treaty.

'I won't be in touch. These are major players. They will soon have tabs on everybody I know. You leave town.'

His friend nodded, reluctantly. There was no point in arguing; Will Hyde had been one of the best. He could take care of himself. Moishe reached forward, shook his hand. By the time Will had mounted the bike, Moishe had already gone.

Will kicked it into gear and headed for the George Washington Bridge.

Chapter Twenty-Five

Lola was not happy. The English bitch had escaped. She had been intelligent and courageous; that was no consolation to Lola. Melissa was a nobody, a history don. Lola, who had killed senators and a president, who had eliminated four rogue agents of the KGB, was being outwitted not just by William Hyde but by his no-account whore.

Worse; she had been seen by one of Hyde's men. There was no doubt she would now be identified.

She was not looking forward to this phone call, but it had to be done. She rang Dimitri, her boss on the job, and gave him a brief account of the facts.

His silence was worse than any cursing or shouting.

'It can happen to all of us at any time,' Lola said. 'I will continue to hunt her.'

'Perhaps you should return your fee,' he said.

She treated this suggestion with the contempt it deserved. He was enraged. There was only one way to deal with that.

'You cannot stop this civilian,' he mocked.

'If you think I am so poor at this, you can try being my next target,' Lola hissed. 'Let us see if you fare so well. I can go off-grid in ten seconds. Do not think to send your men to make an example of me. I can turn and find you, Dimitri. I can hunt *you*. No fee required.'

He was quiet, hating her. The mutual threat hung in the air. Having changed the dynamic, where she was expected to crawl to him, Lola moved on to business.

'Understand. The woman is *good*. She's a natural, while the man is an expert. You have drafted in plenty of other operatives. None of them have succeeded either, even though Hyde has been walking around New York in plain sight.'

He sighed. It was obviously true.

'I'm not territorial. You have sleepers involved now. Activate them. Circulate the picture. Pictures – he has vanished as well. The police want him, for questions over his building.'

'He's gone to save her? John Wayne idiot.' Dimitri coughed. 'This is the least of his problems. In the next couple of days he will be ruined.'

'I have monitors on the phone of his lawyer. The man has been given legal power to make decisions. The bank is to float on the stock market – all of it. His shares go on sale tomorrow.'

'So soon?'

'The markets are scrambling. But yes. Apparently, when he decides to do something, he does it. The bank itself has little significance to him.' She admired this in

Hyde. He had a fine sense of detachment, important for an operative.

'We will see about that, when his shares become worthless.'

Lola doubted Dimitri could do that, but she did not argue. There were money men in the system to deal with financial attacks. Her skills were more basic.

'Until they land someplace, I cannot continue. Your men must find them.'

'Not a problem.' Dimitri was confident; he had secret agencies from more than twelve nations working for him now. Some without their governments' consent. It offered him a massive network of spies and sleepers, his own personal black-ops Interpol. Every bus station and railway stop, even the small ones, could pretty much be covered. When they surfaced, they would be found. It was the age of the internet and the casual surveillance network. There were cameras in every mall, on the carriages of Amtrak, at ATMs. Will Hyde and Melissa Elmet were good, but they were also split up. And working against the clock.

'Keep hunting them,' Dimitri said. 'You will be one of many.'

That was fine, Lola thought. He could assign as many men as he chose. She would make the kill.

Melissa clutched her Diet Coke and her hot dog and followed the crowd. She had no idea where she was going. She'd followed her plan and bought a baseball cap; that was good, she looked like any other fan now. It would be hard for them to pick her out, even if they had people here, which seemed galactically unlikely. For an hour or two she was safe.

'Hey, you.' A fat black woman in uniform was gesturing at her. Melissa jumped out of her skin. She hated being noticed, being accosted. 'Ticket.'

'Sure.' Melissa pulled the ticket from her pocket, proffering it.

'Bleachers,' the woman said sneeringly. 'Don't try to take no alcohol in there.'

'OK,' Melissa replied. She didn't want to pick a fight. She just kept walking.

'Pay no attention.' A young man was walking alongside her, wearing a Red Sox cap. Yankees fans hollered at him and booed, but it was fairly good-natured stuff. Better than an English football stadium, anyway. 'She just hates you 'cause you're a babe.'

Melissa blushed. The kid was probably twenty-six or so, a good few years younger than she was herself. She was not used to being found attractive by random strangers. Particularly not younger men.

She'd bought the cheapest ticket available. The cab fare and tip were almost twenty bucks; the cap was expensive too. She had no credit card, no way to get more. She wasn't like Will, who could probably survive for days with only rats for food or something. She had to conserve her money until she could get somewhere she could find a job.

She'd thought about it and already decided. Waitressing. They often hired illegals if they'd work for less than minimum wage. She would be delighted with an anonymous job working for peanuts. If she did the dishes and swept the floors in some two-bit Italian café somewhere, they would let her feed for free. She could take leftovers home every night. She could probably manage a balanced diet. Whatever let her survive through this crazy situation she'd got herself in. When she thought that only a week ago she'd been in Oxford, preparing for a tutorial, she wanted to laugh.

In the meantime, she'd contact Will and let him know she was safe. That much at least she owed him.

This game was a refuge. A few hours of normal American life, with the sun on her face, a hot dog and a Diet Coke. If she left the stadium with the thousands of other fans, again, she'd be quite safe in the crowd. And after that?

Melissa looked at the kid's Red Sox T-shirt and suddenly had an idea. If Will could do it, why not her? She put on a passable American accent.

'Hey, thanks, man.' She offered him her hand. 'My name's Lisa.'

'Brad,' he said, encouraged. 'You here with someone?'

It was an opening. She took a deep breath and treated him to a dazzling smile. 'Naw. I just split up with my boyfriend.'

'Sorry,' Brad said, meaning he wasn't.

'Don't be.' She remembered a game she'd watched the previous night. 'He was a Mets fan anyway.'

Brad laughed. 'Then the asshole had it coming, I guess.'

Melissa grinned. She had clearly done quite well with the baseball for just a couple of days' study. Both the Red Sox and the Yankees hated the Mets. She and Brad were bonding very nicely.

'What do you do?' Brad asked.

'I was an English teacher, but I quit. I'm taking some time out.' Melissa patted her backpack. 'I'm going to hitch across America, do that hippy thing I always wanted to do.'

Brad beamed. Melissa saw he could hardly believe he was picking her up. She had pleased him, delighted this young American kid. He actually did think she was a babe. He thought she was beautiful. As she registered this, she became aware that quite a few of the men were staring at her as they walked past.

She enjoyed it. She hadn't had that attention since she was in her late teens, not since Will, the first time around. Funny how running for your life could make you so vital. Melissa understood that on some basic level; she relished it. She looked at Brad gratefully. She only wished Will could see her like this . . .

No use thinking that way, her conscious mind told her. But she couldn't help it. It was true. She did want that. She longed to display herself to Will, so that at least he would remember her as beautiful.

'Hell, honey, you can start with me,' Brad said. 'If you ain't got plans after the game.'

She shrugged. 'That's the great thing about it. I'm free. I don't have any plans.'

'If you're hitching, you want to hitch to Boston? I came up with friends. We've got a camper van.'

Oh God. She was saved.

'Won't your friends mind?' she asked innocently.

'Hell no, not when they see how cute you are. Besides, it's my van.'

He had four guys with him, and was proud to show her off. Melissa smiled at them and allowed herself to be flirtatious. They'd had a couple of beers, and laughed and made comments and nudged Brad in a congratulatory fashion. She refused to take off her shades, but it was a sunny day, so they didn't push her. The Red Sox won, which put the boys in a great good humour. They teased her all the way out to the parking lot. They really did have a camper van; Melissa could hardly believe her luck. It was filthy inside, littered with debris from bags of nachos and cans of cherry Coke, but it was one of the most welcoming vehicles she'd ever been in. Brad patted the passenger seat and asked her to ride upfront, which made his friends convulse in raucous laughter.

The journey out of the city was an easy one. Nobody stopped them, nobody bothered them. A few travelling Red Sox fans honked their horns. Some Yankees-loving men shouted obscenities. It was all blissfully normal.

They were big baseball fans, it transpired, the kind who memorised players and their stats. They had a DVD player hooked up in the back and were showing a highlights DVD from the 2004 World Series.

Brad was a good kid, and concentrated on his driving. But he did make conversation. Had she watched the 2004 Series, when they broke the curse? No? There was a total eclipse on the night of Game 4. The moon was coloured Boston red.

'When Doug Mientkiewicz caught the ball from Foulke it was still red . . . you know that?'

Melissa admitted she didn't.

Brad asked about her. She was a nanny and an English teacher, she said, giving private tuition to a rich French businessman from the Upper East Side. She'd outstayed her visa so she wasn't legal, but she'd get a job waitressing, figure something out. Brad asked if she was Australian. Melissa made up a family in Canberra. The Americans really couldn't tell the difference in accent sometimes.

Where would she stay in Boston? A hostel, Melissa thought, somewhere cheap. She had a little money so she'd be OK. Brad recommended the YWCA on Berkeley Street; they would let her share with some other students for ten bucks a bed. No AC, so it was a little sticky, but hey. You couldn't have everything . . .

She agreed. Brad asked her how long she'd been dating. Melissa spent a little time on her fake relation-ship. Dan, her ex-boyfriend, had turned out to be quite the cad. Brad was all sympathy. He was a personal trainer right now but he was planning on going into the army. Maybe she'd like to get a cup of coffee sometime? Maybe she would, Melissa said. He was kind to offer her a lift. No, it was no hardship ferrying around a pretty girl in front of his friends. She'd given him bragging rights.

Melissa laughed. She liked Brad. And she was intensely grateful. It was good to find that the world was full of nice, decent people who would offer to help you. Not everybody was a killer with a gun; there were some good kids from good families who were going to make money, get married and raise more good kids. She relished the boy's optimism. She hoped he had a great life. She was not going to compromise his safety by sticking around longer than she had to.

Finally they reached Boston. The boisterousness had simmered down to quiet satisfaction. Brad drove round some neat suburban neighbourhoods, dropping his friends off. They said goodbye to her, waggling their eyebrows and wishing him luck. Melissa blushed; they made her feel young too. Brad took her into the heart of the city and pointed out the hostel to her. She picked up her backpack from the floor of his van and took his phone number. He climbed out, and stood there, a little awkwardly.

'You don't have a cell number?'

She shook her head. 'Technically I'm illegal. Don't want the cops to be able to track me.'

He looked deflated. 'I won't hear from you again, will I?'

'You might,' she said. 'You're very nice.'

'No guy wants to hear that from a beautiful woman. Nice is the kiss of death.'

'I'm too old for you.'

'Let me be the judge of that,' he said, with swaggering bravado.

She smiled. She hated to disappoint him. She was grateful for the lift, grateful to be out of New York. Grateful that a twenty-six year old found her beautiful.

She put down her backpack and offered herself to him for a kiss. Brad took advantage. Burly arms encircled her slight frame, and he kissed her long and deep, and pressed her against him. She only pulled back when he started to get aroused.

'Bye,' she said. 'Thank you.'

'You're something else, pretty lady,' he said. Then he climbed back into the van and drove off.

Melissa walked into the hostel. She was too old to be here, but she looked like a student and they gave her a room anyway. It was night, and late. Another girl was already sleeping in a bed in the corner. Melissa took a shower and fell into bed, and slept almost instantly, utterly exhausted.

Will sat at an outside table at the Barge, a lobster and seafood restaurant on Front Street, Perth Amboy, thirty miles or so out in New Jersey. He was looking over the water towards Staten Island. It was dark, and the street lamps glinted on the water's surface. The night was a little cold now, but his food was good. He was eating the fried soft-shell crabs for $20.95 and drinking a bottle of Budweiser, and he liked it better than any of the fancy meals he'd eaten with Olivia lately. He was glad to be in New Jersey. It was peaceful here. There was a bed and breakfast down the street, and he would sleep in that.

The alcohol relaxed him after a rough day. His chin was prickling, and he needed a shave, but he wasn't going to get one. A small beard would mean that most of the general public would not recognise him. The professionals were different. He worried about Melissa. She couldn't grow a beard. He kicked himself for not teaching her anything, even the basics, about flight. Presumably she knew not to use credit cards, if she noticed what he did in their time together.

He wanted to find her. And after that . . .

They could not run for ever. He'd have to go back, Olivia had been right about that. Will considered his options, savouring the crab, letting the alcohol free his mind from the cramp of anxiety and promote some solutions.

He would soon have money. Incredible amounts of it. He could track whoever had hired Lola and perhaps buy him off. But no, governments were involved. They were almost impossible to buy off.

He could hire security for Melissa. Find some literal fortress and staff it with an army. Again – not feasible.

She had already said she would not stay. And if she did, one day somebody would succumb to bribery, get sloppy or careless. There could be no long-term defence of her.

She could run, and keep running, until whatever they were hunting her for went away. But Will did not think that would work either. Melissa Elmet had been targeted by professional assassins whose reputations would suffer if she remained alive. Therefore they would keep coming for her. Lola Montoya was inexorable. She never gave up. She was one of a few females whom he knew for a fact had undergone torture and not cracked. She was a sociopath, and arrogant. She would try to kill Melissa even without a price on her head.

Will had never killed a woman in his life. He had never even hit a female. He began to think that would have to change.

There must be an answer, he thought. He drank his beer and looked over the dark water, with the light from the neon lobster sign sparkling on it, red and blue. His food was delicious. There must be an answer. Melissa's life was precious to him. The thought that she was dead had proved it.

He would find her, and take her with him. He would go to where her father was killed, where she lost contact with that asshole. He would find out whatever they did not want Melissa to know, and publicise it as widely as possible.

Yes. That was it.

Remove the incentive to kill her. Of course, there was revenge. But he could do something about that, too. If states were involved, state actors were involved. Publicity would help. If she was slaughtered, somebody would be blamed. He drank some more, pleased. It was coming together now. He registered that this plan was impossibly difficult, but it still had to be done. Because there was no other way out.

For the first time since this whole thing began, Will Hyde turned his analytical mind, his brilliant spy's mind, away from Melissa. And towards her father, the common thread. He should have done this before. He understood that now, quite clearly.

Richard Elmet was a pompous old fool, but undeniably intelligent. Still, even in the academic world, he had made no great mark. He was at Oxford, but had not risen to head a college, or been admitted to All Souls. No American university had offered to poach him, tempting him with a fat cheque and tenure . . . What could he possibly have done to disturb so many people?

He would ask Melissa.

He wandered inside, paid with cash, then took the bike down to the small hostelry half a mile away. They had a room, and since he wasn't drunk and had money, they rented it to him. It was small and clean, with twin beds and a tiny shower. The warm water of the shower was sensationally enjoyable. Moishe hadn't included any fripperies in his box of clothes, so there were no pyjamas. He had some jeans and a black Jack Daniels T-shirt to wear in the morning. Moishe had picked biker clothes. It helped to work with pros.

Will cleaned his teeth and got into bed. It was early, but he wanted to wake at first light. His lawyer did. Melissa would call in. She had no idea how to reach him, but she was a clever girl. He was confident she would find a way. If necessary, she would leave a message on the switchboard of Virginian Prospect. When she tried to make contact, he had to be ready to find her. Because as soon as she called, they would know.

Chapter Twenty-Six

At eight the next morning, Will dialled a number.

'This is Bob Katz.'

'It's Will. Listen and don't talk.'

'OK.'

'Is there a warrant out for my arrest?'

'Not yet.'

'Good. Assume your phones are bugged. If you can, get them swept daily.'

'Shit, Will. OK.'

'I think a friend of mine will be calling the bank.'

'She called here, ten minutes ago.'

Will blinked. 'She called you? She doesn't know who my lawyer is.'

'There's a report on the sale of Prospect in the *Journal* this morning. She was looking through it for articles about you. So she called my office.'

Goddamn, Will thought admiringly. She really was thinking on her feet. Smart, smart girl.

'She's in Boston. She says you can call her on a payphone there. 857–555–7834.'

Will hung up immediately and dialled.

'Hello?' she answered on the first ring.

'Melissa, it's me.'

'Will,' she said, and her voice was a half-sob of elation. 'Will.'

'Sweetheart, you did so well. Listen to me. They'll have had Bob's calls bugged, they'll be on their way to that phone. Run, Melissa!'

'Where?' she asked. She didn't argue. He loved her for that. He thought fast.

'You said you always wanted to see it, Missy. Do you remember?' It was a remark she'd made that day in the Meadows, when he proposed. He did not mean to be cruel, but he had to pick something she would definitely recall. Only she would know. It was between them, and no long-range transmitter in the world could pick up her thoughts.

'I do remember,' she said, after a pause. 'I remember it quite clearly.'

'I'm coming to get you. I'm not in Massachusetts. It will take a little while. I am coming. Remember.'

'I'll be there, Will. I might leave if I have to, but I'll go back.'

'Run!' he commanded. 'Now!'

She hung up. He fastened the helmet about his face, mounted the bike, and started to drive, full throttle, heading for the New Jersey Turnpike.

They were coming. The slightest thing, and they were coming. A call to Will's lawyer. Melissa didn't waste time on pity. She had a pushbike, which she had stolen from inside the hostel in the early hours of the morning. She didn't even feel bad about it. You did what you had to do.

Her emotions churned inside her like butter in a dairy. Fear – she was getting used to that. Joy, at hearing Will's voice. Loss, because he was gone, marrying another. Excitement, because he would be here soon.

But mostly, as she swung her leg over the bike and started to ride, the powerful muscles pushing her off, fast, down the street, faster than she could ever run, Melissa just thought about her destination.

Yeah, she remembered. When they were sitting on the long grass, halfway down to the river, away from the dirt track that led to the college, and she was playing with a daisy and drinking some cheap red wine out of a plastic glass, and it was hot and sunny, and Will was with her, and life seemed utterly perfect, and she remembered, even before he proposed, wanting to take that moment in her head and preserve it for ever, like a film, the youth and happiness of it. He was talking about some concert he'd seen, the college choir doing *Judas Maccabeus*. The time he'd spent at Oxford had exposed Will to culture and grace, refinements she took for granted but which he had not had access to, growing up, dirt poor, in an orphanage. He had a zest for life which blew Melissa away. She had yawned at the classics; Will dived into them. And she went with him, and loved the music again, because she wanted to please him. If he liked Handel, she liked Handel.

'There's a Handel and Haydn society in Boston,' she had said, eager to show off. 'One of the oldest in America. They play at the Symphony Hall. We should go some day.'

He rolled her to him, kissed her lingeringly. 'We will. I'd love to go to America.'

'Me too,' she'd said, her eyes shining.

Now she laughed. Go to America – she'd wanted to for as long as she could remember, even as a kid, before Will. Never thought it would be on a trip quite like this one.

Her heart sped as she rode. Not just from the exercise. Melissa remembered that kiss. She remembered every one of his kisses. She remembered that day.

But so did Will.

He could only have been referring to that comment. And it was a passing remark. She had treasured every second of that day, the day he proposed, in her heart. But Will Hyde had done so as well.

Through all the years, and the army, and his life on the run, and his meteoric rise. After all the models and society women and magazine covers and limousines.

He still remembered.

She tried not to have false hope. What could possibly be more damaging? But it was very difficult. If Will remembered that . . . he must have cared, more than cared. Did he, could he, love her . . . ?

She biked on. No point going to the Symphony Hall yet. He wasn't in Massachusetts. It could be hours, probably would be. She would go elsewhere, out-of-the-way places that they wouldn't look. She was in the centre of town, Park Street. There was an attractive red-brick church with a white spire. Melissa climbed down from her bike, parked it against the railings; she had no lock, it would be gone when she came back. That was no problem. Just conceivably, the police might be looking for a stolen bike. She would walk everywhere, moving from church to diner to store, staying out of the picture, heading slowly towards Massachusetts Avenue. She would be patient. It was a sunny day, and you could eat well cheaply. She was good at nursing cups of coffee, and it would be soothing to kneel down with the believers and pray. She had a lot to pray about.

When Will got there, she would be ready.

It was supposed to be over four hours to the centre of Boston. He made it in under three. Back through Manhattan and slicing through Connecticut, speeding and weaving through the traffic jams. Man, it was perfect to have a bike. It got you places a car could not. It had perfect anonymity and queue-busting freedom.

Will couldn't drive fast enough.

It was a great bike, responsive. He only stopped for gas once. Enough time to eat a sandwich, gulp some water, use the bathroom. Then straight back on the bike, in less than five minutes. He had to force himself to do that, as well, but keeping his strength up and his blood sugar steady was important.

Melissa was waiting, and they were coming for her.

Olivia's anger, the problems at the bank, the New York police; everything fell away, and that was all that was left. He did not waste time analysing it. His thoughts were on other things. Method. Every airport would be being watched. But there was no other way out. And he would not get away with a military flight a second time.

Melissa emerged from the café, where she had managed to make a mint tea last half an hour, and looked again across the street . . .

Her heart stopped. Somebody was there. A man, casually loitering, looking up at the tall pillars of the Symphony Hall as though he were a tourist contemplating whether or not to take a photograph. He wore a black leather jacket. It was Will. She could tell at a distance: his build, the way he carried himself. Everything about him was familiar. He was imprinted in her bones.

She struggled with herself. The impulse to cry out, to run to him, was overwhelming. She fought it. They would be looking.

Melissa walked across the road. Her heart was thumping harder now than when she heard the gunshots, back in her apartment. How pathetic, she thought, how like a girl, to get all worked up over a man you can't even have, when your life is in danger . . .

It didn't matter. Her body was a traitor. Just to see him made her weak-kneed with wanting. She moved deliberately, so he wouldn't see. He might pity her, if he did see. Pride at least kept her strong.

He had stopped off at a biker store, just outside of Boston, and picked her up a basic helmet and leather jacket. He got a long length; it would also help insulate her if they slept outside.

The bike was around the corner. He opened the basket, handed her the helmet and jacket. She put them on without speaking. Will mounted the bike, scooted forward.

'Ridden a motorcycle before?'

'No,' she said. She smiled at him shyly. 'But I want to try.'

Back in Oxford, Melissa had been a quiet, studious girl, afraid of her own shadow. He had put that down to her awful parents. If he coaxed her into stuff, punting on the river, climbing the old church tower at Carfax, then she enjoyed it. But without pushing, she had never let herself go.

All that was changed now. 'Show me how,' she said.

He marvelled at the change in her. Yeah, she really was picking this up. She had dyed her hair. No longer mousy and flat, it was a rich red, shades of auburn and the odd strand of golden blond. And her self-administered cut was sexy as hell; her new curtain of hair, freed from all that flat weight, swung around her sharp cheekbones. Her pallid English skin was golden. All that stuff had been in his apartment, and she'd used it. Her body, he assessed in seconds, had been training, and training hard. She was more slender, and her waist and arms were defined.

He had only left her for a few days. She was a different woman. A far more attractive one.

'Climb up here.' He turned to her, checked the strap under her chin was belted securely. Hell, she looked good. It wasn't just the hair and the tan. Her eyes sparkled. Her skin was glowing. She looked so intensely vital and alive, he longed to take her into his arms and kiss her mouth so hard it bruised.

He knew that feeling very well. It was the paradox of being hunted. You could be terribly sick with fear, under extreme duress, but every step you walked free of a bullet you were glad to be alive; deeply, exultantly glad. The most mundane activities were imbued with a terrible pleasure. Drinking a cup of coffee, even washing your face. Life was precious. You learned to savour each second of it. They were here together now, and it was bad, very bad. But there was a perverse pleasure in the immediacy of life. If he was honest with himself, he liked it better, much better, than sitting in his office analysing some Fortune 500 company for one of his M&A clients.

Melissa looked back at him. He could sense the struggle in her. Her eyes could not hold his. She looked down, and blushed. She wanted him, it was written all across her body.

Thank God they had to run. He didn't know if he could have controlled himself.

'Put your arms round me, hold on tight. Press your body against me.'

She did so. He could feel the smallness of her, the softness, her body so slight against the muscles of his back. He gritted his teeth against her desirability. 'OK, now lean with me, never fight it. Just go with my movements. And hold on to me.'

'I will. Let's go,' she said, her voice muffled by the helmet. 'Tell me where we're going, in case something happens.'

She had a right to ask that. And he had no hesitation in telling her the truth. She'd earned it.

'Logan International Airport.' Will put the bike in gear and pushed off. It was more dangerous now. They would be in Boston, searching for her, hunting in all the wrong places, at the train stations and tram stops, combing through hotel reservations. But they would also be at Logan. And the word would go out to find a man and a woman, working together. Melissa clung tightly to him as they sped out of the city. Will tried to concentrate on the road.

Chapter Twenty-Seven

'Mmmh. Mmmmhhh!'

The man struggled in his bonds. His eyes over the gag were wild. Melissa shrank back from him, terrified at his fear.

'Will . . .'

'Be quiet, damn it,' he hissed at her.

The woman was on her stomach, sobbing. Will's hand went around her mouth and tied the T-shirt expertly in a gag. She had tried some self-defence moves on him when she saw the body of her colleague, tied up and gagged, his knees by his chin, his feet lashed together.

The two of them were both quite strong. They worked in a warehouse for Federal Express. They were uniformed employees, with jumpsuits and badges. The jumpsuits and badges now lay in a heap at Melissa's feet.

Will had picked them off one at a time, crouching behind a forklift, his hand round the mouth of the man first, muffling him perfectly, his other arm immobilising him, dragging him away from the gate of the gigantic warehouse. Nobody had heard a thing. Nobody had looked twice. Melissa, lying flat amidst the long grass, had been terrified to watch, but Will was so quiet he might have been a ghost. The man stood no chance. He was gagged and bound before Will went back for the woman

They were out of sight, in a patch of tall, scrubby grass down the side of a bank, on the field behind the warehouse. She had used karate and tried to hurt Will in the solar plexus. It was instructive to Melissa to see how fast he flipped her to the ground and warned her to silence. It was done in a second, with no apparent effort. The woman, Melissa gathered, had thought she was highly trained and able to fight. Her tear-stained face on the ground had registered complete shock before being flooded with terror.

She was gagged. The man mumbled to her, behind the cloth stuck under his teeth. Will took a length of twine, cut it, and lashed her hands in front of her, then her feet, over her socks. They were not naked; both wore a T-shirt, which was fortunate, underwear, shoes and socks. The woman, in her mid-thirties, had been wearing a thong, but there was no way to spare her modesty any further.

She made a desperate pleading noise. She was crying and snuffling. Melissa came up to Will.

'Please, Will,' she whispered. 'Please . . . do we have to? They're hurting . . .'

'Not really. It's necessary to bind them securely, we need the delay.' He turned around and spoke to them. 'I'm not going to kill or hurt you.'

The man groaned with relief.

'I'm sorry. This is probably going to be a little frightening for you, and unpleasant. I've bound you because I need some time to get away from this warehouse. I'm going to call your supervisor and tell him where you are, but it won't be for about another eight hours. You will be home by midnight. It's a warm day, but if you huddle together when the sun goes down you will feel warmer. There's no danger of exposure tonight, it isn't cold enough. I apologise for the inconvenience, but you'll be able to sell your story to the papers.'

Melissa looked at him gratefully. The woman had stopped being terrified and was now just bewildered, blinking, gulping back tears behind the gag. The man was angry; he tried to shout.

'Our lives are in danger,' Will told him. 'I am sorry.'

Then he beckoned to Melissa, and she followed him out of sight, into a small copse of scrubby trees.

'Put it on.' He threw her the woman's FedEx uniform and began to strip off his own clothes. Melissa tried not to look. Will's body was incredible, hard and muscular, his chest broad, covered in wiry dark hair. He must have worked out every day since he had left the service. Embarrassed, she looked away, hoping he would not catch her staring. It made her terribly self-conscious, to be peeling off her jeans before him in this way. There was no bathroom here, no privacy . . .

Will's eyes slid across to her; Melissa felt his gaze flicker over her, once. Then he turned his back.

'Hurry,' he said.

She tugged the clothes on, did up the buttons. He had looked away from her. How stupid to be disappointed. She had to get a grip; she was mooning over him like a teenager.

'Ready. Where now?'

Will led her away carefully, out of the copse of trees, walking in a natural depression in the grass. The bike was parked some distance from the warehouse.

'The airport. We need to get to Europe.'

Melissa began to understand. 'You're going to use these uniforms to sneak into the airport?'

'We'll use them to get on a plane. A Federal Express cargo plane.' Alarm was written across her face; he made a soothing gesture. 'It's fine, FedEx planes are fully pressurised up to eight thousand feet. We'll be in the hold. It might be a little bumpy but you'll be perfectly safe. I'll be with you.'

'OK.'

'I've done this before,' he said gently. 'And I didn't have a company uniform that time. It will get us across to Europe without the use of passports. We'll be untrackable.'

'But they'll find out.'

'Yes. When we land I'll call the factory so they can go untie those two. As soon as the story hits local news, those guys will know what happened; they'll start looking at every cargo point that FedEx flies out of Logan. But we won't be in the area by then. We'll be long gone.'

'And where are we going?'

'We're going to Rome,' he said.

Melissa flushed; excitement, fear, relief, she wasn't sure. Will was putting the puzzle together. It was the only way out for her. But once she was safe, she would never see him again.

'To my father's old university?'

'Your father owned something, or knew someone or something, that made him very dangerous to a lot of rich people. They think you might know it too. They think you have the secret. The only answer is for you to actually get the secret. Then we may be in a position to bargain.'

They had reached the bike. Melissa took up her black leather jacket and helmet from the ditch where they had left them and strapped them on.

'Are you sure about this, Will?'

'Sure? I can't be sure of anything. But this is the only answer I can see.'

'Then it'll have to do, won't it?' she said, and climbed on the bike behind him, glad of the excuse to put her arms around his chest and cling to him tightly.

They dumped the bike, their jackets and helmets at the back of a freight terminal at the airport. Will rummaged around and pulled out just a couple of things: an envelope, his toothbrush.

Melissa reached for her carefully supplied backpack. Will put his hand on hers.

'Leave it.'

'But we need . . .'

'We'll have to get what we need. If you have money, put it in an inside pocket with your passport.'

'OK,' she said.

He smiled at her, and for a second she thought he was going to pat her head, or stroke her back, touch her reassuringly. But he held back.

'What matters is that we get away. On the road, you learn not to form attachments. Not even to people, and certainly not to things.'

She sighed. 'I can believe that, Will. I don't know how you could stand it. I own nothing now, I have nothing.'

'You've got your life. Anything else is replaceable. Now stop feeling sorry for yourself and follow me.'

He didn't have to do this. She told herself she had to be grateful, never forget what he was risking.

'Coming,' she said.

The plane juddered and shook. She pressed herself back against the wall, frightened. It wasn't like a commercial flight, where you were nicely strapped into your seat, with a pretty stewardess coming to check the fixtures were tight enough. Melissa's feet were wedged against some hard metal runners that lined the surface of the cargo hold. It was a heavy plane, full of pallets. They were almost the last on board. Will had seized his opportunity and attacked the last baggage handler, knocking him out from behind; the man did not see who had hit him. Will had removed his wallet, giving a motive. Melissa, standing in the shadows, her cap round her ears, had run forward up the ramp. They were inside now. Nobody had opened the ramp. The plane was actually moving.

Was he right about pressure? If not, this could be a horrible way to die. Her frozen corpse would be delivered to Paris with a stack of overnighted packages. Were they here? Would they shoot? Maybe they had been seen, maybe the killers had noticed, even if the airport security hadn't . . .

Will reached over and pulled her down; there were a few windows here and there in the lower hold.

'Just in case,' he said. 'But it's OK, really. They're not coming.'

She trembled; it was so loud in here. She could actually feel the wheels rumbling as they sped up beneath her. There was nothing impersonal about it. She was in a big DC-11 aircraft, and it was going to take off.

Will grabbed her by the shoulders, made her face him.

'Melissa. Slow your breathing. It's OK.'

'It's not . . .' Her panic was rising. She tried to stifle it, but she couldn't. 'Will . . .'

'This isn't going to be like one of those movies, is it?' He smiled at her, trying to calm her with a joke. 'Where I have to slap you for getting hysterical?'

She tried to laugh, but it came out as a ragged sob. The plane was going very fast now. They were slipping and bouncing as it raced into gear. She could not be rational.

It felt dangerous, and it was completely out of control. Her stomach was bouncing and lifting with every new bump.

He pulled her close and frowned, looking into her face. Her heart was thudding, thumping, racing with sheer terror. Fear rose up in her. She broke into a sweat, and gasped.

'I can't have you scream,' he said. 'There are people in the cabin, just up that ladder. It has a flight crew like every other plane. And there are side-arms in a locker.'

The cargo plane juddered and lurched. Melissa simply could not help herself. She let out a moan of fright.

'No,' he said firmly, and tilted her face up to his, bringing his mouth down across hers, covering it before she could scream.

Kissing her.

Melissa stiffened for a moment, in shock. He was kissing her. Her fear vanished, as though somebody had thrown iced water over her. She wanted to push back from him. She didn't. His arms were around her, firmly, holding her. The plane beneath her shivered, moved, lifted into the air. She hardly registered it. Will's grip on her was complete.

He held her perfectly still. Her body was crushed against his chest. Her panicky heart rate slowed. He was still kissing her, his lips moving over hers, brushing against her face.

She flushed. A wave of desire pulsed across her entire

body. Her belly tightened, her breasts, her groin, every part of her responded instantly to his kiss. She was open, literally hot. Her skin against him was hot.

No, she thought weakly. *No*. She must not do this. He belonged to Olivia now. She was in love with him – she might as well admit that. She would not allow herself to become Will Hyde's last fling, his one-night stand . . .

She wrenched herself away, breaking the kiss. His arms were still around her. Melissa pushed back. She could not move unless he let her.

'What are you doing?' she demanded.

'Sorry.' He moved, letting her go, opening his arms. 'I didn't want you to go into hysterics. We have to remain undetected for a little while. It would be too easy for them to turn the plane around.'

'I get it.' She sat down on the hard metal cargo tracks, furious. 'You were simply silencing a hysterical female. Very effective.'

He sat down by her side. She shifted away from him a little. She could not risk her body touching his.

He was silent for a few seconds. Melissa felt tears of humiliation spring to her eyes. Angrily, she looked to one side.

'It was no penance to kiss you,' he said. 'I didn't want to stop.'

'Don't tease me,' she said.

'Tease you?' he laughed shortly. 'Tease you. With the way you look, Melissa, with what we're doing? I can hardly . . . hardly take my eyes off you.'

She turned to face him. 'You hate me,' she whispered. 'You've hated me for years.'

'I don't hate you any more. I like you.' He could say that, it was true, it was not a complete betrayal of Olivia. He did like her; God, how he liked her. 'You're not the woman that's been in my head. You've been tough, you've been incredibly brave. You're amazing. You're so alive.'

'And you're in love with Olivia Wharton,' she said. She wanted to be firm. But her voice caught in her throat. Hating her weakness, she turned around, her back to him, and lay down. 'Don't touch me, Will. I won't sleep with you. There's too much history. You are engaged to this woman. If I can't be your wife, I won't be anything.'

'Melissa . . .'

'There's a long time till we get to Paris. I'm going to try to sleep.' She shut her eyes, ignoring the tears that rolled out of them. Perhaps he couldn't see. She waited a few seconds, but he didn't say anything. The plane bumped a little, with the turbulence. She didn't care any more. Her entire body pulsed with longing and emotion, like a violin string trembling under the bow. Darkness would give her a little privacy, help her recover her composure, stop her from turning to him and begging him to kiss her again. She was determined. She lay very still, and distracted herself, figuring out routes away from Paris. In a little while her desire subsided, and she sank into a fitful sleep.

Chapter Twenty-Eight

'Wake up. Are you awake?'

She sat up immediately, bolt upright, and got to her feet.

'Whoa. Don't hit me,' Will said, grinning.

Right. She blinked. The plane. It was dropping, she could feel it dropping.

'We're coming in to land. Obviously we don't want to be in here when the freight handlers open the hatch. So we're going to lower ourselves through the floor of the plane. There's an engineering door there, by the wheels.'

'Sounds dangerous.'

'Very dangerous. As the air hostesses like to say, you need to wait until the plane has come to a complete halt. Even a slight forward motion of the wheels could catch you and kill you, no problem.'

Melissa nodded. She was deeply relieved that Will was talking practicalities.

'You go down first, then, and catch me?'

He came closer to her.

'Sure. If you trust me.'

'I don't have a lot of choice,' she said, looking out of the window.

Will's finger was under her chin. She caught her breath. He turned her head back towards him, made her look at him. Her knees weakened.

'Missy, we have to talk.'

There was no mistaking the intent in his eyes.

'For God's sake,' she stammered. The plane shook, the landing gear dropped. They stumbled; Will held her by the upper arms. 'We're running from this airport, hopefully without getting shot by armed French soldiers. We don't have time for this.'

'Tonight,' he said. 'And just follow me when you get to the ground. I know where I'm going.'

'OK,' Melissa managed.

The plane had landed. It was taxiing forward, losing speed nicely. She tried to concentrate. It was very serious, everything was serious, they were in France, they were criminals, they had robbed and assaulted . . .

But there was nothing for her, nothing in her world, but the gaze from his eyes, the longing that was rising again in her heart, inexorable as the tide.

She was deeply, wholly in love with Will Hyde. In love again . . . maybe. Maybe she had never stopped. And whatever pain was going to come, whatever heartache when he married someone else, she simply could not lie to herself for one more second. He would know it. He could read her. So be it. She was past caring now, past humiliation, past trying to be strong.

The plane ground slowly to a halt. Will, crouching on the floor in front of her, waited one second. Then, without the slightest hesitation, he opened the security hatch with its internal handle, put his hands on the sides, and dropped through the hole. Melissa rushed forward. He was on the ground, waiting for her. She did not hesitate either. She jumped.

He caught her easily, like her weight was nothing, and set her on the ground.

'We're walking this way. Keep talking to me, like we're two employees having a conversation. If you think somebody's watching, start arguing with me. Get pissed off.'

'That should be easy.'

He started walking. Melissa went with him, baseball cap tucked down on her head. She began to chatter about European hubs and scheduled delivery flight times. Out of her peripheral vision, she could see they were walking through a large fleet of parked FedEx jets. They got closer to the edge of the tarmac, and passed men and women in similar uniforms to their own, in suits, airline uniforms, baggage handling gear. Melissa didn't make eye contact. She was with Will, and she just kept talking. Every moment she expected a hand on her shoulder, a shout, a warning gunshot. But it didn't come, and in under a minute, Will was walking her calmly out of a car park and on to a main road.

'Keep going.'

'OK.' She was elated. 'Where are we going?'

'Out of the airport. Little town called Roissy-en-France. Mostly airport hotels, but it's got a few shops and bistros of its own. About a couple miles' walk. One moment.'

There was a payphone by the side of the street. Will punched in a few numbers; a code of some sort, a corporate thing perhaps. She heard him calmly giving a report about the two Federal Express workers. He repeated himself slowly, several times. When he was sure the office at the end of the line had understood him, he hung up and kept walking.

Will led her across busy roads and past several major airport hotels. There was a bank on a corner; he went inside, queued up and emerged with a sheaf of euros. Melissa just hung back. Never once did he look lost. He was so purposeful. When he walked out of the bank, he just gestured for her to come, a slight motion of the head. She saw he was walking into a large French supermarket, a Carrefour Express. He moved quickly, not consulting her, buying basics cheaply. He selected clothes from a rack for both of them. Without asking her, she saw he had her size exactly right. He could tell, just by looking. He paid, chatted to the checkout girl in fluent French. Melissa blushed, and just hung out with him. She did not trust herself to speak.

'Now what?'

He gave her a bag. 'Round the corner. You walk a little

way more, into the old village. I know this bed and breakfast. They take cash, no questions asked.'

Roissy was neat and compact for an airport town; Melissa noted the colourful houses and painted shutters. Will's place was tucked away down a side street by a modern-looking church. He walked in, yawning, negotiated with a surly guy at reception, and passed over a couple of banknotes. The man gave him a key without even looking at them. Will led her up a narrow staircase covered in dingy flower-patterned carpet. The door at the top was chipped and stained, but when he opened it, the double room was reasonably sized and clean. There was a small shower room with a loo and a window.

'Please tell me I have time to change,' Melissa said. She was wearing somebody else's uniform, had been sleeping in it, and it stank.

'Sure. Clean yourself up. Here.' He opened the bags and passed her a toothbrush, paste, a disposable razor, a travel-sized deodorant, a comb and some conditioning shampoo.

'Heaven,' she said, clutching them to her. Amazing how the simplest things became the most precious luxuries. 'You remembered everything.'

'You have to look normal doing this. You let yourself go, and people remember you. Clean and neat is unre- markable. That's good.' He handed her a change of clothes: cheap jeans, a T-shirt and a little sweater. 'They give you towels in there, but they're the size of a handkerchief.'

She nodded and fled into the little bathroom, peeling

off her clothes. The sun streamed through the small, cracked window, set high into the wall. It was open, to let out the steam; extractor fans hadn't got here yet. Melissa didn't care. The plumbing worked, there was hot water. She would have preferred a bath, but it was blissful, simply blissful, to wash herself, to feel her face and hair getting clean, the glorious hot water sluicing away the dirt and stress. She showered efficiently, washing her hair and combing it through, then brushed her teeth and carefully scrubbed her underwear and socks in the sink with the little sliver of cheap soap provided. They could dry while she wore the new stuff Will had got her. He had not exaggerated about the towels, which were tiny and scratchy, but Melissa worked with what she had. She was dry in seconds and tugged on the new clothes. They felt so good, clean and fresh, more enjoyable than any smart dress she'd ever treated herself to. And she looked good in them. Dirt-cheap sweatshop outfit, but made for French women; she was slim enough and strong enough that the little clothes clung tightly to her body, chic and presentable.

When she got out, Will was sitting on the bed, speaking into the phone in rapid-fire French. He'd bought a local paper and it was open on the coverlet. Melissa bent down; he had ringed a few private ads for cars.

'*Oui, nous y serons, à tout à l'heure,*' he said, hanging up. 'Be right back,' and he went to shower.

Melissa packed up carefully. They were leaving for

Paris. They weren't going to talk. He regretted that kiss, that mind-blowing, brilliant kiss. Whatever had happened, it was over now. She tried to think things through, but the torrent of emotion had drained her. She waited, running her fingers through her hair, air-drying it; the local paper was leading on a small-town mayor arrested for corruption, and the closure of a local hospital. She read it, trying to practise her French, but the words slipped past her. She could not concentrate. She was in suspended animation.

The bathroom door unbolted. Melissa jumped out of her skin. He was carrying his dirty clothes in his hand, neatly folded, and wore a cheap blue shirt and polyester trousers. Nothing could disguise his body, his dark hair, the muscled arms and chest. The dark hair on his chin had been trimmed, but not eliminated; in another day it would be a proper beard.

He looked strange with a beard. Just as handsome.

He glanced at her. 'Who did you think was coming out of there?'

'You startled me,' Melissa said weakly. She picked up the paper. 'Let's go.'

Will moved over to her. He put his hands on her shoulders.

'We're going into Paris on the bus. I'm buying a car. We'll stop at O'Meara's on the Seine; they sell camping gear. We'll get out of here and head south towards Switzerland.'

'OK.'

'And as soon as we're in the car, we need to talk. But let's get out of here first.'

Will could move fast. He was tired – she could see that; Melissa had no idea how long he'd slept on that plane – but he kept going. The car was a Renault Espace, old and battered but in working order; the guy haggled with Will, then let them have it for a couple of hundred euros. They got petrol and bottled water, and Melissa sat behind the wheel while Will went into the camping shop. He came back with a solid amount of gear, and dumped it into the boot. They drove back to Roissy in mutual silence. Will collected the shopping bags from the room, and dropped the key at the front desk. It was unmanned. Better and better.

She watched him climb into the car, navigate out of the village and swing south. They were soon on a motorway, massive, grey, perfectly anonymous, the cars moving at a hellish speed.

'What will we do when we get to the border?' Melissa asked timidly.

'They never check passports when you drive. Incredibly rare. If it happens,' a shrug, 'we'll figure it out.'

'OK.'

'Melissa.'

She caught her breath at his tone. Oh God. She could not bear it. Could not.

'Look, you don't have to say anything, Will. I understand. We're under pressure, it was a mistake, this will be over soon and you have your fiancée to go back to. Let's not talk about it. I was out of line.'

'Melissa. I'm going to call Olivia the next town we stop at.'

'Do you have to tell her?' Melissa asked. The humiliation burned in her. All she had left was that only Will knew how weak she had been. 'Calling her is dangerous, isn't it? You could be traced.'

'I have to take that risk. She has a right to know, immediately. I'm calling off the engagement. She's going to be heartbroken.' He sighed. 'I feel like a bastard. She's done nothing wrong. But I don't love her, and I can't live that life. I cannot marry her, and so it must be done as soon as possible.' He shook his head. 'If they're listening, and they know I've left her, she'll probably be safer. That connection to me is dangerous.'

Melissa put her head back against the headrest. She opened her mouth, but nothing came out.

'You hurt me,' he said, his eyes on the road, his voice low and sure. 'You broke me. You shattered everything I thought was good in the world. You were the sun, the moon and the stars to me, the only family I ever had, and you betrayed me.'

Tears rolled down her cheeks. He would not even look at her.

'I had to.'

'You did not have to. You didn't even try to talk your mother round. You didn't even test whether she was telling the truth.' His fingers clenched on the wheel. 'You left me, you betrayed me. You didn't fight for me, Missy. Not once.'

'And you punished me, didn't you?' Melissa demanded, rage surging in her. 'You punished me well. I was young! So I was weak. Maybe I should have stood up to them. But you never gave me a chance to put it right. I called, you never answered, you ignored my letters, you just *left*, damn you. You were so self-righteous, Will! You made damn sure I couldn't find you. I called your college, I asked your friends, I humiliated myself looking all round town. But you'd left. You'd gone. You never came back, never called, you never showed me mercy even once, Will, you unforgiving stubborn bastard! God, I hate you! Do you know how many years I cried myself to sleep, how it felt like my life was over! You might as well have slammed me into prison, because you've been off fighting to save the damn world and making millions and I've been suffocating myself, suffocating every last flicker of hope, for years! I loved you – I loved you so much! And you buried me alive!'

Will's knuckles went white. He glanced across at her, and his eyes on her burned. Melissa could not hold his gaze.

'*Loved* me?' he said. 'You still love me, Melissa. You love me. You want me. Every time I touch you I can feel it.'

'So what if I do?' she said. 'I won't die of a broken heart, whatever you may think. Even if you do hate me, I'll survive this.'

He put his foot on the accelerator, and laughed, startling her, a deep laugh of pure joy. 'I don't hate you, foolish girl. I love you. I thought I was over you. Guess not.'

Melissa looked at him disbelievingly. The motorway rushed past her. 'You mean that?'

'Why did I come to get you, really? I told myself it was my duty. But the truth was, I couldn't bear to think of you hurt or dead. When I saw you . . . you were different, Melissa. You looked beaten down by life. Disappointed. The beauty had all gone.'

'I thought so,' she said, but she really didn't care any more. He loved her. Nothing mattered but that.

'When I saw you I was almost relieved. Maybe this thing in my head was my own creation. Maybe I'd been in love with an idea, not you. Maybe I could move on, settle down, enjoy marrying Olivia instead of just assuming it was time.'

'Oh, Will . . .'

'Then we started running. I wanted to kiss you on the train, the first day. In Rotterdam, it was difficult. I couldn't tell if you resented me, or hated me. But I wanted you.'

He spun the wheel a little, turned to look at her, and grinned.

'And then after a while, I could see that you wanted me, Melissa, and you couldn't help yourself.'

'You arrogant bastard,' she said, smiling.

'You know it's true. I've been with too many women.

347

It only made me want to take you more. By that time, I was fighting myself.' He pushed the accelerator, weaving between lanes. 'Have you been very passionate, with men?'

She blushed. 'That's a personal question.'

'It's me,' he said. 'And I'll ask you all the personal questions I like.'

'There's only been Fraser,' she admitted. 'He thought I was cold.'

Will laughed again. 'Cold? You? You are the most helplessly hot girl I have ever had in my arms.'

Melissa blushed again. Hearing him talk like that sent a wave of lust rocking through her. 'I was a lot younger then,' she protested.

'Makes no difference. If anything, you're going to be even hotter. You've been waiting longer.'

'I should . . .'

'You should do what, exactly? You know how we're going to sleep?'

She shook her head.

'In a tent. By the side of the road, under trees, where I can find them. Near rivers and streams. They won't be expecting that. They'll be hunting through hotel registrations and calling their contacts in national police services to look out in the little villas and bed and breakfasts. And the foliage means you can't be seen with satellites or helicopters.'

'OK.'

'So you'll be in a tent with me, honey. Just us. Nobody

around for miles. And every night I'm going to exact something from you. I'm going to make you pay for every evening I had to spend without you.' Will took one hand off the wheel, and casually placed it on her lap, pressing his palm against the slight cradle of her belly, feeling the heat and the longing.

Melissa half sobbed with desire. 'Can't we stop?'

He removed his hand. 'I want to get out of France. They'll be hunting us by now, they'll be looking where FedEx flies from Logan. Let's get somewhere safer. I must call Olivia, too. She's a victim here.'

'Yes,' Melissa said. 'She thought she was going to be your wife. Poor girl,' she said, with feeling.

'She could only have been my wife in one sense. In another, you still are.'

'What?'

'You got a civil annulment. You didn't get one from the vicar, or did you?'

He had noticed that, she thought, he actually noticed.

'No, I didn't.'

'Then we'll get the civil ceremonies done, Melissa, but you're my wife still.'

She longed to kiss him, hold him, but she had to wait. They were driving, barrelling down the autoroute at an almost terminal speed. Powerful people out there wanted her dead. But Melissa did not care. She had been reborn. She was almost dizzy with love and joy. And frightening, insistent pure animal lust.

Chapter Twenty-Nine

Olivia Wharton sat in the front room of Will's townhouse and attempted to exude poise and composure. She crossed her long legs, snugly clad in Wolford hose, and stared coolly at the policeman. She was carefully dressed in a tailored olive-green Prada suit, with her dark hair elegantly blow-dried and her make-up carefully applied, a gorgeous palette of berry and plum. A quilted Chanel bag rested on the floor, and she wore red-soled Louboutin pumps. Her enormous diamond ring sparkled in the soft light from the porcelain lamps.

She had dressed up to the max. On her ears, to match the suit, were some terrific jade-and-emerald flower earrings, and there was a gleaming string of South Sea pearls the size of marbles, with exceptional lustre, glowing at her throat. Her entire outfit cost several times more than the combined salaries of the three men sitting opposite her.

'So you haven't heard from him?'

'I've told you already, Officer,' she snapped. 'I don't keep tabs on my fiancé. His work takes him all over the world.'

'Tell us again, ma'am,' the senior detective said.

Fucking Cops! They thought they could flash a warrant card and she had to jump through hoops. God*damn* Will and his stupid ugly British chick. She was *so* going to put her foot down when he got back. Next time he could hire somebody to look after her. Hollywood stars had bodyguards. She could too.

'No,' she lied. 'I haven't heard from him. Do I need a lawyer?'

They looked at each other.

'Don't know, ma'am. Do you?'

'I haven't done anything wrong.'

'OK. But so long as you know that aiding and abetting a fugitive is wrong.'

'A fugitive,' Olivia said slowly. This was supposed to be her moment of glory, her week in the sun. She had landed the most eligible bachelor on the entire New York social circuit. And now they were talking about Will like he was some common criminal? 'Is Mr Hyde a fugitive? Has he committed a crime?'

'The SEC have stated they are investigating financial irregularities in the Virginian Prospect Bank.'

'I know that.' Her phone had hardly stopped ringing. On the flat-screen TV behind them, the muted Bloomberg anchor was mouthing something else about Virginian's disastrous rights issue. Yet another picture of Will, in a headshot, came up on the screen. Olivia turned her gaze away. This was a nightmare, it was all a horrible nightmare . . .

She did not understand what the hell was going on. Will had gone and left her in chaos. The lawyer had come round, Jack Sansone had come round. They were all frantic. The shares had been issued for sale, and then the Mexican government had demanded repayment at once for an investment in a natural gas plant. The price had plummeted. Three other foreign institutions had cut off lines of credit. The rumours went out that Virginian Prospect was not solvent. The SEC issued warnings. Lines of depositors started to form at branches of Virginian Prospect up and down the country. In one branch in Pasadena, they had closed when the pressure of bodies grew too much, and then there was a riot. She'd seen it on CNN, with the cops getting involved and everything.

The bank was failing. There was a commercial run on it, other banks were pulling their loans. Meanwhile, there were unexplained payments from the bank to one of Will's private accounts in the Cayman Islands. Somehow they'd found that. And it was being tied in to the incident at his building on the Upper West Side. Nobody knew where he'd gone or why he'd gone. They were comparing him to Marc Rich, calling him a fugitive billionaire.

Olivia was no finance expert. But she knew her man was all over the TV, the bank was falling apart, and the police had their squad cars parked in front of her house. Already the maid had been in to complain that her wages hadn't come through that Friday, because Señor Hyde's account was frozen. Could she, Olivia, pay them?

Olivia wanted to fire her, but that would have caused another scene. She felt desperately sorry for herself. Why should she have to have another scene? Even Jack Sansone had been *nasty* to her. Like this was anything to do with *her*.

'We believe that Mr Hyde may have attacked a couple of employees of Federal Express out in Boston.'

Olivia blinked. 'What?'

The cops exchanged more meaningful glances. This time in her favour; Olivia had clearly been shocked.

'They were tied up, assaulted, and robbed.'

She laughed hysterically. 'You have to be kidding me, Officer. My fiancé's worth about three billion dollars. What the hell would he rob a FedEx guy for?'

'I'm not sure if he's worth three billion any more, Ms Wharton,' said Detective Gaines heavily. 'Not sure if he's worth anything at all. Guess you'll have to wait till the dust settles, but yeah, I do get your point. I doubt he'd do it because he needs the money. Maybe for kicks. Is he having a mid-life crisis, ma'am? Any signs of that at all?'

She thought of Melissa Elmet and hated her with all her heart.

'No. None.' Olivia stiffened her back and asserted herself. 'Detectives, I appreciate you've got a job to do and I've certainly tried to be co-operative, but I feel Will's good name is not best served by my continuing with this conversation. I've told you everything I know.' There. He'd be proud of her. 'I'm going to have to ask you to leave, and since Will's not here, only to return if you have a warrant. In the meantime, I can put you in touch with his lawyer, Mr Katz, if you have any further questions.'

She stood up, and they got the message.

'OK, lady,' Detective Bell replied. She was an older woman and looked at Olivia with a particularly intense loathing. Probably lived in a tiny little tract house in Queens, Olivia thought contemptuously. 'We're going. We may well be back with a warrant, though. Depends on what comes through from Massachusetts. Meantime, we would ask you not to leave the state, please. You may be an important witness to an ongoing inquiry.'

'Sure,' Olivia replied, with a toss of her head. She signalled to the maid. 'Raquel will see you out.'

The maid moved forward – she had been paid, after all – and ushered the detectives from Olivia's presence. Olivia flopped back on to the antique Chesterfield sofa, exhausted. The door closed.

'Raquel. Don't let anyone else in unless they have a search warrant or they're Mr Katz. I am not available otherwise.'

'Yes, ma'am.'

'And shut these doors and tell the staff not to bother me,' she added.

'Yes, ma'am.'

Raquel quietly closed the large oak doors and Olivia rolled her head back against the cushions. She wanted some peace and quiet, and to decide what on earth she was going—

The phone rang. Olivia jumped. That was their private phone, the one only he had the number to. Not the house phone. Flustered, she grabbed at the receiver and almost dropped the handset.

'Yes?'

'It's Will.'

'Oh, thank God,' she said. 'Will – are you all right? Are you safe?'

She wanted to shout, rage, scream at him. What the hell was he *doing*? But it had to be serious. Olivia wasn't sure if she loved Will Hyde, not right this minute. But she did still care about him.

The doctor in her remembered that gunshot wound. 'Tell me you're safe!' she demanded.

'I'm fine,' he said.

Well if you're fine, why aren't you here? That goddamn English girl again! Her anger returned.

'So no wounds, Will?'

'Physically unharmed, Livvy. Look. I must tell you something.'

She ignored his tone. 'If you'd called just five minutes ago . . . the cops were in the house.'

'What did they want?'

'To know where you were. If I'd heard from you. They said you might be a fugitive. They said you robbed some FedEx guys.'

He sighed. 'OK.'

Olivia rolled her eyes. 'Tell me you didn't actually rob some delivery men, Will!'

He was silent. That enraged her. 'You need to talk to me,' she hissed. 'Don't you get it? You have to get back here. The bank is breaking up.'

'Breaking up?' He sounded shocked.

'Yes! Breaking up! As in a run on the bank, the shares crashing! I have MSNBC on, Bloomberg on. They say Mexico called in a loan, all the other banks are calling in loans. Your shares – they've been suspended *twice*. The people are queuing at the banks for their money. Will,' she said hysterically, 'the cops said you might not be a billionaire any more! You might have lost it all!'

He sounded detached. 'I see. Thanks for telling me.'

'Don't say thanks for telling me, get *back* here and *deal* with it! You're losing everything! *We're* losing everything! All your money is in those shares! Jack Sansone is going absolutely crazy, he was rude to me just now . . .'

'Tell Jack Sansone to get lost. Listen, Olivia, I'm not coming back.'

'Of course you are!' she almost shrieked. 'You don't have a choice! You have to save the business, save what you can!'

'I guess they froze my accounts?'

'They said you took an unlawful payment to your account in the Caymans. They've frozen all your accounts and the cops said they're working on a warrant for your arrest.'

'I don't have an account in the Caymans.' He sighed. 'Olivia, this is not easy for me to say.'

'But it's your *money*,' she insisted, hardly hearing him.

'Forget the money. It isn't important. I cannot save the bank. Some people have taken a decision to wreck the bank; it doesn't take much these days. National governments are involved. Fake money trails are being set up, like this Cayman thing. By the time I untangle it, the bank will already have failed.' He was furious. 'Sons of bitches, there are a lot of ordinary families out there who are going to lose their homes.'

'And that's real sad, but what about us?' Olivia asked plaintively.

'Olivia, I'm sorry. I wanted to say this to you first, but you surprised me. I shouldn't have allowed myself to get distracted.'

Her stomach flipped, horribly, inside her chest. She had heard that tone before. It was not good.

'I can't marry you,' Will said.

Oh God. Oh God. He'd actually said it. Her eyes darted to the ring on her finger, the colossal rock, worth more than her own entire bank balance.

'You can marry me,' she said. 'I'll stand by you . . .'

Maybe, maybe not; she hadn't signed up to be wed to some irresponsible jerk who crashed his own bank, but Olivia had seen the way that Will performed, and something told her not to give up on him, not yet . . .

She knew the law. If she married him, the ring was hers. No matter when the divorce came. Better to keep her options open.

'It's not that. You're a good woman, Olivia. I am truly

sorry for how I must be hurting you. I didn't mean to do it. But I realise I still love Melissa Elmet.'

Anger, a righteous, boiling anger, started to seethe in Olivia Wharton. He had run off. He had sworn to her Melissa Elmet was just a friend. She had shown off her rock on TV, she had told all her friends, put it in the papers . . .

Wasn't it bad enough that he was humbling her by destroying his fortune, *their* fortune? Now he was even taking from her the one scrap of dignity she had left, of the suffering society beauty nobly standing by her man . . .

Now she was just one in a long line of fools that Will Hyde had duped.

And he'd dumped her for an older, fatter, poorer girl, a goddamn schoolteacher or something! Melissa Elmet was nothing. She'd dropped Will like a stone when he was a poor British kid, and now he was – well, famous at least, and Olivia would bet there was still some cash squirrelled away somewhere . . . now he was *the* Will Hyde, she, Olivia Wharton, his faithful girlfriend, was being shoved out the way for some old flame.

'You're not yourself.' Olivia fought to control her anger. Don't let the mask slip. 'You've had a mental breakdown . . .'

'Don't make this any harder, Livvy.'

'Damn you! You don't have the right to tell me what to do!'

'I'm sorry,' he said. 'I really am. Keep the ring. I did

not understand how I've felt all these years. You did nothing wrong.'

'Damn straight I didn't,' she hissed. 'You announced our engagement. You're going to make me look like a fool!'

'It's better now than later. Look. It seems I'm losing all my money and the cops are calling me a criminal. Say I called and you dumped me.'

'That's a great idea,' she hissed. 'You fucker. If the police call again I'm going to give them everything they want.'

'I'm sorry, Olivia. You'll marry somebody better for you than me. I have to go now.'

'Where *are* you?' she demanded, torn with curiosity, despite herself.

'We're safe,' he said, and hung up.

She stood there, holding the phone, almost choking with rage. *We're* safe. He dared to dump her in a phone call, and then refer to 'we'?

Olivia moved into the bedroom she had shared with Will and grabbed a Louis Vuitton case. She would take every one of the jewels he had given her, the furs and the haute couture dresses. She had gowns in that closet that had cost over twenty thousand dollars apiece. The Manolos and Louboutins would come with her, the rest of the shit his damn valet could send to her house. She packed in a frenzy, stuffing in as many clothes as she could carry. Not one thing over five thousand bucks would she leave in this guy's house. Even the little Prada backpack was coming with her. She would pack, then summon his fucking chauffeur and drive back to her own, far more modest place, her little one-bedroom in a good part of the Village. And then, damn it, she would figure out her revenge.

Fuck him anyway, she thought bitterly, as a strand of emeralds slipped into the suitcase, followed by a Dooney & Bourke briefcase. He had gone nuts. He had lost all his money. She didn't *want* to be married to a loser.

Chapter Thirty

Lola sat in the bar and sipped her orange juice. She would be on a plane out of America very soon, travelling on one of her multiple passports, her features disguised with a latex mask and some contact lenses. Nobody would recognise her. They never did. She had false fingertip patches with different fingerprints recorded on them; no matter how sophisticated the technology grew, she was ahead of it.

She preferred getting back into Europe. She hunted better there, where it was more familiar. The man, Hyde, was getting sloppy. He had left without securing his house. She had entered it days ago and placed bugs in every telephone receiver.

How emotional, that he had felt the need to call the woman he was repudiating. She did not understand men. The woman was a gold-digger, a type of female Lola particularly disliked. She herself had earned great wealth through her talents. This whore, like so many, earned it from dressing well and splitting her legs. It annoyed her that even an operative like William Hyde, one so good at the game, so impressive, could ever have been hoodwinked by such a bland, overpriced hooker as Olivia Wharton.

A man like William Hyde deserved a firebrand of a woman, an equal. Someone like Lola Montoya. His affection might even be worth having, she thought briefly. Men had lusted after Lola, but none had ever loved her. Nobody had, in fact, not family, not since her birth. So maybe the shrinks had her wrong. If she'd been given love, she might have been able to return it . . .

She shook her head, clearing out the cobwebs. No place for sentiment on the chase.

Not only had Hyde called Olivia – as though he owed her something – he had stayed on the phone. Long; too long. Long enough for her to trace him.

He must be very distracted.

She ran over the operation in her mind. Like music, like a symphony, it was all coming together. She sensed, a killer's sense, that they were moving towards the end game. His money and prestige had been removed from him. Listening, it was clear to Lola that Will did not really care. That fitted his psychological profile. He was a spy, essentially, and not a banker. How dull the last few years must have been for him. He would feel free now, she was sure.

But while they were destroying his money, he had got the girl and they had stowed in a cargo jet and gone to Paris. And the phone call said they were now in the vicinity of Rue de Bavoir, Voiron, southern France. She was full of admiration. He didn't wait, or mess around. He was in motion, with transport, and the girl, and he was moving south, purposefully south. She could tell Dimitri what she knew, but chose not to. They had bought two heads from her, nothing more. The kill must be hers. She would not permit another agent to do that work.

Let Dimitri's new web of goons look around France. They would be studying CCTV cameras, hotels, borders, everything. She already had the scent, although the prey was not stupid. Lola was hunting.

She thought some more about Will Hyde. He had been a constant surprise. He had amazed her. She could not recall the last time that had happened. He was strong and inventive, unattached to money, absolutely fearless. Exceptionally handsome.

He aroused her. Few enough men did anything for her at all, but this one, this one was different. She remembered the phone call. She was glad he had dumped the vapid little social climber. Her target, Melissa, was at least somewhat worthier; not a professional, but brave, and with a certain natural cunning. She had stayed alive long enough to meet her rescuer. She had jumped off the roof. That was something, indeed.

Thinking about Will fucking Melissa made Lola want him more. If he admired courage and skill in his females, he would certainly desire Lola. Imagine the curiosity of it. Most men did, fucking the killer. She was greedy for sensation. Hard to obtain when you saw most men as sheep. But Will Hyde was nobody's sheep. In bed, close up, he would be able to control her. She knew perfectly well what their relative strengths were.

He was her match.

She toyed idly with a fantasy. Killing the woman, her original target. Offering Hyde protection. She could provide them with a perfect corpse. And disappear, with him, to South America. He would not go willingly with Melissa's assassin, so she would make it seem like somebody else had slain the girl. What would life be like with him?

Annoyed, she shook herself. Perhaps there would be an opportunity to fuck him. If so, she would take it. She was the match for Olivia, Melissa, any of these insipid women. In his bed she would make him scream with pleasure.

But afterwards . . . there were no relationships, not in her business. She would soon tire of him. And the possibility of revenge would always be there.

She stood up. He was her match. Desire, like all her bodily needs, she felt strongly, on the rare occasions that it came. She was slippery, wet. She thought of Melissa Elmet lying in his arms in some flophouse, some French motel. He would make her leap well, she was sure of that.

The thought was annoying. She was jealous. She wanted to punish Melissa, but Melissa was in France and would have to wait.

Instead she would punish Olivia, and that would be a

lesson to Will Hyde, too. Nobody defied Lola Montoya.

She walked back to the little grey building on West Fourth Street. Olivia Wharton had flounced in here just a short while ago. It would be an easy break-in; a tree-lined street, low windows close to the ground, a fire escape in the back, nice and solid, made of wrought iron. But she chose to amuse herself. Lola walked up the stone steps and rang one of the bells.

'Olivia Wharton?'

'Yes?'

The girl had not been crying. Good. She'd be more likely to come out.

'Ma'am, this is Ellen Post. I'm a pool reporter for the *New York Times*. Ma'am, there's a rumour going around that Will Hyde has broken off your engagement today, dumped you.'

A sharp intake of breath. 'Not true at all, I have no comment.'

'OK then, well if you have no comment, that's the story our society section will be running, because we have confirmed it with staff at the Hyde residence. But my editor wanted me to give you the chance to rebut.'

'Is there a photographer with you?'

'No, ma'am. I could call one.'

'Not yet. Hold on.' There was a buzz, and the door swung open. Man, Lola thought contemptuously. Moronic female. And she had dared to aspire to Will Hyde!

She was standing in the corridor, wearing a pretty

little dress of white jersey wool, her tanned feet in open-toed cream leather pumps by Dior. Lola noticed she was still wearing the ring, but had switched it to her right hand. What a statement. And how convenient.

'Come in, so I can make a statement,' she ordered.

'Sure,' Lola said pleasantly. 'That'd be great.'

She held open the door and let Lola enter. Lola shut it behind her.

'I broke it off with Will Hyde,' Olivia said imperiously. 'Get out your pad! I want this in print.'

Lola smiled sweetly. 'No you didn't. You're a money-grabbing whore, and he dumped you.'

Olivia gasped. 'What?'

Lola sighed, bored already. She took her scarf from her own neck in a lightning-quick move and looped it around Olivia Wharton's throat, her strong muscles pulling tightly, cutting off the air supply. Olivia's eyes were terrified; her fingers scrabbled futilely at her neck, trying to free herself, like they always did; her legs started to thrash about . . .

Lola could have played with her, but there was no time. She needed to get to the airport. A knife would have been faster, but this way there was no blood. She tightened the noose and moved forward, one hand on Olivia's temple, the other under her chin, and snapped her neck to the side. It broke. Her head lolled forward, and she died.

Lola had brought a couple of things with her. Samples of blood and hair. She splashed the phial around the apartment and placed some hairs under Olivia's fingernails. It was a pity there was no semen, but Will had never donated any; there were no samples in his doctor's office. The operation took her just a couple of seconds. She had done it so many times before.

'Thanks for your co-operation,' Lola said merrily. She reached out and slipped the ring off Olivia's right hand. It was a beautiful stone, a good price for the job in itself. Plus, it reminded her of Will.

She opened the door and let herself out, walking calmly down the steps. It would probably be forty-eight hours, at least, before they found Olivia's body. By that time she would no longer be in the United States.

The sun on her back was pleasant. Lola walked to the end of the street and hailed a cab. They had no cameras, unlike the subway or buses, and it was the best choice for her right now. She slipped into the back, settling against the ripped black leather seats, and told the driver to take her to JFK. On her right hand, Will Hyde's huge diamond ring glittered in the afternoon light.

The planes arrived at the airport at Fadiz one by one, unnoticed. It was the perfect place to hold a summit of this kind. Off-radar, too small for the world's media to notice. Even the Arab papers did not pay too much attention. It was another tiny, oil-rich sultanate, with no desire to move and play in even regional affairs. It was a holiday destination for many of them, a curiosity of a nation, like Liechtenstein or the Maldives.

Heads of state did not attend. Heads of government stayed away, although in some cases they desperately wanted to come. The Nigerian president had to be cajoled and flattered into staying in Lagos. The men who attended were unknowns, functionaries, senior lieutenants. In many cases they thought of themselves as the true powers of their nations. Once you got sucked into government, you had to deal with the mundane: your voters, or other subjects; roads, hospitals, water pipes. These men did not deal with the mundane. They were unconcerned with tax rates. They dealt with the money, the sources of wealth that kept everything afloat. Their focus was narrow. Other men feared them, even their presidents. Without these men, it would all fall apart.

There were too many present for the meeting to be totally off-radar. If the politicians did not notice, the business analysts would. It was announced as an ethics conference: improving the sector's global image, corporate responsibility, charitable sponsorship. Haroun had suggested that, and he was proud of it. Almost nothing could have been a more effective disguise. Journalists covering the sector yawned and went back to writing output predictions.

They staggered the arrival times, and unmarked black Lincoln Town Cars, a fleet of which formed the Nadrahi government's private chauffeur service, wound their way up and down the baking heat of the white cliff-edge road from the Sultan's complex to the airport.

Haroun was waiting to see them. He had visited his wife earlier in the morning, in a fit of marital virtue, and they had endured each other. After a while, he could arouse her to some mild level of enjoyment, but it took a few minutes. He did not particularly object. If she was a cold fish, there would be fewer opportunities for scandal. That they slept together regularly was still gossiped about. He wanted no lese-majesty. The royal family would remain a unit. She could then return to her shopping, her charities and her tennis, while he dallied with the models and other concubines waiting for him in the lodge.

He liked to have sex most days. It was not particularly good with Fatima, but that was not her purpose. And when he was done, he had at least received some relief. Perhaps she would become pregnant again, which would do wonders for his image. The people enjoyed a royal birth, a warm family photoshoot. And Haroun was most concerned to keep them happy. Life in Nadrah was perfect. The paradise promised to the faithful could be no better than this. His concern, today, was to ensure that his anxieties rose no higher than such ephemera: keeping his hot little harem of sluts away from the photographers, keeping the Sultana happy, another child, the narrative of sun-soaked happiness spinning down another year in the Gulf.

All such things were teetering on a giant precipice.

They could not find them. They could not catch them. A simple clean-up operation had become an epic nightmare. The Russian was useless. He had allowed some dull English academic with no training of any kind to outwit him. In the States, her banker ally had protected her with magnificent skill. And now what they all feared, the incipient nightmare, was breaking over them. The hunt was gathering press. It had been necessary to remove financial support from this William Hyde, but you could not break an American bank in secret. Hyde's photograph had been all over American television. He was a fugitive billionaire now, and that was the sort of juicy story that would have journalists panting. The sand in the hourglass was getting low. They must find these two. They must kill them.

'*Ahlan wa-Sahlan*,' the Qatari emir said, kissing Haroun on both cheeks. The Sultan nodded, moving to shake hands with Feliz Torrealba of Venezuela and greeting the Algerian emissary. There was full attendance. Some had arrived the night before, and slept in luxury in the palace; others were fresh off the plane. All ready to get on with it.

He gestured and the men sat down. There was no chairman or moderator. They were not here for intricate policy discussions.

'Let us begin.' Haroun did not bother with ceremonial welcomes, and there was a nod of approval around the table. 'He is waiting.'

The doors to the palace swung open. Dimitri entered. His eyes were hard. There were powerful clients at that table, and they were under the impression they were about to ream him out for failure. They were mistaken.

He thought of Lola Montoya. She had stiffened her back and acted defiantly before him. In turn, he must now do the same.

'Why is this man not dead?'

Dimitri looked at the speaker, a young princeling from the House of Saud. Others were opening their mouths, preparing to chime in.

'Because he is a first-class secret agent, and luck has been with him.'

'Agents have been killed before. Chiefs of station. Heads of service, even.'

'That is true. But plenty of others have been hunted and have escaped. If I, for example, were to go off-grid, none of your men would catch me.'

'Perhaps you have employed the wrong people,' Haroun said mildly.

'No.' He did not bother with the 'Majesty' this time. He was sick of this job and tired of deference. 'I have four of the world's best hunting them individually, but it has moved on from that. After Rotterdam you have all put your security forces on tracing them. Not one has come up with the kill.' Dimitri shrugged. 'It is not as simple as it sounds to eliminate a highly trained and motivated agent on the run. You could, of course, have killed him when he went back to New York, but the decision was taken to eliminate the woman first and avoid unnecessary publicity.'

They muttered, unhappy. That had been their

decision, not Dimitri's. A wrong decision. The woman had escaped and the man had instantly disappeared. The opportunity to kill him had vanished. He had defied them, appearing in plain sight, attending charitable balls, daring them to act, and they had hesitated.

'Now we have the worst situation, of publicity and both targets loose. I believe there are some causes for optimism, though.'

'Name them,' the Saudi said.

Optimism. They all wanted to hear that.

'Firstly, the wealth of the Englishman has been confiscated. It will soon be utterly destroyed. It's true there is now press, but it was almost impossible to hunt a man with many friends and infinite resources. Enough money can buy you safety. Secondly, more important perhaps, Mr Hyde is now wanted by more people than us. Interpol are looking, the Americans are looking. The news coverage means his face is known. It will be harder for him on the road, because the number of eyes hunting him has just doubled.'

Nods. They could see that.

'He may choose to go to ground. Take the woman and hide. In that case it could be some years before they are found. But they will be too scared to emerge and divulge the information.'

'How can you tell?'

Dimitri smiled; this was his trump card. 'Because they don't know it. They don't know why they are being hunted or who is hunting them. If they knew, they would already have broken the story, as wide as possible. It is the only solution for them: the spotlight to be turned on all of us, when we need the assistance and goodwill of the Western powers. Then they would be safe. Who would risk assassinating them? We would all have bigger worries at that point. The world would.'

There was a low growl of fear.

'My operative Lola Montoya has killed Olivia Wharton, the fiancée of Will Hyde.' Gasps of surprise; he had prepared some shots from the morgue, and now passed them around. 'Her body was found this morning, spattered with Hyde's blood and with her hair under his fingernails. He is now the subject of a murder warrant and an international APB.'

'Excellent,' Haroun said. 'Does he know?'

'Not yet. Things are moving fast. He is probably only now discovering that his wealth has vanished. The death of the woman will strain things between him and his protectee. She is responsible for it.' Dimitri stood up. 'Your job, gentlemen, is to provide me with as many watchers as you can manage. There is no point now in trying to hide the manhunt. Nor should any agent try anything cute, like capturing and torturing them. If they are seen, they should be shot at once. They must be eliminated if the slightest opportunity presents itself. Encourage whoever is willing to trade his own life for the kill.'

He looked around the room, holding the eyes of each client in turn.

'If anyone thinks they can do better, they should ask their security forces to move in. Meanwhile, I am going to Roissy-en-France, where they were last seen.'

Chapter Thirty-One

Will moved a little about the camp, and Melissa watched him. They were deep in the woods at the side of the road, near Voiron. The car was parked a short distance away. It was hard going, climbing up the embankment, but they had to do it fast, before another car tore round the bend and might notice them. He had carried the camping gear on his back and was lost in the trees before she even scrambled to the top of the bank.

It was a pine forest, and therefore especially dark. Melissa liked that: an added feeling of safety. The canopy was dense. No aircraft would see them. They were far away from paths, and camping sites. The air was heavily scented, a beautiful cloud of resin and water; even the fumes from the autoroute nearby could not reach them.

The town huddled together on the low sloping land behind the road. They were removed from it here, where nobody would walk a dog or go picnicking. Long fissures of sunlight streamed down through the dark avenues of conifers, giving the wood an unworldly look. The lack of light meant the forest floor was scrubby, with few bushes and a springy, golden-brown carpet of pine leaves. An occasional moth fluttered past them. Incredible, Melissa thought, how you could go steps away from civilisation and be so alone. The world was full of nooks and crannies, places people simply did not think to look.

Will had found a more or less level patch of ground and erected their small tent in barely a few minutes. He had laid out food, all of it cold: some cooked chicken thighs, a couple of oranges, ham and tomatoes with salt, a baguette, a bottle of olive oil, some miniature Edam cheeses in their little wax wrappers. He tossed Melissa a small plastic zippered bag; inside were their tooth-brushes, some disposable razors and deodorants, and shampoo.

'Go and clean up,' he said.

She glanced around her. 'In what?'

He pointed. 'There's a stream down that slope behind us.'

The sun was already sinking through the trees; the wind was fresh. It was starting to get cold.

'I'll be freezing,' Melissa protested.

'That's right. But you'll be clean. You can't do this without bathing, like I said.' He looked her over. 'Here.' He tossed her a small, thin towel. 'I would hurry if I were you. The later it gets, the colder the water will be.'

'OK,' she said reluctantly. A second ago she had been thinking, frightened, of what it would be like when he touched her, if she would be frigid, if it would be any good for him after all those pliant models . . .

There was nothing like the prospect of icy water to distract her. She stumbled down the bank, slipping on pine cones. The stream moved fast, but it was shallow; about a foot in depth, she thought. She took off her clothes, stripping to her underwear, hanging everything carefully over the branch of a tree so that it did not get filled with needles.

She moved to the edge of the water, slipped her foot in. It was cold, burning cold. She hurriedly took it out again.

Will came running down the slope. He was naked. There was an outcrop of rock next to where Melissa was standing, perched over a deeper pool of water, a swim-hole where the gravelly base of the stream dipped away. He grabbed his knees, jumped, and plunged in. She watched with fascinated horror. He swam up, his golden body strong in the water, his slight beard and dark hair flattened to his head.

'Get in.'

'I can't! I'll catch pneumonia.'

'Unlikely. Get in.'

She shook her head.

'Then at least pass me the bag,' he said, exasperated.

Melissa zipped it up and tiptoed forward on to the outcrop, extending her arm, leaning forward to him . . .

Will grabbed her wrist and neatly pulled her down into the swim-hole. Melissa was swallowed completely by the icy water. Her entire body was in shock. She was too cold to scream; she gasped and spluttered, trying to get her frozen limbs to move.

'You bastard,' she chattered. She made to move to the bank, but Will slipped one hand around her waist, pinning her to him.

'Stay still,' he ordered. She struggled feebly against the cold. He had rested the bag on a rock, and now his hands were in her hair and his own. She felt him apply a little shampoo to them both. 'No, please,' she gasped, but he had pushed her under the water. It was dark and freezing; she shuddered as he hauled her back up, rinsed, and handed her a razor.

'Be quick,' he said.

'Let me out,' she demanded. 'God! Let me out, Will!'

'The longer you argue with me, the longer you stay here.'

Cursing him, her hands shaking, she leaned forward and began to clean herself up. The water was still freezing, but now fractionally less brutal. She was acclimatising herself. Her hands stopped shaking. She drew the razor across her legs. When she had finished, Will took it from her, shook it in the current, and carefully trimmed his beard. His hand was still on her, preventing her from moving.

She was so cold it hurt. She sobbed, needing to move. Her lips were turning blue.

'Please, please,' she chattered.

'We're done,' Will said.

Melissa was shuddering in the water. She suddenly found herself scooped up in his arms, as though her weight was nothing; a good thing, she didn't know if she could walk. On the bank he paused and reached for her towel. She was shivering wildly against him. Her teeth chattered. She pressed herself to him, craving the heat from his skin. Little rivulets of water sluiced down the muscles of his chest.

He moved fast, back to the tent, and set her down. She was still shaking. Will grabbed the small towel and rubbed it briskly over her, drying her, then himself.

'The tent must not get damp,' he said.

'You froze me,' she managed. 'It hurt – I'm so cold . . .'

Will put his hand on the small of her back and pushed her inside the tent. It was well insulated, and there was a large, flat blanket made of some silver material in there. Melissa trembled.

'Can – can we have a fire?'

'No fire,' he said. He moved towards her, and with one hand tugged off her soaked panties and unhooked her bra. She was too cold to object, too cold to feel anything. He knelt by the door, holding them outside the tent, wrung them out, and then tossed them on to a bush to dry.

Then he zipped up the front of the tent. It was cold outside, now the sun had disappeared, and the twilight was deepening. He moved next to her and beckoned. Melissa crept into his arms.

'If you had listened, it would have been quicker.' His arms circled around her back, pulling her in tight. Her breasts and stomach, and her icy legs, were pressed into his body, warming her, heating her up slowly. 'You have to learn survival skills. We use streams and rivers. You make yourself clean on the road. If not, you will be noticed. Forget hot showers, Missy.'

She nestled closer, her frozen skin warming, thawing against him.

'You also go in naked. You need to be thoroughly clean.' He moved his hand, then, gently down to the base of her spine.

She gasped, not from cold. He was warming her, but he was also touching her. His hand stroked gently over her lower back. She felt herself respond at once. He chuckled. 'Not that cold,' he said. 'Are you?'

She bit her lip. His other hand traced a line from her shoulder, down across her arm, on to her left hand. His callused fingertip made a circle there.

'Where is your wedding ring?' he murmured in her ear. 'You need another one, Missy. You are my wife, still my wife.'

Melissa could hardly see straight. She lifted her body to him. She was no longer cold, or if she was, it did not matter, she couldn't feel it. There was nothing but Will, his lips, his hands, the incredible strength of his chest. When she had loved him he was a handsome boy. Now he was a man, virile, muscular, a warrior, one who had risked his life and all he owned to save her.

She felt weak and slight in his grip and it aroused her. She wasn't used to the torrent of longing raging through her. Her body was not the only thing thawing. Her passion, her need that had lain dormant for years, was now burning in her, making her open and receptive, making her totally hot for him.

'Will,' she whispered. 'Will . . . please . . .'

He scooped her up again, lifting her lightly and laying her down on the floor of the tent. He kicked the blanket to one side and looked down at her, holding her eyes.

'I have waited for this for years,' he said softly.

'No pressure,' she said, trying for a smile. But he didn't laugh.

'I should tease you,' he said. He moved his hand up, running the tips of his fingers up her shin, over her knee. The pleasure was incredible. Melissa moved, half sobbing, reaching for him, but his right hand was on her chest, firmly, casually holding her down. 'I should make you pay for every second you made me suffer.'

A soft moan of lust escaped her. Will moved his hands, and came down lower, kissing the skin at the side of her neck, under the earlobe, raking at it so she could feel his lips and teeth.

'You're not going to get off easy,' he said, 'Melissa, I'm going to work you out,' and he ran his tongue lightly down the back of her neck, kissing the top of her spine. She leapt, wildly, uncontrollably, off the ground, flinging her arms round his neck, pushing herself towards him . . .

And he kissed her hard on the lips, and pushed her back into the ground, and took her, and everything fell away, the whole world fell away, and all that was there for her was how she moved with Will and what he forced her to feel.

'What time is it?' she asked.

Will had gone outside and thrown some more fabric over the top of the tent. He came back inside, zipped it up carefully, and took out a match, lighting the kerosene in a small tin lamp. The flame licked up into life and sent dappled shadows dancing around the walls. Melissa smiled; it was warm and cheerful. There was something primal and good about fire, even a tiny one in a lamp.

She was not cold, not any more. The tent had good insulation and the blanket was made from some space-age warming material. And she had been nestled against Will for an hour now, just kissing and talking, after the frenzy of their lovemaking finally subsided.

'Late. But we've got to eat.' He passed her some food, and she took it from him. 'Keep up your strength. I buy food that's cheap and nourishing. Oranges for vitamin C.' He gestured at the bread. 'Carbs for energy. Olive oil for fat – butter doesn't keep. Chicken and cheese, fats and proteins. Tomatoes . . . they just taste good.'

She laughed softly. They were dressed again now. Will had left the tent briefly, while Melissa was still lying on her back, panting, recovering, and gone down to the stream; he said he could see in the dark, and she wasn't used to it. He had washed their towels and clothes and hung them out on bushes to dry. Then he had come back inside with fresh outfits: T-shirts, underwear, jogging bottoms and their trainers; you always slept clothed, he said, in case you were attacked, or needed to run.

'It's delicious,' she said, and it was. Cold or not, she was now ravenously hungry. The flight, the water, the sex . . . she needed calories; everything tasted sublimely fresh and delicious. When they were done, Will offered her the water bottle. She drank deep and used just a little water to brush her teeth.

He blew out the lamp.

'How did Olivia take it?' Melissa asked, nestled close to him in the darkness, loving him, breathing in the male scent of him, his strong arm curled around her shoulders.

'Not well.' He kissed the top of her head, and she felt him toy with the strands of her hair. 'But she was mostly concerned for her image. She'll get over it. And besides, I think she'd have walked anyway.'

'Why?'

'I lost all my money today.'

Melissa blinked in the darkness. 'What?'

'The bank – there was a run on it. They planted money in fake accounts to smear me. The bank failed, my stock went down the pan and they froze my accounts. I've got nothing left. Not a billionaire, a millionaire or any other kind of aire.' He stiffened, just slightly. 'Does that upset you?'

'Upset me?' She was half crying, half laughing. 'No, no! It's wonderful, Will, it means we can start over, we can make it together. I'm glad,' she said fiercely. 'Now you'll always know how much I love you, how hot I am for you. Not the money. You.'

He rolled her to him and found her lips in the dark, tugging up her T-shirt, his hand over her breasts, feeling them, cupping them.

'We have to sleep,' she protested.

'Sleep later,' he said, kissing her face and neck. 'Later.'

The early light came up gently in the east, and Melissa was woken by Will, on top of her, stroking her, teasing her.

'Mmm,' she breathed. She emerged from sleep, and it was true, like waking from a good dream and finding it actually was your birthday . . .

He was there, Will was there, on her, kissing her. The memory of his touch, of clutching him, lost in it, came back to her, and she breathed in her arousal, and he took her wrists and pinned her arms to the ground over her head, his lips moving down to her collarbone while she squirmed, holding her in place . . .

Chapter Thirty-Two

Lola sat in a tiny internet café on Montee du Boulord, La Murette, France. She was very tired; her sleep on the plane had been unusually fitful. Next to her was a small china cup of good black coffee and a couple of tiny *pâtisseries*. Even a shitty little place like this, where bored local kids came to get on the net, the food was still basically good. She needed the caffeine and sugar. Soon she would have to sleep, there was no getting around it. But she thought she could push her body for a couple of hours yet.

She had access to certain things other assassins didn't bother with. That was what made her so effective. All her skills were honed, of course; she was an excellent shot, she could mix various poisons, she was strong for her size and could strangle and snap a neck efficiently. But Lola did not concentrate on technique. More or less any competent could do that. It was easy to kill another human being if you had a knife or a gun. The body is fragile. She knew how much.

No, her success stemmed from something they did not

do. She was a huntress. She could track down the prey, find them when other operatives made excuses, insisted they had gone to ground. Will Hyde was better than most – any – of her targets. But he was not Superman. He couldn't push his feet off the ground and fly. He needed vehicles, and where you had vehicles, you had tracking.

She used distance-based codes. Technology had made things much easier. Half the kill was in your mind. A few strokes of the keyboard and she had accessed the desktop of a regional supervisor of motorway traffic. She zoomed her mouse around his screen. He was a lazy fucker and invariably took three-hour lunches. Impossible, she thought, disappointed; no resolution. The cars on her screen streamed past. It would be tough to get a numberplate capture, let alone faces. OK. She tried something else. A few more strokes and the toll stops for the commune of the Isère popped up. She glanced at the atlas next to her, the road map of Europe. They must have come down the autoroute A43, towards Grenoble. That was a toll road. Tap-tap-tap. She brought up the toll bridge and calculated in her head. It was a guess, it was such a guess. Had they slept when they came into Roissy? A long flight, juddering around a cargo hold. A long walk to the town.

Would Lola have slept? Of course not. Fear of death is an excellent motivator. She would look at her own reactions and judge Hyde's by them. A compliment to him. So he would have driven. She doubted he would have attempted to smuggle anything on to the FedEx plane. Take a half-hour minimum for the purchase of supplies, a change of clothing. They would have washed up in some bathroom somewhere, too. That gave her a window of two hours if you assumed five hours for the drive to that point . . .

She tapped again, getting closer. Much better. You could clearly see the faces through the windscreens. She ran the CCTV footage at double speed, sipped her coffee, and waited.

They ate the rest of the food, cleaned their teeth, and washed quickly in the stream; this time Melissa didn't argue. Will only made her splash her body. Her hair was already clean. He packed up the tent, she retrieved the dry clothes, and then Will moved about, kicking up leaves and twigs, hiding the evidence of their camp.

'Come on. We've got to go,' he said, kissing her on the cheek. He ran both hands up and down her rib cage, and Melissa felt another instant surge of desire.

Will grinned. 'Later,' he said. 'We should have been gone an hour ago. It's my fault. I can't stop with you.'

They buckled up and Will spun the car back on to the road. It sputtered a little, but it was good to go. They had a full tank of petrol. As they found the autoroute again, Melissa sighed with sheer pleasure. She was clean, dry, fed, loved. The car seats were warm and luxurious after the cold water of the stream. She felt inviolate, touched by a star. The killers, that woman's hideous angry voice shouting at her at the apartment, they were all irrelevant. How could they find her? Will Hyde could protect her from the Devil himself.

Lola bit at another tiny macaroon, so light and delicate it was barely there in her mouth. She had not eaten anything so good for quite some time. They sold nougat here, she might take some with her, that was a good source of glucose and kept well . . .

Ah. She leaned forward, tapped at the screen. Rewound. Froze.

There was no way to get in further, damn it, no way to blow the image up. But it was them. She was sure. She never forgot the eyes of a target. She ran her gaze over the figures in the car. Big car, not a motorbike, wonder why they switched from using bikes to cars? The height was correct, the weight was correct. The girl was easier to make out than Hyde. He had grown a beard. Clever boy, she thought. It was so odd how targets neglected the basics. The girl, Melissa, had cut her hair. The image was black and white, unfortunately, but if she had cut her hair she had likely dyed it too.

This was taken yesterday. They were in a Renault Espace and they were driving south, towards the border of either Switzerland or Italy. After this it would have been necessary for them, too, to sleep. Hyde would have hated that as much as Lola did, but the body needed its pit-stop.

*

Melissa was quiet in the car, trying to think. Will had been a spy. He processed so much information, stuff she didn't notice. Perhaps he was being too analytical. Maybe she could cut through some of it, help him out.

'If we go back to the other two murders, do they tell us anything?' she asked. 'You can see why they'd kill Senator Jospin. But why the librarian, what was her name . . .'

'Moira Dunwoody.'

'Right. What about her?'

He thought about it, retrieving information from his mental Rolodex.

'She was the Chief Librarian of the New York Public Library, which is a nice honorific but nothing special. She had no money to speak of. She wasn't a spy undercover, I'd have known that.'

'Daddy had been to the library?'

'For several benefits. I saw him there once, talking to her. Another time he met with Ellen Jospin, who I was watching over a banking business. His name came up on the list of people who visited her office. That's how I made the connection to you.'

Melissa said slowly, 'My father didn't make friends easily.'

'You can say that again.'

'Don't be bitter.'

'I'm sorry.' He casually put one hand on her thigh, controlling the wheel with his other hand, his grip stroking her firm leg. She bit her lip against her immediate response. His slightest touch aroused her. 'Since last night I'm getting over it.'

Melissa gasped, pressing her thighs together. Will's hand was steady on her. 'Wildcat,' he said.

'Will . . .'

'Later,' he said.

When he moved his hand she was flaming hot, shifting in her seat. 'I can't concentrate,' she muttered.

'And I thought you were a cold fish,' Will said, and laughed. 'I shouldn't touch you. I just can't resist you.'

She breathed in deeply, calming herself.

'You're a bastard, you know that?'

'So I've been told.' He shrugged. 'I'm just having my revenge on you, baby.'

Melissa tossed her head defiantly, and he grinned at her.

'My father,' she said, ploughing on, 'was only really interested in socialising with people who either could do something for him, or who looked up to him because of how brilliant he was. He loved the adulation he got at Oxford. He was an exceptional scientist, you know, Will.'

'Yes. I can see that.'

'Did Moira the librarian have a specialist subject or interest, that Daddy would have sought her out?'

Will stared straight ahead, his eyes on the road, thinking. Then he breathed in, sharply.

'My God!' he said, and the car spun a little; Melissa cried out in alarm, but he had regained control in an instant. His knuckles were white on the steering wheel, his face had flushed with blood. The remnants of desire drained from Melissa, to be replaced by fear; she had never seen Will like this. He was so cool, so unflappable.

'What is it, what is it, Will?'

'Your father – you said you didn't know what his field was, exactly?'

'He never said. It was kept quiet. Something to do with conservation, all very boring.'

'Not boring,' Will said. 'Energy conservation?'

'Yes. He was interested in disproving global warming.' She shook her head. 'Anything to get fame, or the academic equivalent of it. But he told me once his work had led him in another direction. I didn't ask why, because I really didn't care. Science never interested me.'

'I think you've cracked it,' Will said. 'I can't believe I was so dumb. The dots were there for anyone to join up. I was too focused on getting you safe. I should have been looking at the why of this from day one, not the how.'

'You're talking in riddles.'

'You asked what Moira's subject was. Good question. *Great* question. Maybe you should go into intelligence.'

'Will . . .'

'Energy,' he said. 'Renewable energy. Solar, wind, hydro. And Ellen Jospin was on the Joint Intelligence Committee. That's what blinded me. Prior to the intelligence committee she served on the energy committee. She was a yellow-dog Democrat, a real liberal. She was the last one to hold out against drilling in ANWR even when oil prices were going through the roof. She believed the United States had not done enough to invest in solar power.'

Melissa leaned back against her headrest. She saw where he was going. Her heart raced. Her breath quickened. 'Will! Before he left for Italy, when David Fell first gave him the grant. He said something then. He said the sun and the clouds were really important and the whole world would know his name.'

'Go on,' Will said. 'Anything you remember. Anything at all.'

'He said these were exciting times in climatology. And there were commercial uses for his work . . .'

Will saw a sign ahead and suddenly moved to the right, heading to a slip road.

'We're near Portofino,' he said. 'We'll park somewhere and eat. I have to think. I have to think.'

'OK.' She was far too excited to eat, but she wanted to get off the endless grey stretch of asphalt. 'Will, you said earlier about the woman assassin. That her customers were Arabs. And the men at the apartment, from South America. Venezuela has oil, doesn't it? Lots of oil.'

'Yes, it does,' he said. 'You get it, my beauty, don't you?'

They had moved into a village, somewhere in northern Italy, Liguria. Will brought the car to a stop on a dusty road bordering an olive grove. There was a taverna a little further down the street, advertising itself as an American sports bar.

They both got out. He half ran round the car to her, his eyes glittering.

'Your father must have invented a solar cell,' he said. 'A solar cell that worked. A solar cell that could do more than power a battery or a watch. It's been a holy grail for years. Imagine a solar cell that could be built into the roof of a car, that would power it.'

Melissa tried. She understood, at once. The consequences would be epic. It could change the world.

'Oil . . .'

Will seized her by the upper arms. 'Oil would plummet. It would have some value, but the stranglehold would be gone. It would drop through the floor. The richest oil-producing nations would become poor overnight.'

She stood there, in his grip, by the side of the road, in the dusty, scrubby countryside of the Mediterranean and laughed out loud.

'My father,' she said. 'My father, the right-wing lunatic, the chief attacker of global warming. *My father* invented the one device that could save the planet?'

'Fuck the planet,' Will said. 'There are men out there who would drop a nuclear bomb on Rome to stop information like that being released.'

She looked at him.

'I'm not joking,' Will said. 'They would lose everything. There are also terrorist organisations, lots of them, outside of governments, who are funded with oil money.'

'Then no wonder they want me dead,' Melissa said. She started to shake. 'What do we do? They'll never stop.'

Will's hands on her upper arms drew her to him. He kissed her lingeringly, and she shuddered and pressed herself against him.

'You're alive. We're alive,' he said. 'Do you think I'd let you go, Missy? After this? Think again.'

She nestled into his chest, but she was terrified. They would kill her, kill him. Just when she had found love it would be snatched from her. This new life, so vital and precious, would be blacked out.

They could outrun one female assassin. The combined forced of the world's oil producers? She doubted that, doubted it very much.

'Maybe if we disappear,' she whispered. 'Maybe if we go somewhere private . . . Iceland, or . . . or . . . Argentina . . .'

Will's arms were around her, holding her. He placed his palm, open, on her chest, over her heart, feeling it beat against his skin.

'There is no running,' he murmured. 'Not against those many people. You have to make their nightmare come true, sweetheart. You have to find whatever proof your father had and publish it. Put it on the internet, send it to the *New York Times* and the *Sun* and the BBC. Send it to Greenpeace. Send it to the White House. And then go to the CIA and ask for protection.'

'But Will,' she said, almost in tears. 'I hadn't really

spoken to Daddy, not for years. I had no idea what he was working on. How can I find that? How can I prove it? We don't even know we're right about this. Maybe it's got nothing to do with solar cells . . .'

'It does,' Will said. 'It fits. Perfectly. And there are very few explanations that would fit.'

'He didn't talk to me,' Melissa protested. 'He didn't give me any details about his work. We had lost touch. How are we going to find it?'

Will shrugged. 'Carefully,' he said. 'You must be prepared, sweetheart. If I have figured this out, they will too. They will know where we're going and why. If they can't catch us on the road they will be waiting for us to turn up at your father's old university. Soon, if not just yet.' He kissed her again. 'Come on, we're in the middle of nowhere. Let's eat. They won't be here, honey, not yet.'

He offered her his hand. Melissa slipped hers into it, leaned close to him, kissed him on the arm. She felt weak, almost dizzy with the love of him.

The taverna was very basic, a menu scrawled on a blackboard with white chalk, Italian, nothing for tourists. Will ordered a *burida*, a Ligurian fish stew, and Melissa chose a simple pasta and pesto. They served it up with glass bottles of *limonata*, fizzy lemon soda, poured over ice. It was cheap and good, and the host grunted with approval at Will's Italian.

There was a dusty TV, a small set, mounted in iron

brackets on the wall. Will spoke to the host, and he switched it on, proudly turning the knobs to find CNN. The news channel was showing sports, a football game between the Jets and the Vikings. The proprietor shuffled off to serve his regulars, and ignored them. They had paid in advance. He no longer cared.

'Eat,' Will said. 'It's good. They invented pesto here, did you know that?'

Melissa didn't answer. She was staring at the screen. She reached out, subtly, and touched him on the forearm, and gestured at the TV. Will waited a moment, and took a swig of his soda; he turned, very slightly, towards the television, as though hardly interested.

The blonde newsreader was speaking over footage of Olivia and Will, standing on the red carpet, Olivia's hand extended, a diamond ring sparkling on her finger.

Melissa glanced furtively around the room, but nobody was looking at Will; he had a beard, he was not recognisable as the rich man in the tuxedo.

'. . . *when the body of socialite Olivia Wharton was found in her apartment. Ms Wharton, the fiancée of disgraced financier William Hyde, had been strangled. Police sources say that Mr Hyde's blood and hair have been found on the young woman's body. Hyde disappeared from Manhattan a week ago and is now wanted for questioning in regard to the death of Olivia Wharton and assault on two workers from Federal Express, as well as for international money-laundering and bank fraud . . .*'

Will sipped his drink again and deliberately ate three

more spoonfuls of stew, but Melissa could see the shock in his face, the tears brimming in his eyes. He stood casually, throwing down a few euro coins on the table, and then walked out. She followed him, her heart full: fear, guilt, pity.

Will didn't say a word. She followed him to the car and slipped inside it. He reversed and drove down the narrow road, away from the autostrada, towards the coast.

'We'll take back routes,' he said.

Melissa bit her lip. 'I'm so sorry, Will.'

'I failed her,' he said. A tear rolled down his cheek, startling Melissa; she had never seen Will Hyde cry. 'I used her. She was fun to be with, good in bed, socially desirable, didn't argue with me. And I thought it was time to marry, so I proposed to her. I never loved Olivia and she deserved better than me. When we split up, I was so bloody self-righteous. Told myself she only cared about my money and her status. Maybe that was so, maybe not. But I was just as bad. She wanted my money; I was looking for a piece in a jigsaw puzzle, an accessory to my life. I was worse, because I'd never got over you. I used her.'

'Not deliberately,' Melissa said. 'You wouldn't have seen it like that. Don't try to rewrite the past, Will. You'll drive yourself insane.'

'What a goddamned waste,' he said bitterly.

'She was popular and beautiful,' Melissa said. 'She was well respected in your society. She glittered and dazzled. She would have had a wonderful life up until the last few days. Not many people can say that, Will.'

'When I went to get you I never thought they might come for her.' His palm struck the top of the wheel. 'What a stupid, selfish fool I was. I endangered an innocent woman. She paid for me with her life. It's my fault, Missy, I'm the reason she's dead . . .'

They pulled into traffic at the mouth of a mountain tunnel and Melissa touched him on the chin, forcing him to turn his head towards her. She leaned over and kissed his tears away, softly.

'Will. The reason she's dead is that one of these bastards strangled her.'

His eyes focused, and she drew back, frightened. There was dark hatred in them, rage she had never seen before. Will transformed in front of her eyes. For the first time in her life, Melissa saw him as a killer, as an enemy agent must have seen him, long ago, staring at him down the barrel of a gun.

'Yes,' he said. 'You're right.'

'What are you going to do?' she whispered.

'I'm going to stop running from them,' he said. 'And I'm going to start hunting them.' He held her gaze. 'You should leave me for a while. I can call friends to pick you up, military friends. I can put you in one of the safest places in Jerusalem, guarded by their secret service.'

She shook her head. 'I cannot let you go, Will. If you die, my life's over anyway. I just don't want to live without you. Let me go too. What will we do?'

'Dump this car,' he said. 'Book passage on a cruise ship. No registration, I just bribe one of the crew to stash us in an empty cabin. It's the last place they'd look. Cruises stop in Portofino and they will have checked the vessels, if they're that thorough, at the embarkation point. We're hopping on mid-sail. The next stop will be Rome. It's a port, on top of everything else.'

'OK.' She tried a small grin. 'I could live with a cruise cabin.'

'We go to the university campus. Find your father's papers.' He kissed her. 'Then you leave.'

'I refuse.'

'You will leave,' he repeated. 'You will go and publicise your father's work, somewhere safe. Maybe from Israel. They will help. They were my colleagues in the trenches. Remember, Melissa, it's not just Olivia. They killed your father for this. You can avenge him, without firing a shot.'

Anger flooded her. 'They did kill him.'

'And if you're with me, you will inhibit me. I would be thinking about protecting you. Let me hunt, Melissa.'

'Who are you hunting?' she whispered. 'You can't take out all these agents from all these different countries, Will. You're just one person.'

He put back his head, and she saw the frustration. There were too many targets, he knew that. But his eyes narrowed, and he turned back to her.

'I will kill the woman,' he said. 'Lola Montoya.'

'But she's a woman,' Melissa protested.

Will shrugged. 'Don't expect chivalry, Melissa. She is a killer. If I do not take her out she will kill again. She tried to kill you. She probably killed Olivia. It sounds like her work, the planting of the evidence to implicate me. Whoever got my blood broke into a vault in my doctor's office on Fifth Avenue. That is seriously professional work. It matches Montoya.' His eyes were hard. 'She dies. And not just her. This operation has a chief, all of them do. He must be an exceptionally powerful man. He will be dealing with heads of service, ministers maybe. Money guys for sure. Various nations and players. The man selected to do that would be amongst the absolute elite.' His eyes narrowed, thinking. 'I would have a shortlist of about twenty. Lola Montoya would not report to anyone less.'

'If he's that good, can you stop him?'

He looked at her, and again she shuddered. 'Oh yes,' he said. 'Believe it. I can kill him.'

The car emerged from the tunnel, and Will took it down a narrow side road signed for Portofino.

'I will kill him,' he said.

Chapter Thirty-Three

Dimitri waited as his driver opened the door to the limousine. He was prepared to be patient. It might take several minutes to reach the Sultan, the *Malik*, Haroun. He did not object. Haroun was among the clearer sighted of his clients. And finally Dimitri had good news.

'Follow me,' the white-coated vizier said, conducting Dimitri through the cool marble halls of the palace. There was the quiet hum of air-conditioning fans everywhere. Dimitri suddenly wondered how much it cost to maintain an oasis like this, staffed by the best and manned with soldiers. The Sultan kept his wife and children in suffocating luxury, and Dimitri knew all about the house at the bottom of the manicured enclosed park, stuffed full of female diversions. Haroun kept a harem. His appetites were prodigious. Dimitri liked this about him. It made him easier to understand, and control. And it was a weakness; women were best used anonymously and then discarded.

'His Majesty is in his study.'

Dimitri nodded and moved forward. Whatever he said

to Haroun would be discreetly and efficiently dispersed within the ranks of the oil-drilling nations. Haroun himself was the only head of government, even government minister, involved. The rest were the shadows; officers of the intelligence services, with plenty of investment in their countries, even, sometimes, the motivation of patriotism. The surveillance operation and the threat were presently below the radar of the nominal rulers of many of these states.

Malik Haroun of Nadrah was the exception.

Dimitri moved into the study, which was lined with imported European walnut and looked as though it might have belonged in 10 Downing Street. Haroun was on the phone, staring at a computer terminal, behind an antique mahogany desk, a genuine Chippendale, Dimitri thought.

'Majesty,' he said.

Haroun looked up. 'You have progress to report?'

'I do. They landed in France and have fled across the Italian border. They appear to be moving directly south. We traced them to a provincial town in southern France, Voiron. Then they were photographed passing through the Italian border.'

'Why were they not killed?'

'Road stops are typically not used, Majesty. There are few passport checks.'

Haroun frowned, and Dimitri wanted to kill him. He was tired of reporting on an operation to these clowns, even the more moderate ones like this Arab. What did they know of tradecraft? Less than nothing.

'How did you pin them down?'

Dimitri answered this one carefully. 'We tracked them through our operative Lola Montoya.'

Haroun did not follow up the point. 'And what is being done to eliminate them?'

'The man, Hyde, is skilled.'

'I tire of being told that,' Haroun said coldly.

'Yes, Majesty. I have a vast network reading check-in on every hotel, even every bed and breakfast, in France. They did not stop overnight. Therefore they slept either in their car or rough in the bushes. This tells me Hyde has worked out the nature of the hunt, that he understands the range of people looking for him.'

Haroun shrugged. 'How can you infer that?'

'It requires massive manpower to cover every hotel in a country. Ordinarily, on the run an agent will go to some lesser-known flophouse and pay in cash. That's standard practice. The fact that Hyde avoided it means he understands we have that level of resource. He will have inferred that more than one country is involved.' Dimitri held the eyes of the Sultan. 'You should assume, Majesty, that he has worked out why we want him eliminated.'

The Sultan leaned forward, his dark skin flushed; his heavy hooded eyes were bright with fear.

'If he knows, the world will end,' he said, with perceptible malice.

'No, Majesty. There is a difference between what he knows and what he can prove.'

'Where is he now?'

'Off-grid.'

'*Ibn il tinayich*,' Haroun swore. 'Is this man a *djinn*? How does he disappear from us?'

'Years of training,' Dimitri replied, matter-of-fact. 'But it is no matter. I know where they must come. Lola Montoya has provided the evidence to us.' Strictly speaking, true enough. 'We will await them when they get there. We will prepare a trap.'

'Then where are they going?'

Dimitri hated having to tell him. 'Rome, Majesty. My belief is they are heading south. They must be close to the solution, at least. They will visit Richard Elmet's place of work, they will talk to his friends, they will attempt to discover exactly why we hunt them. When we know where they are going, we can find them. I will have command of the force.'

Haroun pressed the tips of his fingers to his forehead.

'How many men will you take?'

'It's delicate. I could have the use of several thousand, but that will be noticed by the Italian authorities. Also, Hyde will notice. When you multiply the numbers, some are not careful. He could go to ground for weeks or months. I want to take one hundred hand-picked men, computer experts and snipers. I can hide a force that size in the city.'

'So Montoya was useful after all,' the client mused. 'She found these two rats scuttling towards the south.'

Dimitri nodded.

'Her picture shows she is beautiful.'

'Yes,' Dimitri said neutrally.

'I want to have her,' Haroun said, making a slight gesture. 'Would she co-operate? I would pay her fee, whatever it is.'

Dimitri grinned. 'She would not take a fee, Majesty, for that.'

'I can hire her to kill, not to sleep with,' Haroun remarked. 'I see. But surely, Dimitri Petrenko, at the end of this mission you will eliminate her? She knows too much, does she not?'

Dimitri's brows lifted in genuine surprise. Sometimes Haroun would come out with things like this, perceptive little remarks that made him almost worth talking to.

'She is more than some common soldier who may be court-martialled. She will be expecting a move of that sort.'

'You did not answer the question,' the Sultan pointed out.

Dimitri inclined his head. 'As a precaution, yes, I plan it. As long as she is unaware. The woman would be a highly dangerous enemy.'

'And you yourself are an agent with an impeccable pedigree. The assassination of President Montaigne, and the kidnapping of Yitzak Wasserman.'

Dimitri smiled. 'And others more famous that you do not even know were kills,' he said.

'Then you will be capable of extracting her here, will you not? I wish to put her in my harem. Not with the other females, of course, because she would kill them. I will keep her isolated and ensure her compliance.' His face twisted into a grin; Dimitri had no doubt of the savagery behind the words. Haroun was not as civilised as he liked to pretend. 'She will supply me with pleasure. When I am finished with her, I could hand her to you or have her killed and disposed of here, myself.'

Dimitri's lip curled, just a little. Haroun was so decadent. 'You might waver, become fond of her. If a woman like that escaped, she could do great damage.'

'You need not fear that.' Haroun shrugged. 'I find her activities revolting. Unwomanly. It would be interesting to have her.'

'I intend to do so,' Dimitri admitted. 'I will see what I can do. But I would want to wait and kill her when you were done. You make a mistake thinking of this girl as a woman. She is an operative. She has escaped from harder places than your palace without breaking a sweat, and then she would come after me.'

Haroun nodded. 'Then do what you like.' He looked at Dimitri. 'I am surprised you do not object. The woman has been working for you, hasn't she?'

'You think me unjust?' Dimitri said. 'She has taken a fee, and withheld some information. Whatever protection she might have had as a professional evaporated at that point. Not that I am sentimental, but there is a certain code to these things. It's not good for business to hire a player, then kill her. Makes it very difficult to hire someone else for another assignment.'

'But if she has betrayed you, then it's different?'

'Then you practically have to kill her. Because if you do not, word goes out that you are weak.'

'Does she suspect your anger?'

'She suspects a little dissatisfaction that she is late. She doesn't know how much I am aware of her movements.' Dimitri smiled. 'She does not even know I am going to Rome. I will make her aware later.'

'Very good,' Haroun said, and his eyes glittered with lust. 'First, of course, eliminate the man, Hyde. Once he is gone, the daughter will be easy to pick off. And then you may return here with the woman.'

'It is outside the terms of reference,' Dimitri said, referring to his commission.

The Sultan shifted in his seat. 'Of course. For the woman alone, as long as she is unmarked and conscious, I will pay you two million dollars.'

Dimitri nodded. It was to be a private arrangement, then. Nothing to do with his mission. It suited him very well; he had planned to take Lola himself anyway. Now it would be profitable, as well as pleasurable.

'You know my account details. Have the money transferred tonight.'

'And what guarantee do I have that you will bring me the female?' Haroun asked.

Dimitri grinned. 'I have said that I will.'

The Sultan also smiled. They were half playing now. The tiresome month of chasing the English couple was almost at an end, and normal service could be resumed. Haroun worked hard at a life of pleasure, of deep sensation. Now the threat to his lifestyle was ending, he had decided the whole tense business was rather enjoyable.

'Does Your Majesty have an intercontinental jet available among your fleet?'

'We have three.'

'I would like to take the smallest. I wish to fly directly to Rome, after I leave here. It will be better not to waste any time.'

'By the time you get to the airport, it will be fuelled for take-off. I will have a couple of envoys fly with you.' Haroun chuckled. 'They will pay a courtesy call to the Italians. We have had few domestic niceties this year.'

'Thank you,' Dimitri said, and nodded his head. Haroun made things easy for them. He was an excellent focal point for the clients, and a lucrative side customer. The Russian turned and walked out of the palace, back towards the chauffeur-driven car still waiting for him on the gravel, as he had ordered. It was good that the Sultan could so readily supply a plane. He too was weary of this chase. In Rome, they would not be able to avoid him. William Hyde was good, but Dimitri was better.

'Airport,' he said to the driver. 'I am to leave in a jet of the royal fleet.'

Lola Montoya had led him to his quarry, but not exactly in the way he had expected. He had tracked her with two watchers, very good men, ex-Georgian agents, not part of this operation. They knew nothing about the solar machine. They thought the woman was a beautiful psychopath, and she was to be executed on the orders of a Russian oligarch, at his convenience.

They were good, solid agents. She wasn't looking for them. She was focused in one direction. They hung well back, only approaching her car, or following her, to a two-block distance. It was clear enough to him that Montoya had caught the scent. Her movements were too purposeful. She was not calling or asking for help. She was following. And she had not called it back to Dimitri, or to any other agent or office.

He had the tech guys on her. Her principal error was to go on-grid, using the traffic software. That was a nice piece of work. He smiled as he thought of it. She was the rare agent who could still teach him something, who had fresh ideas that he had not exhausted. A man inside the road monitoring system. That was a good one; he would start to incorporate such checks at once.

When they fed the image through to him, after a few minutes' delay, Dimitri Petrenko had been flooded with adrenaline, going cold as though a wash of iced water had hit him. *That was why he had hired her*. Her price was five million dollars. And it seemed she was worth it. Even with thousands of eyes scouring Europe for these two, none of them had hit gold. Lola Montoya had.

He waited for the call, but he knew already it would not come. She was hunting solo. She did not want to surrender either the kill or the credit. That was a problem, sometimes, with the big-name killers. They let ego get in the way. The stupid little bitch was smarting from presenting her report to him on the yacht. Dimitri could see inside her head, quite clearly. Because it was his head, too.

Understanding why she did it did not mean he would tolerate it. She had followed them through to the Italian border, and then she had lost them. He would be glad to summon her to Rome. She still had several uses. But she had lost sight of the fact that she was hired by him, on his job.

Fucking her would be fun. She might even enjoy it. Killing her would be a waste of talent in several senses. That wouldn't stop him, though. After this job, he intended to disappear. Dimitri had no illusions. If they wanted Lola dead, they would want him dead as well. His money would be disbursed, they would never trace it, and he would fall out of sight.

These clowns would never be able to track him. But Lola Montoya knew too much about him. As he watched her track Will and Melissa at the toll gate, in that car, the shiver of adrenaline had a little fear to it. If Lola could get a ghost like Will Hyde, then she could certainly also get Dimitri.

There would be lots of death in the next few days. He was unsentimental, but he was also getting older, and more tired. It would be good to leave Haroun with his blonde whores, and disappear from the face of the earth.

What would his new occupation be? Something that involved money, something portable. He idly wondered if he might deal in diamonds.

But that was speculation for another day. He would fly to Rome and finish the job. And then tie up the loose ends that other, lesser men might leave hanging.

Lola sat at the table placed neatly in the centre of her private terrace. The hotel, the Victrix Roma, was one of the best in the city. She had worked it out early, and abandoned her little car, dumping it in a car park near Balzano airport, in the Dolomites. In less than forty-five minutes from take-off, she had landed in Rome. She took a cab to Via Veneto, and indulged herself with some Gucci luggage and attractive clothes. Then she headed straight for the Victrix, where a pretty young woman with expensive suitcases would not be even slightly out of place.

There was no need for tradecraft, no need to deny herself. Will Hyde and his female would be heading for Rome. They could not fly, therefore they would come here slowly. But they would come here. Meanwhile, she would wait, in the luxury that she surrounded herself with when not working. It was good to sink into scented baths in an enormous marble tub, to work herself out in the basement gym, to eat outstanding food. She toyed with the idea of getting a man, for sex. There were plenty of soldiers around the city. She liked those, soldiers and policemen. It was good to seduce one, to drag him off. But in the end, she decided against it.

The dead girl's ring glittered on her finger. She was charged with the idea of Will Hyde. Of course, it was a fantasy; she would have to kill him, no doubt. But she wanted him to see her, to be attracted to her . . .

Maybe, Lola thought, looking out at the Colosseum. The Roman Forum, to its left, was floodlit against the dark. She had always loved this city. Its savagery soothed her. She would have done well in Rome, she thought, thousands of years ago. Her profession had thrived even then. Maybe she was wrong. Maybe, if the woman was removed, and she could blame another. What did she owe the clients? Melissa Elmet was the target.

On the table, behind her, her pager buzzed.

She pushed her dinner plate, a small helping of fragrant *spaghetti al'herbe*, to one side, a little aggravated. She had been enjoying the food, and the glass of wine, a fine Brunello, was the first she had drunk in weeks.

'Lola.'

'This is Dimitri,' he said. 'Where are you?'

She was not about to tell him. 'In Italy,' she compromised.

'I want you to go to Rome,' he said. 'They are travelling there, we think, moving south. They appear to have put some things together. They will resurface around Richard Elmet's laboratory.'

She winced. Damn it. Now Dimitri's classless goons would be crawling all over the city. Will Hyde would see them from miles away.

'I will go there and take them out,' she replied. 'You don't need anyone else.'

'Your lack of results tells me differently,' he replied.

'My men are coming in for general surveillance. You see the targets, kill them.'

She hung up, and stood steady for a second, to control the anger that seethed up in her. Dimitri Petrenko treated her with disdain. If he were less of an agent . . .

But he wasn't, he was exceptionally dangerous. She knew it. She would simply have to hope she got to Melissa before those others did.

Dimitri's plane was taxiing on the runway. He had issued his orders, and men had appeared, strung out across the city, driving in, flying in. Some were already Roman sleepers. Dimitri had hand-picked the list, the best of the Arabs and the Venezuelans, two young kids from Algeria, and one Kazakh. At his word they had fanned into the rail terminals, the bus stations, the major streets around the university. Some were in the offices of the tourism department, scanning hotels and hostels. Copying Lola, he had two analysts working with the *carabinieri*, in traffic, looking at screens until they went blind.

He was here. He would catch them.

Will lay on the narrow bed in their cabin. It was an internal room, close to the ship's boiler. There was no natural light, and the noise never stopped, but to both Melissa and himself it was the height of luxury. She had practically groaned with pleasure when she was able to step under a warm shower again.

He propped himself up one elbow. He was naked; she

too. She was asleep. He looked down at her body, her head turned to one side, red hair spilling out over the pillow. Her breasts were beautiful, the curve of her stomach exquisite, her legs shapely and toned. To look at her was to want her.

Of course, considered objectively, she didn't have the intense model beauty his ex-fiancée had possessed.

He didn't care. To a red-blooded male, she was far more attractive. Defiant and brave, strong, slender, well curved, a girl who liked her food and liked to joke and liked to argue. He never once had wanted to get away from her when sex was over. That was one difference; she was so intelligent, so much fun. She could be a friend.

But more important, perhaps, sex with her was spectacular. It wasn't her technique; several girls he'd had recently knew their way around the male body with the kind of detached skill he ascribed to a pro. Melissa was so much hotter than that. It was her responsiveness. All he had to do was run his hand lightly down her rib cage, and she would shudder and gasp. Her desire was a match for his, maybe more so. If he kissed her, her body leapt underneath him, her skin flaming, the heat of her blood easy to feel. It was so simple to ignite her. Her passion gave him such intense pleasure. When he saw her body react to him like that he could barely control himself.

And she was aroused by strength, too. That was plain to see. Their love, when he was a teenager, had been pure and a little naïve; it shattered him when she broke it off. But now she was so different, so much richer. She was a woman; she felt deeply. She had been starved of manliness, he thought. She had fought it in herself, but she was a woman who responded to a dominant male. And it was particularly intense with him, because she had never stopped loving him.

He sympathised with her torment. They had put themselves through peculiar punishments. But now, while she leapt to every motion from his hand, he revelled in what it meant to control her body and love her mind.

She was so beautiful.

He loved her a million times over. He thought of Olivia with pity and he would avenge her mercilessly, but even mourning for her could not diminish his love of Melissa; his woman, his wife. Still his wife. He wanted to get this done, to free her of all the terrors that were hunting her. More than one. Her wonderful, vital body was holistic. Will loved everything about it.

The thought of sending her into danger – extreme danger, lurking in Rome – almost made him ill. But there was simply no other way.

He loved her with a fever. It was a love for which he was prepared to die. And yet the only way to safety was to risk everything: not just his own life; hers too.

Will lowered his head and gently started to kiss the hollow of her neck, letting his teeth lightly rake her skin, his tongue trace patterns over her skin. Melissa stirred. She moved deliciously, half asleep, murmuring with pleasure. He put his hand on her. She was already aroused. Her eyes fluttered open. She gasped, and arched her back. 'Will,' she said, reaching for him, lifting herself to him.

She is my wife, he thought, with fierce pride. Love of her blazed in his chest. His lust for this girl was so deep. All the other women, the models and actresses, the pretty, bland, skinny little girls, seemed so distant now, just grubby fumbles in the dark. Sex with Melissa was profound. Already she was writhing under him. He had to struggle to control himself, so he could tease her a little. So hot, smoking hot . . .

He reached down to her and kissed her, roughly, his mouth on hers, moving over her. There was fear for her, and heartache, but not now. Nothing mattered now but her. Nothing mattered now but this. His woman. His passion.

They stumbled out on the docks at Civitavecchia. The sun beat down on the tiles. Melissa looked right, left. There were medieval ruins and an old town next to the harbour, jostling with modern structures, vans selling overpriced Coca-Cola and ices.

'Walk with me,' Will said. 'Stick close.'

'OK.' She looked up at the harbour signs. 'Are we getting the train to Termini station?'

'No,' Will said. 'We'll stick around here at first.' He lifted his callused fingers and ran them through her hair. 'I want to get you to a *farmacia*, get you some hair dye. They may have an image of us by now.'

'But we've seen nobody,' she said, worried.

'That's not how it works. They will have images from security cameras, maybe footage from the airport at Charles de Gaulle. It could take days to feed back to them, and we'd be out of the area.'

'But they will still know what we look like.'

' 'Fraid so,' Will said. He squeezed her arm. 'There are lots of them, Missy. Thousands. We might not make it. I don't want to lie to you.'

'I don't care,' she said. The Mediterranean sun was beating down on them. The tourists and street hawkers were smiling. Life was rich to Melissa. She would gladly exchange the last few days with Will, reunited, for those dreary, lonely years in Oxford, frustrated and bitter. 'I love you. I'll always love you.'

He kissed her lightly on the lips.

'You're crying,' she said wonderingly.

His gaze narrowed, despite the tears she saw brimming there.

'Idiot girl,' he growled. 'I don't cry.' He turned away from her, and Melissa saw his back stiffen; when he faced her again, his eyes were dry and cool.

'Let's go,' he said shortly.

'You don't think anyone's here?' Melissa asked. 'You said they wouldn't be expecting us by boat.'

'Take no chances,' Will murmured. He strode off purposefully along the quay, and she hurried after him.

Chapter Thirty-Four

His name was Ali al-Maktoub, and he served in the intelligence forces of Qatar. The government did not know he was here; they knew nothing of this operation. It was being run by Rashid Dagreb, the man they called Sheikh although he was not one. Rashid was a hard-liner and a secret friend to fanatics. He was also hyper-protective of the oil of the emirate.

Ali was one of Rashid's very best men. He had been given this assignment as an honour. He had prayed over it. He hated the decadent Hyde, and not just for his money. Two of Ali's brothers in arms, men he had trained with, had been personally killed by William Hyde when he was working for the British.

He had pleaded to be assigned. He had reported often and well to Dimitri Petrenko, even when his hunt had come up empty. He had been selected to be one of the hundred men assigned to this final chapter. And his vigilance had never slackened for an instant.

Ali had a soldier's attitude. It was not for him to determine tactics. There were better places to be sent than the harbour of Civitavecchia. The two *kuffir* were known to have used motorbikes and cars. Ali wanted to be in the city, walking about, scouring the parked vehicles, looking for plates. He had caught agents in Jerusalem that way, old-fashioned legwork, searching for a stationary target first to which your prey would then return.

But he had been sent to watch the boats, just in case, and he had not objected. If it was written in the book for Ali, he would find them and slay them.

He did not have photographs with him. The present lineaments of the woman Melissa and the bearded face of William Hyde were already burned into his brain. He would recognise them with his eyes shut, he thought.

His eyes scanned the crowd as they had done for the last four hours, relentlessly. He had only shifted a position a bit, here and there, a few yards at a time, just so he would not be obvious amongst the crowds. But nobody was paying any attention.

It got easier being a surveillance agent every year. People hurried and walked and minded their own business. They did not care about their neighbours, or anyone but themselves. The world had shrunk into tiny bubbles.

He looked again, at the packed crowd descending from the German cruise ship. Many of the passengers were a little drunk. Their white skin had been reddened with sunburn. They could not tan, they looked like lobsters.

He disliked these northern Europeans and their aversion to sun. Ali had served missions in their countries, and shivered for weeks.

Then he saw them.

The moment was almost like orgasm, like taking a woman. The flood of adrenaline, the unstoppable gasp of surprise. Wild elation ripped through him. It was the female academic with her new red hair. She was tanned now, lithe, a beauty, quite different. Yet Ali had seen the photographs, and he recognised her.

They were walking along the quayside, not heading for the train station. Interesting. He was not directing her straight to Rome. Maybe they had other business. Maybe Dimitri was wrong.

He glanced around. If there were agents here, or police, he could see few of them. He reached into the pocket of his backpack and felt carefully for his gun. As he started to walk towards them, his fingers closed over the cold metal.

Will was conscious of Melissa by his side. None of the sadness he felt hung over her. She was looking around, glad to stretch her legs, trusting him totally, trusting wherever he might take her . . .

He leaned to one side, to kiss her, his fingers on her back. Already he wanted her again. When it came to this woman he was insatiable. She made him feel like he was nineteen years old again, a teenager with infinite stamina and greed for sensation . . .

He straightened up carefully, making sure his eyes were straight ahead.

'When I say run, run,' he said to her quietly. 'Not yet, baby. Just keep walking . . .'

He had seen him, in his peripheral vision, out of the corner of his eye, by chance. The man was following them. No question. He was good, but Will was too highly trained. The agent was too deliberate in his steps. And he was staring.

Melissa tried to obey, to walk casually, but she had stiffened. Will saw it. The guy would see it. . . .

She was scared, and her breath was coming raggedly. Casually he moved behind her, his body shielding her from the guy's line of vision.

'Oh!' Melissa cried. He had shoved her down to the tarmac, to her knees, violently. There was a scream and yelling from the crowd. A bullet had whistled over her head, missing her by inches. A woman moaned in pain; her arm was hit, she was bleeding . . .

A tourist was screaming now. Lots of them were screaming. Will had hit the deck and already his hand was by his sock and the gun was withdrawn. It was loaded. He cocked it and lifted himself to one knee. The guy was there, aiming. Will's reflexes were lightning. He fired, fired straight at the head.

It split, like a watermelon. Blood gushed everywhere and the corpse fell to the ground. Will hooked his hands under Melissa's arms. 'Run!' he shouted at her. 'Run!'

He started to pound the pavement. The gun was in his

hand. The crowd, hysterical, scattered to let him pass. She was with him, keeping up with him. There were whistles, the sounds of *carabinieri*, now, screaming and shouting. Will turned left into Via Luigi Cadorna, a narrow street overhung with pink-washed stucco buildings. People stared, moved aside. He heard Melissa's footsteps, right behind him. She was fast, a sprinter. He turned right into Piazza Fratti. It was packed, full of shoppers. He slowed instantly, a hand on Melissa's upper arm. She moved to be with him. There were stalls here, a market. He thanked God. He walked swiftly between them, heading right, left. He was lost in the market now. A slight turn of his head saw blue-uniformed policemen come to the end of Via Luigi Cadorna, and now he walked straight ahead, down another alley, turned left. They were in a street, Regina Elena. There was a pharmacy at one end. He took Melissa inside, casually. She pressed close to him. He bought some razors and hair dye, sunglasses and a hat.

As he was paying, Italian police ran past on the road outside. He left quickly and doubled back. There was a cab coming down the street. Will hailed it.

'Terme di Traiano,' he said, and added lightly to Melissa, 'they have some terrific Roman baths right here,' in a good Australian accent.

She nodded, not daring to speak.

The ruins were pleasant, but deserted. Melissa tried to compose herself. But she had not yet felt that she had been that close to death. Will had moved so fast, as fast as a cat pouncing. And his shot, on the moving target, was perfect. She had seen a man die not eight yards away from her.

It was impossible to look at Will the same way. Of course she knew he'd been an agent, but that was all theory. Now she saw what it really meant. A young man's head, split open, his shirt drenched with black blood, the sound of screaming.

And Will had done it in a second.

She knew the man was pointing a gun at her. Had actually shot at her, would have killed them. But that didn't change the brutality of his own death. Will had aimed with practised ease. He took the guy out, and saved her life.

'Come round the back here,' Will said quietly. She followed him into a scrubby coppice. There was the sound of water, a stream running.

'You've been here before?'

'Couple of times. But these were the baths, remember. There's often a natural water source or an aqueduct when you see that name. Come down here.' He pulled her down to the banks of the water. 'Lie on your back. Get your hair wet.'

She did as he said, feeling sick, dizzy. Will ripped open the packet of dye, mixed it expertly and applied it to her head.

'We'll wait for it to set,' he told her. Then he leaned down in the stream, splashing his own face, took one of the packet of razors and started to shave. 'They're looking for a redhead and a guy with a beard. Now you're a blonde and I'm clean-shaven. It won't slow them down, but it will put off the Italian police.'

Melissa watched him, the razor hugging his cheek.

'You look better clean-shaven.'

He smiled, then held her eyes. 'I'm sorry you had to see that man die, Missy. I had to do it.'

'I know.'

'And I may have to do it again. In Rome.'

She nodded. He glanced at his watch; he was keeping track of the time. God, it seemed so absurd. Sitting out here, in a dusty little Italian copse of trees, by some Roman ruins, dyeing her hair blond. Suddenly, passionately, she wanted to solve the mystery. She hated these people for what they were doing to her, doing to Will. She hated them because the young kid was dead. She hated them because he'd tried to kill her.

'I want this to be over, Will,' she said quietly. 'I'm tired, tired of all of it.'

He finished with the razor and came and sat beside her.

'Only you can end it, Missy, I'm sure of that. You have to think. They wanted you dead because they thought your father had told you.'

'But he didn't.'

Will looked at her. 'Maybe he did, though. Maybe that's why they came for you. Maybe that's why they're chasing us so hard. What if Richard did try to tell you what he'd found out?'

427

She clasped his hand. 'You think he did?'

'Makes sense, doesn't it? They fear you because they know he tried to tell you.'

Will sprang to his feet and paced about in the trees like a caged leopard, excited, looking at her, thinking aloud. 'There's no point in us going to the university. Not just because they'll be expecting us there – they'll have agents everywhere. No, because they will already have gone through his rooms and his papers. I'll bet most of his colleagues in the faculty have died over the last summer, one thing or another, a car crash here, a heart attack there.'

'He worked alone,' Melissa said. 'He hated the idea of people being able to steal credit for his ideas.'

'Just as well for them.' Will stood over her, his eyes boring into hers. 'Were they right, Melissa? Did he reach out to you? Try and think. Try!'

'We spoke, two months before he died, but it wasn't important,' Melissa said.

'I'm betting it was.' Will nodded. 'Think. Hard. Cast your mind back. Try to remember every detail of the conversation, no matter how trivial. Any kind of remark, even about the weather.'

'OK,' Melissa said. The excitement was communicated to her. 'OK. Well . . . he did sound edgy.'

'Good. Go on.'

'He was always a little short on the phone. Conversation wasn't his big skill. But I guess he did seem upset.' She drew in her breath sharply. 'He was at the airport – he said he wanted to ring from a payphone. That they were easier.'

'And not bugged,' Will pointed out. 'Hard for ambient mikes to pick up the conversation there, too. Too much background noise. What did he talk about?'

'He said work was going very well. He hoped to be home soon. He said things were going to be different, and we could try to start over. I yessed him to death.' Her eyes filled with tears. 'He was trying to say sorry and I brushed him off.'

'You didn't do anything wrong. Go on, anything you can remember.'

Melissa shut her eyes, and a tear rolled down her cheek. Her poor father. She still loved him, after all. She reached back into her mind, groping for the memory of his voice . . .

'Will!' Her eyes flashed open. 'He said – he said he wanted to show me where he met my mother. He told me to remember that. It was like he was making a point of it. I thought he was referring to us – you and me. Obliquely. But maybe he was trying to tell me something.'

Will grinned, then, a wide, open grin. 'And where exactly did he meet your mother?'

'It was here,' she said. 'Rome. All Saints' Church, it's called. It's one of the only Protestant churches in town.'

'I know it,' he said. 'Heart of the city. Via del Babuino.'

'And he said he'd like to introduce me to Father Gregory.'

'A Catholic?'

She shook her head. 'An Anglican vicar. Lives in the rectory there.'

Will checked his watch. 'Wash your hair out, comb it through.'

She did; the sun was now sinking over the warm stone of the ruins.

'We're going to walk to the entrance and get the bus back to town. Then we get a cab. I will have the cab take us to the Vatican. From there, we walk. When the cab approaches town, turn your head to me, kiss me.'

'I can do that.'

'We don't want to show up on their cameras,' Will said.

Dimitri was thrilled. The boy, Ali, had sent a signal to his pager, as requested, before he did anything else. They had killed him – it was all over the TV. Will Hyde had a gun, and that was dangerous, but only to be expected. More important was that it proved him right. This was no random escape. They were coming here, coming to her father's quarters. Walking straight into the trap.

Of course, he received information, but he had dispensed some too. Hyde now knew they were waiting for him. But he had almost certainly known that before. Dimitri shivered with pleasure at the sheer skill of his opponent.

He ordered his men to fan out. They would get him.

Every street and house in a four-street radius of the university was now being watched.

His thoughts drifted to Lola, the female. He had seen her yesterday, briefed her on the final stage of this operation. She was getting older now, maybe twenty-eight. That perhaps explained her lack of success on this mission. Even legendary operatives lost their touch, over time.

But as a woman, just considered as that, she was superbly enticing.

He had had to be careful, the way he looked at her: long legs, voluptuous, curvy breasts, her waist vanishingly small. She had a figure from the nineteen forties. Her ass was round, it jutted out beautifully, and firm from all her running. Like any good marksman, she had grace. And the icy fire of a brutal, remorseless assassin.

He thought about her strangling the woman in New York. The idea got him hard. He couldn't wait to fuck her. He couldn't wait to see that same terror in her eyes she'd put into the eyes of so many targets.

Haroun the Arab had delivered him his money, and Dimitri was quite prepared to ship the hot little bitch back to him, alive, as requested. She would be lengthily raped, then killed. Dimitri was still furious at how her sloppiness had nearly cost him his reputation. Instead, she would contribute to its glory. This would be his last job. He would retire known as the man who had tamed Lola Montoya, fucked her and killed her, for indiscipline.

In his world, that would make him a legend. And the best thing was, she suspected nothing.

*

Lola Montoya walked through the streets of Rome. She wore a black dress and a headscarf, like a devout Catholic on her way to church. She had briefly considered dressing up as a nun, complete with sunglasses; there were enough of them in this town, crawling with clerics and holy rollers. She hated belief in God. So credulous. God had not saved anyone from her, and plenty of them had asked him to.

But an attractive nun would be too conspicuous. She wanted to blend in, especially now.

It was something that Dimitri had said to her, in passing, when discussing the dragnet around Professor Elmet's rooms. That Will Hyde might not have a beard any more.

How did he know Hyde had a beard?

If they had access to CCTV from the road network, the entire road network, they would have found him long before Lola had. But they had only picked him up, apparently independently, after she accessed the still images from her café in La Murette.

Dimitri had seen what Lola saw.

He knew. Somehow he knew. And that meant he knew she had not reported it.

She was angry with herself for underestimating him. He was a major world player. Which was why they had selected him for the job. He was fearless and cruel. She had studied his files. He had begun as a torturer in the dark rooms under Red Square in Moscow. A total lack of

432

empathy and a keen intelligence. She shared both traits. In her world, they were common.

Of course, he had not trusted her. He had had her followed. And she had made an elementary mistake. Focusing solely on the quarry.

There was only one punishment for disobeying a man like Dimitri in a major operation, and it was death. Lola knew that. She also knew the way he had looked at her. He intended to fuck her. She knew his file; he had raped countless women.

Sex and death, in their worlds, often coincided. The kill could be arousing. He wanted to rape her. She understood the psychology, the domination of the assassin. To take the best female operative in the world, and fuck her . . . he would be a legend among his peers.

She moved slowly towards his hotel. The men were watching for Melissa and William Hyde; they would not concentrate on her, another Italian housewife in a scarf. This assignment was not something she relished. But it had to be endured. She was an agent, when all was said and done. If she had to surrender her body . . . it was only a body.

The knock on the door annoyed him. Fucking chamber maids. Why didn't they understand a 'Do Not Disturb' sign?

'*No, grazie*,' he half shouted.

Reports were coming in from every side. Couples spotted all over the city. Of course, he wanted to say, it's a fucking city. They had to find the right two. They had to be able to use their judgement.

There was a rattle. He hissed in annoyance. You couldn't even kill a maid; they were too precious, too easily noted and missed by their colleagues. He hurriedly slid his gun under the bed. The stupid bitch was using her master key to come in.

The door opened. Dimitri prepared to bawl her out in perfect Italian. But it was not the maid. It was Lola. She held a small metal object, a sort of moulded screwdriver. He gathered she had picked the lock with it. Impressive. Her skills were quite real.

'Shut the door,' he said.

She was luscious. The sight of her dressed so demurely stirred him. There was such a contrast between the headscarf and below-knees skirt, and the luscious body underneath. Lola Montoya had ample breasts, twinned with that gorgeous full Hispanic ass that was high and tight with exercise. He supposed it was Hispanic. He didn't know where she was from. Her hips were narrow, but he did not mind that. If her female hormones had been fully balanced she would not be such an effective killer.

Lola shut the door. Then she raised her hands to her head, unknotting the scarf. This lifted the line of her breasts, jutting them forward at him. She took the scarf in one hand and laid it gently over the back of the couch.

'Dimitri,' she said softly.

He licked his lips. Control, control, he told himself. His

thoughts about Lola Montoya had run in one direction recently. It would not do to be aroused, not yet. She was needed for the hunt before he acted.

'Have you come to report in?' he asked brusquely.

'I have a confession,' she said, shrugging. She unbuttoned the first button on her long shirt dress. 'My hunt required total secrecy. I could not trust the junior agents around you – they come from multiple sources. They might have prevented me doing my job for you. I found William Hyde and Melissa Elmet in traffic, on camera. I kept it to myself. I tracked them. They should have been dead by now.'

He looked at her, his eyes like flint. 'You are meant to report to me.'

'My job was to complete my assignment.'

'They aren't dead.'

'No. the assignment is still open. I will complete it.' She undid another button. 'I always do. That's why you hired me.'

He could not lift his eyes from her dress. 'What are you doing?'

'I want to mitigate your anger,' she said softly. 'I know you knew about the images. And Dimitri, I have been on this hunt for weeks, without distractions. I need a distraction.'

She slipped the shirt dress from her shoulders. They were lightly tanned, olive-toned. Her skin was smooth and slippery with baby oil.

'I would never have betrayed you,' she said humbly. 'I

just wanted a little time to get them. You know how it is when you have to work with a crowd.'

Of course. Any one of them knew. The potential for errors was enormous. A good assassin was many things. Team player was not one of them.

He didn't care. His orders had been clear.

It was nice to watch her supplicate him, though. He enjoyed how her skin glistened. He felt himself harden. It had been weeks since he'd had a woman.

'You want to sleep with me?'

'To relax you, yes. I want a man,' she said shamelessly. 'And it needs to be one of us. I don't touch civilians.' He laughed, and her eyes widened. 'What?'

'You think I would fall for that, Lola? My record is better than yours.' She stiffened. He supposed, objectively, there was not much in it. 'Why would I let a player like you come near me with so much as a lace thong next to your body? I know what you can do.'

'And it excites you,' she said. 'Doesn't it?'

The dress was off her now. Maddening little tease. It slithered to the floor, pooling around her legs. Under her buttoned-up outfit she wore virtually nothing, expensive-looking scraps of lace that did little to conceal her figure. Her hair was glossy, her face open and pretty. If he did not know what she was . . .

Screw that. Even knowing what she was, he wanted her. Dimitri clenched his fists.

'You can't really be afraid,' she said, pouting. 'I'm almost nude. You're dressed. You have your gun.' She turned on one heel, displaying herself for him. There was nothing on her tight, curvy little ass except a G-string. 'See?' she asked, lifting her body a little, rising up on her toes. 'Nowhere to hide a knife.'

His throat was dry. She was indeed completely defenceless. He was clothed, his gun in easy reach. If he wanted to take her now, rape her, he could do it easily.

But she was aroused. He could see that clearly through the pale pink lace of her bra. Better to have her hot and open, at least the first time. No need to take what she was freely offering.

'Take those off,' he said shortly.

She immediately undid the bra and pulled it off, then slipped out of the panties. He smiled, from the sheer pleasure of her body. She was stunning. It wasn't a model's willowy, sexless look. She was shaped like a porn star, narrow-waisted with short legs and outrageous curves, but with her young skin toned and tanned, not tired out from drugs and alcohol.

He beckoned. She came over and stood next to him, close to him. The contrast between her nudity and his being fully clothed was delicious. She was so much in his power. Her breathing was shallow, she was turned on. Dimitri ran his hands down her back, over her ass, squeezing it. She trembled, moaning a little . . .

That was it; he was not made of iron. He ripped at his own clothes, pulling them off, roughly. Buttons flew from his shirt. He kicked off his trousers and pants. She was there, next to him, tiny against his chest, his strong arms.

Her hands snaked around his back, and she came in close. Dimtri was gripped with lust. He shoved her knees wider apart and took her. She gasped in pleasure, moving with him. He took his hands up, finally relaxing, and let them brush against her throat, a clear warning: she had no weapons, and a man could kill a woman quite easily, even a weak man, if she were unarmed. And Dimitri was not weak.

But she was not fighting. She was riding him. Her head was back, exposing her neck, her eyes were shut. She ground on him; she felt so good. Dimitri surged inside her, wanting to laugh out loud. He started to speak to her, in his native Karelian Russian dialect, so she could not understand, moving, thrusting against her, caressing her as she shuddered against him.

'Minx,' he muttered. 'Vixen. You love it, don't you? Insatiable little slut. You won't get off so easy. Next time you will be taken, like it or not.' He hardened inside her; she was incredible. 'Next time,' he murmured, 'and then I will sell you to Haroun, he will enjoy you too. Did you think you could escape me by taking your clothes off? You went solo. And you answer to me, Dimitri Petrenko.' He thrust against her. 'You move well, though . . . ahh . . . ahh . . . very well, damn you . . .'

He enjoyed her. Her nails were sharp now, clawing at his chest. She was bucking wildly. He held her still, controlling her, not letting her pull back an inch from the sensation. Her hair was plastered around her face, her gorgeous body drenched in sweat. She was close now, writing on him, her palms on his back, fingers splayed so those long nails did not catch him. He plunged into her, again, and again.

Lola suddenly stiffened and held very tense. He increased his pace, holding her there. She arched her spine, gave a muffled, sobbing groan of pleasure, and he felt her, shaking, spasming around him.

He gripped her tight. Her surrender had turned him on to the point of mania. Now she was done, but he wasn't. There was nowhere for her to go. He plunged against her. It felt good. Her arousal was subsiding but he was still moving. He would not allow her to draw back. If she tried to resist she would find herself caught.

What could she do? He had her in his grip. He was ten, fifteen times stronger than her. She was ruined as an operative now, he thought, ruined; he could not work with her, he would only see her as this hot, sexy little female. He would cuff her, when he was through, and administer a sedative, and ship her out to Nadrah on the Sultan's jet. There were other good men that could make the kill on Will Hyde. She thought she was so necessary, but she was nothing, good for a lay, good to be ploughed . . .

She was back now, moving hard against him, relaxing him. He knew women could be multiply orgasmic. A hot little bitch like this one definitely so. She was clutching at him, helplessly. Hard. He winced a little, but kept pounding. Her nails were long. He liked to feel her desperation; the pain was nothing. They raked down his back, digging in, digging in – ah, fuck, he thought, and kept driving her. Hot little slut, she had cut his skin, her talons were so sharp they had cut his skin . . .

He slowed a second. He needed to catch his breath. The exertion of fucking her must be taking it out of him. His chest felt tight . . .

She pushed back slightly as he gasped. He looked into her face, bewildered. The pretty brown eyes were sharp.

'I am no man's plaything,' she said.

It took him a second to realise she had spoken in Karelian. Her accent was that of a native. Now, at last, he knew part of the story of Lola Montoya.

'My true name is Olga,' she said.

Dimitri bucked. There was pain now and it was harder to breathe, but worse was the terror, because she had told him her true name, which meant she thought he was about to die. She had administered a poison, that was clear . . . He opened his mouth to bargain, but nothing came out, chokes now, and splutters . . .

'You were good,' she said dispassionately, sliding off him. 'But you let me get close. Fingernails.' She held them up in front of him. 'Cyanide. On the tips. About ten seconds.'

Dimitri gasped. He did not want to die. He had never believed in God. He was confident there was nothing out there. But now, now he was not sure. He was suddenly very afraid. Mostly he was gasping for air. Lola – Olga – had walked to the bathroom, stark naked, and came out again with his nail scissors. She was carefully trimming her nails. His vision of her shook, and blurred. His heart stopped for a beat, then lumbered again. There was no antidote. He tried, half blankly, a prayer. A vague thought, a request for forgiveness. He was sorry. He stumbled forward and fell down. Everything was slowed. He looked at the patterned carpet underneath him; the fibres were large now, close to his eyes, shimmering . . .

The pain swept over him. He died.

Chapter Thirty-Five

The rectory house was set aside, off Via del Babuino. The church, so unusual, was physically unimpressive; an attractive Victorian building, it drowned in the sea of exquisite Renaissance and Baroque architecture that surrounded it.

She liked it. It was anonymous. Will checked out the street while Melissa walked in to the reception. Nobody was following them. They were not here, they were waiting for him around the university. She rang the bell mounted on a little shelf, and when the receptionist appeared, announced that she was here to see Father Gregory.

Will stood just behind her.

'I'll see if he's available,' the woman said. Melissa stood there, her heart thudding, her palms sweaty with adrenaline. How strange it felt to meet a middle-aged woman with an ordinary English accent. She hadn't heard one of those since she got off the Eurostar, an age ago now. She tried to be still, although it felt as though her whole life was suspended in aspic. The woman had turned aside, and was speaking into a telephone.

'Who wants him, please?' She turned back and spoke brightly.

Melissa looked at Will. He shrugged.

'This is Melissa Elmet,' he said. 'Tell him it's Professor Richard Elmet's daughter.'

Melissa tensed. Was he mad? Was he going to give them away now? He put his hand on her shoulder, steadying her. His dark eyes held hers.

This was her father's friend; if he couldn't help them, they were probably doomed anyway. It didn't matter if they knew. It was the end.

The receptionist nodded pleasantly and repeated the name down the phone. She didn't tense; clearly she had not recognised it. Melissa breathed out, just a little. Maybe it wasn't always going to be like this. Not everybody in the world was a killer, or a thug, or a spy. Some people were just going about their lives.

The older woman turned to face them. 'He's just coming down. Take a seat – we've got some magazines.'

Melissa sat down on the couch. Some magazines . . . She suppressed a desire to laugh out loud, hysterically. It was just like the dentist's waiting room, except she was here in sweaty Rome, on the run for her life, next to Will Hyde, who had killed a man right in front of her.

Will sat next to her. Melissa tried not to react. What was wrong with her, what had got into her? He made her feel so alive, so much a woman. His slightest touch, now, and she was aching. It was like waking from the dead.

She had fantasised and dreamed, against her will, of his touch, but he had taken her out of herself, away from herself, and it was better than anything she could have dreamed of. Frightening, almost. What he made her feel. Now she needed to be near him the same way she needed sunlight.

She reached out her hand. Quietly he threaded his fingers through hers, squeezed tight.

He was such a man. She had never known another like him. He would die for her, and kill for her, too. No wonder she was so weak around him.

Melissa never wanted to let Will go. She was suddenly overwhelmed with the desire to bear his child. They were married, still, at least religiously, and now that seemed enormously important to her. She had never had it overturned. But it didn't matter, did it? She could not bring a child into danger.

She stared at the magazine, the *Economist*, without reading it.

'Hello . . . ?'

Melissa looked up to see an older man, in a grey jumper and olive-green corduroy slacks, looking down at her. He wore a black shirt and a clerical collar. A traditionalist, then, she thought. The kind of vicar her father would have preferred.

'Are you Sir Richard's daughter?'

She had stopped thinking of herself that way many years ago. She became aware of Will Hyde, beside her. Will, whose heart she had broken. Because of her father.

Melissa drew back her shoulders.

'Yes, I am,' she said clearly, proudly. She looked at Will, defiant. Her father had not been a good man in many ways, but there was that thread between them still. He was dead, and she would not deny him.

'I'm Father Gregory,' the vicar said. 'And this must be William.'

Melissa shrank back; Will started. But then he smiled. The vicar was not stupid.

'Yes, Father,' he said. 'How do you do?'

Father Gregory's gaze flitted from one to the other.

'A little better than you, I imagine,' he said. 'Come upstairs, come upstairs.'

The rector's rooms were quite lavish, for an expensive area of central Rome; it was a large, lateral apartment with high ceilings and shuttered windows. Melissa felt a tug of homesickness. Her own messy rooms in Oxford, back in the mists of time, her former life, came flooding back to her.

'Will you have a pot of tea?' Father Gregory said. 'Sit down, do, both of you.'

'Father,' Will said. 'I'm going to get to the point.'

The vicar lowered himself into a wing chair and regarded them steadily. 'Yes, young man.'

'Melissa is my wife,' Will said.

She thrilled to hear him say it. It was the first time he had ever spoken about her like that. She blushed from pure happiness.

'It was against Sir Richard's wish, and he was distant from Melissa for some time.'

'I know that,' Father Gregory said quietly.

'There are people – lots of people – trying to kill Melissa and me. Principally because they fear that Sir Richard discovered something, and passed that information on to his daughter.'

Melissa spoke up. 'He called from the airport, Father. He mentioned you.' She looked the priest in the face. 'My father was not a religious man, so I wondered what it was that linked him to you.'

The vicar said nothing. He got up, silently from his chair, and walked across the living room to the bookcase mounted against the wall. He pulled at it, and it came away from the wall. Behind it, there was a small safe.

'This is a relic from the war years,' Father Gregory said. 'A Catholic priest used to have these rooms. He built a safe to hide the consecrated Eucharists for the Catholic Mass from the Nazis. We keep other valuables here.'

He reached inside, and drew out a black metal tablet and a small file of papers. There was an envelope on top of the file. He passed them across to Melissa, and placed his hands over hers.

'You must forgive him, you know,' he said. 'He changed, towards the end. He was a believer. And he did love you, young lady. Very much.'

Melissa looked down. The white envelope had her name on it, written in her father's familiar scrawl.

Miss M. Elmet

She had to smile. Dad. Even in fear for his life, her father could not omit the formalities.

Will was standing by the priest's desk. Without asking, he had picked up his phone and dialled. It was a land line, safer than any mobile. Now he was speaking intently, in a language Melissa did not even recognise.

'Israeli,' the vicar said, in answer to her expression. 'Not so far removed from ancient Hebrew.'

'I'm sorry . . . he needs to do this . . .'

'No need to apologise,' he replied. 'I met your father. I believe you.'

Will hung up and came and sat next to her. Her hands were trembling. What she held in them were the last remnants of her father.

'Thank you,' he said to Father Gregory. 'You took a considerable risk. We will leave before we attract unwelcome attention.'

'Of course,' the older man said, and then, as though it were being wrenched from him, 'will you tell me what it is, Mr Hyde?'

'No.'

Melissa looked at him.

'We know, and we have many assassins on our tail. Once it's out, you'll understand.' Will leaned forward and spoke directly to the vicar. 'Father Gregory, tell nobody of this. Not ever. Their revenge might be very great.'

'I understand,' he said. He reached out and laid his hands on Melissa's head, murmuring something under his breath.

'What are you doing?' Will demanded.

'Praying,' the vicar replied calmly. 'You both need it.'

Melissa stayed close to Will on the street. He walked with her, leading her up to the Piazza di Spagna. Once they arrived there, he stopped.

'There's a guy about to get here. His name is Ari. He's an old friend of mine.'

'Ari,' she repeated.

'He works for Mossad. He's stationed in Rome and armed to the teeth.'

'OK.'

'He's going to take you on a bus from here to the Vatican Museums. It will be full of pickpockets; keep your hands on your stuff at all times.'

Melissa nodded, full of fear.

'Ari will take you to a plane, Missy, and straight into Tel Aviv. He knows what you have. You will scan the documents, put them on the internet.'

'I'm not technical,' Melissa whispered.

'Don't get fancy. Put them on YouTube, film them with a video camera, upload the pages, put them on Flickr, put them on Google. Just put them every-where. Email photos of the pages to the BBC and the *New York Times*. Keep going. Don't stop to analyse. Put it all out there. Everywhere and anywhere. Send it to your damn science department at Oxford. He was one of them.'

'I understand,' she said. She wanted to cry. Scrap that

– she *was* crying. Tears were flooding down her face. 'I'll get it out. And the cell?'

'Give the solar cell to Ari. Nobody will be more motivated to publish this than the Israeli government will. Not even Her Majesty's Government.'

'All right,' Melissa said. She could not help herself. She stumbled against him. 'Will,' she said. She knew she was begging. 'Will, don't leave me . . . don't . . .'

He took her face in both his hands, and kissed her and kissed her, again and again. She lifted herself to him, in love with him, mad in love.

'I only love you,' he said. 'But they killed Olivia. And I owe her, Missy. I owe her revenge.'

She nodded, her eyes full of tears, and brushed them away with the back of her hand.

'I don't want you to leave.' She grabbed his hand and kissed it, desperately. 'I love you, Will. You have no idea how much.'

'There is no peace, no hope for us,' he said, 'unless I kill the one who orchestrated this.'

'But all the other men . . .'

'They know little; only fragments. Bad operational discipline to keep them informed of the whole, you see. Only one man will have access to everything. He has to die. And the woman who killed Olivia, too. Her name is Lola Montoya, and I know her work. If I let her live, she will never stop coming.'

Melissa shuddered, and breathed in deeply. Her eyes were red, but she blinked the tears away. He might be shot;

probably would be shot. And she would not let the last image he saw of her be of some pathetic, weeping female.

'You're a brave man, Will Hyde,' she said. 'You saved my life. You're my husband. I love you. Always have, always will. I let you go before because I was afraid. I can do this,' she said. 'I don't want to be afraid any more.'

'My Melissa,' he said. 'I came across the world to claim you. Don't think I'm going to let you go now.'

He reached to her, and his lips touched on hers, and she was on fire. She moved to him, her hands circling his neck . . .

'Hey,' came a voice.

Melissa pulled back. It was a clean-shaven young man in a preppy American outfit. He nodded at Will. 'Melissa? I'm Ari.'

She collected herself. 'Hi, Ari.'

Will looked at her, like he didn't want her to leave, and her heart solidified in ice, and cracked open, raw, like a glacier.

She grabbed his hand, and spoke low and urgently.

'They didn't just kill Olivia,' she said. 'They killed my father. They killed Fraser. They killed Moira Dunwoody, David Fell and Ellen Jospin. And they tried to kill you. I'm going to go and put this stuff everywhere. We're going to make their nightmares come true. After it's out there, they can just watch their backs.'

Will kissed her lightly. 'That's my girl,' he said.

She gestured to the bland-looking young man. 'Come on,' she said.

'Sure,' he answered, falling in beside her. And Melissa walked away from Will, as fast as she could, keeping her heart steady so she did not cry. Maybe this feeling was what it was like to walk in his world. For her father's handwriting was on the envelope, and it called to her.

He had wanted the world to know, and she would see that it did.

Will Hyde moved lightly through the streets, in a random fashion, ducking through alleys and in and out of buildings. He zig-zagged, he played with the city. But he got closer, and closer. Melissa, his love, was gone. And now he was hunting.

Professor Elmet's house was in Via Calandrelli, and they would be there, in all those streets around there, looking for him. He went in from the rear, slicing the city behind them, until he hit Via Ugo Bassi, far behind their targeting zone, well back from where he would have placed his hindmost man. Lola's runner was here, somewhere. Lola was here. He moved forward, slowly, a baseball cap and sunglasses on, a disposable camera hung round his neck. She was here. He could sense it. He scanned the windows of the hotels and *pensioni*, looking for her, but he knew it was futile.

She was on the ground, moving through the streets, like him. His intuition told him so. There was nothing else now, just her and him.

It was time.

Chapter Thirty-Six

The American University in Rome was surrounded by trees, a lush green in the summer. It was a striking building in the Italianate style, red at the bottom, yellow at the top. It was modern, and surrounded by students. Some of them would be asassins.

Will Hyde looked around him, almost casually, and kept walking. And then he saw her.

She was far back from the kill zone. Hovering around the edges. She wore a backpack, maybe crammed with explosives or grenades, a light summer coat, Bermuda shorts, sandals, a T-shirt. She could pass for twenty-five, for a graduate student. She was at least four blocks back from where he would have placed his men.

Clever girl, he thought, clever girl. Just not clever enough.

Where was the man? he wondered. Where was her runner? He had to kill him.

Will walked on casually, trying to angle his body behind a tree. Possibly he had hesitated for a second. Her peripheral vision caught him; she was exceptional, he thought. She turned, and he saw a pair of brown eyes looking at him.

She was a remarkably beautiful woman. His gaze flickered for a second over the hourglass of her body.

She stretched, languid, like a cat. And smiled.

Will reached to the side of his trousers, his hand resting on his gun. But she was not moving to shoot. He saw her looking around him, searching for Melissa.

He walked forwards, towards her, keeping an eye on the overhead cover. He smiled back.

Lola took a moment to adjust, but only a moment. He was here. It was a shock to see Will Hyde. He was not merely a target. He was one of her kind. And he had showed up behind her, in the hunting position.

The woman was not with him.

Maybe she was dead, and he had come for revenge. She hoped not. Melissa Elmet should be her kill.

She smiled back at Will. It had taken far longer than any other target she had ever been assigned to. He was marvellous prey, really. She would almost miss this job. It was going to take her reputation up to legendary heights. Will Hyde of MI6. Dimitri Petrenko. No assassin had ever had such a double bill, at least not in the past twenty years. And of course, she was a female.

He was armed. Highly dangerous. A legendary shot, better than her. Lola decided to let him get close, as close as Dimitri. She had more than just sharpened fingernails dipped in cyanide; they were now flushed down the lavatory of the dead man's hotel room. She was rather proud of her inventiveness; she would try that again. Dimitri's weaknesses were lust and vanity. Will Hyde was also lustful. And he had another, worse, weakness.

He was a good boy. Chivalrous, she thought with a little contempt. He had risked his fortune and his life for that dull British woman. The most he would try to do to Lola would be to capture her and put her in jail.

She waited for him, turning to one side, casually slipping off Olivia Wharton's ring and putting it in her pocket. His hand was resting near his gun. He was so handsome, she thought, clean-shaven again, his face tanned from life on the run. Where was the girl? Back in some bedsit, sleeping in a car, cowering in a hotel? She was the major kill. It would amuse Lola no end to take care of both this guy's women.

Fucking Dimitri had been good, but this man, this Englishman . . . he was on another level again.

She didn't know if she should kill him. If he could be turned to go with her, it might be very enjoyable. The woman, Melissa, was her original target. Lola could deliver Melissa, and disappear to Brazil with Will Hyde. There was nothing for him in America. He was too good, as well, to go back to being a banker. Perhaps they could mount some actions together . . .

If he was willing. Lola straightened her body as he reached her. She wanted him to find her attractive. His eyes swept over her, assessingly. She thought he liked what he saw. And why not? She was beautiful, she knew she was beautiful.

'I'm Will Hyde,' he said.

'Lola Montoya.'

Hyde gestured, slightly, with his head, for her to walk back the way he had come, out of the hunt zone, away from Dimitri's watchers. She came with him, walking close, next to him.

'What's your real name?' he asked conversationally.

She smiled. 'You don't want to know, do you?'

Of course not; knowing her real name could only be a prelude to his death. He would know that. He would trust her a little more for not revealing it.

'You are exceptionally good,' he said. 'I know some of your work.'

Lola tossed her hair. This compliment pleased her. He was worth being praised by.

'You know very little. Most of my kills are not seen. That's my price.'

'We evaded you.'

'Only so far.' She glanced around again, checking his perimeter. 'Where is your protectee?'

'Not here.'

'Do you love her?' Lola asked. She wanted to know this. It mattered.

Will shrugged. 'I'm fond of her.'

'That's a mistake,' Lola said. 'There's no peace with civilians. The best of us never get attached to them.'

'It is simpler without complications,' Will agreed. They

had walked past the hospital now, and were in the modern outskirts of the city: large, square apartment blocks, the wide road, Via Quirino Majorana. 'Who hired you for this?'

'Don't be stupid.'

He inclined his head. 'Then who is your runner?'

She decided to tell him. 'Dimitri Petrenko.' She wanted him to know, when it came out, her victory. What was the point of glory if none of your peers could appreciate it?

'I am going to kill him,' Will Hyde said, in flat earnest.

'You can try.' She turned and looked up at him. 'He tried to run me in ways I don't like. I always work alone. It's what I'm good at.' She lowered her eyelids slightly, like it was difficult to talk. 'He killed your fiancée, back in New York.'

Hyde stiffened; she saw his fingers clench.

'Why do that?' he asked. 'He knows she has no connection to the solar cell. She was just another girl.'

'To show you that if you continue to oppose his clients, there will be punishment.' Lola didn't try for sympathy or shock; he would never buy that. 'I wouldn't have killed her. Never take out more than you have to. It's indulgent, it's sloppy.'

'You're an interesting woman,' he said. They had come up to a bus stop. The Roman air shimmered and danced, rippling from the heat. It was dusty on the street, and there was a bench. Will gestured, inviting her to sit.

She did, moving close to him. She enjoyed it.

'When I was thirteen, I was living on the borders of Finland and Russia,' she said, looking straight ahead. 'My father died at work, factory accident. My mother was a drunk. She sold me to some men. I was trafficked to a brothel in Serbia.'

'I'm sorry,' Will said quietly.

'It taught me patience. I spent a year there, on my back, looking for weapons, planning, studying escape routes. In the end I got out; I killed two men. Then I trained a bit. I came back for the rest. I picked them off, one by one.' She straightened. 'I killed the other girls, too, but I did it quickly. They thought they were being rescued, so they weren't afraid. Does that shock you?'

He looked down at her. 'They knew who you were,' he said. 'They knew your family background, your real name.'

'Right. I had no choice. It was clean. The men, their deaths were not clean.' Her eyes hardened. 'I took my time with them.'

'I do not object,' Will said. 'Did you go back and kill your mother?'

Lola shrugged. 'Why bother? Vodka did that for me. And afterwards, I had found something I was very good at. It gave me power where I had none before.' She looked at him. 'Maybe you could leave the girl, and come with me. We could be a team. You don't owe her anything more.'

His eyes were flint.

'You cannot go back to banking,' she said. 'They

destroyed all that. And anyway, you're like me. You were made for this. I have read your papers.'

'Maybe,' he said. 'Maybe so.'

'If you want, we can hunt them,' she said. 'Nothing to stop a former client becoming a target.'

'And Dimitri?' he asked.

'Him too,' she said, perhaps fractionally too quickly.

He stared into the traffic for a few minutes. Lola looked at him. He seemed to be thinking. She could tell, from the way his body relaxed, that he was here, on this dusty street on the city outskirts, and part of his life was coming to an end.

'I'm sorry about what happened to you, when you were a child,' he said quietly. He put out his right hand, and she slipped her left hand into it. Almost disbelievingly. He liked her. He did want her. She was so pleased, so thrilled. Perhaps, just perhaps, there was something new for her. Lola breathed out, hardly daring to believe it. Perhaps – why not? A fresh life, hidden deep away, somewhere obscure, where they would never find her. Part of her life could also be coming to an end. Maybe it was time to still the rage. Dimitri Petrenko would be her last kill.

'But you took it further than you had to,' he said. 'You're a psychopath, and you kill for money. And fun. You killed Olivia.'

Her blood turned to ice, the mellow satisfaction seeping out of her. Goddamn it, he had her wrist. He was strong. His grip was like steel.

'Dimitri killed her,' she said, trying not to show fear.

'It's your style. And besides,' he looked at her fingers, soft and pink, splayed in his grip, 'that depression matches her ring. It was engraved with her name.'

She looked down, horrified. There were the faintest letter strokes, tiny indentations, in the soft flesh above her palm.

Lola moved fast. She twisted her wrist backwards, attempting to break his grip. Standard move but it could work, if the assailant was surprised.

Will Hyde was not surprised. He held her wrist and brought his elbow sharply down on her forearm. She gasped in shock. He had broken her arm.

A second later, pain flooded through her.

'Don't kill me,' she begged. 'I'm a woman. Are you going to kill a defenceless woman . . .'

He let her go. Lola's right hand flashed down to her left shin. She tore at it. The false skin came off; she had a long knitting needle in there, tipped with Ricin, under the latex pocket. Her back-up weapon for Dimitri. She growled with pain, with rage and disappointment, and slashed it at Will Hyde, waiting for him to fall back, to stumble.

Instead, he thrust his arm up against her, meeting the sharp point of her weapon. It stuck in the fabric of his jacket. It was millimetres from his skin, but it was stuck. She scrambled to try to get to her feet, but his hand was on her, about her head, his left hand on her ear . . .

She was utterly terrified. She screamed. 'No! Don't kill—'

He snapped her neck, twisting the head to one side. People had stopped across the street. Lola saw them staring and pointing, and she knew. It was the end. Her world went black.

Will stood, slowly. He pulled the needle from his jacket and dropped it into a storm drain. The people across the street were pointing now, shouting.

'*La ha danneggiata. Penso che la abbia uccisa!*' yelled a dumpy woman shrouded in a black dress.

A man stepped forward, mobile phone to his ear. Another man, a young kid really, was shrieking and pointing at Will. '*Vada a prendere la polizia!*'

Will took his jacket off and tossed it over the corpse of Lola Montoya. Then he started to run, a light jog, towards the grounds of the hospital. It would be easy enough to get lost in there. He might steal a car, too. Time to get to the airport. She had obviously killed Dimitri Petrenko.

He hadn't enjoyed that task, but nor did he regret it. Lola Montoya could not control her own nature. To leave her alive would be to condemn others to die. And Olivia's blood, Olivia's fear, preached against mercy.

He knew Dimitri Petrenko, knew him well. His client list would be easy to obtain. Perhaps Will would publicise it. He had not decided. The first thing to do was to leave the city, and get himself to Tel Aviv. He would head south, to Naples, a glorious den of thieves, and from there to Puglia, and charter a little boat for Africa.

Nobody would track him from Casablanca.

It would take a week, perhaps, and he would let himself be seen. They had only henchmen, good shooters maybe, in the centre of town now. He was confident Melissa was safe. Until somebody found Dimitri and Lola dead, the octopus had no head and no eyes. It would flail around, catching nothing.

Will would be bait. He would draw them to himself. A passport stop here, a credit card use there, CCTV images in another slot. He would draw them closer and closer. He would distract them from Melissa. It was down to her now, in the few days he could give her, to get Sir Richard's discovery out. To change the world.

But she would do it perfectly. She would be terrified, of course, thinking he was dead. And he could not reach out to her, even slightly, until he arrived to claim her. He wouldn't risk it. If he contacted her, they might trace that, and come for her when he was not around. She'd have to suffer until he turned up in person.

God, Will thought. How far they had come. How much he loved her. More than himself. More than his own life. He was so incredibly proud of her. The thought of them spending the rest of their days together filled his heart with an intense joy.

A little temporary sorrow would not distract her from their mission. Melissa, his wife, his love, would get it done. She would get the information out there.

She was good at this.

Epilogue

Melissa Elmet was transported safely to Israel. She had no need of a passport; a government delegation was waiting for her as she landed. Armoured vehicles and ten soldiers with machine guns took her to an army base inside Jerusalem. She was given access to a government computer, and allowed to keep her papers.

The soldiers took the solar cell from her, but there was little she could do about that.

She heard nothing from Will. She opened her father's papers and put them on to the internet. She asked for a scanner, a camera. The military supplied them. Melissa distributed the information widely, very widely. It was something to do, over long days, when her heart was breaking. She didn't worry about discovery. A military computer in Israel was as untraceable as you could get.

She lay alone, without him, and ached for him. The fear was constant. During the day, she trained in the gym, ate, and kept going back to the computer.

The news stories hit on around the fourth day. The Israeli interior minister showed, live on CNN, a Chrysler

Jeep driving around with a set of solar panels fitted to its roof.

'We were groundbreaking when we introduced electric cars in Israel,' he said triumphantly. 'Now we won't even need the charging station. This can be used all over the world. A magnificent invention by Israeli scientists.'

Israeli scientists? Melissa stirred from her heartbreak to find a moment for white-hot anger. But Ari came to her quarters that night, and told her it was standard practice.

'If they think your father invented it, they may still come looking for you. Now the blame is on us.'

She nodded, her eyes bright with tears. 'Who knows he was the one, though?'

'You. Will. Me. Perhaps five other men.' Ari patted her knee. 'Let that be enough, Melissa. He's dead, he doesn't need glory. He would rather have you safe.'

She kept her father's letter close to her heart. She almost couldn't bear to open it. Once that was done, there would be nothing left to bind her to him.

But on the fifth night, as she was watching the news channels on her computer, watching the global chaos as the oil price collapsed, the gloating of the environmental campaigners, the riots in Jeddah, the uprising in Nadrah, where they had overthrown their sultan, Melissa finally came to a decision. She had to know what her father had said. She had lost him, and she had lost Will. But she couldn't start again, by herself, without proper grieving.

She clicked the computer shut and sat back on her single bed. Her heart thumped as she slit open the envelope. Inside was a crisp blue sheet of paper, her father's signature Smythson's. It had just a few words typed on it, and his scrawl at the bottom.

My darling Melissa,

I hope you never read this letter; if you do, it means they came after you in the end, and you found what they were looking for. If you can, get it to William Hyde. He lives in New York now, where he has become quite successful. My sense is that he will know what to do with it.

I am sorry that I tried to control you, as a girl. It is a fault in my nature. I'm sorry I did not spend more time with you and your mother. I'm sorry for many things, in fact. I may be dead when you read this, but that is no reason to be mawkish. Find somebody you can love, and marry them; or be single, and as happy as you can. At a moment like this, I understand it is all that matters.

If you still love Hyde, marry him if he will have you. I was wrong to interfere.

Try to think well of me. I do, and did, love you.

He had signed it 'Daddy'.

Melissa put the letter aside carefully, lay down on her bed, and wept until she could weep no more. Then, exhausted from pain and loss, she fell asleep.

*

When she woke up, it was the twenty-ninth. Ten days after Will had left her at the Spanish Steps. Now she had to accept the truth. He was not coming back.

She summoned Ari, and asked for help. She wanted a new identity. And to stay in Israel. It was the most secure nation in the world. He was full of compassion for her and offered her various positions. The Israeli government was grateful, he told her. They would provide. A state income, a state pension. A desk job.

She asked for a university position. It was all she knew. A research fellow, and she would retrain, studying antiquities. She would become an archaeologist. That might work to dull the pain a little: the soothing love of the past, to be in the open, in the hot sun, close to all the beauties of death and history.

The irony of it; she had been thinking of something like that, a lifetime ago, before Will's voice on the phone turned her world upside down. Before her heart had healed. Now it was broken open again, broken for good. And here she was.

He promised to see what he could do. There was a slot open in Tel Aviv. Would she like to transfer?

Melissa nodded, dry-eyed. Yes. Thank you.

A soldier would take her in an army Jeep, at first light. Best to get her off the base when nobody was watching.

Melissa nodded. Nothing mattered much any more. That was fine, she was amenable to anything. There was not much point in being alive.

She put her small bag of belongings together and

dumped it in a rucksack. She had toiletries, basic clothing, and an envelope with thirty-five thousand shekels in
cash. Enough to get her through the first month, he said,
and then there would be more.

A female cadet woke her, and Melissa came down the
stairs, in the dark. The car was out there, its engine purr-
ing in the darkness. She could see a driver in sunglasses
and a large military cap. She climbed into the back,
wordlessly; her Israeli was still nonexistent. The Jeep
rolled forward to the gates, and Melissa put her head
down. Then the guards saluted, the vehicle moved
through the gatehouse, and they were on their way.

'Do you speak English?' she asked after a couple of
minutes.

The driver turned round in his seat, and smiled at her.

'Sure I do,' he said.

It was Will.

Melissa opened her mouth to say something. She
spluttered and gasped. She moved forward, her hands
around his neck, covering him with kisses.

'Careful, baby, you're going to kill us,' he said, steering
the Jeep away from the main road, down a little back
alley.

'You didn't say anything. You didn't tell me!' she
gasped. Her heart soared with joy, such unbelievable,
incredible joy. He was back and he was with her, and she
loved him, she adored him . . .

'I wanted to get off-base without them noticing.
Dressed as a soldier will do it.'

'You didn't call . . .'

'I couldn't. They were tracking me. What was left of them. My trail went cold somewhere around Malta.'

She shuddered. 'Where are we running to now?'

'Nowhere,' he said. 'You and I are going home.'

'Home?' Melissa asked. For the first time, a cloud descended over her face. 'God, Will, I don't know if I have a home any more. Or ever can. My father's dead.'

He nodded. 'I understand, Missy.'

'Do you?' she asked. 'I wonder if you can, Will.'

'Oh yeah,' he said flatly. 'Your father's been dead for a year, but with this, you finally feel like you were starting to know him. Now he's gone, your mother's gone and your country's gone. And you wonder if you'll ever sleep sound again. Ever stop looking over your shoulder.'

She was staring at him, his eyes ahead on the road while he spoke. 'How do you know that?' she whispered. 'You scare me sometimes, Will. It's like you can climb inside my head.'

Will smiled slightly. 'No; it's just that we share a head now.'

'Meaning what?'

'Meaning now you think like an agent, Missy, like an operative. You have the same fears we all do. Every field asset in the world has these terrors. It's part of the life.' Will shook his head. 'Why do they work up psych profiles before they recruit anyone? Regular personalities don't make it.'

'So I'm not a normal girl?'

'No. Thank God.'

She leaned her head against the car seat, digesting this. 'Then what is there for us, baby? Can we bring children into this situation? Can we relax together? Or do we always run?'

He pulled the Jeep over at the side of the road, went around and opened her door. Her eyes were bright with tears.

'Take a walk with me,' Will said.

Melissa put her hand in his. Their surroundings were hot and dusty, rather beautiful. She thought of Bible stories from her childhood.

'Do you like Israel?'

She nodded. 'Yes.'

'Then start thinking of it as home. Look, despite the fears, most agents not killed on missions die quietly in their beds. Revenge slayings are rare. Most global actors deal only with the present crisis, whatever it is. We have some things on our side.'

'I'm listening,' Melissa replied. She wanted to believe. She desperately wanted to believe.

And as she looked at Will Hyde, her heart contracted with a spasm of pure love. He wasn't yessing her to death with platitudes. He was dissecting the problem, her fears, and offering her logic. He respected her brain; she loved him for that. He gave it to her straight, like a man with no time for anything less.

'Israel is a nation constantly under assault. As a result

they have the world's best security. They are practised at hiding senior assets from multiple countries and terror organisations that want them dead. Frankly, there is no safer place on earth for you.'

'OK.' She could buy that.

'Secondly, those who hunted us are being hunted themselves. I know most of the names. They'll be preoccupied with their own survival. They will hide in caves, not look for us. Thirdly, our trail is cold. They think we are dead. Our new identities are established in Tel Aviv in a code these guys won't break and wouldn't bother trying to break.' Will turned her towards him, his hands strong on her shoulders, and drew her in for a deep, loving kiss on the lips, till her body melted to him. 'And Melissa, here's the deal. We're safer here than anywhere. Odds are on our side. But no, there are no guarantees. You need to get on living without one, or you hand them the victory. And I'm not prepared to do that. Are you?'

She laughed aloud. 'Hell, no.'

'A little danger adds a little spice.'

'Always the optimist,' she said, but she felt the fear and knots drain out of her stomach, and pure, flowing joy replace them; she was here with Will, they were safe, they *were* going to have a life. A great one. 'So, you're ready to start a job as a librarian or something, nice little semi-detached in the suburbs?'

Will's eyes opened; his turn to laugh.

'What?' Melissa said.

'That's not your life,' he said. 'You think I would permit that for you? I have a villa in Ramat Aviv. It's exceptionally large, it's staffed with military bodyguards, nice pool, lush gardens . . .'

Melissa blinked. 'I thought you didn't have any money.'

He looked at her and grinned. 'I know how to hide my money, baby. I still have access to over two hundred million dollars.'

'You're kidding.'

'And the US government will gradually restore what it can to my new identity. The Israelis have let them know what happened. They understand I didn't kill Olivia.'

Melissa exhaled. 'But the woman . . .'

'She's dead, Missy. The runner is dead, too. And so are fifteen of their best men.' Will breathed out. 'Their clients have a little more to worry about. Frightened people, ruined money men. Most of the people who could connect us to this are going to be killed within the next six months.'

'So we're safe?' she breathed. 'Live-in-a-villa safe?'

'Remarry, legally. Have a baby. Two babies. That kind of safe. The threat's always there. But we'll handle it.'

'I love you,' she said, starting to cry as they got back in the Jeep.

'Good,' he said, putting his foot on the gas. 'Because you're staying with me now. And there's no escape for either of us, no going back.'

'Pull over,' Melissa said. She was hot, burning for him.

He hadn't touched her in two weeks. 'Pull over.'

Will glanced back, took one look at her, and smiled. 'Insatiable,' he commented.

'Don't know about that,' she said. 'Try it. Let's see.'

He smiled, and pulled the Jeep over to the side of the road. Then he climbed in the back, and took Melissa, his wife, his passion, in his arms, kissing her about the throat and neck, kissing her like he would never stop.